TO DO AND DIE

To Do and Die

PATRICK MERCER

ISIS
LARGE PRINT
Oxford

First published in Great Britain 2009
by
HarperCollins*Publishers*

Published in Large Print 2010 by ISIS Publishing Ltd.,
7 Centremead, Osney Mead, Oxford OX2 0ES
by arrangement with
HarperCollins*Publishers*

British Library Cataloguing in Publication Data
Mercer, Patrick.
    To do and die.
    1. Great Britain. Army - - Officers - - Fiction.
    2. Crimean War, 1853–1856 - - Fiction.
    3. War stories.
    4. Large type books.
    I. Title
    823.9'2–dc22

ISBN 978–0–7531–8548–3 (hb)
ISBN 978–0–7531–8549–0 (pb)

Printed and bound in Great Britain by
T. J. International Ltd., Padstow, Cornwall

To Do and Die is dedicated to
'The Pack'

Acknowledgements

A first novel is very special because, even in middle-age, there is so much to learn. I'm especially grateful to Natasha Fairweather, my agent, whom I steered over Crimean battlefields and then who steered me, patiently and kindly towards the finished product; to Susan Watt, my editor, whose help has been invaluable; to my long-suffering friends Heather Millican and Richard Kemp; and my wife Cait and son Rupert who have listened to every syllable with huge self-control.

Lastly, I must pay tribute to the men and women of all nations who fought in the Crimea. Ever since I was a small boy they've fascinated me: I hope I've done them justice.

CHAPTER ONE

The Battle of the River Alma

The chaffing and laughter stopped abruptly: shallow jokes were choked off as the troops listened intently. Every bristle-chinned man in the long, snaking ranks sweated gently into his scarlet coat, shoulders bowed under his load of kit and ammunition, hands cupped around his rifle as he strained to hear the order that would start the killing. The warm, late September breeze carried the snapping and popping of the burning village of Bourliouk to their front clearly now as every voice was stilled, then the captains stumbled over the furrows of the vineyards clutching at swords and haversacks, rushing to be first to give the order to their men. The soldierly form of Captain Eddington, their company commander, stood before them, trim, athletic, just a slight flush on his face betraying the excitement of imminent action. The run had left him almost out of breath: he fought hard to steady his voice.

"With ball cartridge . . . load!"

Eddington was crisp, exact, almost elegant compared with the brass-lunged non-commissioned officers who repeated his orders. Young Anthony Morgan did his best to conquer his suddenly dry throat, to stop himself sounding too Irish and utter the same command that, if truth were known, he had never really expected to say on the field of battle. Here he was, twenty-three and the junior subaltern of the 95th Foot's Grenadier Company, about to see war for the first time and acting as if he'd never heard the words of the drill manual before.

Almost as one, the troops spat out the cartridge paper, then the line sang as ramrods forced home the bullets that were about as big as the end of your thumb. Rifles were pulled sharply back to the order before a gulp swept down the lines — there could be no turning back now. With all forty rounds untied and ready for use in their pouches and hands sticky with sweat on the stocks of their weapons, every man knew that the browny-grey blocks of Russian infantry looking down at them on the other bank of the sluggish Alma had to be faced.

"Officers, to me," Eddington shouted. Both of his subalterns, Richard Carmichael and Anthony Morgan ran from their places by their men to the front of the company.

"Right, you two, the plan's simple . . ." Eddington turned and pointed across the river towards the Great Redoubt, the earthwork at the centre of the Russian position, howitzer barrels just visible, pointing menacingly towards the waiting, British ranks. "The French will turn the right of the Russian position whilst we go straight at them here, across the river Alma, to take that

Redoubt. The Light Division are on our left, Adams's Brigade on our right; Cambridge's Guards are to the rear, in reserve. Once the firing starts it'll be all smoke and chaos, I guess, so if you get confused, just look to the centre of the Regiment where the Colours are. Any questions?" Despite the invitation, Eddington — quite evidently — felt that everything was as clear as it needed to be.

Neither subalterns dared ask anything, merely shaking their heads in reply.

"Right . . ." Eddington shook both of his officers' hands quickly. "Back to your men, remember how much they'll depend on you." Then, less stiffly, "Good luck," before both young men strode back to their places at either end of the Grenadier Company.

The river twisted and coiled between low banks on the northern side and higher ones to the south, then a little shelf gave way to a short, steep climb before the land sloped gently, smoothly up to the enemy positions. The Russian commander — Menschikoff — had given his divisional and regimental officers, in this part of the field at least, all the freedom they needed to plan this position and Morgan could see that they had been thorough. When they had paused at Scutari on their way to the Crimea, they'd visited their own artillery and been told that the most lethal range for guns against infantry was about six hundred paces. He looked up to the brass muzzles that peeped down through the embrasures over clear slopes where no vines grew and the only trees were a dotted line of

3

scrawny poplars along the course of the river: they were about six hundred paces away.

Morgan was just able to make out the far-off rattle of drums before the first shot rasped overhead — he'd never heard that sound before: now his guts and arse tightened — just as the veterans had said. Judging by the way that the whole company ducked, there were another eighty-odd sphincters doing just the same and he fought with himself to look the men in the face and not to turn and stare at the guns whose smoke now roiled across the hillside. The round shot had still to find their mark when the commanding officer cantered forward, his own nervousness carrying to his horse — the animal pecked and sidestepped as the balls shivered through the air.

"Ninety-Fifth will advance . . . by the centre, quick march!" Colonel Webber-Smith's words were echoed down the companies and the regiment billowed forward.

But this certainty was to be short lived — they stuttered to a halt no more than three hundred yards further on.

"Bloody Seventh, just a bunch o' bairns." Colour-Sergeant McGucken was one of the few Scots in the regiment. He'd transferred from the 36th a few years ago and, at six-foot and as hard as a Glasgow winter he'd soon found himself in his new regiment's hand-picked Grenadiers. Now, he damned the battalion to their left whose cursing ranks had first collided with their own and then caused them to pause and have to be untangled.

They'd never made friends with the 'Old 7th' as they called themselves, for these boys had seen no more active service than the 95th, but they would never stop bragging about their lineage and history. The 7th Fusiliers came from the Light Division — the left assault division — and there had been friction between the two regiments ever since the pause at Varna; now an uneasy file of them tramped past, all downy, half-grown beards and haphazard firewood sticking out of their blanket packs. They looked just a little too fixedly ahead, their stares pleading their innocence for this officer-botch that made them seem so clumsy in front of a 'young' regiment. Then the earth spurted momentarily just ahead of them and half a dozen sprawled on the ground, as if felled by some mighty scythe. A brightly-painted drum bounced, a rifle now bent like a hairpin cartwheeled away and one of the 7th sagged, his clothes, belts and blanket awry.

Morgan saw how the jagged iron shards had caught the lad, for a furrow the length of a man's finger had been opened below his ear, yet he felt nothing more than curiosity. Bruised, dark-purple ribbons of chopped flesh laced his neck as black, arterial blood soaked his collar and cross-belts, dripping into the soft earth next to his dead face.

A further soldier sat plucking dumbly at gouges on his wrists and hands. Coins from another's pocket had been hit and hurled by a ball as lethally as any shrapnel, slashing and scoring the man like meat on a butcher's slab.

5

The gunners now had the range. The smoke from blazing Bourliouk helped to hide them a little, but in almost perfect unison shells burst above them and the 55th to their right, hurling jagged iron and shrapnel balls into the red-coated ranks below. From all around came screams and moans as the men fell with ugly punctures to their shoulders and heads whilst splinters bounced off rifles, wrenching them from fear-damp hands.

Then Pegg was pitched heavily onto his face by a crack and angry burst of smoke above them, drumsticks, belts and shako everywhere. At seventeen, Drummer Pegg was the youngest man in the company — now he was their first casualty.

"You two, help Pegg. One of you get his drum and sticks, sharp now." Colour-Sergeant McGucken saw the lad being dashed down, but before the others could get to him, Pegg was on his feet, ashen but gingerly feeling himself for wounds.

"You all right, son?"

"Fucked if I know, Colour-Sar'nt, I think so." Pegg continued to investigate himself bemusedly.

"You're a right lucky little bugger, yous: get your kit and stop sitting down on the job, then." A shaky grin played over Pegg's face as he chased his drum, oblivious to the great gash in the blanket strapped to his back.

As the fire intensified, so the dense smoke from the village blew straight across the face of the company. Order began to be lost as the men looked for solid cover in the lee of farm walls and byres, eyes stinging, and coughing as they did so. Morgan just didn't know whether he should try to restore some form of regularity to the ranks or continue to let the men find their own shelter as they had been taught in the new style of skirmishing. But he had little choice, as the jarring noise of the shells joined with the swirling smoke to make close-order impossible.

Then, emerging from behind a low farm wall came the senior subaltern of the Grenadiers, Richard Carmichael, but he was not his usual poised Harrovian self. Whilst his scarlet coat and great, bullion shoulder wings, even his rolled blanket, haversack and water-bottle still hung like a tailor's plate, there was an unusual distraction about him. He darted hunted looks everywhere, he was pallid, he licked his lips, his self-assured serenity seemed to have been scraped away by the first shot.

"Carmichael, where's Eddington?" bellowed Morgan, but only on the third time of asking did Carmichael reply.

"I . . . I don't know. The company's all to blazes, I shall go and find him." He shrank back behind a protective piece of brickwork.

To their front, the Light Company was fleetingly visible, thrown out in skirmish line to screen the rest of the Regiment. Morgan now realized the popping that he'd heard amidst the artillery was their rifles replying to bangs and puffs of smoke that came from the scatter of buildings and bushes that marked the outskirts of the burning village. The Russians would certainly have their

7

own sharpshooters this side of the river, hidden, he supposed, amidst the scrub and huts, but none was to be seen.

A scrawny little corporal — a Dublin enlistment whose name Morgan had never managed to learn — emerged with another Light Company man from the smoke. Both had thrown off their tall black shakoes and folded down the collars of their coatees: now their rifles were half in the shoulder whilst they peered intently into a tangle of walls and vines as if a rabbit were about to bolt. He couldn't make out what they were calling to one another above the din of the guns, but suddenly both rifles fired almost together and uncertain grins showed that they'd found a mark.

The corporal, peering through the reek, recognized the wings at Morgan's shoulder as those of an officer and sent the private to report to him. This was another lad whom he knew but couldn't name; even as he stumbled through the smoke and over the loose earth of the vineyard he reached behind his hip to get a fresh cartridge. The nameless soldier's lips were smeared with powder sticking to his stubble showing, Morgan noticed enviously, that he'd already been plying his trade and there was a slight swagger about the man, his manner as unlike the parade ground as his once-white belts were grimy.

"Sir, Corporal McElver says to say that we got a couple on 'em, but there's still Russ in the buildings and what do you want us to do now?" How like the men to ask the first officer they saw for orders.

Just as he was groping for something useful to say, the soldier staggered, his head jerking sharply — his weapon fell as he sat down heavily at Morgan's feet, clutching at his mouth. Blood welled between his fingers from a hole in his cheek whilst into his palm he spat a wad of pulp and broken teeth. It was all that Morgan could do to stop himself from dropping down to help the man — but the wounded would be dealt with by medical orderlies — his job was to lead the troops forward to find the enemy.

A gout of smoke and a flicker of movement, though, showed where the Russian sharpshooter had fired from above a wall no more than twenty yards away. All that Morgan wanted to do was to sink into the damp soil beside the casualty, but the unspoken challenges of his men were too strong. Trying to hold his equipment steady with one hand, he gripped the hilt of his sword as he stumbled over the broken ground whilst, he was sure, a hundred judgemental eyes bore into him.

"Sir, wait . . . let me get some lads together to flush the bastard out, don't you go by yourself . . ." But McGucken's words went unheard as Morgan scrambled forwards.

A thin cloud of powdersmoke still hung over the low wall as he tried to vault it, but the top stones were loose and in one ugly, tripping crash, he bundled straight into someone crouched on the other side. The Russian rifleman had been concentrating on reloading his weapon and sprawled beneath Morgan's inelegant arrival, giving the officer just enough time to regain his balance.

Pulling his cap from his eyes and his equipment from around his groin, Morgan instinctively brought his sword around his shoulder to slash at his foe, but the once balanced, tempered blade now sagged like a felling axe — the thrill of action had immediately sapped him of all his strength. Just as he was bracing himself to strike, he remembered the advice dinned into him — always to use the point, but in changing his blow, he gave the Russian time to slither back half a pace through the slime of the yard and he overreached himself. What should have been a decisive swipe turned into a half-spent prod that did no more than tear the cloth of his enemy's coat and cause a yelp, more of surprise than pain, whilst the young Russian recovered fast, his scrappy moustache sticking wetly to his lips. Without a rifle, he grabbed at Morgan's hilt, wresting the blade from his hand and pulling him off balance through the sword knot that still looped it to his wrist.

The boy was big and bulky in his coarse, grey greatcoat and Morgan had spent enough time in the ring to know that if he were to win he had to use every ounce of weight and strength in his muscular five-foot ten and use it quickly. But this fight was in deadly earnest, it wasn't school or regimental boxing, just cuts and nosebleeds; this time one of them would die. As he was pulled forward so he let his full weight barrel into his opponent and in an instant both men were rolling on the ground. Then blinding pain and a blast of stagnant breath — Morgan got the full benefit of the Muscovite's fist square on the bridge of his nose. He reeled back as his enemy's weight was swiftly on top of him.

The pain in his face still raged when his ears, already roaring as the blood pumped round his system, almost split. Then his bruised nose was filled with the smell of powder-smoke and the Russian ceased to struggle. Thrusting the dead burden away from him, Morgan leapt to his feet, groping for his sword that dangled by his hand and desperately trying to rid himself of the stranglehold of the coat around his shoulder.

Standing above him was his Colour-Sergeant — McGucken. He'd judged the shot well, for the powerful Minié round could have easily passed through the Russian's body and hurt Morgan. Now, as if he did such things every day of the week, the Scot was finishing the job. He jabbed viciously with his brass-capped rifle-butt straight into the Russian's face, cracking open the nose, splintering the sinus bones, reducing the flesh to a mass of purple bruises. Finally, he stood astride the body and split the skull with one great blow and a curse.

"That'll teach yous . . ." before turning, lungs heaving, to Morgan. "Sir, will you please stop fannying around? Never do that again — always take an escort, I don't need you cold." McGucken had to yell above the noise to be heard, but there was no mistaking his anger and concern for the young officer. "And get rid of that pox-ridden coat, sir." McGucken was scraping the butt of his rifle along the coarse grass to clean the bloody mess away.

Plunging into the smoke after McGucken, Morgan found the wounded Light Company soldier propped against a mossy wall whilst two bandsmen and a girl were doing their best to bandage the awkward mouth wound without suffocating the man. A great stain spread on the snowy gauze being inexpertly bound around his jaw whilst blood bubbled from his nose.

"Mary Keenan, what in God's name are you doing this far forward?" That his former chambermaid and wife of his batman came to be in the Crimea at all still amazed him. Now the same Mary that had changed his linen, served at table and become closer to him than any other person on earth, was crouching next to the casualty, proffering a useless canteen of spirits. The smallest pair of soldier's boots jutted from below her muddy hem whilst the dark hair that Morgan remembered so well running through his hands was plaited neatly below a scarf.

"Have a care Mr Morgan, sir, it's Mrs Keenan to you." Despite the sharpness of the reply, her eyes were wide with fear, but there was still the same resolute glitter in them that he had seen so often at his family's house, Glassdrumman, in County Cork. There was a determination in this woman that, despite her nineteen years, had seen her become the unelected leader of the handful of regimental wives who had been allowed to accompany the Regiment on campaign.

"I'm sorry — Mrs Keenan. But you're too far forward, please get to the rear." Morgan noticed how her fingers trembled.

"I . . . I'll be fine, thank you, sir." Despite the stuttered formality of her words, Morgan couldn't fail to notice the hand that caught at his sleeve.

"Sir, for God's sake come on." McGucken recalled him to his duty.

All the companies were now stumbling for the lee of the riverbank. The dashing, bounding balls could not reach them here and they were invisible to the gunners, but confusion reigned as men from the regiments of the Light Division plunged off the banks and into the river in an effort to reach the sheltering lip of the opposite bank.

"You lot, keep your pouches above your heads . . ." McGucken was doing his best to stop his men from soaking their ammunition by plunging thoughtlessly into the river. "NCOs, get the men to keep their weapons dry."

Some of the sergeants and corporals heard the Colour-Sergeant and understood him amidst the chaos. A handful of the soldiers, numbed by the noise and fear, had to be grabbed to make them listen, their belts undone for them, their rifles lifted above their heads as splinters and bullets churned up the water.

The few mounted officers urged their chargers into the breast-deep stream. Beach, commanding the 33rd, spurred his dripping little grey mare directly at the bank, but she slithered back, mud staining her knees. He tried again, riding her obliquely up the greasy slope, picking firmer ground in a fine display of horsemanship. Silhouetted on the higher ground for an instant, Morgan saw the 33rd's colonel rousing his men: then the saddle was emptied by a sudden blast of iron as the Russians fired their first rounds of shotgun-like canister.

Below the lip the regiments teemed. The 7th Fusiliers were astounded by the abandon of their commanding officer — Colonel Lacy Yea. "Come on, come on anyhow!" he yelled as his horse, too, wallowed at the bank. The knotted line — muddy red coats, smeared white belts and dark, sodden trousers — now raised a breathless cheer and surged up the rise.

The two ensigns had floundered through the river keeping the 95th's Colours almost dry. A subaltern wrung at one corner of the bright yellow regimental standard as they looked for their commanding officer and gathered themselves for the waiting storm.

"So, that's where you've got to, Morgan." From somewhere in the smoke Eddington was suddenly at his side, "The Colonel's been wounded — I saw him being carried to the rear back there in the vineyards — along with half the other commanding officers in the Division, as far as I can see. Major Hume's in charge, now, but he had a bad fall when his horse was shot." Eddington was looking round in the smoke and crowd of soldiers from every regiment who were splashing into the river, seeking the cover of the bank. "Where's Carmichael and his half of the company?" Even though he had to shout to make himself heard, there was something reassuring about Eddington's calmness. It was as though he had been born to this confusion, that the shriek of balls and shrapnel was a normal part of his life: he seemed to be enjoying himself.

14

Just as he asked, a clutch of their men under Sergeant Ormond came stumbling through the smoke and vines. To their rear and hunched in a curious half-crouch came Carmichael, but his shako and coat had gone, his legs and bottom were covered in mud whilst his normally well-combed hair was everywhere. When he saw his company commander his face lit-up with relief.

"Well done, Sergeant Ormond, I see you've brought Mr Carmichael with you," shouted Captain Eddington.

Morgan smiled to himself. It was Sergeant Ormond and the men who should have been led by Lieutenant Carmichael, not the other way round, but just as Eddington turned to tell Carmichael what to do, a great, thirty-two pound ball skidded muddily off the far bank of the river before hitting him squarely in the nape of the neck. One moment Eddington had a head — the next he had not. So cleanly had the iron done its work that the Captain's body was upright for an instant, the trunk spurting blood in a liquid rope, before the knees crumpled and the corpse fell in a shrunken bundle of rags and straps onto the riverbank.

"Dear God!" shrieked Carmichael, clear above the surrounding noise. He'd been within feet of Eddington when the ball struck, now he was spattered with his blood and matter. A file of their Grenadiers led by a lance-corporal picked up the hysteria in Carmichael's voice and now they edged uneasily by, trying not to catch his eye.

"Christ, Morgan, Eddington's dead . . . look." Morgan was as appalled by the decapitated horror that had been their Captain as Carmichael was, but he knew that they must not let the men see their officers' fear.

"That would certainly seem to be the case." Morgan was surprised, impressed even, by his own *sangfroid*. "You're in charge now. What do you want me to do?" He turned to encourage a young non-commissioned officer. "Corporal Aldworth, well done, get those men down the bank."

"Just . . . get on, just . . . get across to Major Hume and report to him. I'll . . . I'll go and look for the others." Carmichael slipped off to the rear, enveloped by the smoke before Morgan could remind him of his duty.

Hundreds of urgent feet had churned the bank of the river, making it hard to stay upright. He slopped into the mud, forced through the water pistol, sword and haversack as far above his waist as their various straps would allow, watching Hume and the Colour party. The fall from his horse didn't seem to have unsettled Hume, for now he stretched his arms out behind the young ensigns' backs, gently urging them on, uttering calm words of encouragement to the knot of frightened men around the Colours.

With the two Colour-Sergeants alongside, the little band ducked their chins and braced their shoulders as if to face a gale as they slithered up the bank. The advance through the vineyard had been mild compared to this, for as the line of dripping troops thickened on the bare slope directly below the Russian guns, so their enemies increased the fire. A mixture of shell and canister whined from the guns ensconced in the

Redoubt behind big, basketwork gabions that were full of protective packed earth: the whole position was carefully sited to cover the point where the British would emerge from the banks of the river.

"Look there . . ." Morgan pointed at a Russian who was desperately trying to set fire to a tar and straw-tipped pole in front of them, ". . . that rogue's trying to light a range-marker." Even Morgan's crude grasp of tactics told him that attacking into the face of an enemy that had prepared themselves well enough to have range-markers for the guns was unwise — hadn't someone said something about always seeking a flank?

"Quick, Nixon, knock him down." The Russian struggled with flint and steel as one of the soldiers beside Morgan raised his rifle, squinted and squeezed the trigger as calmly as if on the butts back in England.

"Damn me, the fucking charge is wet," Nixon cursed as the Russian scuttled off into a fold in the ground, whilst the marker spat smokily behind him.

The jumbled line of regiments sputtered up towards the Great Redoubt. Sometimes pausing to fire then reload, the men pushed on despite wide furrows being opened in their lines whenever the Russian guns belched, for at their most effective range the canister rounds were deadly even when fired almost blind through the clinging, grey powder-smoke. Above the tangled, yelling lines Morgan could see the blue Colours of the 23rd and the 7th, the deep green standards of the 19th and his own jaunty, canary-yellow beside the big Union flag, but in an instant they were down, swept away by another sheet of canister.

"Sir, Major Hume's shouting for you." McGucken had seen the senior major hauling at the fallen flags, pulling the Queen's Colour from beneath its stricken ensign, passing it to one of the Colour-Sergeants before taking up the Regimental Colour and bawling for the closest officer.

"Mother of God, he can't want me."

"Just get over there, sir."

Morgan ducked past the levelled rifles of some of his own men, fumbling with his wet sash to find the scabbard for his sword. As he approached the muddied Hume, a ball hummed through the major's haversack, spilling biscuits and a razor — it was coolly ignored.

"Ah, Morgan, why the deaf ear? Grab hold of this, get onto the high ground with the colour-sar'nt and for God's sake show front whilst I try to rally them."

On a hillock, Colour-Sergeant Baghurst had dug the butt of his Colour pike into the ground whilst brandishing his rifle at the enemy entrenchment and shouting encouragements. Then Morgan saw the shot-holes and rents in the bright silk, realizing that he was about to become a magnet for every rifleman and gunner on the field. But with no belt to carry the Colour, he raised the pole that bore the six-foot silk square with both hands, immediately struggling to control it in the breeze.

As if to confirm his fears, no sooner had he drawn close to Baghurst than the Colour-Sergeant yelped, let his flag sag to the ground and grabbed his ankle, barging into one of the men who was hurrying forward. He wasn't alone for long, though, for his servant and fellow Corkman, Keenan, left the ranks and ran to be beside his master — quickly slinging his rifle and picking up the fallen Colour.

"So, your honour, bet you never expected to see me doing an officer's job, did you?" Morgan agreed: there were a number of things that surprised him about Keenan, not least his wife, Mary.

Death loved these sparse, scarlet files. No more than two thousand British had climbed out of the riverbed and now the guns were whittling at them so hard that it would be madness to pause to dress the line. Like a tangled piece of string, the troops plodded up the slope, the perfect target for Russian riflemen who were now forming to one side of the Redoubt.

The stolid slabs of Russian infantry were just visible through the smoke, their bayonets glittering above them, whilst hovering about their flanks was a cloud of riflemen. Active men wearing soft green caps, they sped into cover, kneeling behind the scrub, firing, disappearing to reload and then emerging from a different spot. One was handling his ramrod with fluid movements — he paused to adjust his sights then cuddled his butt into his cheek.

Keenan's tongue flicked quickly over his stubbled lips as the pair saw the rifle barrel deliberately swing up towards them. At two hundred paces, every detail of the Russian's uniform and features were clear and both men unconsciously drew their shoulders up to shield themselves as the marksman disappeared behind a cloud of smoke. The bullet snatched at Morgan's wing, holing the bullion and opening a gash in the scarlet cloth at his shoulder through which a pennon of white lining now peeped. Next to him Keenan, without a sound, sank to the ground, the great yellow flag shrouding him for an instant before it was snatched up. Morgan fancied that he saw a smile on the Russian's face.

"He'll cook you with his next round, sir." Sergeant Ormond — one of those steady, likeable men, the backbone of the company — had appeared beside him, giving words to his own thoughts as the ramrod flew down the barrel of the distant rifle.

"Thank you Ormond — you're a great comfort, you are. Luff, pass me your rifle . . . is it made ready?"

"Sir, an' it's dry an' all. Sure you know how it works?" It wasn't much of a joke, but Luff's words made them all smile amongst the danger and noise. Morgan, like most officers, had been brought up with gun, hounds and rod and took a pride in being more skilful with the new Minié rifle than the soldiers. Despite this, officers didn't carry such weapons in action; gentlemen were expected to arm themselves only with a chivalrous sword and pistol.

Now Morgan glanced at the sights and drew the chunky rifle into the shoulder. The Russian was just starting to kneel — he aimed at his belly and as the pale disc of his face swam above the foresight, he squeezed the trigger. He was always surprised at the kick of the new weapon; a few rounds would leave your shoulder black and blue.

Even above the din, Morgan recognized the sound. He'd first heard it as a boy when shooting seals off

Bantry with his father's heavy rifle — the solid, meaty thump of a soft lead ball tearing flesh. The Russian jerked forward onto his face, invisible now amongst the low scrub and the young officer marked the spot as he would for his dog and a downed pheasant.

Had Morgan been able to hear above the pounding of his heart, he would have sensed that the din was less. As they'd raced up the lethal slope splinters and balls had sliced the men around them and Morgan had been conscious of holes and rents suddenly appearing in his Colour as the artillery banged and roared its hatred at them. But at the crucial point, when cool, disciplined gunnery would have won the day, panic seemed to have struck the Russians and now the brass-barrelled howitzers were being manhandled and tugged away by teams of horses to save them from being overrun.

"Right, come on you lot, they're all in a pother, get amongst 'em," Hume recognized the moment. The Russians were confused by the whining shells and bullets and the screaming British: dash and boldness now would carry the position.

Gasping, Morgan crouched with Sergeant Ormond below the bank of gabions, Colours across their laps, gathering themselves for the final rush into the heart of the enemy, whilst the troops around them scrabbled through the unaccountably empty embrasures, boots rasping on the basketwork as, rifles at the ready, they leapt into the gun positions beyond. Catching Morgan by the arm, Ormond led the way up and over the breastwork, brandishing his Colour as soon as he was steady and helping the officer over the obstacle.

21

Inside the Redoubt everything was in uproar. Four horses plunged and shivered, anchored at one end of their harness by a heavy howitzer and at the other by a subaltern of the 23rd who, clinging to the tack with one hand, had a pistol firmly in the ear of the Russian driver. The man was clearly terrified by the demented youngster and his revolver and he was leaning so far out of his saddle that he was in danger of falling and losing control of his horses, yet still the boy yelled and threatened.

Another gun remained. Morgan saw how Alfred Heyland, commander of Number Six Company, and a handful of his soldiers went surging towards it. There was blood all over Heyland — it dripped from his nose and whiskers and one arm hung uselessly by his side. Later, Morgan was told that Heyland had been blown over bodily by a discharge of grape just yards from the centre of the gun-line in the Great Redoubt — everyone thinking that he was dead, yet he'd risen up like a torn and bleeding Lazarus, determined to lead his men on. Now all that Morgan saw was a crazed thing, chopping at one of the gunners with his sword whilst the men dealt with the others in a mad lust for blood.

Three Russians had been surrounded beside the gun's trail. They all had short swords, but none had drawn them before their attackers pounced. None of the British had reloaded their rifles, nor were their bayonets fixed, so the Russians met death in the most brutal way as butts rose and fell whilst boots kicked and stamped, despite the cries for mercy. Eventually their victims were silent: chests heaving, the executioners looked down at the red splashes on their feet.

But the trophy was theirs. Some men cut away the hastily placed tow-ropes whilst Heyland clutched his sword by the end of its blade and scratched a crude '95' into the green paint of the carriage to confirm its capture. Faint with lack of blood, Heyland was swabbed with bandages and then led away by two of his men. Morgan remembered how well Heyland had danced at Dublin Castle last year — and how jealous they had all been of the flock of women around his elegant form. Now, how could any girl find this broken, bruised creature attractive again?

"Good men, get those Colours up on the parapet." Major Hume was now commanding the Regiment. Just as collected — though even more tattered than when the pair had seen him last — he was bareheaded, quite unarmed and utterly in control. The same self-confidence that Morgan had noticed when they were in the river was asserting itself over every man to whom he spoke, regardless of regiment or company, calming, reassuring and helping frightened boys to become men.

"We've done it, sir, we've taken the Redoubt." Morgan had thrust the butt of the Colour pike hard into the parapet; now he looked round up at the bushy slopes to the horizon no more than three hundred paces above him.

"Aye, Morgan we have, but there's plenty more Muscovites: look there." Hume pointed up the hill.

Although a few hundred British had bloodily taken the centre of the position, they were now pinioned between the unprotected rear of the Great Redoubt and a mass of fresh, Russian infantry who lay on the smoke-laden slope above them. Meanwhile, the British commander, Lord Raglan, had moved forward with a tiny group of his Staff until he was well to the fore, almost in advance of his leading troops with the foresight to order-up a battery of British guns that could fire right into his enemy's flank.

"Now we'll need some help to hold it." Major Hume was so hoarse he could barely make himself heard, despite the fact that the guns and rifles had fallen quiet for an instant right across the battlefield.

"Yes, sir, Cambridge's Guards are in reserve right behind us, aren't they?" Morgan knew what was supposed to be the plan, but Hume looked anxiously back towards the river.

"Well, if they are in reserve, they're a bloody long way away; we need them up here now before the Russians counterattack," Hume replied.

The Duke of Cambridge's division had, indeed, been held in reserve, untouched by the fire that had so damaged the Light and Second Divisions during the advance to the river and now he was determined not to let his command fall into the same ruptured state as they crossed the Alma. But Cambridge's caution meant that his Division lay too far to the rear of the troops that were now so horribly exposed in the Great Redoubt. They should have been closely supporting the first wave of attackers, on hand to deal with whatever the Russians planned to do next.

The unnatural quiet ended as suddenly as it began. As the last few men seeped into the Redoubt and caught their breath, the danger of the position became more and more obvious. The sergeants busied themselves redistributing ammunition and clearing fouled breeches with their combination tools whilst trying to calm and steady the men. Despite their every effort, though, the troops started endless, ragged cheering that Morgan was raw enough to mistake for a sign of confidence rather than one of near panic. He and Sergeant Ormond had been relieved of the responsibility of the Colours by two uninjured sergeants, so they bawled with the best of them until a spatter of bullets sent them to ground.

"Where's that fire coming from, Sar'nt Ormond?" Morgan felt useless as he crouched on the ground with no Colour, no troops to command and only a sword and pistol.

"Must be them lot, sir, there." Ormond paused for a moment whilst reloading his rifle and pointed through the smoke to a slab of Russian infantry about three hundred yards up the hillside beyond them. One half were firing whilst the other half plodded obliquely across the rear of the Great Redoubt, bayonets twinkling, the sun flashing off the brass spikes of their leather helmets.

That morning, Morgan had taken the Tranter revolver from its case and carefully loaded the six chambers before clipping it to his narrow sash — he thought he could remember holding it above the

25

current but, as he drew it, he had no confidence that the thing would work.

"You'd be better off with one of the casualties' rifles, sir, wouldn't you?" Ormond asked.

Morgan looked around him — none of the other officers had picked-up rifles, they were sticking to the unwritten rule that gentlemen left the sordid business of killing to the rank and file — a rule that he'd already broken. So now he contented himself with his pistol, balancing it carefully on his forearm as he aimed at the coatskirts of a crossing Russian and pulled the trigger. He was rewarded with a bang, a jolt and a face full of smoke followed, much to his surprise, by five more faultless detonations, yet the Muscovites tramped on untouched, apparently oblivious to his fire. How his father would have scoffed.

Heads and hearts more hardened to war may have been able to resist the spark of panic that now fanned through the mass. Two Staff officers scrambled through the position, waving their arms, yelling, "Don't fire, they're the French" then "Fusiliers retire" in chaotic succession.

"Retire be damned, stand fast and fire low." Hume had almost lost his voice, but other officers echoed him. "Morgan, put that wretched thing down; get amongst the boys, won't you?" Stung by the words, Morgan thrust his half-reloaded pistol away.

"Here, sir, help me with these." Colour-Sergeant McGucken thrust a clutch of paper cartridges into the young man's hand, gesturing him to calm the troops from the hotch-potch of regiments around him. Within the Great Redoubt were men of the 7th and 23rd Fusiliers, both as keen as anyone else to hear and obey an order that would get them out of the horror with their honour intact and once a bugler took up the 'Retire' all was lost. Some men paused, firing sullenly into their enemies, but most bundled back through the embrasures that they had seized just a short time before with barely a backward glance. The troops streamed down the hill, trying hard to avoid their dead and wounded comrades who studded the slopes.

Morgan never really knew whether the Scots Fusilier Guards had broken or not. He could certainly remember their Colours standing fast amongst the smoke and shot and, later, the body of a young Guards officer in the hospital riven with bayonet wounds. He could recall Russians too close for comfort, his imperfectly loaded pistol and then the whole Guards Brigade in close and perfect order as the survivors of the first attack on the Redoubt eddied around them, but none of this left the same impression as Hume did. Somehow he'd retrieved the 95th's Colour party and reformed it; somehow he'd clubbed a score or so of his own men around him; and somehow he found the sheer gall to persuade them to face the Russian fire once again.

Morgan wondered if Hume's exaggerated courtesy was natural or whether he was simply trying to master the surrounding bedlam. It hardly mattered, for there wasn't a man in sight who could have failed to notice a senior, shot-holed and tousled major approach an

27

ensign of the 3rd Grenadiers, brace to attention and ask the youngster's permission to fall Her Majesty's 95th Regiment in on their flank. Mere theatre, perhaps — but it worked. The boy in the bearskin stuttered his approval and now no one in the 95th could fail to get into step behind Hume and beside the sweeping line of Guardsmen.

Without the heavy guns in the Redoubt, the fire was certainly lighter this time, but the fear was worse. Just a few minutes before, Morgan had found himself all but oblivious to the hum and crack of shot knowing that all eyes were upon him and the Colour that he carried. Now, though, he was amongst the bloodied, those who chose to face the horrors of those slopes again and who no longer needed a mere subaltern's bravado. Regimental pride was a powerful thing. With the Guards file-firing as they advanced, the knot of 95th steadied and began to ply their weapons with the precision that they'd been taught.

"Come on show-soldiers, it's this way to Mr Russ." The boy, Pegg, seemed to have recovered sufficiently from his earlier fright not only to be beating a creditable tattoo on his dented drum, but also to be taunting the line of bearskins to his left.

"So when we take the position for you will you be able to hold it this time, short-arse?" One of the Guardsmen snarled back at Pegg.

The rifles sickled the Russians. The enemy musket-fire was feeble in return and as each volley smashed home, so low mounds of moaning or motionless bodies began to pile up. Morgan saw a

Russian officer come running to the front of his troops, sword point down, waving his men on. A line of bayonets were lowered and a brown-grey wall of men began to trot down the hill towards them.

"You five, kneel," croaked McGucken. "Three hundred — but aim at their knees, it's not that far. Get that bastard officer." One fouled rifle failed to fire, but four rounds and a pointless one from Morgan's pistol flew straight and true and when the smoke from the muzzles had cleared, the officer had disappeared and the bank of Russians had stalled, their muskets touching the ground as they goggled at the approaching British.

Some unheard message pulled the 95th to a halt. The Guards to their left had stopped, all looking expectantly to the centre of their line, whilst the other two battalions continued on their steady tramp. Then flashing metal, a sibilant rasp and six hundred long, needle-like bayonets were fixed over the muzzles of the men's rifles. Another pause, and then with a mute command, the Guards stepped out.

The Russians stood in the same dense columns that had served them well at Borodino, little expecting that at such close ranges a Minié bullet would pierce not just the front rank but find the second and sometimes the third. As the lead squashed and distorted on the first impact, so it became all the more damaging on subsequent strikes — no troops could stand against this.

As the Guards' pace increased, so the Russian columns dissolved. Harried now by French and British horse artillery, the great, grey masses started to peel away, leaving just their dead and wounded to face the bayonets.

"Here you are, Mr Morgan, sir, I'm sending one to Marn." He wondered just how grateful Mrs Pegg would be for the brass eagle with its big "31" from the front of a Russian helmet and whether she would approve as her boy lifted an icon from around the rapidly cooling neck of one of their foes.

The earth and sandbag walls of the Great Redoubt gave welcome protection as the British surged back into it for the second time. The Allies' guns had played on the Russians as they massed for the counterattack there and now the red coats of the earlier casualties were all but submerged by their dead and dying enemies. There on his back, arms outstretched, head lolling back and mouth wide open was Private Peter Luff — he was as pale as milk, the river water still dripped gently from his clothes, mingling with the great brown stain that spread below his body whilst two flies crawled over his lips.

"God help us, Pegg, it's Peter Luff, ain't it? Did you see him fall?"

"No, sir, only just seen the poor bastard. Save him from a flogging though, won't it?" Now, Private Luff would never receive the punishment that he'd been awarded a few days before. With scarcely a glance at his dead friend, Pegg ransacked another corpse.

Then, just feet from them a shot cracked out. Without a sound, a subaltern of the 95th toppled over, banging his face hard into the earth. His dead fingers still held the water-bottle with which he had been trying to slake the thirst of one wounded Russian, when another had shot him in the neck. Now both blood and water spilled into the ground, but before Morgan or Pegg could properly grasp what was going on, two of their soldiers were upon the Russian, thrusting at him with their bayonets. The Muscovite cried once, twice and then was silent as the men wiped his gore from their blades.

The Guards battalions were quickly brought in hand, stoically pushing past and beyond the earthwork in an attempt to turn their enemy's defeat into a rout, but Hume ordered his clutch of 95th to check and rally the rest of the troops.

The guns still thundered but at distant targets now. For the first time in what seemed weeks, Morgan was conscious that the air was not full of metal and that death, for him at least, was slightly more distant. The men sank all around him, deaf to the cries of the wounded, as they pulled out their stumpy clay pipes, some of the younger ones falling instantly asleep, lips still black with powder. Even the sergeants, moving amongst the survivors trying to find out who was and who was not answering the roll, staggered, exhausted.

Morgan sat down heavily. He rooted around his haversack until he found the silver-topped brandy flask that he had bought in Dublin on the way out and, hands shaking with the sheer relief of being alive, he unscrewed it and took a long pull at the raw spirit. Looking between his soaked and muddy legs and boots, he saw the grassy hillside below him covered with scarlet and grey cairns. It seemed like an eternity since that farewell dinner at home when he'd been asked if he could take another's life, if he could widow wives and orphan children. Well, now he had and it gave him no pleasure. The smiles of those at the table were still vivid, but now James Keenan was torn by shot, Mary was stained with her own husband's blood and had seen things that no teenage girl should have to see whilst his own courage had been tested to the full. As he sat and pondered, Colour-Sergeant McGucken lowered himself wearily to the ground beside him.

"Well, Colour-Sar'nt, that will be the first battle-honour on our Colours." Morgan forced his gloom and tiredness away.

McGucken pulled out his pipe and poked and prodded at the bowl before answering, "Aye, sir, an' let's pray it's our last."

CHAPTER
TWO

Glassdrumman

The young moon winked through the shutters. Glassdrumman, the warm, shabby, peeling Georgian hall that was the Morgan family's Cork home was deep in sleep. Mary Cade pulled her nightshift down to cover her bottom, wrapped an errant blanket about them both and moved herself a fraction on top of Tony Morgan, their passion spent. The chambermaid and the young officer had had their fill of one another and now was the time for talk.

"Maude Hawtrey's lovely — she sits a horse so well, almost like a man. And it's obvious to anyone that you're getting on famously, so much in common, scriptures and the like." Mary held Morgan's face in both her hands, his dark-fair hair and whiskers tousled, her nose an inch from his, murmuring, smiling so that he'd have to search for the barbs.

"Mary, please, why are you always like this afterwards?"

"Mary, please." Even in a whisper she mimicked him well enough, catching the Englishness that he'd cultivated over the past couple of years. "And why are you always like this afterwards? You're all promises and passion with me here, but downstairs I'm nothing to you, am I — d'you think I'm some sort of eejit?" In an instant the warmth and smile had disappeared. Her face was now serious, the honey had gone from her voice and she neglected that little gesture of sweeping a jet-black lock of hair from out of her eyes.

Without warning her sticky weight was off him. She slid from under the blanket and onto the woollen rug beside the bed, hands on her hips, a curling mane of hair down her back, chin and breasts petulantly thrust forward. Morgan recognized the signs and unconsciously pulled the covers up against the storm.

"What happiness d'you think you'll get there, Lieutenant Mister-bloody-Morgan? Your Da will end up with some Prod stronghold and you'll be at his and the Hawtreys' beck and call for the rest of your days, like a wee puppy." Mary hissed her venom. He lunged and tried to grab her wrists. Occasionally she could be tamed, won round by kisses and enveloping arms but this time she wouldn't be turned. She left the dawn-lit room as swiftly as her pleasure had cooled.

Morgan winced as the bedroom door banged — did she want everyone to know? And she was wrong of course. Maude would never glance at Tony Morgan whilst he was soldiering; besides, a war could change his world. But whatever lay ahead with stringy Maude, the smell, warmth and sheer sparkle of Mary would stay with him. He groped to find his watch.

"So, the young lion's awake and prepared to grace us with his presence at last." Billy Morgan, a widower at fifty-nine, grey curls hanging too long about the collar of his badly-starched shirt, his waistcoat unbuttoned and loose, greeted his son as he came into breakfast.

The big dining room was barely warm from the peat fire that the servants had started before any of the family were awake, lighting up the walls and heavily decorated ceiling where the grey March morning light hardly penetrated. Silver *entrée* dishes jostled for space on the sideboard, little spirit lamps flickering below them to keep the porridge, eggs, bacon and kidneys warm for the Morgans and their guest.

"I am, father: good morning, Colonel, I hope you slept well?" Tony had learnt not to encourage his father's heavy jokes, particularly when others were there; to do anything else would only spur him on. Now Billy's oldest friend, Colonel Dick Kemp, grinned across the table at him.

"I slept as well as your father's lumpy mattress would allow: I've had better nights in a snake-filled storm ditch with jackals licking my balls; I only stay at Glassdrumman out of pity for the old boy." When Tony had come back for home leave a week ago, he'd found Kemp deeply ensconced there, staying for a full three months of his furlough from India where he commanded a battalion of Bengal infantry. The two officers, despite the gap in age and rank, had soon formed an easy bond in the face of Billy Morgan's wit that sent the banter crackling between the three of them.

"Less of the 'old boy', Kemp. Just because I was a-soldiering before you'd thrown a leg across a drab, don't come the 'Victor of Aliwal' with me!" As a very young man, Billy Morgan had seen some gentle service in the West Cork Militia, patrolling the Atlantic coastline against the last vestiges of Napoleon's hordes whilst Kemp had just been starting on his career as an ensign of the Honourable East India Company. And that career had been a placid one until Kemp, if his accounts were to be believed, had beaten the Sikhs almost single-handed, smashing them as effectively as they had snapped one of his legs at the Battle of Aliwal eight years before.

Tony knew the signs by now. Kemp's sharp, black eyes were shining, he was full of piss and vinegar, keen for fun at any price, but if the two, older men started one of their verbal skirmishes now, there would be no end to it: distraction was the answer.

"What have the papers to say today, Father?" Tony asked as he sprinkled cinnamon and sugar over his porridge.

"Well, those fools in London and Paris have finally declared war." Billy shook the paper out, the headlines bellowing the formal recognition of a war that had been underway for several months already.

"Tell me something that surprises me, Father. Here, Keenan, look at this: at last we're at war." Private James Keenan, Tony's batman in the 95th whom he'd selected for the post as much for the fact that he was a fellow Corkman as for his competence, had brought more coffee for his master. When the Regiment was sent on leave before embarking for foreign service, Keenan had chosen to spend the time comfortably fed and watered by his master in Glassdrumman rather than with his own family scraping an existence from the soil just a dozen miles away in Clonakilty. Now he narrowed his eyes and laboured over the letters of the headline.

"So, we're to have a fight, then, your honour. But where will it be?" Keenan asked the question to which none of them knew the answer.

Six months before, the Russian Admiral Nachimov had sunk an ageing Turkish fleet at Sinope in the Black Sea; since then war had been an inevitability. The Turks had already been hard at it with the Russians, each pounding the other inconclusively: now the formal entry of the Allies meant that war could start in earnest, plunging Europe into her first serious conflict since Waterloo.

"Good question, Keenan." They all deferred to Kemp for he knew the Russians well — or so he claimed. "We saw more than enough of the Russians' tricks up on the Frontier after that nonsense at Kabul in forty-two. They're crafty buggers an' John Turk will need all the help he can get if he's to throw them out of Moldavia and Wallachia. You'll be scampering up and down the Danube, I'd guess."

The mention of two such exotic names stalled the discussion for a moment, adding to Kemp's stature, before Tony cut in, "You're probably right, Colonel, but everybody seemed to have a different view back in Weedon."

The 95th were stationed at the newly-built barracks in Weedon in Northamptonshire. Just six weeks before the commanding officer had ordered a general parade and told them all that they were to start, "warlike preparations".

"All we've been told is that we're to be ready to go to, 'The East' and there's been some *craic* over that, I can tell you. Kingsley, the adjutant — you remember him, Father, he transferred in from the Cape Mounted Rifles — says we'll go wherever the Turks want us, but Hume, the senior major, reckons that the French will want us to have a go at the Muscovites' fleet in Sevastopol up to the north, in the Crimea."

"The French," Billy Morgan said it as if he were clearing phlegm, "how in the name of God have we got involved with those rogues?"

"Father, before you start, those poor fellows have had their necks stretched enough: I'd say that Colonel Kemp and Keenan can probably name every last one." Tony was trying to stop his father from treating the whole room to another account of the highpoint of Billy's Militia service when, at seventeen, he'd arrested and strung-up a boatload of shipwrecked French sailors. Local society was still undecided whether they were spies or not, but Billy was convinced and still delighted in the story.

"Aye, well it's all right for you an' your clever pals loafing around in barracks without a hand-span of proper soldiering to your name," Billy Morgan was warming to one of his favourite themes, "but if you'd seen what those damn Frogs and the Croppies did to this country when I was a boy, then that so-called revolution of theirs in forty-eight — and now they've got another of those Buonaparte fuckers back at the helm, you'd be getting ready to fight the Frenchies and not the Russians who helped us to thrash 'em last time." His voice fell before adding, "They're just a parcel of bloody Papists."

There was a flicker of embarrassment as Kemp and Tony looked at Keenan — the only Catholic there — but the soldier-servant was too used to this sort of talk from his betters to take any notice or offence.

"What d'you, think, James Keenan?" Billy Morgan sensed the others' slight discomfort and tried to cover it by bringing the man back into the conversation, "Wouldn't you prefer to go at the French and leave the Russians to their own devices?"

"I couldn't care less, your honour . . ." Keenan poured more coffee for Kemp, "I'm just a soldier an' I'll go wherever I'm told an' put a lead bullet into any head that Mr Morgan asks me to, Catholic, Protestant, Musselman or Jew, they're all one to me. Besides, they say Turkish tail's worth a look."

There was a shout of appreciative laughter at Keenan's simple philosophy and it brought an end to talk of war.

"Now, I'm off to have a peep at this horse you've got for me, Billy," said Kemp, rising from the table, wiping heartily at his lips before letting his napkin fall to the ground. "I'll see you in the tack room in, what . . . five and twenty minutes, shall we say, Mr Morgan?" Keenan pulled the Colonel's chair away for him and retrieved his discarded cloth.

"That's fine, Colonel, I'll be with you as soon as I've finished my breakfast," Tony half rose from his chair respectfully as his senior left the room.

"You'll be taking Kemp for a canter over Clow's Top, will you, son?" Billy pushed more bacon home as a slight smile lit his face.

"I will and don't fret, I know that Miss Hawtrey and her cousin are expecting to see us up there. I'll show them that fox's earth that Finn's been talking about all winter."

"Aye, well mind you do, you'll get bugger-all time between now and the end of your leave to speak to young Maude with anything like privacy, an' I've told Kemp to give you both a bit of breathing space, so make the most of it." With no mother to corral suitable young women for Morgan during his rare leaves, Billy had to do the job instead, the most promising target being the eldest daughter of Judge Hawtrey from Leap. He'd first introduced them last year; what Maude lacked in beauty and warmth was more than compensated for by her family's wealth and position.

A sudden crash at the sideboard made both father and son jump.

"Mary, have a care, won't you? Those are the last few bits of Mrs Morgan's favourite china." Neither man had noticed the girl glide in from the scullery to start clearing the plates and dishes. She must have heard all of the last conversation and now she banged away with none of her normal care, her usually elegant lips pursed in a tight, cold line. She said not a thing, almost snatching the cups and saucers from their hands, her face set and expressionless until James Keenan held the door open for her. Then she smiled: she smiled a great, lovely beam straight into the young soldier's eyes before both servants left the room.

"Don't know what's got into her this morning — though I've a fair idea what got into her last night . . ." Billy looked hard at his son. "Any ideas, boy?"

"No, father, but she can be awfully cussed sometimes, you know."

"Yes, I do, son . . . but please be careful."

Tony paused at the back door of the house to buckle his spurs to his polished, brown, riding boots and take his crop from the mahogany stand. As he clicked over the setts towards the tack room, he could hear Colonel Kemp's excited voice.

"They came on like bloody French did the Sikhs — mind you, half their officers was *école* trained — and it looked bad until the guns put some canister amongst them. I never expected natives to stand against our sepoys, but I was wrong. Sir Harry used the infantry well, but it took you and the Sixteenth Lancers, Finn, to really finish the day."

Morgan entered the big, leather-smelling room just as Finn, at forty-two still as slender as the lance he'd once carried, took to the floor. Legs bowed, imaginary reins and weapons in hand, the former sergeant bobbed below the razor-like cuts, jibbed his mount to the left and dug hard at his invisible foe,

"I tell you, sir, a big turbaned fellah came up to our officer for to bayonet him, bold as you please. But like

41

the griffin I was, I pushed my lance too hard — the fucking pennon came out the other side and I was left capering like a damn fool round the poor man, so. I shoulda dropped the thing and used my sword — that's when I got this."

Morgan had seen the three-inch weal across Finn's shoulder often enough, but as he peeled back his collar, Kemp hissed between his teeth in admiration.

"Ah, Morgan, Finn and I were just recounting the delights of Aliwal. I bet you haven't seen as smooth a job as this, though?" Kemp rolled up his trouser leg to show a purple, mottled, scaly shin-bone deeply etched across.

"I'd ordered our boys to form square to keep the Sikh horse at bay when their guns caught us on the nose. I went down like a sack of shite — poor Goldie was dead before she hit the ground and me stuck below her. Tricky moment, that, but the doctors did wonders. If we'd had the boy surgeons that some of the Queen's regiments did, I don't doubt I'd have lost it. Beautiful job, ain't it?"

Colonel and sergeant preened and bragged. The bond of shared experience quite overcame any difference in military or social rank, both men grinning with an almost childish pleasure over their mutual brushes with death. Morgan pondered their casual acceptance of the pain and destruction that they had both suffered and inflicted, remembering the fearful casualties that the Sikhs and British had imposed on each other. In the depot at Fermoy he'd seen young men, some without limbs, one blinded, another with a face that looked as if it had been scythed; then he'd watched the guns at Chobham firing canister and shell at paper targets: Colonel Kemp had been just such to the Sikh gunners only a few years ago. Now he wondered whether Keenan and he would have to face such horror and how he would react. Kemp and Finn were just about to put the Sikhs to the sword again when James Keenan bustled into the room.

"Sable's ready for you outside, your honour an' we've got Thunder for you, Colonel Kemp, sir, like you said, Mr Finn," Keenan had fitted very easily into life at Glassdrumman, accepting Finn's experience and authority and hanging on his every word when war or horseflesh was being discussed.

"Aye, lad, we'll be with you directly . . ." Kemp waved him away, he hadn't yet finished his war story.

"No, sir, the Master's keen that you're not late for your meeting with the ladies . . ." Keenan spoke with surprising firmness: Billy Morgan had told him to hasten Kemp and Tony and hasten them he would, officers or not.

Kemp paused for a moment, not used to being gainsaid by either soldiers or servants, before remembering in whose house he was a guest.

"Quite so, James Keenan, we're at the ladies' command. Come on young Morgan, stop delaying us with all that gammon, you've a gusset to sniff." Kemp's crude familiarity was greeted with a peal of laughter from all the men, taking the edge off the atmosphere. In his middle fifties, Indian living had given Kemp a generous figure: now it filled the doorframe as he stumped outside with Morgan.

An under-groom held Thunder's stirrup for Kemp whilst Keenan steadied Sable, the big gelding, for Tony. He levered himself aboard as he thought about the colonel's words: it was an odd thing, but in all the time he'd known Maude Hawtrey he'd never even thought about her gusset. Her inheritance, certainly; her place in society, for sure; but he could never remember lusting after her. There was none of the constant ache that he felt for Mary Cade who, even now, was crossing the stableyard with a great bunch of freshly-cut daffodils in her hands. Tony smiled across at her, but she looked straight through him.

"There, your honour, don't let Sable run away with you . . ." Keenan tightened Tony's girth and smoothed the saddle-leather back into position as he noticed his master's look, "an' she's a great wee girl, ain't she? Have a grand day," and he turned away to follow Mary inside.

"God, I love these mornings, don't you, Morgan?" Kemp turned to Tony and yelled above the noise of their horses' cantering hooves as they vied with each other over the rich, Irish turf, "I never thought I'd want to see a drop o' rain again when I left Ireland, but you get so goddamn bored with the dust and the sun and the constant smell of shit in India that you're almost glad to be pissed-wet through and perished just for a change." They cantered over the field towards the rendezvous with Maude and her young cousin that Billy Morgan had arranged.

"Aye, Colonel, but it must be good living and an easy command with sepoys, ain't it?" Morgan asked more out of politeness than curiosity, for he'd never wanted to serve with one of John Company's regiments, despite the better style of living and the supposed adventure of life in India. No, he'd been quite clear with his father when the question of what he wanted to do for a job came up a few years before, it was one of the Queen's regiments or nothing at all. Why, he'd prefer to be a damned vicar than be marooned in Hindoostan.

"It's suited me well enough, but I miss the old country and have never been able to afford to be in a smart regiment like yours." Kemp had reined back a little, keener to talk to his friend's son than to run him ragged.

"There's nothing smart about the Ninety-Fifth, Colonel, we're not like the Guards or cavalry, just ordinary Line, and 'young' Line at that, not a battle to our name so far." The 95th had only been raised in 1823, every soldier and officer being acutely aware of the absence of honours on the regiment's Colours.

"But there a good lot, ain't they? You fit well enough, don't you, or are you full of those bloody merchants' sons who take a rise out of us Paddies?" The more lurid papers had been obsessed over the past few years with snobbery amongst the officer class; the friction that it had caused and the bullying in regiments that had become infamous for the "hazing" of officers who didn't quite fit. Kemp had obviously been following all of this from India.

"No, not really, Colonel. There's one or two cads about, but nothing like the happenings in the Forty-Sixth . . ." Despite the news of war, the papers were still full of the scandal of a young officer from a "new money" background whose peers had treated him so badly that he'd become demented, challenging even his commanding officer to an illegal duel. "We rub along well enough. The Bible-punchers are more of a bore."

"Aye, we get more than our fair share of those twots out east . . ." Kemp had eased Thunder right back now, keen to hear what Morgan had to say, ". . . always trying to impose their damned religion on the sepoys, never understanding how much offence they can cause to both Muslim and Hindu."

"Yes, you've got to be so damned careful with the men, though. You expect some of the officers to be full of that righteous stuff and know to steer clear, but then some of the boys will pull the 'good book' out of their haversacks and sit about reading with a face like a smacked arse rather than chasing tail an' drinking like normal men." Most of Morgan's men were the products of the overcrowded slums or had come straight from the plough, their vices and attitudes being wholly predictable. But a handful of them were different, usually the better-educated, Scottish boys who tended to band together when off-duty, often gravitating around a particular pious officer or sergeant: no better or worse soldiers for it, just a bit different.

"And we've even got one or two who are keen on this damn teetotal nonsense," Morgan added.

"Thank Jaysus there's little enough of that in the Punjab just now," replied Kemp. "Why, you need a good belt of grog just to keep the sun off. Never can understand how the natives manage without it. What are your non-commissioned men like?"

"For the most part they're really good, Colonel, steady and loyal as you like. They lack a bit of imagination, sometimes — too keen on the manuals and they can be rough on the private soldiers, but we're lucky with our Colour-Sergeant, McGucken who's got fifteen years' service already."

"Well, take it from me, young Mr Morgan, you don't need imagination in battle, just plenty of guts and unquestioning obedience. When the iron begins to fly, take my tip and stick close to this Colour-Sergeant of yours, he'll do you well." Kemp spoke with all the authority of a man who had been tested on the anvil of war already: Morgan envied him. "Now, there's the ladies, enough of this war talk, you've got your other career to think about." Kemp smiled and winked at Morgan.

Now Morgan saw just what Mary had meant in bed that morning, for Maude Hawtrey sat stiffly, very mannishly, despite her side-saddle. Her dark hair was pulled back in a bun below her low-crowned hat, the veil exaggerating rather than hiding her jutting nose. Laced and stayed, her figure had none of the ripeness of Mary's. With her was her plump fourteen-year-old cousin, Charlotte Foster, whose pony was a little too big for her; now she was fighting to control it.

The two women had heard the men approaching, had measured their distance from the barred wooden gate that led into the next pasture and slowed to a walk to let Kemp or Morgan dismount and open it for them. The colonel, remembering his instructions, broke into a trot and got there first, swinging down from the saddle with more grace than might be expected of a man of his girth.

"Good morning Colonel, that's civil of you." Maude tilted her head to Kemp with a slight smile as he swung the big gate open for the other three.

Morgan edged up alongside Maude — Kemp was giving him every chance. But as the two riders walked to the gate Charlotte's skittish pony decide to have its own way, suddenly breaking into a canter and trying to squeeze between Morgan and the rough-hewn gatepost as the girl hauled uselessly at its bit. With a shriek that echoed back off a nearby spinney, Charlotte scraped her leg along the post, her velvet cap falling from her head as she dropped her crop and reins and clung to the mane. The pony trotted on, raising its nose and snorting at its freedom as the reins hung loose, before the rider tumbled slowly from the saddle and landed with a damp thump on the grass.

"Gracious me, that wee devil's killed Charlotte!" exclaimed Maude, and she pressed her gloved hand hard against her lips.

Certainly, petticoats and habit lay motionless on the grass, but the child's outraged moaning suggested that the diagnosis was probably wrong. In an instant, though, Morgan was out of the saddle and alongside the girl, her cries subsiding almost as soon as he wrapped his arms about her.

"There, Miss Foster, there. Are you hurt or just winded, jewel?" Tony could see that it was more shock than actual harm.

"It's my leg, sir," Charlotte sobbed.

"Forgive me, please, miss, but can you point your foot . . ." Morgan reached as decorously as he could below the backless skirt of her riding habit, gently holding her calf through the corduroy breeches that she wore below, ". . . and wiggle your toes?"

The pony cropped the grass a few yards away, looking pleased with itself.

"Yes . . . yes I think so." Charlotte's tears had quite subsided under the young officer's touch.

There was the smallest rip in the leg of the girl's breeches where the gatepost had scored the cloth; now Morgan helped Charlotte to her feet and she hopped a few paces, gingerly putting her weight on the suspect leg before stepping a few paces more whilst still clutching firmly to Morgan's arm.

"Well, Mr Morgan you're quite the man for a lady to have around in an emergency, aren't you?" Maude had her horse well in hand as she gazed down at Morgan from her saddle.

"I try to rise to every challenge, Miss Hawtrey," he replied, ignoring Kemp's suppressed guffaw in the background.

"I'm sure that we're both very grateful to you. I think I'd better get Charlotte home now — that fox's earth can wait for another occasion, I hope. In the meantime, we look forward to seeing you both at dinner tonight," said Maude as she held the pony's bridle as Morgan helped Charlotte to mount.

The two cousins walked their mounts away across the spongy meadow and Morgan didn't have long to wait for Kemp's assessment. "Well, young Morgan that was a nice piece of work, but I can think of challenges that would make me rise more quickly than that ice-cube."

The starched white collar was always tricky. No matter how many times he fiddled with studs and pins, no matter how much help his servant gave him, Morgan still found it difficult to shoe-horn himself into the simple black and white of evening dress without time in hand. Father had wanted him to wear his regimentals for his final dinner party, but he'd resisted, settling for Keenan's waiting at table in his scarlet. Father's friends would be attentive enough without his having to flaunt his gallantry.

In an unusual fit of competence, the servants had lit the drawing-room fire in plenty of time. Despite the damp peat, the blaze was almost too much for a spring night and the guests quickly migrated to the cooler, less smoky end of the room. Kemp was reserved, for he realized that the evening should belong to Tony and that there was little interest in wars past.

50

Billy Morgan had every intention of thoroughly lionizing his son. The glory that Tony would reflect upon his father could only be increased if attention were lavished upon him on this, his final night at home. The difficulty was that Mrs Amelia Smythe was one of the guests. Tony could quite see the attraction of the young widow whose husband had failed to return from the Cape last year, but he hadn't realized just how interested his father was in the woman. In fact, he could be excused for wondering just who the main guest of honour was.

Desultory enquiries were made of the young hero whilst they drank. His father's friends asked endless questions about weapons and horses, all designed to display their own militia experience, whilst Kemp restricted himself to opinions only upon the Russians and their antics on the Afghan border. The warlike talk cooled, though, as Billy concentrated the full force of his charm upon Amelia. Imperial ambitions soon gave way to domestic ones, sabre-rattling to numbers of acres, fleets of ships to stables full of hunters.

The silver had been polished almost entirely clean. Whilst the candles were a little uneven, at least they were all burning, shedding a gentle light on the only slightly smeared crystal. Perhaps Morgan's expectations had been raised too high by the standards required in the Mess, for his father seemed oblivious to the corner-cutting, purring over the display and making great play of finding Mrs Smythe's seat for her.

Sitting opposite Amelia Smythe, Morgan gazed at Mary who stood ready to serve her. The girl had on a muslin dress passed down from some lady guest and she had carefully rouged her cheeks whilst her hair, Tony was sure, had felt the deft fingers of Mrs O'Connor, the housekeeper. The ribbons and ringlets were strangely similar to those that adorned Maude Hawtrey who was sitting next to him — but there was little doubt upon whom they looked better. Whilst Mary made the impression that she intended, Tony tried to avoid her glances, but he couldn't fail to notice her smiles. From behind him darted the yellow cuff of Keenan's regimental coatee as plates and glasses were whipped away. The young soldier's movements seemed strangely in tune with those of Mary across the table.

Tony did his best with Maude and the bruised Charlotte. The little sallies that he tried with Miss Hawtrey seemed to tell, but her polite enquiries about the typical temperature in the East, whether he would have to keep warm or cool and how trying the indigenous snakes and flies would be were hard to endure. To her the "East" was a definite place, populated by a distinct and loathsome tribe with the absolute intention of making his life as uncomfortable as possible. Try as he might, he could not convince her of the reality of the Russians, the certainty of their trying to kill rather than simply discommode him and the absolute gallantry with which he would confound them. No, to Maude war was no platform of valour, merely a plain of banality. On the other hand, Charlotte's accident at least gave Morgan something plausible to talk about whilst reminding Maude of another sort of gallantry.

The courses seemed endless. Billy stuck to the old custom of feeding early and feeding plenty no doubt hoping to impress their guests. Soup gave way to ices, savouries to meats, jellies to slices of offal on toast and finally puddings, the whole accompanied by the finest that the Morgan cellar could provide. There would have been every temptation to lighten the burden of his neighbours with drink, but with Maude at such close quarters he hardly dared.

Finally, the toasts. The Queen and Albert began the cavalcade, the army and the navy came next, respective regiments followed hard: then the Tsar and Pope (eyes well damned) brought up the rear.

Warming to his role, Billy called for silence again: "Friends, it's been some time since a Morgan answered the call to war." Father must have a wonderful memory, thought Tony. There had been no whiff of powder for the old captain and the West Cork Militia along Bantry Bay forty-odd years ago. "We don't know where this great war will take Tony, but we do know that it's made new enemies of old friends and new friends of old enemies. In my day you knew where you stood."

A long way from danger, thought Tony. It was impossible not to like the man, but he made such a show of his militia service all those years ago that the guests could have been forgiven for thinking that it was Billy who was about to go and humble the Tsar, not him.

"But in this pell-mellery all I can do is to show my son our admiration with a gift that we pray he does not have to use — at least, not against Christians."

53

The last phrase drew a snort from the men, but had Tony not been concentrating so hard on the unexpected present he would have noticed a frown from Amelia. Finn, smart as paint in his bottle-green suit of livery, moved from the shadows and passed a slender mahogany box to Billy Morgan. Tony, quite forgetting napkin and chair leg half stumbled as his father beckoned him forward to accept the gift. A little brass plate let into the top was inscribed, "A. Morgan Esqre, Gren Coy, 95th Regt." The box contained a steely-blue, walnut-stocked Tranter with patches, powder and enough lead to quench the ambition of any Muscovite.

"That's a fine-looking thing. May I?" Now alongside the Morgans, Kemp's fingers took the pistol with an almost lascivious grace, coiling themselves around the chequered stock whilst gently tickling the trigger. Supporting it on his beefy left forearm he aimed at the curtain. "Only some of us had revolvers in the Punjab and they were nowhere near as fine as this. Remember, Mr Morgan, you'll have the advantage with a repeater, but don't go wasting shot at long range. Wait til' your man gets up close then stick the thing hard into his face before you fire. At Aliwal I had a pepperpot that Charteris — you remember him, Billy? — had urged me to try. All the barrels failed and I ended up using the wretched thing like a club. Oh, I do beg your pardon." Kemp cut himself short, realizing that he was marring Billy's moment.

The generosity and unexpectedness of the gift quite silenced Tony. He'd rehearsed a little speech that he expected to give once the toasts had finished — it was brief, self-effacing yet poignant with suggested danger and valour, honed to beguile both lady and maid — but in the event it was still-born. He tumbled out some almost adequate words before resorting to a toast to his father's and friends' health.

Extra peat had redoubled the effects of the drawing-room fire. A lacklustre enquiry or two from the vicar and his wife soon ran into the sand and Tony was desperately seeking another topic when Amelia Smythe appeared at his side. She was a shapely, almost pretty woman who suited the black dress and sparse jewellery that she wore. She was carefully groomed, her hair piled high, powder subtly applied, simple clusters of diamonds at her ears and throat, yet there was a sadness in her grey eyes and at the corners of her mouth. Morgan saw immediately that she was not bent upon platitudes, for she thrust her chin forward, strong opinion bubbling to be set free.

"Mr Morgan, forgive my seeking your views, especially as we hardly know each other — oh, forgive me. Thank you for inviting me to your party, but have you thought what war will really mean? Are you quite sure that you will be able to send some other poor creature to eternity?"

"Mrs Smythe, I'm a soldier — death is my trade." Tony immediately regretted his gauche reply, remembering how hollow the same phrase had sounded when Richard Carmichael had used it, trying to impress some miss at a ball in England. Why hadn't he managed a thoughtful reply to a serious question, for as he'd handled the pistol he'd wondered just the same thing? If he returned from this campaign would he and Keenan be full of that same lethal joy that he'd seen in Finn and Kemp? Could he rejoice over death and injury? Might he join the gouged veterans in Fermoy — or, like Mr Smythe, not return at all?

"You heard Colonel Kemp, exhorting you to fire that awful gun — I mean no disrespect — only when you could be sure of killing with it. Have you prayed about this, can you tell me that Christian nations, today, are really not able to settle their arguments in some other way?"

"But this war is a just one, someone must protect Turkey from being bullied." Morgan was struggling now. He'd read the Parliamentary debates in the papers and whilst he would much have preferred to adopt Keenan's stance that, as a soldier, he'd go anywhere and fight anyone he was told to, he knew that wouldn't do for the intense Mrs Smythe. Where were the barrack God-botherers when you needed them, Morgan thought, and why couldn't this comely woman pester his father and not him?

"Can any act of war or killing be described as just, Mr Morgan? If you really believe that God could smile on those who seek to kill in his name, then I can only pray for you. Forgive my saying such things in your home on this your last night here, but I have to let you know how much I hate the idea of war and all the unhappiness it will unleash." The strident note had quite gone from Mrs Smythe's voice and her eyes were cast down almost demurely.

Tony wondered if his father had seen this side of Amelia. She'd made her points with a persuasive passion that had made him think seriously about what he was embarking upon for the first time. Could he continue to hide behind the simplistic arguments that his brother subalterns used and the jingoism of the press? Keenan and the other soldiers might be able to shelter behind the claims that they weren't paid to think or reason, but he was an officer who, if all this talk came to anything at all, would be required to lead men to their deaths.

Later, when cleaning and balancing his gift he questioned whether he would be able to do the things that war required. Would he be capable of taking this elegant tool and bludgeoning another man with it as Kemp had done?

Dinner finished late and Morgan was almost immediately asleep. Every creak of the house, though, every dream-grunt from Hector in the kitchen below woke him, making him check the half-hunter by the light of the moon, but still Mary didn't come. On this, of all nights, he wanted to see her to say a leisured goodbye, to store up memories that would warm him in whatever solitude and latitudes lay ahead. Then, with the first signs of light, his door opened and Mary — stepping wide in her bare feet to avoid a squeaky board — was with him. Cold beneath the eiderdown, her kisses covered his mouth and face, as she slipped from her nightdress and reached for him in one well-practised movement.

"I'm sorry to be so late, your honour, but the table and kitchen won't clean themselves and James Keenan had a wee party as well as you!" Her mouth tasted of drink.

"I hope the Staff were kind to him . . . Oh, Mary." She smiled up from the shadows deep below the sheets.

"We were, and herself said that we had to find you a gift, just like your father did. Trouble was, we had nothing to give you, so I thought this might answer."

"I'm glad that you came to give me the present and not Mrs O'Connor." The joke was old but Mary trembled silently as only she could. When she laughed her whole body was consumed by it. Her eyes screwed tight shut, the lines about them deep-etched. It delighted Morgan.

"Tony, take me with you, I can't be without you." The mirth quickly faded. All the bounce, all the confidence had gone from her, her face crumpled as she pushed her head into his shoulder.

A great surge of joy and pleasure welled up through Tony as the idea seized him, but then it died as quickly as it was born. "Don't be daft, girl, we're going to war. There'll be time enough to catch up once I'm back."

It was as if he'd punched her. From sweet softness and warmth she turned to blazing fury, hurling herself from the bed, her eyes alight, her whole body shaking with anger. "If I'm not good enough for you, Lieutenant-almighty-bloody-Morgan, I know someone who thinks I am. Well then, I shall accept ordinary

James Keenan of Clonakilty's proposal of marriage —
he's twice the man you'll ever be!" She gathered her
clothes around the gifts that nature had so generously
given her and stormed from the room.

Morgan winced as the bedroom door banged yet
again in the early morning. There was no denying how
he felt about the girl, but he had hoped that the war
would somehow magically resolve things. Knowing
Mary, though, she would certainly carry out her threat
and no doubt conspire to embark with the regiment for
whatever adventures lay ahead, married — goddamn
her — to the soldier who would always be at his elbow.
He groaned and turned into his pillow.

Handshakes, then Finn driving the jaunty. More
goodbyes and stowing of gear before the coach took
them on to the station at Cork and then to the Dublin
packet which was full of officers and men from the Irish
garrisons and others, like them, who were returning
from leave. In the last, easy familiarity before the
tendrils of the regiment coiled round both of them,
Keenan and Morgan smoked together at the rail.

"So, sir, Glassdrumman will miss you and I expect
Miss Hawtrey will as well."

"Well, Keenan, we'll have to see, there's much
ground to travel. And what of you, I was surprised that
you didn't get down to Clonakilty to see your people.
Did you write?"

Keenan tinkered with his stubby, clay pipe. "I did,
sir, Mary gave me a hand with the letter, so. Jewel of a
girl, that Mary."

Morgan darted him a look, expecting some embarrassing reproach. But no, Keenan's face was set and sincere.

"Sir, I need to ask you something. Mary's coming to join me in England and we're to marry. Will we be allowed to live together in barracks?"

Morgan couldn't believe what he was being told. So, Mary had been true to her word yet Private Keenan gave no sign of knowing what his future wife's actual relationship with his master really was. His departure for war, for deeds and glory, should have simplified things. Instead, the piquant little treat that he'd been pleased to dip into every time he came back to Ireland on leave was going to follow him back to the Regiment, married to his own servant.

"You will, Keenan, but if we do get sent to war, there'll only be a handful of wives allowed to come with us and you'd better get used to the idea that a newly wed wife is unlikely to be selected." But even as Morgan replied to Keenan, he knew that if Mary was half the girl he thought she was, then she would somehow manage to be with them. He sighed deeply to himself.

CHAPTER THREE

Weedon Barracks

There was a stamp of feet as the sentries stepped smartly from their wooden boxes outside the barrack gates and presented arms. Morgan touched his hat in acknowledgement of the salute whilst noting how both men had been alert enough to see an officer in plain clothes approaching in a civilian carriage. What he had failed to see was James Keenan's silent but frantic signals to his confederates from the open top of the vehicle: anything to avoid an officer's displeasure.

As they rattled through the gates of the modern, red-brick and tile barracks, Keenan couldn't resist the time-honoured greeting to those whose lot it was to stand guard. "It'll never get better if you pick-et, you bastards!" whilst he flicked the oldest of discourtesies.

"For the love of God stop it, Keenan," Morgan had half-expected something ribald from his servant as they approached Weedon Barracks — he had been in tearing spirits ever since they had boarded the carriage at Northampton station a couple of hours before.

"We're not at Glassdrumman now and I've trouble enough with the adjutant without you adding to it!" He was more giving voice to his own thoughts than trying

61

to reprove Keenan, who in any event ignored his master, leaping from the carriage as it approached the Officers' Mess and busying himself with bags and cases.

"Your honour will want to be in uniform? The other gentlemen are wearing their shell-jackets, sir, so I'll lay yours out with your sword and cap. Try not to tear that trouser strap again, sir, I had a devil of a job with it last time!"

Keenan's veneer of discipline had always been thin. The time at home in Ireland together had only helped to erode it further, but he could at least be trusted to help Morgan get the all-important details of dress right. He'd noticed that other regiments didn't seem so particular about things as the 95th, but then they had a depth of history and *savoir-faire* that his corps didn't. Raised only thirty or so years before, what they lacked in self-confidence was made up for by what was officially described as "attention to detail" but which often translated into military myopia.

Keenan prattled as he stored Morgan's clothes and kit in his rooms in the Mess. The doings of this cousin and that, the purchase and subsequent escape of his mother's new sow and Mary Cade's near-perfection — as if Tony needed to be reminded — were a distracting enough backdrop to his dressing. As he levered himself into his plain blue overalls, they both became aware of a commotion below his window. A single voice bellowed encouragement, then others rapidly joined in.

"That'll be Mister Carmichael: some boy him. Must be the new draft he's got his hooks into." Keenan, a second-best sash half-coiled around his fist, stared out of the window into the brassy March-morning sunshine.

Richard Carmichael, paragon and fellow subaltern of the Grenadier Company, stood there in Harrow colours and the lightest and most expensive running pumps. Steaming gently, he bellowed encouragement at the assortment of soldiers who bundled in behind him. Some wore canvas slops, others football shorts and pullovers but all were spattered with mud from the cross-country run. Carmichael had obviously raced them individually over the last part of the course. Fit as a hare and knowing every inch of the route, he'd had no difficulty in coming in a long way ahead of the new men. But why, wondered Morgan wryly, had he chosen to finish the race outside the adjutant's and colonel's office?

"Where are the new boys from, Keenan?"

"I don't recognise any of 'em. Sir, but most have come from the Eighty-Second and some from the Sixth, Forty-Eighth and Thirty-Sixth they say. Bag o' shite says I."

Shite or not, they looked pretty good to Morgan. All volunteers, they seemed big and healthy and would more than plug the gaps left by the 95th's sick. Throwing the window open, he was about to shout across to his brother subaltern when his ear caught a strange thing. As each man came puffing home, Carmichael seemed to be addressing them in their native accents. The Irish and Scots were simple enough to imitate, the odd Geordie got a passable greeting, those from the slums of Derby and Birmingham probably recognized their own flattened vowels, but he saved his best effort for the pair of West Countrymen. They were yokelled in fine style, the young officer having been sharp enough even to learn their names. Carmichael was obviously delighted with his efforts, but Morgan couldn't help but notice the men's wooden faces.

As all the others trooped away a lone figure wheezed in. Younger, smaller, fatter and redder than any of the others, he panted across the finish line. His chest and shoulders heaved as he stooped, hands on thighs.

"Hey, Pegg, you fat little sod, what about ye?"

"Keenan, will you kindly remember where you are?" Morgan elbowed him away from the window but not, he fancied before he saw a movement in the adjutant's office opposite.

Podgy Pegg even at seventeen, he had a man's appetite for ale and women that had him constantly in trouble, but his cockiness usually saw him right.

"Now then, Mr Morgan, sir, welcome 'ome." Pegg braced his chubby arms to his sides — he was just about able to control his breathing enough now to speak coherently. "Mr Carmichael's got me showing the new 'uns around the place. Didn't know that meant runnin' with the bleeders an all." The warmth had gone from his voice, but instantly returned. "How's that Jimmy Keenan twat got on, sir?"

"Less of the twat, lardy." Keenan's hayrick head now jutted from the other window and he was back at full volume. "I'm to be wed to Mr Morgan's maid."

"Keenan, please, the adjutant has no desire to know that; just get my things ready, will you?"

The commanding officer wanted to speak to the officers in the Mess. Many of the bachelors had been asked to find rooms in the town so that space could be made for a dining room where they could all eat together. Now it was to be used for Colonel Webber-Smith's address and it buzzed with talk as the officers assembled. Almost all of them were there, including the captain and both subalterns of the Grenadier Company.

Morgan pushed his sword and cap onto the growing pile of others on the table in the hall. The officers were simply dressed in short, red jackets that flattered youthful figures but damned the portly — at thirty-two Captain James Eddington looked very much the part. Whether he had simply fallen lucky was open to question, but as far as the world was concerned, the Colonel's decision to give him command of the premier company in the regiment — the Grenadiers — was no mere chance. Now he lounged studiedly against a table, teacup in hand and whiskers just on the fashionable side of proper, curling around his collar.

"What are your impressions of the new draft, Carmichael?"

Carmichael's hair was still wet from the tub, his skin glowing from the run.

"Good enough, sir, but I wonder if their own regiments will have given them the discipline that they'll need to stand up to shot and shell?"

"Well, we'll have to see about that." Eddington replied. "My only worry is that by the time we've got stuck into this war, wherever it's going to be, all those regiments that have sent men to us will need them themselves. Mark you, whatever bit of 'the East' we're going to, the Russians will fight like fury and every bit of the navy and the army will be needed."

Morgan agreed with Eddington. The newspapers had all been warning of the power of Russia, her tenacity against Napoleon and the lack of preparation within the British forces for a sustained campaign. Certainly, there had been talk of military reforms for two or three years now and improvements were being made, not least to the weaponry and commissariat, but little would be ready by the time that the troops set sail.

"I know it goes against the grain, but thank God that the French are on our side this time . . ." Eddington continued.

"You can't mean it . . . the Frogs?" interrupted Carmichael.

"Yes, I do. There's lots of 'em — big conscript army with plenty of recent battle experience in North Africa. They gave my father a run for his money and I guess we'll be glad to have them alongside."

Anyone else would have been laughed to scorn by Carmichael, but Eddington was not only his immediate superior, he would also deploy a lashing tongue to deflate his senior subaltern when occasion demanded it.

"And if the Frogs let us down, we've always got the bold Ottomans to help us out." Morgan's joke was met by a weak laugh from everyone within earshot.

"Well, you may mock the Turks and point to their defeat at Sinope . . ." the sinking of an entire fleet by the Russians a few weeks before had caused a mixture of outrage and disdain for Britain's ally in the press, ". . . but what d'you know about Oltenitsa?"

"Er . . . didn't the Russians get a bloody nose there a few months back?" Morgan could just remember an account of the battle written by a British correspondent.

"Yes, last November, a body of Turko cavalry and infantry whipped a much larger force of Russians up on the Danube." But before Eddington could continue, the commanding officer and Kingsley, the adjutant, swept in.

"Well done today with those new lads, Carmichael, you seem to have a grip of them." This encomium was accompanied by a quick tap on Carmichael's chest from the Colonel's folded gloves as he passed.

"Thank you, sir, we'll soon have them up to our standard."

"Quite so, quite so. By the way, I see that your uncle has been given a prime job." Carmichael beamed with pleasure. His uncle, Sir George Cathcart, the only major-general who had seen recent active service in the Cape, had been given command of a Division. Carmichael was going to play the relationship for all that it was worth, whilst the colonel was far from ignorant to the cachet it ought to bestow on his regiment.

"Why yes, sir, do we know yet whether we'll be in my uncle's Division?"

"Who knows, Carmichael. It'll do your career no harm if we are." The Colonel laughed indulgently. "Now gentlemen, I've brought you all together to tell you about the realities of war."

Morgan and the others knew that Webber-Smith was one of the few present to have seen any fighting, yet he rarely mentioned it. There was no doubt that he ran a smart and taut regiment but, with the exception of the last few weeks when the accent had, indeed, been more upon tactical matters, most of their time was spent in the drill yard. Joining just too late to be with the Regiment at the last big manoeuvres at Chobham, the stories persisted of their being foxed by the 48th, embarrassingly, the commanding officer's original corps. Expecting now to pick up some real tips on leadership in battle, they were all to be disappointed.

There were hints on the selection of sutlers, the best ways to find clean water, the need for regular inspection of the men's feet and — everyone cringed — their members, the most effective way of rigging an awning in a downpour and, in short, any number of other tricks of the trade that would stand them all in good stead during the rainy season in India. Sadly, they weren't bound for India and, spellbinding though the sixty minutes were, none of them was any the wiser about the business of death at the end of it. Morgan wondered if an ancient forty-nine-year-old shouldn't be turning his mind to dog-breeding rather than tropical agues.

As the Colonel left, Hume, the senior major, brought the room to attention and then strolled to the fireplace at the front.

"Gentlemen, you've heard what the colonel has had to tell you about, er . . . campaigning: I have little to add."

Hume was short but what the Irish would call "well-made". His jacket was slightly too tight and his overalls bagged a little at the knee whilst his hair was unbrushed. But there was a composure about him that was reassuring. They all had to strain to hear what he said. He would arrange for them to see and handle the nine- and twelve-pounders of their own artillery for they were bound to need to understand them. Then, at his word, one of the Mess servants produced the new rifle which, it was rumoured, they were about to receive.

"I trust you all know what this is . . ."

"Ask Charlton, his dad makes them," half-whispered Carmichael to the subalterns around him. One or two sniggered at the snobbish little dig, but the others were intent upon the new weapon.

". . . and the principle upon which it fires its ball?" Hume frowned at Carmichael but wasn't going to be distracted. There followed a ten-minute discourse on a rifle that, if they ever got their hands on it, would reduce their enemies' life expectancy very dramatically indeed.

Morgan wondered if all this talk would ever really translate into war. There would be little difficulty in loading, gauging the range, aiming and firing one of these weapons — but at another Christian?

In the name of all that was holy why had he agreed to this? The rite-of-passage that was regimental boxing usually came round once a year but this was an extra ordeal. In an effort, Morgan supposed, to draw the new drafts into the 95th's family, the Colonel had not only ordained an additional session but he had let it be known that young officers would be very strongly encouraged to fight. He'd milled well enough at school, well enough, at least, to keep him out of trouble in the ring with the soldiers.

Every year he swore not to go through it again. Private Pug-Ugly — invariably half a stone heavier and two inches taller — would come out swinging, jabbing and bashing him round the ring. Morgan usually found a reserve of fitness and skill that allowed him to survive and not disgrace himself. That, at least, was how it had gone the last three times: plucky young officer faces his man, gets as good a hiding as he gives, wins narrowly, then wears his bruises gamely round the barracks for the next few days. Subaltern and soldier-honour satisfied, everyone was content.

Everyone except Morgan. He agreed that the officers should muck-in with the men, he knew how good it was for officer prestige to chance their arm with one of the regimental bruisers — but why did he always have to be the one? The whole business appalled him, not so much the fear of getting hurt — though that was bad enough — but the dread of making a fool of himself. No matter what the commanding officer encouraged, no matter what the adjutant said, no matter how much flattery tinged with sadism he got from Carmichael and the other subalterns, he would simply refuse.

So effective had his refusal been that he now sat on the simple stool with the light, leather slips bound at the wrist. Predictably, the Grenadier's Colour-Sergeant, big, florid, Glaswegian Andrew McGucken, was a veritable pugilist. He'd immediately taken the young officer into training — all twenty-four hours of it — and now stood behind him, chafing him with a grubby towel.

"He's just a lamb, sir." McGucken's view of the thug who'd just leapt into the crude, rope ring was rather different from Morgan's. Rather than gambolling, the creature bounced about his corner, thumping the air, emitting little "tsh-tsh" noises like one of the new steam engines in human form. His opponent was called John Duffy and he'd recently volunteered from the 6th. His colleagues from his former corps stood as close around the ring as possible and as the bell rang, a sallow, curly-haired confederate yelled, "Break his face". Duffy clearly heard, for the next four minutes were some of the most punishing that Morgan could recall.

Almost at once his nose bled. Then a splendid hook sent him staggering into the ropes in his opponent's corner, followed by a bruising jab or two to the ribs. Realizing that Duffy was more skilled than most of the men, Morgan rallied, put together some good combination punches that marked his opponent around the eyes and started to get his confidence back.

It didn't last long. Just before the bell rang to end the round, an uppercut felled him. He was suddenly on all fours, gazing at the packed dirt floor and listening to the referee counting down the seconds. He heard "four" and realized that he must stand. On "five" he did, brushing his gloves and coming on guard just on "seven". The referee patted his shoulder and he flung himself onto his corner stool.

"That's it, Morgan, let him exhaust himself by running round the ring after you and punching you silly. The idea is to hit him, you know." Carmichael, smooth, clean, brushed and polished, sneered through the ropes.

"I don't see yous up here in the ring, sir, so shag-off unless you've got something useful to say to Mr Morgan." Subalterns signified little to Colour-Sergeant McGucken.

"You've got to keep away from his right, sir. Keep circling to his left, your right, and jab with your left as hard as possible. You're doin'grand". The red-stained towel that was pulled away from his nostrils suggested something different, but at least the bleeding had stopped.

The second round was bruising. Morgan did his best to keep his flowing nose away from Duffy's flicking left hook, but without total success. Every time he came forward to deliver one of his crushing rights, Duffy found his mark, stinging him hard and making the bleeding worse. Just as the round was in its last seconds, though, Morgan pushed his opponent onto the back foot. Duffy tried a desperate lunge, allowed the young officer to get inside his guard and paid the price. Morgan pushed with his left, another left, both punches rocking the burly private back, before he caught him with a very creditable right on the point of the jaw. Duffy reeled; his gloves came down, but just as Morgan was closing in for what he hoped would be the kill, the bell sounded and the round ended. His opponent slunk back to his stool, bloody but determined to redress the balance. What did a fucking officer know about scrapping anyway?

The next two rounds were not the happiest of Morgan's life. What he'd achieved in round two was more than undone by his now-angry opponent. Whilst he wasn't knocked down again, Duffy concentrated on his already flooding nose, closed his left eye and seemed impervious to all of his blows — or almost impervious. At the end of the fourth, Morgan made him stagger with a left jab and stopped him with the hardest right he could muster just above his enemy's belt. More would have followed had Duffy not held him in a clinch and pushed him hard against the ropes.

As Morgan stumbled back to his corner he noticed the black drips of blood soaking into the ground. All over his torso were red weals where Duffy's punches had smeared his own blood yet with his one, good eye he could see nothing similar on his foe.

"Well done, sir, you've got him now. See how he's slumped over?" to Morgan's surprise, McGucken seemed to be delighted. Certainly, Duffy's head was down and his second — a corporal from the Light Company — was working overtime with towel and sponge. Morgan suspected, though, that Duffy was just husbanding his strength.

"Get out there, Mr Morgan sir, and belt the twat in the ribs, you've broke a couple already, he's on the run."

Now it was the last round. Morgan had four minutes to salvage the honour of the Officers' Mess, four minutes to burnish his reputation. The leaning, apparently broken Duffy, however, had other ideas. The young officer ran into a barrage of punches that made his nose fountain and blocked any vision at all from his left eye. A flurry of blows had him covering up as best he could in his own corner when broad Glasgow was bellowed into his ear.

"See his ribs there, sir, leather the bastards!" And leather them he did. The best right he could find landed just where the earlier blow had and Duffy faltered, both gloves came down, and he sagged back into the centre of the ring. All that now remained was for Morgan to step forward and punch mechanically at a target that could no longer defend itself. Within seconds a towel flew into the ring, within another few seconds the referee had the victor's hands above his head and seconds after that he was receiving the cheers and slaps of every officer and soldier there. He'd never do that again.

A good, hard run was just the way to shift bruises, Finn always said. Got the blood pumping round the system

and washed the contusion away from the skin, Finn
always said. Certainly, when he'd fallen off his horse as
a boy or been in one scrape or another, the groom back
at Glassdrumman had always insisted that a run was
the treatment; that's why Morgan had risen early,
earlier than his aching limbs and muscles would have
liked, to run the four miles out of the barracks, up over
Todd's Hill and then home. Now he was back,
agreeably blown and with his bruised face and ribs
complaining in time to the pulse of his heart. As he
padded back to the Mess past the stables, though, there
was a hubbub of excited voices: men laughing and
hooting before breakfast suggested something intrigu-
ing.

"Stand up!" As Morgan rounded the corner of the
stable block still panting in his shorts and jersey, half a
dozen men in undress, brown, canvas trousers and
shirtsleeves braced to attention.

"Leave to carry on, sir, please?" A well-muscled lad
whom Morgan recognized as a lance-corporal from
Number Three Company, bellowed with a confidence
that Morgan knew was designed to hide something.

"Please do, Corporal . . ."

"Fitchett, sir, Number Three."

"Sorry, yes of course," Morgan replied. "Who's this?
You're a jewel, ain't you?" In the arms of one of the
other men was the gamest little Jack Russell that
Morgan could remember seeing in an age. His coat was
dappled and smooth, his ears short, well-pointed and
alert and his eyes like the blackest of coals. As the
young officer stretched forward and stroked his muzzle,

a tiny pink tongue flicked out and gave him a perfunctory lick, the salute of one sportsman to another.

"Mine, sir, name o' Derby," the soldier, whom Morgan didn't think he'd ever seen before replied, smiling at the officer's obvious interest.

"Well, Derby, shall we see you at your work?" At this all the troops relaxed. A circle of bricks three high and about ten feet across had been improvised for the ratting session which, as long as no money changed hands, was winked at in the regiment. But it was quite clear from the time of day and the bearing of the men that this was a serious, commercial affair — quite against Queen's Regulations. That's why they had been worried by the approach of an officer, until Morgan had made his tacit approval clear.

"We shall, sir," the dog's owner replied in a flat, midland accent. "Bobby Shone, tell the officer the stakes."

Shone, saturnine and curly, the shortest of the group, held a leather bag that squirmed and squeaked as he shook it gently. "Twenny rats in 'ere, sir. We fancy Derby could earn a penny or two if he gets the practise, so we thought we'd give 'im a bit of a run." Shone waggled the bag again. "Half-a-crown a shot, Miller's the shortest stake on nothing more than three minutes; Corporal Fitchett's on the clock."

This was the crudest form of rat-baiting, but excellent training for the serious matches when one dog was pitched against others, with weight taken and handicaps allotted. The rules were simple: the dog had to kill a specified number of rats as fast as possible, the winner taking two-thirds of the purse, the runner-up the rest with a whip-round for the owner. The referee might poke a rat about to see whether it was quite dead or even shamming, but it was no more complex than that.

"Half-a-crown's a lot of money, boys . . ." Morgan replied — and it was. In barracks a private soldier could expect to see no more than ninepence a day, ". . . and I've not a penny-cent on me."

"Gerraway, sir, you're bloody made o' money," challenged Shone. "Anyway, your word's good. You in?"

Morgan couldn't resist. It may have been quite against the rules, but it was more than sporting blood could bear — his rank could go hang.

"Aye, of course I am. Three minutes, five and twenty seconds for me, is it free?" he asked, any concerns about discipline or over-familiarity with the men quite forgotten.

"Free as a hawk, sir, but you'll be skinned by Derby, he's a terror." One of the other men wrote Morgan's time down on a scrap of card.

"Right, let's see the rats." Corporal Fitchett craned forward over the ring as Shone emptied the bag.

Twenty black, brown, sleek forms tumbled on to the earth floor, collected themselves in less time than it took to blink and shot for the edge of the circle, clawing at the bricks to find a scrap of cover. Their pink noses twitched — sharp, yellow teeth bared, scaly tails flicking in anticipation of something terrible.

And terrible it was.

"Go on, Derby, me bucko!" Morgan was rapt, fists clenched, yelling along with the rest of the men as the dog became a vortex of teeth, tail and death.

Furry forms were grabbed by the neck and shaken with one, two or three swift flicks of the neck till their backbones broke; then they were tossed from Derby's mouth against the bricks, flopping dead on the grit floor below. One rash rodent had the temerity to sink its fangs into Derby's lip and grip there whilst the terrier tried to rip it free. Cling though it did, the rat couldn't survive the dashing of its body against the rough bricks and after a few short but bruising seconds, it let go and fell with its comrades, cooling quickly.

"Thirty seconds," bellowed Fitchett.

"Nineteen!" replied the throng, as each death was exulted. "Twenty!" They roared as the last rat had the life snapped from it.

"Two minutes and fifty on the nose, goddamn!" Corporal Fitchett's watch was held for all to see. "Why, the hound's a bloody goldmine."

Great silver half-crowns were produced as the brick circle was dismantled and Shone dabbed at Derby's bitten nose with a drop of brandy.

"Thanks, Corporal Fitchett, that was a grand few minutes, quite unexpected." Morgan had hardly noticed the sweat chilling him. "Are there any other dogs around who might challenge him?"

"Doubt it, sir. The Armourer-Sar'nt reckons his hound will be better over thirty or more rats than Derby; says he's got more stayin' power. Anyway, sir, we'll try 'em out against each other in the next couple o' weeks," Fitchett replied, formal and regimental now.

"Well, let's hope they delay the war for a wee bit then." The men smiled. "Let me know when the match is to be, if you would. I'll send James Keenan to you with the money, Corporal Fitchett, if that's accept-able?"

"Fine, sir," and as Morgan left, "Stand up: may I have your leave to carry on, sir, please?"

The gabbled formula reminded Morgan that he'd broken every rule that it was possible to break. Not only had he connived at the men's gambling, he was now in debt to a non-commissioned officer with plenty of witnesses — and he didn't give a damn.

The rat-baiting had made him late. If it had been an ordinary wedding back in Cork then a few minutes here or there simply wouldn't signify, but because soldiers were involved and because he, an officer, was invited then everything had to be organized as if life itself depended upon it.

"Well, it'll be a hard thing to see that prime little maid of yours married to one of the 'sons of toil', won't it?" Carmichael lolled against the post of Morgan's door, clicking the cover of his watch open and closed. "You wouldn't catch me letting a piece of fluff like that off my mattress." The watch was slipped back into Carmichael's pocket, as a sly little grin slid across his face.

"Well, she ain't been on my mattress, has she?" Morgan replied just a little too quickly. "She's to be married to James Keenan and will have to shift for herself back here when we sail. Or, I suppose she might go back to Ireland and fall back into my father's clutches."

"Hmm, I wonder. You think I haven't seen how you look at each other? Mind you, if you're not man enough to keep her content, I'm quite happy to volunteer for the post myself. You certainly cut quite a dash today, why did you let Duffy give you such a hiding?" Carmichael looked with mock concern at Morgan's cuts and rainbow bruising.

"You weren't in too much of a hurry to chance your arm, were you, Carmichael?"

"Why keep a dog and bark yourself? I leave that sort of brutish stuff to the likes of you and those with horny hands — proper officers should lead, not brawl. Also — hope you don't mind me saying it — it's one thing being manly with the troops and letting them thump you about, but should you really be rattin' with them? Bit familiar, don't you think? Give your darling Mary my very fondest wishes." Carmichael sauntered off down the back stairs of the Mess.

How the hell, Morgan wondered, had Carmichael found out about this morning's sport so quickly?

Pegg strode as hard and as fast as he could to keep in step with Morgan. Fiddling with belts and sashes with no servant to help him had made him late for the self-same servant's wedding. Now the only two Protestants to be invited to an otherwise exclusively Catholic service were racing to be on time, with poor Pegg in an ecstasy of unease. He was to accompany the two Irish fiddlers from another company on his fife at James Keenan's wedding.

He'd arrived to escort his officer in plenty of time. He'd scuffed the gravel loudly outside Morgan's room; he'd cleared his throat so hard and so often that he now worried that he wouldn't be able to sound his fife; he'd even considered trying out a tune or two just to hurry the young gentleman along. Then, as desperation overtook him and he was about to leave Mr Morgan to his own devices, the officer came out of the Mess like a rabbit with a ferret on his scut.

"Come on, Pegg, stop hanging around, we'll be late, boy."

They pelted off to the little church about a quarter of a mile from the barracks. Keenan had enlisted Morgan's help to find a priest to marry them at short notice and he'd lit upon one of the few Catholic deacons who were to escort the troops to the East. As luck would have it, there was a nearby Catholic church whose incumbent was delighted to allow it to be used for a regimental wedding, especially with the promise of war.

"Jesus, sir, lucky fucking Jimmy Keenan."

As they rounded the corner thirty seconds late, it was obvious that the groom, bride and the knot of guests were waiting for himself to arrive. The men were all in uniform, scarlet and blue bisected by white belts, their shakoes set with flowers as the only civilian concession, and at their centre stood Mary. Morgan's stomach tightened at the sight of her. Again, she'd contrived to look entirely out of place beside the men yet totally relaxed with them. A light blue, narrow-waisted, satin dress printed with sprigs of flowers was complemented by the garland set in her hair and the posy that she carried. At her throat was a beaded necklace that could have passed for sapphires whilst her hands and wrists were covered in snowy-white buttoned gloves that Morgan knew to be the height of fashion. She could have strolled arm-in-arm with him in Phoenix Park or, come to that, Hyde Park and been more than a credit.

Mary smiled at James Keenan. A handsome-enough man, his rough scarlet serge and his weather-reddened, calloused hands contrasted uneasily with his wife-to-be's elegance. He had asked Morgan if he might borrow some of his pomade for his hair and whiskers and applied it liberally. Now he stood on the church steps with his betrothed, his hair glistening in equal measure to the beam on his face.

"Ah, sir, it's yourself, thank you for coming." Keenan, bareheaded, brought his heels together and stiffened whilst a dozen hands flew to the peaks of the shakoes around him. Mary executed a mocking little curtsey whilst she stared into his eyes from below her lashes. She said not a thing.

"Keenan, I'm so pleased for you both," Morgan lied as he pulled off his glove and clasped the groom's hand. "May I kiss your future wife?" Morgan saw how Mary bridled, but such a gesture was required.

"Go on, Mr Morgan, sir, help yourself." For a split second Morgan wondered at Keenan's choice of words, but no, they were innocent enough.

One peach-like, gently powdered cheek was presented with a coolness that struck him like a slap. As his lips brushed against her he caught that same scent that haunted his bedclothes back in Glassdrumman.

"You've made a wonderful choice of husband, Mary, but I don't know how my family will manage without you." None of the meaning was lost on Mary and Tony could almost feel the lash of the reply that such a comment would receive in other circumstances. She said not a thing.

The service was short and the hymns were few. Any lack of melody amongst the singers was disguised by the skill of the fiddlers and the shrieks of Lance-Corporal Healey's toddlers. The poor priest had to contend with their babble whilst the first note of every hymn set them howling.

"Can't Mrs H tek the little sods out, sir?" whispered Pegg to Morgan.

He made no reply, for the Irish audience would tolerate outrages from children that no English one would. Earlier, Morgan had had to suppress an oath when one of his glistening toe-caps had been scuffed by a rampaging Healey brat. His mother had paid not the slightest attention.

There could be no honeymoon. With the regiment preparing for war, the best that Private and Mrs Keenan could manage was a ceilidh in the other ranks' canteen. A handful of the wives and their husbands had set about the barn-like structure, weaving ivy and other greenery through some bunting, then setting up Union flags and an enormous, crêpe shamrock. A somewhat crumpled, slightly crookedly-painted banner read, "Good luck to you both". Morgan remembered it from the last wedding party he'd attended there.

The group was pathetically small, clustered around the fire at one end of the hall. The priest came, grinned, downed two glasses of whiskey and fled, leaving Morgan as the only impediment to a wholesale onslaught on the liquor. But the group's temperance lasted about as long as it took for the priest to disappear from sight. As soon as his cassock had floated out, the fiddlers and Pegg started to play. Now tots of whiskey many times the size of that given to the divine were handed round.

It was clear to Morgan that the novelty of his presence would very soon wear off. Taking the first opportunity, he drained his whiskey and strode over to Mary, for it had to be done. "May I be the first man to dance with Mrs Keenan?" He gave a little bow.

"I'd be delighted, Lieutenant Morgan, sir." She stood and dropped him a much deeper curtsey than earlier, smiling and bobbing her ringlets most becomingly.

Morgan did his best at the reels and steps, never a natural dancer. The soldiers and women looked on indulgently, just pleased to see one of Themselves mixing with them. His clumsiness was at odds with Mary's easy grace, a grace that he remembered so well from an entirely different setting.

The dancing done, he pumped hands, slapped backs and left. His walk back to the Mess was the loneliest of his life.

★   ★   ★

"Come on, Morgan, there's no point in loafing here."

The days since the wedding had been frantic as last-minute preparations were made for departure and this was to be the regiment's last evening in Weedon, for tomorrow they were to leave for Portsmouth and embarkation for the mysterious "East". So, Morgan had accepted Carmichael's invitation to join him at his rooms in Weedon to "raise Cain".

Carmichael's idea of Cain-raising held little appeal to Morgan. He already spent more than enough time with the regiment's foremost scion and self-appointed rake and, besides, any quiet moment allowed his thoughts to drift back to Mary, of seeing her all the time yet knowing that she was beyond his reach. But Carmichael had chivvied and cajoled him in the Mess in front of the others. The invitation was issued only to him and whilst he knew that he would have to endure a battery of stings and innuendo, even that was better than being alone.

Meanwhile, Keenan had been in an almost indecent rush to get his master respectably into civilian clothes, out of barracks and off his hands. Normally, there would have been much smoothing of Morgan's beaver hat, the watch chain would have had to be fixed just so, and there would be a final rub of a duster over his boots before the young officer was fit to be seen in public. The married Keenan was a different, more perfunctory creature. Morgan found himself adjusting his own braces, fitting his own cuff-links and pulling his stock to just the right position whilst there was little of the barrack tittle-tattle that made such occasions so invaluable.

Now, instead of learning why Private Ghastly felt himself so aggrieved when Lance-Corporal Nasty told him off for kitchen fatigues (after all, they had been good mates when they were privates together, hadn't they?), there was little except a few scrappy questions about what Russ would look like and whether Turkish girls chewed tobacco. His soldier-servant seemed to be in a tearing hurry to get back to the barrack corner that had been screened off with an army blanket for the newly-weds. Morgan understood the urgency only too well.

Carmichael's rooms were a cliché. A bedroom, sitting room and bathroom looked from the first floor of a small hotel onto the cobbled main street of the town below. The wooden floor was awash with coloured woollen rugs whilst the furniture was old but studiedly comfortable. He'd had the walls redecorated in a fashionable lemon (as advised, Morgan recalled, by some London society piece) and on them hung a selection of hunting, boxing and naval prints. His greatest conceit, though, was a pastel nude that hung above his bed.

Morgan's already failing interest in Cain had dwindled to nothing by the time that he arrived. Carmichael's man had just been sent home and with a fire blazing and the gentle light of the oil lamps, Morgan hoped that the next few hours could be spent in an alcoholic cloud, forgetting his gloom and discussing the adventure that lay before them. He might learn Carmichael's secret of shining whenever the colonel or the adjutant were about — he might even learn to like the ambitious, arrogant bastard a little. But no, Cain was a creature of the streets. In high spirits, Carmichael stepped out, dandified in strapped trousers, a waistcoat of the darkest green, stock and pin and a coat cut fashionably long.

They sank a tot of whiskey apiece in the Rodney and the Granby. But in both there were some of their own corporals or sergeants toping steadily. The young officers passed a civil few sentences with them, trying not to make it look as though they were bolting their liquor before moving on. There would be plenty of time to rub shoulders with the men in the next few months.

They settled, unrecognized, in the snug of the the Plough. More drink came and went whilst their talk gathered pace. Carmichael, though, had been distracted from the moment that two unescorted girls came into the room. They sat down a little way from the fire and began to commune in a geyser of giggles and whispers. Sitting in another corner were four young men, farmers or their sons judging by their clothes. Their volume, too, increased as they drank until one of the braver ones rose, very slightly unsteady, and approached the girls.

Despite a lively, good-natured exchange where the farmer's boy did his best to impress both women with promises of untold largesse, he was rebuffed. With a shrug and upturned palms he walked back to his friends.

"Missing a bed-warmer now that sweet Mary's tucked up with Keenan, Morgan?" But before Morgan could react to this jibe, Carmichael had lost interest, sensing a different and much more interesting diversion.

The next hour or so were to remain a whiskey blur to Morgan. The girls joined them, they drank, they laughed a little too loudly at the young gentlemen's wit, showing their teeth too readily behind their too-red lips and in no time the four of them found themselves in Carmichael's rooms.

"Just get some more coal would you, Morgan? We can't let the fire get any lower." Carmichael made it quite clear that Morgan had no choice. He knew where the coal hole was, but in the few minutes that it took him to refill the bucket in the dark and to clatter back upstairs, Carmichael and Jane — by far the prettier of the two girls — had disappeared. With wits dulled by drink, Morgan was just about to enquire of Molly where they had gone when a burst of laughter from behind the firmly-closed bedroom door betrayed them. Restoking the fire bought him a few minutes to think whilst Molly, silent except for a few rustles and sips from her glass, sat on the sofa behind him.

The lamps had been trimmed low. As he turned, their forgiving light played over Molly who lounged back on the cushions, glass in hand and breasts quite naked. She smiled and did her best to look attractive.

"Get dressed, girl." Morgan was irritated with himself for being drawn into Carmichael's scheme; he reached into his pocket and put a silver crown in Molly's hand. "Here, there's better ways of earning

88

money than that," and he rattled down the stairs and away as quickly as he could.

By halfway back to barracks Morgan's canter had slowed to a quick-step. The sentries came to the salute, and raising his top hat, he went over to speak to them. Whilst he had no desire whatsoever to talk, he remembered his first captain's advice when he joined the regiment — always be bothered with the troops: one day they'll save your life or your reputation. They weren't from his company, but he recognized them both. In their early twenties they were older soldiers — Morgan mused on why neither was a lance-corporal and how such old hands had managed to get caught for a greenhorn's duty like this.

"I'm sorry, I can't remember your name, nor where you're from." The taller of the two had a round, pock-marked face that split into a surprised grin now that an officer was talking to him.

"Francis Luff, sir, Number Five Company." The man's breath wisped into the cold night air as his gloved fingers played on the stock of his rifle.

"No, I know that, where's your home town, man?"

"Oh, sorry, sir, Hayling Island — our Pete's in your company." Luff seemed to have no neck at all. His head jutted straight out of the thick collar of his greatcoat, bobbing now with pleasure, the moonlight reflected off the brass "95" on the front of his soft woollen cap.

"I know him well, he's a good man, up for a tape I'm told. What about you, you must be due promotion soon?"

"Only thing Luffy'll get, sir, is a bleedin' tape-worm." One of the oldest jests in the troops' lexicon was delivered in a flat Manchester accent by the other man, provoking dutiful laughs.

"You're doing well, lads: stand easy and for pity's sake keep warm." Men cheered, bonhomie dispensed, easy, pleasant little job done, it was a good point to leave. Both men snapped their left foot forward, clasped their hands across their bellies and pushed their rifles into the crooks of their arms. The cosiness of the banter was stark against the long, lethal gleam of their bayonets.

"He's a decent bloke, that Paddy Morgan. Pete says 'e'll be all right when we get to fight." The conversation had pleased Luff disproportionately.

"Don't s'pose it'll come to that. We'll go down to Portsmouth tomorrer an' be stuck there for ever, knowing our luck. Mind you, Mr Morgan did well in the ring t'other night, wouldn't mind having him as our officer, not a stuck-up sod like some o' the others." The sentries' muttered conversation helped to pass the long hours of their watch.

The heavy metal key clunked into the back door of the Mess. Morgan's room still felt warm against the cold of the night and as he stripped off coat, hat and muffler he twitched back his curtains. The barracks slept — but not entirely. Over there, at an end of the Grenadier Company's lines he fancied that he could see just one light burning dimly.

CHAPTER
FOUR

Bulganak

"Now look, yous . . ." Colour-Sergeant McGucken held the heavy rifle across his waist and pointed at the graduated rear-sight, ". . . it's no good buggerin' about adjustin' the bloody thing if you don't know how far away the target is, so you've got to be able to estimate the range accurately, or it's all a waste of fuckin' time."

The Grenadier Company gaggled about him as the sun beat down on the eighty-odd men, all of whom swiped to keep the flies out of their eyes, ears and noses. They had been waiting in Varna on the west coast of the Black Sea for a fortnight or more whilst the politicians decided what to do next, nobody quite knowing whether they would be sent inland to help the Turks on the Danube or embark on their ships again.

"Luff, tell us how we estimate range." McGucken picked the boy out from the rear of the crowd where his attention had begun to wander. He was looking at the scorched, brown Bulgarian fields and hedges where they stretched down to the sea and thinking how different it all was from the green of Hayling Island.

"At five hundred you can make out colours; at four hundred limbs and the head become distinct; at three hundred features become visible and at two hundred all details can be discerned." Luff intoned the rubric that they had all been taught.

"Good, well done Luff; why were you being so fuckin' thick about things in Turkey?" McGucken had almost despaired of Luff and some of the others when the fleets had paused in Scutari where the Allied forces had been gathered before the voyage into the Black Sea. It was there that the new Minié rifle had been served out to most of the regiments and the first tentative shots been tried against paper targets pinned to wooden billets. Instructors had been sent from the units who had received the weapons first, amazing everyone with the accuracy and penetration of the half-inch-wide lead bullets that were so very different from the round balls of the old, smooth-bored muskets which they carried up until then.

"Dunno, Colour-Sar'nt . . . just difficult to get the hang of, ain't it?" replied Luff, who had struggled more than most to understand that the new weapon was so very different from the one that they had been used to. He'd been quick enough to understand that the bullet spun and was more accurate due to the rifling, that it dropped in quite a steep curve the further it flew and that you had to allow for this by tinkering around with the iron sight at the rear of the barrel. But he and several others had a real problem with estimating range.

"Aye, well just think about what you repeated to me, don't just chant it like some magic bloody Papish prayer: understand it and keep practising." McGucken discovered that the boys from the land and the plough had picked the idea up quite quickly, whilst townies like Luff had taken much longer to grasp things. So, he'd taught them the words of the manual by rote, but whether they understood it properly was quite a different matter.

"S'pose that pair yonder were Russian infantry . . ." McGucken pointed across the fields to two elderly peasants who were digging in a field, ". . . what would you set your sights at to hit them, Luff?"

The boy held his hand up to shade his eyes against the sun, revealing a great wet patch at his armpit. The troops had been allowed to parade for training in their grey shirtsleeves to spare them from the heat and to save their already shabby scarlet coatees from further wear. They had just received the order to cease shaving as well, apparently in an effort to save water, but as far as McGucken was concerned, it had just given the men an excuse to let their smartness and turnout drop off even further.

"'Bout four 'undred, I'd say." A general mutter of agreement greeted Luff's estimate. "But are we ever goin' to shoot at any bastard, or will we just arse about 'ere gettin' cholera, Colour-Sar'nt?"

"A very good question, son." McGucken had been having just the same discussion in the Sergeants' Mess last night. They had arrived in Bulgaria fully expecting to be in action alongside the Turks in no time at all, but they had done nothing for weeks now except train and move camp every time there was another outbreak of cholera. Some said the Russians had surrendered and the whole shooting match would be packed on its boats and sent home, but the papers insisted that the Allies would sail against the Russian ports in the north. "I reckon we'll be off for Sevastopol once the high-ups can get the politicos to make their minds up."

"See . . . vas . . . tow . . . pol . . ." The men played with the word, liking its exotic sound.

"Where's that then, Colour-Sar'nt?" Luff voiced all of their thoughts.

"Couple of hundred miles that way." McGucken pointed out to sea where three French men-of-war smoked past. "It's the Russians' great big bastard anchorage for their fleet and the papers say that there's no point in comin' this far an' then goin' home without a fight. So, you'd best learn how to estimate range then, hadn't you?" There was a tepid hum amongst the men.

"Now, how far away's that haystack . . . Shortt?" McGucken was as bored with the lounging about as his men were, but as he looked around their downy, sunburnt faces and their earnest, furrowed brows he wondered just how many of them would live to tell their mothers and fathers what a Russian infantryman really looked like.

"They've got to land us south of Sevastopol, it makes no sense to go to the north." Carmichael seemed very sure of himself as Eddington and both his subalterns pored over a chart showing the coast of the Crimea.

"Well, you'd think so. All these rivers that flow into the Black Sea will be perfect defensive positions and the captain tells me that there's no really suitable beach much south of here." Eddington's manicured finger hovered on the map just south of Eupatoria, thirty miles at least from the Allies' target, Sevastopol. Like a stepladder, the rivers bisected the coastal plain, each one a major obstacle to the 60,000-strong French and British army.

"But if we go to the south we'll be that much closer to Sevastopol and we might catch Russ off guard?" Morgan saw how unlikely that was from the deep, coloured contours of the map. There were only a couple of points where a landing from the sea would be possible and those, according to the chart, were well-established ports.

"Closer, certainly, but we would have to force either Balaklava or Kamiesch and the Russians will have made that very difficult indeed. No, the captain reckons we're for the north — that's where the only suitable beaches are — and then we'll have to tramp down parallel to the sea. There's so little cavalry that we won't be able to go too far inland and the colonel says that if we do land northwards then the plan is to hug the coast. That way we've got the fleets to victual us and we can march under the lee of their guns. The only question is, who gets to march closer to the ships?" Eddington looked at the pair with a slight smile.

"It'll be the bloody French, pound to a penny. They'll turn us inside out every chance they get, you see. My uncle, sir George Cathcart, says his people almost came to blows with them in Turkey." Carmichael was never slow to remind people of his connections, nor to criticize the French. Only the Turks had proved more unpopular with the troops than the

French so far and all but a handful of the officers followed the fashion of berating Britain's ally whenever they could.

"Yes, my father got a boatload of 'em in Bantry back before Waterloo. They said they were ship-wrecked but they turned out to be spies. Hanged the lot." Morgan could hear the relish in his father's words as his only bit of real service against Napoleon was rehearsed time and again during long dinners at home.

"Just be glad that the French are with us this time, they've had much more recent experience of campaigning than most of us and what I've seen of them so far looks pretty businesslike. We'll see how they fight, but my father learned to respect them in Spain and at Waterloo, so hold your scorn for the Russians." Eddington could be infuriating, sometimes.

The fleets surged on across the Black Sea. A pall of black coal-smoke hung with them on the following breeze, the steamers deliberately slowing to stay abreast of the sailing ships. The coast of the Crimea was distantly sighted, a lookout in the masts far above assuring the captain that what they could see was Sevastopol.

"And if we can see them . . ." Eddington snapped shut his glass, ". . . then they can see us. We must be heading north, and there'll be no surprise for Russ. So, gentlemen, we land tomorrow and must be ready to fight. Inspect every weapon, every round of ammunition and take a good look at feet, socks and the men's shoes. Colour-Sar'nt, please check that Braden has enough leather and nails with him for running repairs once we're ashore." Eddington had gone over all these fine details a dozen times already, Braden, the company's cobbler having his scraps of leather and hobnails scrutinized more times in a week than in the last five years.

As dawn broke, there it was. The armada rode at anchor almost a mile off shore, gazing at a low line of dunes topped with grass in a crescent-shaped bay that the chart told them was known as "Kalamita". The lead-grey sky loured over a scene that few would forget for the rest of their days and when the papers subsequently dubbed it "Calamity Bay", most agreed.

"Just remind me what our good captain had to say about this wretched landing?" Major Hume had squelched up to the Grenadier Company's three officers as they lay in the grass-studded sand-dunes. "'Still as a mill-pond' and 'dry as a bone' wasn't it?"

The captain of the *Himalaya* had told them all how smoothly the landing would go and how they would all be ashore in no time, simply stepping from the improvised landing rafts onto the beach.

"Are all your men as soaked as I am, Eddington?" Hume had been scurrying about between the companies checking the state of equipment and ammunition at the commanding officer's request.

Eddington's company was amongst the last to land and, like the others, they had first been thrown about by a boisterous surf and then floundered into three feet of chilling water, despite everything the navy had promised. Now they all sat amongst the tussocks, boots off, wringing the salt water out of their socks.

"To the skin, sir." Eddington had produced a towel from his haversack with which he was rubbing vigorously at his feet. He'd undone the straps that held his trousers tight below the instep of his boots, now the bits of leather and tiny buckles flailed around his ankles. "But Colour-Sergeant McGucken had the presence of mind to tell the men to keep their pouches above their heads, so our ammunition should be sound; he's just checking it now."

In the background McGucken, apparently totally unaffected by the ordeal by brine, stalked amongst the sprawling troops reminding the sergeants to inspect every man's supply of wax-paper-wrapped rounds.

"You're lucky to have McGucken, you know, Eddington." Hume looked over as the Scot went quietly about his business.

"I know, sir, we got a good deal when he came to us from the Thirty-Sixth," Eddington replied.

"He was particularly good on the rafts, sir." Morgan interjected. "Most of the boys were bloody terrified of the waves but he just took the rise out of them and kept them calm." Morgan had been surprised how scared the men had been of the sea, until he realized how few of them could swim. Every officer had been taught the gentlemanly art of swimming just as surely as they had learnt to ride a horse, but other than for some farmers' boys, it was a skill that few of the soldiers had mastered.

"Yes, he's a good fellow," Hume continued, "I have to say, if any of the boys had been dunked with sixty-five pounds of shot and kit on their backs, I don't suppose we'd have seen them again — not alive at least. Now, let me know when you're ready to move, Eddington, I'm amazed that we've had no interference from the Russians thus far," Hume added before moving off to have much the same conversation with Number Six Company close by.

As the 95th had come ashore, they had seen the Rifles in the sand-dunes above the beach, their dark green uniforms bobbing about the rough grass on guard against an expected counter-attack, whilst the French skirmishers had done the same, their bugles shrieking incessantly in a way that was to become all too familiar to the British. But only a few seedy Cossacks on hairy ponies had looked on until the first Allied troops appeared — providing just enough excitement to distract the men from their sopping clothes.

"Dear God, it's starting to rain, now . . ." Eddington looked up at the dark, Crimean skies, ". . . as if we're not wet enough already. Right, you two, I want sentries posted and the men in their blankets as soon as we're stood down by the adjutant. Don't let the men sit around yarning, it'll be a hard day tomorrow and they'll need as much sleep as possible."

The two subalterns saluted and moved off to join their men. Soon, with their weapons piled in little pyramids, the troops were bedded down, all of the regiment's seven companies stretched next to each other. Morgan looked at the blanket-wrapped forms and was reminded of one vast farrow of grey piglets. Nobody was going to get much sleep with the enemy to hand and the rain setting in, he thought, but at least they looked tidy, a sergeant's dream.

Men settled and sentries posted, Morgan flung himself down next to the spitting camp fire that the servants had managed to light for the officers. Keenan and the other batmen were stirring at a stew made from the pork that everyone — officers and soldiers — had been issued before they disembarked, the smell of which seemed like ambrosia. The light played off their faces. Collars turned up against the wind and wet, soft caps pulled down hard, from almost every pair of lips jutted either pipe or cigar. Keenan had adopted the old soldiers' wheeze of smoking his little, black, clay pipe with the bowl pointing down away from the rain, bits of tobacco stuck to his stubbly lips.

"Dear God, I shall never be able to wear this in Dublin again." Morgan, like all the other novices to war, was doing as he was told and wearing "Review Order", his best set of everything. His swallow-tailed, scarlet coatee and heavy, bullion wings had made a serious hole in the Morgan family coffers and he could remember how he was made to twist and turn around for Father and the Staff at Glassdrumman in his new regimentals, self-conscious and suspicious of their smiles. He wore those very clothes now, strapped about with belts, bottles and bullets and topped by a soaked greatcoat.

"The men seem happy enough now we're off that wretched ship." Carmichael, predictably, had the slimmest, most expensive of cheroots in his mouth. Even the smoke slid stylishly onto the breeze.

"I'd be a damn sight happier for them if they could get a decent night's sleep, though. The bloody cholera will be back unless we keep their strength up. Any sign of it, either of you?" Captain Eddington was as much checking that his officers had done their jobs as showing concern for the men of his company.

The men's health had been much better at sea, but despite the kindness of the captain and the crew, it had become fashionable to complain about them, the ungainliness of the ship and about all matters nautical. Carmichael had been amongst the most vocal.

"Carry out your normal rounds, you two, better make it every two hours this close to the Russians, and which one of you wants the stand-to slot?"

"I'll do it, sir." Morgan knew that if the men slept little that night then the officers would sleep even less. It would be far better to be supervising the dawn ritual of every man standing-to-arms, kit packed, weapons cleaned and ready, than trying to get a last few minutes in drenched blankets.

He was right. Both subalterns took turn and turn about to visit the sentries — all of whom were gratifyingly alert — before rolling themselves up on the ground in an attempt to drift into unconsciousness. But when they rose in the dark just before dawn everyone was stiff, soggy and bug-eyed. They struggled almost gratefully into their belts and equipment, wiping the water off their rifles and checking their ammunition to make sure that the bundles of cartridges had kept dry. For half an hour they waited, poised, ready to fight until daylight was fully there, then they stood down. Damp charges were drawn from barrels, breakfast fires were lit, little domestic scenes sprang up everywhere.

The men's morning bacon was just starting to sizzle when two shots rang out. Hard in front of where the men were cooking and inside the chain of outlying sentries, the bangs had men scuttling for their kit and weapons, sergeants and corporals shouting, kettles knocked over, the whole company in a lather.

"What in Christ's name is going on? Sar'nt Ormond, stop dithering and get the men back to their stand-to positions." That was precisely what the Sergeant was doing, but it didn't save him from a tongue-lashing from Carmichael.

"Beat to arms, Pegg." Colour-Sergeant McGucken's crisp order to the drummer seemed to steady Carmichael a little until, it was discovered that the boy was missing. "Where's bloody Pegg, has anyone seen him?" McGucken's voice was already tinged with concern.

"His drum and kit's here, Colour-Sar'nt" shouted one of the other drummers who had gone in search of the boy.

"Just beat to arms then, son, he can't 'ave gone far."

As the tattoo rolled out, the hubbub in the Grenadier Company's lines soon infected the rest of the regiment. In no time, all of the other companies were standing-to, Colonel Webber-Smith was calling for his horse and the

102

adjutant, the transport ponies were having their bran and oat nosebags snatched away, the buglers taking up the call whilst damp, smoky cooking fires were stamped to embers.

The drizzle had cleared but the light was still not good as the sentries saw two figures, one tall and lean, one small and fat — and weighed down by the hare that he carried by its hind legs — come galloping towards them. Only the scarlet of their coats saved them from a jumpy volley, both pickets having cocked their rifles and brought them to the aim at the sight of movement where only Russians should be.

"Don't shoot, it's us, Pegg and Luff! What's going on?" The two hunters breathed hard as the sentries lowered their rifles.

"God knows. You must have heard them shots over yonder, more or less where you came from?" A skinny, sallow-faced lad, the senior of the two sentries, eased the hammer of his rifle forward before absently brushing at his running nose.

"Aye, that was us, just got this." Pegg held up the hare: it was almost as big as he was.

"Well, no fucker knew you was out there, the whole lot's standing-to. Best report to Jock McGucken, he'll skin you sooner than he does that bleeder. Sure there's no Russians out there?"

"Not that we saw," Pegg shouted over his shoulder as the pair trotted guiltily back towards McGucken and wrath.

And wrath they got. There seemed to be no end to the pair's sins. First they had neglected to ask a corporal if they could go out to look for game. On top of that, they'd been half-witted enough not to check out with the same pair of sentries through whom they would return. What did they expect the company to do when they heard shooting to their front? And what about the rest of the regiment? Hadn't they made Captain Eddington and himself look utter fools in the eyes of everyone? Didn't they realize that the company commander, even now, was having a strip torn off him by no lesser mortal than the colonel?

Then, in the name of all that was holy, what would they have done if they met a clutch of bleedin' Cossacks out there just waiting to stick their lances up their fur-framed hoops? How would he have explained that to their mums and, more to the point, Luff was senior enough not to let silly little knobs like Pegg get them all into trouble. They were just downright fuckin' eejits. He was going to rip them a second arsehole, worse, he had a good mind to fuck-them-off-out of the Grenadiers and back to some "hat" company!

McGucken's riftings were known to be impressive. The two privates stood trembling to attention whilst the storm flickered about them. Minute flecks of foam from the Colour-Sergeant's lips landed on their cheeks but they dared not wipe it away, they just stood there, watching the others — amused yet appalled — go about their business. Then the squall seemed to have abated. McGucken paused, eased his leather cross-belts on his shoulders, pushed his bayonet scabbard back against his thigh and drew breath.

They were half hoping that they'd get away with just a bollocking and that the ordeal was over. But then another thought occurred to big Jock McGucken.

"What the bloody hell did yous pair of clowns use to kill that hare? It wasn't buck-shot, was it?"

"Yes, Colour-Sar'nt," the miscreants muttered.

"Right, that's it! I've had a gut-load of you! You're on company commander's report for damaging your weapons. Now shag off back to your place of duty and get that pox-ridden rabbit out of my sight!"

With the old, smooth-bored muskets it was quite normal to use buck-shot for killing game, so all the soldiers had brought some pellets with them for just that purpose. The trouble was, the spiral rifling with which the barrel of the new rifle was etched — the very secret of its range and accuracy — was thought to be delicate. Firing even soft lead pellets from it was ordained a sin — though this, Pegg and Luff claimed, had been made far from clear. The only good that might come from the embarrassment of the Grenadier Company, McGucken reasoned, was that the men wouldn't abuse their rifles again.

Company commander's report, though, was not good. Discipline McGucken-style usually resulted in extra duties or fatigues being awarded, tedious but bearable. Being put in front of Captain Eddington — with all his cold authority — was quite another matter for at the very least their records would be spoilt and the possibility of promotion delayed. They might be stopped pay or their ration of spirits, but much worse, now that they were on active service, a flogging was a possibility. It made sense: the officers would want to underline the fact that discipline had to be sharper in the face of the enemy, that things that might be overlooked in barracks were unacceptable in the field.

"Ever seen a flogging, Luffy?" Such punishments were almost unknown in the 95th, so it was a fair bet that Luff had no such experience and that its very mystery made the prospect all the worse.

"No, mate. One of the new draft from the 82nd got twenty lashes couple o' years back, he said. Got busted from lance-jack an' all. He reckons it don't hurt that bad, it's just that you feel such a twot if you yell out with everyone watching."

The hare had been stuffed into Pegg's haversack as soon as they got back to where they had left their equipment. Now the pair were desperately trying to light a fire. Despite shaving twigs to get finer tinder, the scraps of branches were so wet that everyone had had the devil's own job to get their cooking fires lit. One or two of the older NCOs had lodged bits of lint in their shirt pockets to keep them as dry as possible for the flints and steel. Once their fires were lit, kindling was brought by others and very quickly the whole company was fanning and puffing smokily. Luff and Pegg's episode, though, had ensured that everyone had to start the laborious process again whilst the pair could be sure that no embers would willingly be passed in their direction. Luff had already spent ten minutes with his coatee undone as a windbreak, desperately trying to get a spark to take.

106

"This'll never work, the wood's too bleedin' wet." Luff continued to strike his tinder box disconsolately.

"We'll have to use a cartridge." Pegg suggested exactly what was on Luff's mind.

"So long as we don't get caught, we've got enough drama as it is." Luff knew that they would have to account for each round.

"We won't get caught. We'll be firing them at Russ tomorrow then no bugger will know how many we've got." Pegg's logic was impeccable. He reached into his pouch, took out a bundle of ten waxy paper tubes and split one open, sprinkling the gunpowder over the twigs. The pair crouched over the pyre, Luff tinkering away until a spark took, the flash making them both jerk back in surprise. But the billow of white smoke drifted right through the knots of kneeling, blowing men who were trying to get their own fires going.

"Right, you two, I seen that, you've been told not to use cartridges for fires. You're both on report, get your bodies over to the Colour-Sergeant now!" Sergeant Ormond had seen exactly what happened — he had little choice: Pegg and Luff had little hope. As they trudged over for their second interview with McGucken in half an hour, they could almost feel the bite of the lash.

"See, I was right, wasn't I?" Carmichael had indeed been right, the French were marching next to the sea and the support of the ships whilst the British stumped on further inland.

107

"Yes, we've been seen off again by the Frogs," Morgan answered distractedly. Ever since he was a boy he'd hated long walks. Mother had supposed them to be "improving" and dragged him about with her as she visited the estate cottages apparently impervious to the incessant Cork rain. After her death when he was six — and thoroughly at home astride a horse — he had rarely walked any distance at all, until he'd joined the regiment. Then he'd really learnt to hate walking.

Now the long columns crept forward over gentle, rolling hills that were covered in rough, herby grass whilst larks rose and fussed overhead. Here and there they came across odd, isolated villages of shingled cottages with some larger stone houses dotted about, herds of skinny cows and flocks of hairy goats, but it hardly relieved his boredom.

There were great, leafy vineyards everywhere, heavy with fruit. Carefully cultivated over many acres, the ground was criss-crossed with shallow trenches designed to allow the vines to grow up the wall facing the sun. These were topped with sticks and light poles along which the sinewy vines grew, and on them were bunches of green grapes ripening in the autumn sun. But other than the vines and the odd bit of rough plough, the country was remarkably untouched.

"Wouldn't you just love to be in the cavalry, now?" Carmichael had come beetling up from his place at the rear of the company column to pester Morgan.

"Well, I'd love to have a better horse than Shanks's mare, if that's what you mean, Carmichael, but this fight will be decided by us and the guns, I reckon, not that lot." Morgan nodded past the Light Division that marched to their own — the 2nd Division's — left towards the dust cloud that marked the progress of the Cavalry Division. They had been pushed out inland to guard the Allies' flank. "Anyway, if I did have a horse I would miss all this grand marching, wouldn't I, and all the fun of dealing with the men and their precious, bloody feet." Morgan knew that at the end of the day's march, when weapons had been cleaned but before food could be prepared, there would be the ritual of foot inspection. All those who were not on sentry would sit by their kit, boots and socks off whilst the subalterns peered at spongy soles, poked at burst blisters whilst the sergeants scribbled in notebooks beside them.

"Do I detect a slight *malaise* in the house of Morgan? Is the bold officer bored of *la vie militaire* before it's even started?" Carmichael could be especially annoying when he put his mind to it, thought Morgan. If he kept his mouth shut perhaps the wretched man would leave him alone.

As roads and tracks were crossed by the horde so gawping villagers gathered, apparently totally unafraid of the invaders. The local people were Tartars, broad-eyed, coarse-haired, accustomed to the hard life of field and plough but occasionally they would glimpse some of the managing classes who dressed and looked more like Europeans. Straddling the same squat ponies as the peasants, everyone expected these folk to hare off at the sight of the Allies. But no, they seemed as content as their workers to watch the columns stamp by, even exchanging some civil words in French with the Staff officers.

For three days this continued with, as each dawn broke, everyone expecting a brush with the foe. But of him there was hardly a sign. Stuck in the middle of the dusty phalanx, the 95th saw nothing of the occasional hussar or light dragoon who came flying into headquarters to report the sighting of a distant cavalry vedette. They just plodded on, any thrill of excitement quelled by the weight on their backs, any spark of anticipation quenched by the pain of their blistered feet. One or two men fell from the ranks clutching at their stomachs, cholera never being far away, but for the most part the troops just trudged, living for the order to raid the precious water from their big, wooden canteens.

There wasn't much help for the sick. If a man fell out with disease or heat-stroke, his comrades would do all that they could before leaving him to be picked up by the regimental surgeon and his Staff. In battle, the band were expected to provide stretcher-bearers, but on the line of march they had music to play so the task of collecting the sick fell to the handful of wives. Only eight of them had been selected by ballot to accompany the regiment and now two were themselves sick. The others, though, had been equipped with locally purchased carts drawn by sturdy little ponies. Just big enough for two casualties and all their weapons and kit, the little traps did a brisk trade amongst the plodding companies.

110

There had been some heart-wrenching scenes back in England when the wives whose names had not come up in the ballot parted from their husbands but, just as Morgan had predicted to himself, Mary had been one of the lucky ones. Now he glimpsed her only rarely, his throat constricting with desire whenever he saw her dashing about in her cart.

A boy from Thirsk called Almond, never the strongest, had been one of the few sick in the Grenadier Company. On the second day, he'd simply plonked himself down in the grass, grey in the face and all resistance gone, just letting his rifle fall like so much scrap. He'd sat for a few moments whilst his comrades got a bit of water past his lips, but as soon as the NCOs decided that he had to be left for "the quack" he'd just lain down flat, moaning pathetically. Quick on the scene was Mary. Where Almond was grey she was vibrant, where he was weak she was strong. Morgan could see that this life suited her perfectly. Gone was the chambermaid — in her place was a confident, blossoming young woman totally in control, all faux-servility forgotten.

It was the first decent river they'd seen. By the time they got to it the Bulganak was terribly muddied after cavalry, guns and the leading divisions had splashed through. This didn't prevent some of the younger soldiers from trying to fill their canteens with the gritty liquid, NCOs roundly cursing them for greenhorns. But whilst the early autumn sun shone with a ferocity that no one had warned them about in England and

111

burnt necks were sponged in the dark but cooling water, bugles suddenly shrieked from way to the front.

"Colour-Sar'nt, unless I'm very wrong, the cavalry have got a bite. Get the men out of the river and listen out for our bugles." Captain Eddington was right. The cavalry screen had seen Russian horsemen in far greater numbers than ever before lining the ridge to their front and now horse artillery was being called forward to support them. As the 95th cleared the river and fell into disciplined rank, trotting up to where the rest of the 2nd Division was forming, so the horse gunners came pelting into the ford.

From the slightly rising ground, Eddington's company was to get a grandstand view of the little drama that was to be played out in front of them. The men first formed in their three ranks, then they were allowed to stand at ease, then when it became clear that the fighting would all be done by horse and guns, they were allowed to sit down and smoke. In minutes the martial atmosphere had changed to that of a race meeting.

"Here, Colour-Sar'nt, have one of these." Carmichael offered his pigskin cheroot case to Eddington, to Morgan then McGucken, all of whom had gathered in a knot in front of the lounging troops.

"No thanks, sir, I'll stick to me pipe." Stooping to take a light from a nearby private who was already puffing happily, McGucken rested his rifle against his body before shading his eyes with his hand.

"The Eleventh Hussars are dismounting." Eddington had taken one of Carmichael's offerings, but it remained unlit in the fingers that were curled around his telescope. In the distance the 11th, distinctive in their cherry-coloured pants, swung out of the saddle.

"Yes, they're going to use their carbines, I guess." Morgan also had his glass trained on the action.

"Doubt it, they'll be itching to charge old Russ." Carmichael too looked down his telescope, but his prediction was turned on its head by a long line of white puffs of smoke followed, a second later, by far-off popping.

Morgan exchanged a knowing glance with McGucken before returning his gaze to the distant marionettes. The Russian cavalry declined to dismount, but they, in turn, fired their carbines at the kneeling British hussars. One toy-like charger dropped to its knees and then slowly keeled onto its side whilst the Russians, as far as the onlookers could see, went unharmed.

Splashing through the ford below them was the first battery of British six-pounders. The brass guns bounced behind their ammunition caissons, six sleek horses towing each one out of the soft ground mounted by busbied, blue-clad riders. The guns strained up the slope to join the cavalry, but not before the Russians got their blow in first. Unseen by the watching infantrymen, Russian guns had moved up to just behind the opposite ridge. Invisible except for their barrels, they had waited until the British guns had presented a target before sending a ripple of shot at them. To warm their bores, each enemy gun started with a solid, round, iron shot that burred and bounded over both cavalry and guns. There would be time enough for more lethal shellfire once the true range had been found.

The first volley fell well short. Earth and clods were thrown up harmlessly whilst the round shot bounced then embedded itself in the boggy ground around the Bulganak. For their second volley the Russians made a bold correction and sent a covey of rounds flying a little too high. Morgan had been watching one gun that, if his telescope wasn't lying, seemed to be pointing exclusively in their direction. Now it belched smokily, then as its ball grazed the slope below them its report reached their ears. Another spurt of earth in front, then the lump of iron hummed over the group to bound playfully away.

"Jesus, that was close!" All four had heard the lofty sound, but only one seemed to be alarmed. Flinching almost double and quite white in the face, Carmichael appeared to have noticed a danger that none of the others had.

"Drop summat, sir?" An urchin voice rose from the sprawled line of soldiers behind the officers as another ball sang far overhead. There were sniggers.

"Who said that?" Carmichael whirled to confront his accuser but saw nothing but ranks of whiskery, grinning faces.

"Leave it, Carmichael . . ." Eddington knew that the senior of his two subalterns had lost the moral battle with the troops, the very men whom he would have to lead into action, ". . . look yonder at our guns."

Three of the six-pounders were now wheeling hard against the slope whilst the nearby cavalry did their best to cover them with carbine fire. This was one of the most difficult manoeuvres possible for horse artillery as they would present a vulnerable flank and tail to the enemy guns as they brought their own pieces into action. Turf flying, all three teams turned away from the enemy to bring their guns into line with his. Before the horses had been brought to a skidding halt the men were off their seats or saddles, running hard to unlimber the gun, to get staves, rammers and sponges off its carriage and to sprint ammunition up to their brassy master. The commands of the gunner officers and NCOs could just be heard on the breeze as the whole performance unfolded mechanically before them.

Morgan focused carefully on the ammunition party. A bombardier threw open the lid of the wheeled ammunition caisson then rapidly handed shot to the two waiting gunners — "gun-numbers" as he'd been taught to call them — who raced forward, black, glistening balls held in that odd, folded-arm way. Like ants, the men went through their drills. The guns were sponged, primed, rammed and loaded just as the Russians fired again. Rounds bounced and furrowed past the British guns doing nothing more than showering the little blue figures with grit until one lucky shot bowled into the 11th Hussars.

"First blood to the Muscovites, then." Eddington had just caught the chaos in a mounted troop at the edge of his glass. He pointed and the others swung to look more closely. A Russian ball had swept through the ranks passing mainly between the horses' legs but

115

catching some mounts and their riders — it was hard to say exactly how many at that distance — and tumbling them into a mass of limbs and saddlery. Cherry-red overalls flashed in the tangle, the wearers horribly limp.

Then the British guns replied. Three fired almost as one — there was a relieved cheer from the 95th and chirpier individuals called for odds on which side would get the better of things. More bangs and smoke from the Russians and more furrowed earth, but this time without any hurt. The balls rattled past the gun crews unnoticed as they sweated with staves and rammers to get a better rate of fire than their opponents — then the order was given to fire shell. With only a couple of ranging shots, the British switched from solid shot to explosive rounds, the ridgeline being suddenly garlanded with black, smoky smudges cracking angrily just above the heads of the Russians.

"That'll sort the sods out, sir!" McGucken spoke for them all. But just as the British seemed to get the upper hand, bugles blared, the cavalry mounted and as quickly as the guns had come into action they were being limbered-up and moved to the rear.

"What on earth are the cavalry up to now? Can't they see that they got Russ on the back foot — Lord-bloody-Lucan needs a bit more ginger!"

A group of mounted Staff officers were directing the battle. Mostly in blue with cocked hats, one figure stood out in fur busby and pelisse, Lord Cardigan, commander of the Light Cavalry Brigade. His animus towards his brother-in-law and divisional commander,

Lord Lucan, was infamous, even here amongst the infantry, and Morgan fancied that he could see both noblemen straining with dislike for each other.

"I suspect he'd ginger you if he heard that, Carmichael." Eddington spoke quietly but with an edge. "I have no doubt that he has his reasons to withdraw the cavalry and guns. I expect it's just a screen force that he's discovered, not the main body. It'll take more than a few donkey-guns to dislodge a well-defended position — and Lord knows, they've had the time and we've shown them exactly what our intentions are. No, it'll be up to that bunch behind us."

Eddington cast a wary eye over the mass of beefy, scruffy boys loafing behind him. They sat or kneeled now, belts undone, shakoes cast off, their muddy trouser bottoms rolled up to just above the ankle. The white-laced scarlet coatees were beginning to fade whilst their leather equipment hadn't seen pipeclay for an age. Sunburnt, stubbly faces either grinned back at the company commander or were instantly asleep, cushioned on their blanket packs.

"Aye, sir, and they'll do just fine." McGucken said this not as an opinion, but as a simple fact.

As they were soon to learn, the price of a little excitement was a lot of boredom. It took for ever for the army to sort itself out after what instantly came to be known as "The Cavalry Affair" and whilst the Light Brigade aligned, re-aligned and then eventually trotted off over the near horizon, the 95th just hung about. No orders were given to relax, so no cooking fires were lit

117

nor could equipment be fully taken off, for everyone felt that an order to dash to support of the hussars would come at any moment.

Meanwhile waiting wooden-wheeled, squeaky pony carts brought the Light Cavalry Brigade's casualties back through the ford. A prurient curiosity drew Morgan and Carmichael like a magnet — real war meant real blood and real death and they must see it for themselves. Pegg trailed after them, as morbidly interested as his officers.

The carts were driven by medical orderlies of the 11th. Both of them were pointedly sombre — they were still wearing their blood-spattered white aprons and cuff covers like battle honours. In the back of the first cart sat a Sergeant, bare-headed but chewing at a pipe. Over the back of the little cart dangled one good cherry-clad leg whilst his hands clasped the remains of his other. Where his foot had been there was now a swathe of crimson bandages, whilst the bottom of his overall dripped a darker red.

"Well done, Sar'nt, you got the better of that lot on the ridge," Morgan lied bravely. Two glassy eyes slowly swivelled towards the subalterns, smoke idling from his nostrils as his pipe stuck out from below a scrappy, gingery moustache. That was all the answer they got.

Morgan had seen plenty of corpses in his life — the famine of forty-eight had killed half Skibbereen — but never one that had died violently. In the back of the second cart was a young, mousey hussar lying on his belly, his face turned to one side. His right shoulder was a mess of blood and butchered tissue, a roundshot had smashed the arm bones which now stuck out like something from Hector's bowl. The spurs at his heels joggled gently to the rhythm of the cart, but it was his open eyes that held the young officer. As the cart moved so his eyelashes trembled — it was as if the boy were listening intently, quite awake, one ear pressed to the boards of the cart. Black blood had dried around his nostrils.

The three of them silently watched the sad cavalcade.

Eddington was right, of course. But that was why he was a captain, Morgan mused as they settled down again to sleep in the open. Just like the other nights, the boys had stood to, stood down, cleaned their weapons, cooked then wrapped themselves in their blankets — but tonight was different. Across the next river — the Alma — on the slopes that lined the far side twinkled myriad fires. There hadn't been quite enough light to see the Russian trenches and earthworks when they had marched into their night-time positions, but now the whole landscape seemed to be covered in little pin-pricks of light, the firmament of a mighty army. The soldiers were excited, chattering, cleaning their rifles, checking their ammunition with unusual zeal.

The padre and the volunteer priest wandered amongst them but instead of the usual affable, banter from the men, there were odd, earnest little conversations. Here the padre helped boys from the slums to read passages from letters, there the priest mumbled, head-to-head with a couple of lads from the bogs who toyed with their rosaries.

119

The officers, as usual, had gathered around their own fire. They had learnt to waste no time before getting into their blankets — an exhausted sleep now came easily between watches — but tonight they had visitors. A trio of subalterns from the other companies were prowling about, seeking out friends, measuring others' nervousness against their own. Morgan joined the group just as Boothby was expanding on the desirability or otherwise of losing a limb in battle.

"It would be a damned nuisance, for sure, but it'd be bound to get you noticed by the *filles* wouldn't it?"

"No bloody use having a bunch of lovelies hovering around if you've had your eyes put out, though, is it?" burly McDonald from the Light Company objected.

"All right, I accept that, but a missing limb gives you a certain *je ne sais quoi*, don't it?" Boothby plugged on.

"You'd be pretty unhappy if your *je ne sais quoi* had been shot off, wouldn't you though?" Carmichael added.

Morgan immediately thought of today's crippled hussar and the veterans he'd seen in Fermoy and Dublin — now just husks and as likely to catch the eye of one of Boothby's *filles* as he was to kiss the Pope.

"No, but really, if you had to lose a limb which one would you prefer?" Boothby directed this at Eddington.

"I've never heard such damn nonsense in my life, but if something has to go you'd better hope it's one of my legs, that's the only thing that would stop me kicking your arse all the way back to your own company. Now cut along and get some sleep."

CHAPTER
FIVE

Alma to Balaklava

"Christ, Colour-Sar'nt, the Regiment's taken a beating, ain't it?" Morgan looked at the headless body of his former company commander, Eddington, that was being carried by two soldiers from the Grenadier Company, one holding him below the knees, the other below the shoulders. As the lifeless, waxy white hands swung in time to the men's pace, so the soldier at the rear tried to keep the sticky gore from the dead officers' shattered neck from staining his uniform.

Morgan stared as the corpse passed. Could it only be last night that Eddington had sent the subaltern's packing when they were discussing the glamour of being wounded in battle — although none of them had reflected on the merits of a bloody death? And was it only a few hours ago that the same man had lead his troops with a dash, an *élan* that he doubted he would ever have, Morgan wondered?

"Aye, sir, the adjutant's kilt as well, sir; half the subbies are cold meat, the commanding officer'll lose a leg, the Sergeants' Mess is eight good men down and as many wounded, an' over two hundred of the boys are dead or wounded an' we're still counting." Even

McGucken seemed stunned by the loss of so many of his officers and comrades. "Bastard of a way to win our first battle, ain't it, sir?"

"That's what Wellington said wasn't it, Colour-Sar'nt?" Morgan surveyed the scattered parties of men carrying the dead and wounded. "'The only thing worse than a battle won, is a battle lost' or something like that."

"Aye, sir, something like that," Colour-Sergeant McGucken answered distractedly.

With Carmichael — now the acting company commander — nowhere to be seen, McGucken had organized the burial parties on his own initiative. He gathered the sergeants and corporal who were still standing around him and detailed them off to find their own dead and do their best for the wounded. For most, it was a long haul as the casualties stretched right back over the river and far into the vines on the north side. Little groups of men toiled with the bodies — if they had some vestige of life in them they could be left at the surgeons' tents down by the river but the stiff, cold corpses had to be carried up the hill to the Russian trenches in the Great Redoubt that were now being used as mass graves.

At first great care had been taken to identify, remove and then bundle up the casualties' effects, but this soon faltered in the face of sheer weight of numbers and leaden fatigue. As soon as a man was clearly recognized he was pushed in with his regimental comrades — boots, clothes, belts and all — regardless of the instructions to return everything useful to the quartermaster. No sooner had the last spade of soil been heaped on the shallow pits than the men sank down, almost too exhausted to eat.

"They reckon half the regiment's gone, Frank. Did you see your Pete?" Pegg, haversack now full to bursting with his spoils, had sought out Francis Luff, the brother of his dead friend. To ease Luff's grief, Pegg had busied himself about a fire, stripping musket barrels from their stocks to create an iron grid above the flames. His tin kettle was just beginning to boil as dusk turned to night and the flames painted their faces.

"Aye, don't s'pose he knew much about it. Got his prayer book and a few letters for Mam, but they're all covered in his blood, can't send them home like that can I?" Frank gathered his greatcoat about him, took his pipe from his mouth, spat half-heartedly and pushed at the burning wood with his boot.

"No. Did you take a bit of his hair for her?"

"Didn't think, an' it's too late now, I saw him being covered over," Frank muttered miserably.

"Come 'ere, give her this." Pegg sawed an inch or two of greasy hair from Frank's head before tying it with a bit of string and a tiny Russian icon from his haversack. "She'll never know it's yours an' it'll mean worlds to her." A stumpy pencil and a scrap of paper were produced and Pegg worked away at a note before wrapping the little bundle up and passing it to Frank. In the light of the flames he could just make out the laborious, printed words. "From the head of Private Peter Luff, Grenadiers, 95th Regiment, 20 Sep 54. He fell in the great victory at the River Alma". Frank tucked the token away in a deep pocket — when the post arrived in Hayling Island it would tear a mother's heart.

The hills behind the Alma rolled even more gently in the long march down towards Sevastopol. Where before the going had been dull and unobstructed, now forests and thorny woods sprang up that wasted not just time and energy but caused the troops to curse most horribly, almost poetic in their profanity. The plodding infantry saw the occasional horseman go tearing by, directing them, it was universally assumed, up the wrong track or through the wrong ford out of sheer badness. Whether it was the utter monotony of the march or the heaviness of heart that hung over the men after the battle was hard to say. They all knew that life could never be as carefree again.

"I never thought I'd call a bit of scabby hillside 'home' Sar'nt Ormond."

Morgan had thrown himself down next to Ormond who had taken off his belts and pack, scrabbled around in his haversack and was pruning a toenail with a pen knife. All around them the footsore, grubby troops were lighting fires, taking long pulls from their water bottles or just sitting vacantly, hardly believing that this was to be their camp. They'd had no change of clothes since they left the ships fifteen days ago and had spent no more than two nights in any one place. Now they refused to believe that the last week and a half of constant movement and marching since the battle at the Alma had come to an end.

"Aye, sir, the last few days have been a bit 'ectic, 'aven't they?" Brows knitted, Ormond dug away at his foot. "I thought we'd get a bit of rest when the Rifles took Balaklava couple of days back, but we've been buggered around from pillar to post ever since, ain't we, sir?"

After the long march down and around to the south of Sevastopol, both the British and French had tried to use Balaklava as their main port once it had fallen, but it had proved too small. So, the French had pushed further along the coast whilst the British sorted out not just their camps and gun positions, but also the exposed and vulnerable route from Balaklava up to the siege lines on the Sapoune — the great horseshoe-shaped ridge that dominated Sevastopol.

"What do they call this place, anyway, sir? I can't read a blind bit of their funny writing." Ormond wriggled his toes, cleaned scraps of grey, doughy, dead skin from between them with a stubby finger and turned to look at Morgan.

"Well, the colonel says the Staff insist on calling it 'Inkermann', because that's what that village down there . . ." Morgan pointed into the valley at a thatched and shingled hamlet just on the other side of the bridge that spanned the River Tchernaya, ". . . is known as, apparently. You know the army, Sar'nt Ormond, they'll take the damndest little spot on a map and make it something it isn't — look at Fermoy."

"No, sir, you look at Fermoy if you like, I thought it was a pox-ridden dump. Anyway, d'you reckon this is it, or will we be moving again?"

125

For the last week Brigadier-General Pennefather's Brigade, to which the 30th, 55th and 95th belonged, had been told to wait first here and then there all over the eastern part of the Sapoune. Before the siege could start, however, the infantry had to be arranged to the Staff's satisfaction.

"Well, the Pope's a pig if I'm wrong, but the Thirtieth and the Fifty-Fifth are starting to lay out their tent lines yonder and the gunners have laid claim to those huts."

Morgan looked across the scrub-covered saddle that was bisected by a packed-dirt road as the other two regiments settled into camp routine. The Division's artillery, meanwhile, were rapidly digging and scraping drains for their stables around a clutch of buildings.

"The gunners can have the bloody things for all I care, sir. Let's just get the tents up and let the lads get some rest." Ormond said what was on everyone's mind.

"I hope you're right, Sar'nt Ormond, but I guess we'll be busy soon enough." Morgan nodded through the scrub towards Balaklava. "You see, every damn bit of kit we use, every morsel we eat, every shot the gunners fire will have to come up from Balaklava and the route will have to be guarded. You remember when the cavalry bumped into the Russians a few days ago when we were just outside Sevastopol?" Morgan paused to see whether Ormond was still with him and got a tired nod in reply. "Well, the newspapers say . . ." Morgan had eagerly devoured the latest copy of *The Times* that one of the other subalterns had produced in last night's bivouac, ". . . that General Menscikoff has now got thousands of troops ranging across the interior of the Crimea and they can be re-supplied from Russia proper whilst there's not a damn thing we can do about it. Those troops are now free to operate against Balaklava and against us here. We'll have to do all the digging and bag-filling for the siege work — as the infantry always have to do — but we'll also have to protect the whole of the Allied flank; you see, the hard graft hasn't even started yet."

As Morgan finished his gloomy speech, two men arrived from battalion headquarters to guide the company to their camp site.

"Right, on yer feet you idle lot, there's the whole of the Allied flank to protect so let's be havin' you." Ormond gently mocked his officer. Wearily, the troops rose and buckled on their kit before tramping off through the brushwood.

"Well, I suppose it means that we'll be in reserve next time." Morgan looked at the mass of officers of the other two regiments of the Brigade, the 30th and the 55th. Compared with the remains of the 95th, they seemed to be plentiful.

"Aye, it'll be their turn to lead the next attack." Carmichael, now acting as the Grenadier's company commander, echoed the thoughts of all the 95th's officers who had survived the Alma.

The whole of Pennefather's Brigade was shocked by the number of officers and men that the 95th had lost, for on parade they looked like a couple of strong companies rather than a whole battalion. The other two regiments seemed to have got away lightly, now the Brigade commander, Pennefather, assembled them to reconnoitre the approaches to Sevastopol. The infantry were to be put to work constructing parallels and trenches whilst the guns would batter any defences of the soon-to-be besieged city.

"Gentlemen, we're going to have look at a bit of ground that you'll get very familiar with over the next few weeks. The guns will knock away at Sevastopol, but *we'll* have to take the place and the sooner we can do that — and it's got to be before winter — the better. There be a whore of a lot of digging to do an' everyone will say the Staff don't know their arse from their elbow, but I can assure you that a steady advance with trenches and parallels is the only way to do it. Now, it's Shanks's Pony from here on." Pennefather, light, wiry, grey-haired, whose triumphs in India were never far from his lips, had yet to make an impression on the 95th. He'd been far away from them at the Alma and whilst almost every man had been able to hear his oaths and curses as the battle started, they'd soon been parted in the smoke. Now he told the senior officers to dismount for the Russians would be on the lookout for such parties.

"The Brigade will be responsible for a series of parallels on what's being called the 'Right Attack'. Over to the left the other divisions will be constructing the 'Left Attack' and beyond them, stretching right round the city, the Frogs will be carrying out similar operations. First, I'm going to show you where the gunners are starting their batteries, for we shall have to fit in with their misbegotten plans."

Carmichael was foremost in the polite laughter as the brigadier damned — as infantrymen always do — the artillery.

The thirty or so officers, no two of them now dressed alike except for their stained red coats, crept up the rocky fissures on the lip of the great Careening Ravine that led right down into the heart of the city and the bay that was cleverly adapted to allow Russian warships to have their keels cleaned there. The ravine itself was deep and sinuous, its sides rocky and steep and it served as a perfect, natural delineation between the Left and Right Attacks. The autumn sun still shone intently and as they stalked forward the band of Morgan's cap and the too-long hair at the nape of his neck became very wet. He longed to pull at his water-bottle.

The officers stumbled around the steep hillsides for a good half-hour before there was an unexpected, muted challenge. A sentry from the most advanced artillery battery was covering the path that led to his position, whilst all around gunners dug and filled basketwork gabions and sandbags, sweating into their grey woollen shirts, leather braces swinging freely around their knees. Now the man looked down the barrel of his carbine at the gaggle of officers.

"Sorry, sirs, no one told us you was a-coming. You'll be wanting the major, he's up there." The grimy gunner returned his carbine to the crook of his arm, tapped its sling in salute and pointed in the general direction of his officer with a flick of his new-grown beard. As they

129

passed, Morgan noticed how the young soldier scratched at the crack of his bottom: so it wasn't just the infantry whom the lice favoured.

The gunner major was busy, too busy to be impressed by a mere brigadier-general and a gang of infantrymen. With great science his battery was taking shape and he made it clear that there would be little need for inching cautiously forward with trenches and earthworks. He spread out his chart on a low sandbag wall.

"Now, sir, gentlemen, you can't quite see the town from here, but our guns will be able to once the battery is complete. Just over that rise . . ." he pointed to a near horizon no more than a hundred paces away, ". . . is Sevastopol. It's practically undefended right now, and if we get a move on I have no doubt that we could be in the place in a month at the very most." Instantly aware that he'd overreached himself in the presence of a general-officer, the Gunner quickly back-pedalled. "At least, that's our view, but I have no doubt that you're full aware of the situation, sir?"

"Aye, well, Lord Raglan will have a view as well, Major — forgive me, I didn't catch your name — perhaps we ought to listen to him." The mention of the commander-in-chief had the desired effect and the gunner shut up. "Now, gentlemen, follow me but beware of the Muscovites' marksmanship. I almost lost a goddamn aide here day before last."

They snaked up the low rise, fumbling at telescopes and compasses. Carefully the group of officers walked forward until they had a good view of the port, a glimpse of the very reason for all of them being there. Below them in the sun winked Sevastopol. The mighty, shimmering harbour that divided the north part of the great arsenal from the south stretched across their front with the deep, harsh-sided ravines fingering towards them. Toy-like ships swayed almost imperceptibly at their anchor-cables, gun ports open and alert. From a ravine deep below them came incessant hammering from what, Morgan guessed, was a gang of shipwrights hard at work on a keel, whilst ribbons of freshly-dug soil seemed to be everywhere in front of the city. The officers all stared intently through their glasses. Trenches, embrasures and great banks of spoil were being dug but with the exception of one, white tower there seemed to be no masonry defences.

"That wee tower's what they call the Malakoff." Their telescopes all swung in the direction indicated by Pennefather's pointing blackthorn stick. "See how the Russians are throwing up other works to support it with cross-fire." The faster Pennefather spoke the more marked was his brogue.

A careful look at the grey worms of packed earth showed hosts of men at work with shovels and picks, sweating as hard as anyone on the Allied side. In each line gun positions were being prepared, giant basketwork gabions were already in place at many of them and Morgan fancied that he could even see a group of women hard at work shovelling dirt into sandbags.

The scene mesmerized him. Grand, golden domes reflected the sun back at him whilst milky white

131

barracks topped with deep red tiled roofs stretched serenely along the quay sides. They had all been told of the Russian men-of-war that had been scuttled across the harbour front to prevent the Allied fleets from thrusting deep into the anchorage and with a careful adjustment of his telescope, Morgan could just bring into focus a line of masts sticking forlornly from the water. He let his glass drift further towards the north of the city. It was from here that they had approached on that weary march.

Morgan suddenly realized how difficult their job was going to be. They only had enough troops to lay siege to the southern side of the port, whilst the north side was wide open. They needed at least twice the number of men and guns to invest the place properly. Worse still, with an army free to operate beyond the Allied line, the besiegers would be mighty lucky not to find themselves besieged.

Then that horrid, too familiar sound. With a screech and whirr iron shot skidded and bounced around them, closely followed by two bangs and — though none of them saw them — blossoms of light grey smoke from one of the enemy batteries. A shower of grit anointed their backs and rumps. Morgan found his fingers twisting into the coarse, chalky grass, the horror of the Alma back with him in an instant. With his eyes tight-shut and jaw clenched he was suddenly more frightened of being the only one to have thrown himself down than of anything that his enemies could do to him. He needn't have worried. Less than a month ago they had all smiled at one another, falsely confident, as the first Russian rounds had sailed across their heads at the Alma. They might even have chuckled — "What, afraid of a little iron? Not us." But those few, bloody hours had harrowed them all. Whilst their bodies might be whole, they all knew just how fragile they were and what a little iron had done to so many.

"Get up you idiots and get back into cover." Even Pennefather was white. He brushed the dirt from his clothes, clutched at his glass and led the little stampede back down to the half-dug, half-safe, battery.

"So, gentlemen, you've had a goddam' good look at where you're going to be digging over the next few weeks." Brigadier-General Pennefather had recovered a little of his composure. "See to it that none of your men exposes himself needlessly to Russian shot, we're short-handed enough as it is."

Like he's just done to us, thought Morgan.

The slightly dusty, slightly chastened group of officers moved back down the track rather more quickly than they had arrived. The sweaty, grimy gunners paused in their labours and smiled.

"Bet you'd prefer to be tucked up with sweet Mary rather than mooning around out here, wouldn't you, Morgan?" Carmichael muttered quietly as they looked out over the dark, drizzly hillside.

"I just hope her husband's wound heals fast and we get him back to the company soon. Keenan did great work with the Colours once we were across the Alma — did you not see him?" Morgan's quiet sally had its intended effect, for Carmichael quickly moved on.

"Just make sure you keep those forward pickets on their toes tonight in this muck, Morgan. These are just the conditions that the Russians like for skulking about."

Morgan said nothing, wondering just how Carmichael knew such things for he had rarely seen his acting company commander visit even the main pickets on Shell Hill let alone the most exposed positions.

At first, the troops had thought that anything must be better than digging trenches under the Russians' eyes, back-breaking work made worse by having to do most of it either on their knees or bent double. The naval gunners in Sevastopol had proved uncannily accurate and even working at night attracted well-aimed fire. So, when it was announced that the 2nd Division would divide its time between entrenchment and watching the hilly approaches to the exposed Allied flank at Inkermann, many of the men had welcomed it.

"Meks a change to see Carmichael up 'ere." Shell Hill was only a couple of miles from the heart of Sevastopol, just out of sight of the Russians' outlying earthworks and half a mile from the 95th's camp, but, on a night like this, it seemed to be the most desolate place on earth. Now Pegg pulled the cape of his greatcoat around his ears, screwed his dark-blue woollen cap further down on his head and tried to settle his back more comfortably against the earth bank.

"Aye, saw no sign of him once we was across the Alma, an' you should 'ave seen him scuttle when Russ opened up on us digging party night before last. He were like that." Private Pacey skimmed his flat, mittened hand out of the deep cuff of his coat. "It's Paddy Morgan on duty tonight, ain't it? Never knew what to mek of 'im at first, but 'e's the right man to have out 'ere."

Pegg and his friends had soon realized that picket work was dull, hard and dangerous. Pairs of men had to loiter, always alert, in the brush and broken ground watching for the Russians to sneak up from the gullies surrounding the harbour for if they managed to get guns up on the high point of Shell Hill, then the whole of the British position on Fore Ridge would be untenable. At first men had prowled forward to see just what the enemy was up to, but shells from two warships moored in the far reaches of the harbour had soon dampened their ardour. Two men from the 55th had disappeared some days ago. Shots had been heard, probably from their wraith-like Russian counterparts who could be trusted to spot any movement just as quickly as the British would.

Meanwhile the weather got colder and wetter. Whilst the drummers could keep a fire and kettle going behind one of the walls or banks that served as rally points just to the rear of the forward pickets, it was a desolate, tedious duty that bored the men yet left them uneasy and insecure.

"What are yous pair purging about now?" Colour-Sergeant McGucken, slid quietly in through the dusk to the little sheltering bank. He had with him two men who had just been relieved from picket. They were all

135

soaked by fine drizzle, greatcoats hanging dankly on their spare frames, collars turned up, broad leather cross-belts now a soggy, dun colour, completely free of the white, parade-ground pipeclay. All three had the muzzles of their rifles well down, the locks tucked closely under their armpits against the damp and rain.

"Not much, Colour-Sar'nt. We was just saying what a treat it was to see Mr Carmichael, almost forgot what he looks like." Pegg hunched forward over the smoky fire, poured hot water over the crushed coffee beans in his tin jug and swirled it around. "Give us your mugs, then," All four produced their dented, stained tin cups before Pegg poured the precious liquid carefully into each. The party squatted down next to the bank, warming their cold, clammy hands on the metal, blowing the steam into the night.

"Don't know what you're whining about, young Pegg, Mr Carmichael never got round to that flogging that Captain Eddington ordered, did he?" One of the others crossed himself unobtrusively at the name of their dead officer, whilst Pegg busied himself, filling his kettle for the next brew.

Promotion had quite changed Richard Carmichael. His confidence, far from being dented by his unexplained absence during the fighting at the river, had soared. The company had been used to Captain Eddington's attention to detail, to his insistence that weapons, ammunition and the like were kept in good order, but they could see the point in this. What they couldn't understand was Carmichael's fussiness. Water bottles had to be worn on the right hip, the right hip, mind, not the left. Firewood could only be carried to the forward picket positions by every fifth man rather than by them all because it made the working parties look "slovenly". Each muddy, sloppy tent area was inspected daily, clotheslines and soaking kit having to be cleared away just so that the position would look, according to Carmichael, "soldierly". But they didn't feel very "soldierly" when they struggled back into dank, clammy clothes that should have been dry.

The troops might have forgiven all this if Carmichael had shared the dangers and hardships. Checking the forward sentries was left to Morgan and the colour-sergeant whilst Carmichael enjoyed several straight hours between his blankets most nights. He'd even been heard to say that for commanders, "sleep was a duty". He occasionally swept round the reserve positions up on Shell Hill, but he'd never yet been known to venture forward to the picket line to chaff the troops on watch and to get a glimpse of the enemy. Predictably, the conversation drifted back to a recent company-sized working party in the forward trenches that Carmichael had led.

"'E wouldn't 'elp carry any of the bastard big gabions, nor the piles of piss-wet sandbags. You remember those star-shells and then more iron flying around than a Bolton scrapyard, don't you? 'E just buggered off. It was only Jock McGucken and Paddy Morgan who stopped the whole bleedin' lot on us from running all the way to Balaklava." It was a favourite theme for Pacey and the others.

"Stand up!" McGucken, with a quiet authority brought the party to its feet as Morgan shuffled into the circle of light around the fire. Like all the others, he was wet and cold, his pistol and sword hanging heavily round his narrow waist, drizzle speckling the deep leather peak of his cap. The colour-sergeant flicked a quick salute onto the stock of his rifle. "Now then, sir, I've just got a fresh brew on for you." The flames reflected off Pegg and the others' frank, admiring smiles.

"Carry-on, Colour-Sergeant, relax, lads. I'm grateful to you, Pegg. You two been out on picket?"

"Sir," both privates replied.

"See anything odd, or hear any movement from the Russians?"

"Nothing, sir. I reckon Russ has had enough. We'll be in the town in no time once the gunners get goin' properly and the navy lads have a go at the harbour forts. Then there'll be more grog and quim than we know what to do with. Don't you reckon, sir?" The taller of the two sentries hadn't let the drizzle quench his spirits.

"Well, Taylor, we shall have to see. I know Sevastopol seems to be guarded by no more than a park wall, but you've seen how the Russians can shoot and we don't know how well they'll hold up to our and the Froggy guns when the bombardment starts."

"They'll just wrap their hand in, won't they, sir?"

"I hope so, Pegg, but what really worries me is that we won't be able to make the siege tell before Russ has a go at Balaklava. Don't forget General Menschikoff's

138

lads that got out of Sevastopol just as we arrived, there'll be the devil to pay if they interfere with the lines of supply. Our guns have got to have enough rounds to fire at Russ, if they attack the port there'll be real dramas." The damp little group seemed downcast. Morgan realized that he'd probably been more honest with them than they wanted him to be. "Well, lads, there's a carrying party needed for Balaklava tomorrow, they need more powder and shot for the bombardment. So, Taylor if you've any strength left after tonight's picket, volunteer for it and we'll see if we can't scare up enough grog and quim for all of us."

"Always ready for a bit of either — or both, come to that, sir." They were a good lot that could laugh in these conditions.

"Oh, you lovely little thing!"

"Run away to sea with me, darling!"

A gang of beefy sailors voiced their appreciation as Mary and Mrs Polley trundled down the Col Road towards Balaklava, the reins of the two squat local ponies barely needing to be held as they trotted gently downhill. Mrs Polley was the other Grenadier Company wife whose name had come out of the hat during the ballot in Weedon, much to the delight of her husband, George, a lance-corporal from Lincoln whom she looked after with cheerful zeal.

"Oo, those matelots can't get enough of us, can they?" Mrs Polley was under no illusion about which of them was attracting the sailors' admiration, and she was rewarded by a sparkling laugh from her companion.

The two long lines of seamen heaved at the ropes. Dripping, stripped to just their shirts despite the sharp wind that blew up onto the ridge from the river valley below, they pulled the barrel of a heavy naval gun on a two-wheeled sledge up towards the siege lines facing Sevastopol. Mary was always impressed by their cheerfulness, the easy, self-confidence about them and the relaxed discipline that would never have worked with soldiers. Solid, ruddy, happy, they never let her wagon go by without making it quite clear how they intended to provide the next seafaring generation for the nation.

"Get on, you lubbers! You've only gone to sea 'cos you're frightened of your wives." Mrs Polley cawed with delight at Mary's riposte, even attempting a coquettish wave.

"Come aboard the *Sphinx* then, my duck, an' I'll show you something that frightens even my missus — but leave yer mum behind!" Gales of laughter swept down the lines, Mrs Polley's smile broadened and Mary twitched the reins. As they trotted past, the midshipman in charge scooped his cap from his teenage head and executed a tiny bow, a flush on his downy cheeks.

"They don't mean any harm, ladies, you know what they're like."

"They're good lads, sir, but just get that piece up to the ridge, will you, an' give Russ a battering?" Mary replied.

"I was thinking of giving you a batt . . . sorry, miss, I'm spending too much time on the lower deck, good

140

day to you both." The midshipman clapped his cap on his head and trotted off to rejoin his party.

The last week had been busy for the women. The long-expected Allied bombardment had started well, French and British guns opening fire almost as one, making the air shiver with detonation after booming detonation — Mary even had to soothe her ponies with precious barley sugar and much stroking of ears. The crescendo had steadily grown, but then a great rumbling roar that seemed to go on for ever, had overwhelmed every other sound. A lucky Russian round (some said it was an old-fashioned red-hot shot) struck home at the main French magazine, blowing laboriously stock-piled ammunition sky-high.

Mary had been in the hospital tent at the time tending two lads whose trench-side had collapsed on them. The canvas had billowed tautly inwards as the shock-wave struck, and she'd rushed outside to see a dirty geyser of earth and odd little specks that Mrs Polley poetically described as "fragments of Frog" plummeting to earth. A great cloud of smoke wafted along the French positions to their left and soon all of the guns in their sector fell silent.

At the same time, the fire from the Allied ships were making almost no impression against the harbour forts and whilst the British artillery tried to cover for the silence of the French, it was obvious that any attempt on Sevastopol would have to be delayed. During all this, of course, the Russians had been far from silent. A steady trickle of wounded and the odd corpse had been ferried back to the regimental hospital where Fergusson the surgeon and his team of orderlies and soldiers' wives had done their best.

It had taken Mary and the rest of the women some time to learn the rudiments of cleaning, sponging and picking wounds clear of any bits of cloth that had been driven into them. Fergusson was at pains to explain how the lethal gangrene would soon set in to any puncture that hadn't been properly probed not just for the projectile that had caused it, but for any wad of cloth that had been driven in as well. They were shown how careful teasing at a scrap of lint that poked from the edge of an oozing hole might produce a patch of material from deep within and, perhaps save a life. Some of the women and orderlies had no aptitude for the work, being clumsy or just careless, needlessly rough with the injured and cack-handed with delicate work.

At first Mary had recoiled from the blood and pus. Some of the girls in the kitchens at Glassdrumman had always been squeamish with joints from the butchers, but that had never bothered her. This was different, though. In the heat of battle at the Alma, she had just been able to steel herself to the screams and immediacy of wounds and death, but this deliberate nursing was entirely different. The men would come to the hospital usually mute with pain, their eyes speaking more than their lips. Many of them had been lying under fire for hours after being hurt, vital blood seeping away, healthy, robust men turned to shrivelled, suffering boys. At first the waste had appalled her. Too many would sink into death before her eyes and be borne away like so much offal, but like the others she had become accustomed to it, had come to accept the reality of war and overcome it. Unlike the others, though, Mary always saw the ripples of grief and dismay in every house and family that death visited.

As the bombardment dwindled to a rhythmic, routine drumming, so the flow of casualties lessened. Fergusson, as a reward for hard and skilful work asked Mary to take a wagon the seven or so miles to the port of Balaklava, pick up some medical supplies, find out what she could about regimental casualties in the main hospital there and ". . . take a wee while to herself".

"Right, come on Mrs Polley, who's that friend of yours in the cavalry this side of Balaklava?" Mrs Polley had worked harder than most but she would never get the same recognition from men that Mary did.

"Why, Betty Martin from Stockport. We was girls together. You remember her, we met her in Varna. Her husband's with the Eighth Hussars, just got a tape, said the kettle's always a-boiling and there's a bed for the night for friends."

"Well, let's go and see her, then, chances are that we can pick up the mail an' get any news from Turkey."

Mary had barely mentioned it. She'd last seen her husband, James, loaded onto a litter at the Alma, unconscious with the blood from his shot-torn throat soaking through the bandage that she and Tony Morgan had applied. News came through with a litany of other snippets that he was recovering slowly in the Turkish base hospital at Scutari. Most assumed that she bore the tragedy stoically — it wasn't the place of a soldier's wife to be free with her emotions. But Mary knew the truth. Beyond guilt and duty she felt little for James Keenan.

Now she and Mrs Polley barged through the press of bodies in the cramped post office on Balaklava's quayside. Everyone was here, from officers at Lord Raglan's headquarters, to post NCOs from every regiment in the siege, to ragamuffin cabin boys off the merchantmen that crowded the harbour. The stone-tiled roof building had been a Russian official's office for the administration of the port's fishing — now it handled every communication for Britain's army and navy in the Crimea. The floor was awash with mud and horse dung, the air heavy with bustling humanity that hadn't glimpsed soap and water for a month or more.

"Here, Mrs Keenan, here's mail for the regiment from base hospital." Mrs Polley held a narrow sheaf of envelopes tied about with a piece of brown paper and red ribbon.

"Let's get outside into the light."

It may have been brighter in the open, but the harbour was an appalling sight. The steep sides of Balaklava's fjord reached up above them, scree set with the odd bush leading up to a series of ancient Genoese towers that dominated the approaches to the anchorage. Marines and sailors toiled upwards carrying every piece of military kit needed to build forts and earthworks to defend the place. An ingenious series of pulleys and ropes lofted gun barrels from a bomb-ketch in the harbour to the surrounding heights whilst mules brayed and whinnied their loads up the narrow tracks.

Below them, though, the harbour slopped and stank. Men-of-war of all types were moored alongside a maze of merchantmen, all busily unloading equipment, disembarking more troops and horses or taking the sick and wounded on board. But this press of living creatures had only one place to deposit its waste — the harbour waters. A sheen of filth floated there. Rubbish from the galleys vied with sewage and slops, whilst dead mules, horses, pigs and sheep drifted and bumped against the sides of the ships. Mrs Polley turned her eyes away from what she swore was a bobbing, shrouded, human head and both women clasped handkerchiefs to their noses against the reek.

"The official report says your James is 'poorly, recovering well'." Mrs Polley read the long list of the 95th's casualties through her handkerchief. "You haven't got anything from your husband, have you?" she asked. Mary had riffled through the other letters, all of them addressed to other soldiers, none for her.

"No, James is no great hand with a pen, but I'd hoped that one of the others might have helped him." She remembered how her husband's hair was slick with blood, how his head had lolled as Tony Morgan helped to put him in the cart with its solid wooden wheels. Most of her never expected to see Private James Keenan alive again — a part of her hoped not to. She pushed the thought away. "Any letters there for Mr Morgan?"

"Yes, quite a handful." Mrs Polley shuffled the letters for the young officer, throwing a knowing eye over them. "Mostly bills and boring stuff; but there's a couple from Ireland and one from India." She passed the lot over for Mary's inspection.

Mrs Polley was right — there were half a dozen written in the official-looking copperplate of agents, tailors and saddlers, one franked in Delhi that she guessed came from that old lecher Colonel Dick Kemp and two sent from Cork. One was certainly from Morgan's father, Billy, but the other was a mystery.

"Why, that's nice, rounded hand-writing, ain't it?" Mrs Polley was as interested in the letter as Mary was. "Does it smell of scent?"

Mary hadn't thought of that. She ran it under her nose and, sure enough, there was a trace of something floral. "It does, Mrs Polley. I was afraid that it might be from some grand Proddy woman that's got her eye on Mr Morgan; but it can't be, it smells too nice. If it had come from Maude-bloody-Hawtrey, it would have reeked of church candles and horse sweat." Both women laughed.

"Come on Mrs Polley, if Mrs Martin's as free with her hospitality as you say she is, let's get to her before dark." The pair gathered up their papers and package of medical supplies and found their wagon, swiftly removing the ponies' nosebags and heading away from the harbour. Mary's visits to Balaklava were infrequent enough for her to forget the stench of the place — now it hung at the back of her throat.

146

The 8th Hussars had aligned their tents perfectly. Sitting in the bottom of the Balaklava valley, each of the Light Cavalry Brigade's five regiments had pitched their tents symmetrically so that the prevailing wind would carry the smoke of the cooking fires away. Now the two 95th wives walked their covered hospital cart through empty horse lines whose troughs were being filled in preparation for the return of the regiments. Like every other Brigade, as dusk fell the eight-hundred horsemen had moved to their battle positions in case the enemy attacked at the most vulnerable time of the day. The women saw the camp flags of the 4th and 13th Light Dragoons and the skull and crossbones insignia of the 17th Lancers.

"Bet the Frogs don't like to be reminded o' that, Mrs Polley." Mary smiled ruefully at the flag.

"Aye, all those lads that our boys lanced at Waterloo." Mrs Polley was as keen as Mary to believe the fallacy of the latest anti-French story.

"Where d'you think Mrs Martin will be?"

"Not sure, but she'll be somewhere near the farrier's lines, so look for a forge. There it is." Mrs Polley shot a coarse finger towards a box-bodied wagon and a low, smoky, stone hearth.

As they approached a pair of tents a generous back and shoulders came into sight, chopping steadily at billets of wood. Mrs Martin wielded a saw-bladed Russian pioneer's sword with precision, each blow splitting packing-case pine into kindling for the cooking fires. No more than twenty-three, she wore the same bun and full skirt as Mrs Polley, but there the similarity

147

ended for she was florid, sturdy, broad of thigh and rump, a podgy hand easily hefting the chunky brass sword hilt. Her dull brown bodice strained to contain her, almost hidden by the soiled cotton apron that she wore above. Mary pulled the wagon to a halt beside her.

"Mrs Betty Martin." Mrs Polley's greeting brought the chopping to an end. There was a brief pause whilst Betty stared hard at them through the gathering gloom.

"Well, Mrs Victoria Polley, as I live and breathe, and one of her chums from up on the hill; I've been waiting for you. Tether those nags yonder — have you feed enough for them? There's coffee or tea and just time for a cup before the men get back — will you stay for the night?"

The torrent of welcome continued. Mrs Martin's plump arms flew from kettle to cups to dainty, crockery milk jug in the tent next to the forge, for the cavalry had managed to make themselves considerably more comfortable down in the valley than the infantry and gunners on the hill. Then, just as night had fallen, the jangle, scrape and smell of many horses overwhelmed the camp. Subdued voices muttered low commands.

"Ah, they've stood-down. Tom will be in once they've got the tack off but, pound to a penny, he'll be out during the night. He mithers the poor loves to death, that Lord Cardigan of ours; real gentleman, but, oh, he does delight in the slightest alarm. Tom says some God-forsaken Turk up in the Redoubts on the ridge there has only got to imagine Russ frolicking about and its 'boots and saddles' and poor Tom and the rest up and out, half-perished and the wretched horses, Tom says, out of condition and, Tom says, off their fodder and . . ."

Betty would have overwhelmed them had Mary not cut-in hard. "He may be a so-called gentleman, this lord of yours, but isn't he the one that had his regiment taken off of him a few years back and has only got command again 'cos he's a favourite at court or some such nonsense? What makes him fit to order the likes of your husband or mine around and get them hurt or killed?"

There was a shocked silence from the other two women at Mary's outburst.

"But, Mary, Mr Cardigan's a lord. He's used to telling folk what to do." Mrs Polley did her best to cover up for Mary in front of her friend.

"That's as maybe, but that Richard Carmichael of ours is related to some general, went to a grand school and, as you say, has been used to telling folk what to do all his life. Didn't stop him running at the Alma though, did it, when my James went straight at Russ and got a bullet for his trouble." Mary's cheeks were flushed with anger. "But that's the point, love, the Cardigans, Carmichaels and the officers are just different from the likes of us . . ." But Mary wouldn't be soothed by Mrs Polley.

"Different? Different, they're all the same on a mattress, I can tell you."

But Mary had gone too far. If there had been a shocked silence before, there was now mute, scandalized astonishment.

Luckily, Betty Martin's tongue was equal to the occasion and hardly drawing breath for the next twenty minutes, she continued her description of Tom's torments. She paused long enough to ask the ladies if they didn't mind sleeping beneath the canvas of their own wagon due to Tom's "being very particular about his privacy", then the tea gave way to rum, a full beaker being poured just as the man himself pushed the canvas to one side, blinking in the light of the lantern. Short, wiry, whiskered, the farrier-corporal pulled the damp, furry busby from his head, the cloak from his shoulders and belt from around his waist before passing sabre and carbine to Betty.

"There, my sweet, dab a bit of oil on them, shall yer? Oh, how rude I am, ladies, I didn't know we had company." Tom, tired as he was, couldn't forget his manners. "Will you not introduce us, Betty my love?"

"This is my girlhood friend from Stockport, Mrs Victoria Polley and her companion Mrs Mary Keenan." The two women curtseyed — the whole scene might have been enacted in a Methodist church hall rather than a wind-swept tent. "They're from the Ninety-Fifth who are up at the siege."

Tom bowed theatrically low, whilst shooting his wife a sideways glance that told her that he knew quite well where the 95th were. "Ladies, I'm glad to meet you."

"They're both working as nurses with the regiment, they are." Betty was bursting to show off her friends. "In the thick of it at the Alma, they were, poor Mr Keenan got 'urt — back in Scutari 'e is now — and the Ninety-Fifth's in the trenches all day and night . . ."

150

"Aye, Betty I know what our gallant infantry do." He certainly did. Every time a patrol of the 8th Hussars trotted past a scruffy group in scarlet on the Balaklava Road, they were reminded. "Seen any Russians yet, donkey-walloper?" or, "Get down off of yer 'orse 'an burn some powder" and other, similar sneers seemed to be the only words the foot-plodders knew. The age-old contempt of the common man on foot for his mounted better was made even more acute by the fact that the Cavalry Division had yet to see any proper fighting.

"We're out day and night keepin' an eye on Russ, you know," Tom added, unnecessarily. "That Menschikoff'll come sneaking out of the hills an' have a crack at Balaklava before long, you see if 'e don't."

The two women nodded their agreement. They had heard their own officers saying just the same thing, how the force under General Menschikoff that had marched out of Sevastopol and into the interior of the Crimea as the Allies approached, was a real threat.

"Then all there'll be between Russ an' the port will be us and Scarlett's Heavies." Tom was suddenly aware how defensive he sounded. "But never fear, we'll show 'em how to fight — just like your husbands have done," he added tactfully.

But this was all the gallantry they got from him. Farrier-Corporal Martin's rum lasted no more than a gulp or two, then he stood and ushered the visitors from the tent as politely as he could, asking Betty to guide them to their wagon. Even before the pair had climbed over the tailboard into their chilly blankets

151

there wasn't a light to be seen in the camp of the exhausted Light Cavalry Brigade.

CHAPTER
SIX

Balaklava

"I dunno if it's just another bloody flap, sir, but they do seem to be squaring up for a fight." Sergeant Ormond spoke for all of the carrying party.

Twenty-five men, one sergeant and five mules under Lieutenant Morgan had set off from the Inkermann position just as daylight broke on the long haul down into Balaklava to pick up supplies, powder and shot. Although the trip downhill was easy enough and time in the harbour always gave the troops the opportunity to gather news and a few luxuries, the return was backbreaking. Coarse, wet, empty sandbags, wooden staves, barrel hoops and all manner of awkward, heavy, dead-weight kit were bad enough. Worst of all were the square, painted wooden boxes of rifle ammunition that were specially designed, everyone knew, to take the skin off your shins whenever they could. When they were combined with obstinate, ignorant, farting asses that were as likely to throw their loads as to carry them, the whole journey became just an exhausting, bruising chore.

"I guess you're right, Sar'nt Ormond. We'll just sit down a while and keep off the road until this lot sorts

153

itself out. Tell the men to smoke and try to get those mokes under control, will you, whilst all this lot's on the move."

It wasn't quite fully light when Morgan's party had come over the ridge. As the road turned, the Balaklava valley and the River Tchernaya were laid out like a chess board below them. All of the earthen Redoubts that protected the approaches to the harbour were now clearly visible as gun flashes lit the whole scene, unnaturally bright in the grey half-light. Staff officers — Morgan thought he saw the commander-in-chief, Lord Raglan — fussed around on the higher ground behind where they were sitting whilst horse artillery rattled down the road, sparks flying from their iron tyres and the hooves of the horses.

"Hey, sir, I can hardly believe it, but the Turks seem to be putting up a bleedin' good fight." Sergeant Ormond, like most others, usually damned anything Turkish, thoroughly doubting the reliability of the Ottoman garrisons in the vital Redoubts. Someone in authority had the same reservations, for all of the four forts that were manned had a stiffening of British artillery NCOs whose job it was to lay and fire the guns. But whether it was now British or Turkish gallantry that was responsible for their spirited defence was irrelevant, for the further ones were giving as good as they got. Russian artillery flashes were everywhere.

"They are, Sergeant Ormond, but just look at the number of guns that Russ has brought up. I fear he's having a real go at the harbour this time — as we said he would — it ain't just another scare."

154

Even up on the plateau where the talk was about nothing except the siege, they had all been aware of Balaklava's vulnerability and just how brittle the defences were. Every time they had any contact with the cavalry who were responsible for the mobile defence of the valley and the outer reaches of the harbour, they were left in no doubt about the strain that the horsemen had to endure. Although there was much mockery of their hanging back at both the Bulganak and the Alma, and whilst their commander, Lord Lucan, had been dubbed, "Lord Look-On", none of the infantry envied the constant alarms, standing-to and idling in the saddle that was the lot of the Heavy and Light Brigades of the Cavalry Division.

Now the road behind them drummed with running feet. They all looked round to see two companies of riflemen trotting down the hill at the double. Their rifles were held parallel to the ground, black slings hanging loose — quite unlike any Line regiment — their green uniforms pale with the chalk dust that their shuffling boots threw up. As they ran a babble of Cockney and Scouse reached their ears as weak or sickly soldiers were pushed, prodded and cajoled by the others to keep up.

"Bloody Rifles, full of mouth, as usual," Drummer Pegg gave voice to another prejudice.

As the green-clad columns drew away, though, three more men followed behind, two dragging and shoving a bareheaded, moaning lad. The little gang slowed to a standstill when they noticed Morgan's party at the roadside, the casualty falling to his knees.

155

"Here, you lot, can you look after Sam till we get back?" A lance-corporal of the Rifle Brigade tried to get Sam to his feet, furious at having to expose this weakness to another regiment.

"Less of that, Corporal, officer present." Sergeant Ormond pointed to Morgan, whilst making his own chevrons obvious.

"Sorry, Sarge, didn't see the officer. Can you take care of Private Crabb 'til we get back though — we've just come off trenches an' he's got a touch of fever?"

"Aye, leave him with us, we'll get 'im back to you." Sergeant Ormond took the stricken greenjacket's rifle as his mates laid him on the ground.

"Thanks, Sarge, we're Second Rifles from Four Div, by the way." The NCO and rifleman sprinted to catch up with their column.

"Looks like this touch of fever came out of a whiskey bottle, sir." Ormond shook his head over the already snoring Crabb. "Bloody Rifles have a real talent for the grog."

"Aye, that's as maybe, but the Turks will be grateful even for that lot if they're to hold Russ off. Look at all those flashes, there's one whore of a lot of 'em down there." Morgan could see many stabs of flame arcing towards the Redoubts and speckling, rippling musketry.

"Look there, sir, can you get your glass on that furthest Redoubt?" The Redoubts ran right along the Causeway Heights, the line of hillocks that bisected the valley. Now Sergeant Ormond's naked eye had seen something moving in the dawn light.

Sure enough, as Morgan swung his telescope onto the further earthworks, it was clear that the doubters' fears had come true — the Turks were running. Down the slopes they scampered, some stopping to fire, some plodding doggedly, but most throwing their weapons away and just trying to save their skins. A broken black swarm poured out of the forts, immediately set upon by Russian cavalry, lances and swords rising with a lethal urgency.

Morgan focused on one turbaned figure, gamer than most. His pounding white spats shot up little puffs of dust as he pelted from bush to bush to avoid the two lancers on his tail. He paused behind one shrub, brought his musket up, there was a billow of smoke, clear but silent in Morgan's glass, and one of the mounts crumpled throwing the rider over its head. The other horseman hesitated, but as the Turk dashed from cover, he couched his lance under his arm, and cantered in pursuit. There seemed to be no contest as the cavalryman bore down on the foot-soldier, but then the target stopped dead, turned, ducked and brought his bayonet sharply up under the Russian's guard. He ripped the spike out of his foe's chest, pulling the dead man from his saddle, but just as the body slumped to the ground, one foot still in the stirrup, two more men galloped from nowhere. A lance caught the Turk above the kidneys, the green and white pennon almost disappearing then re-emerging with each piston thrust. Morgan gasped, rapt by the silent death.

"We'd better get ourselves down into the valley to lend a hand, Sar'nt Ormond."

157

"'Ow, sir? There's only an 'andful on us — there's a stack of Jocks an' cavalry by the harbour 'oo've done fuck-all fighting so far, sir. We'd just be a bleedin', nuisance, especially now we've got that drunken Greenfly to look after."

"Maybe, but we'd better get down there just in case. Besides, what would Mr Carmichael say if we missed a fight?"

"What indeed, sir . . ." said Ormond flatly, seeing that Morgan was not going to be persuaded, ". . . right, you lot, get on the road in three ranks. Just leave that drunk bastard there . . . get the bloody mules at the back, we're doubling down to the valley, so secure your equipment." Sergeant Ormond's professionalism overcame his doubts — the officer had spoken so the officer would be obeyed, even if it involved getting the shit scared out of him for no good reason that he could see.

The little band bundled themselves into rough files, rifles at the trail in their right hands, left hands pushed back over their water-bottles and above the heavy ammunition pouches on their right hips to stop them bouncing, just as the manual said it should be done and, at Ormond's word of command, off they trotted down the gravelled road to Balaklava.

Despite all the gloomy predictions, the two ladies had a peaceful night. The hospital wagon made a fair couch and there were no disturbances until about an hour before dawn. Then the camp arose. Men stamped about cursing the cold and trying to light fires, horses were saddled with much snorting and clashing of bits whilst pails of water were banged against any and every solid object that came to hand. At least, so it seemed to both women. They had determined to avoid the dawn stand-to for just one day, to luxuriate in getting out of bed in daylight rather than in the dark. But no amount of blanket-pulling around the ears could deaden the noise of a full cavalry regiment starting their day's business around them.

"Will this noisy lot ever clear off and do some soldiering?" Mrs Polley's breath smoked in the dark, cold interior of the wagon.

"Aye, soon enough, I hope." Mary mumbled back as she fought to stay just under the surface of sleep, snuggling deeper into the coarse warmth of the blankets.

Then, for a few precious minutes there was some quiet. The troops formed into their squadrons, then the regiment walk-marched out to join the rest of the Light Brigade trotting through the vineyards to their forward, dawn positions. The hooves and rattling gear had gone and just a few voices remained around the cooking fires, making sure that the cavalrymen would have something to fill their bellies once they returned. Blissful sleep swept over them both.

"Now then, my dears, here's a cup of coffee for you." The wagon's canvas snapped back sharply showing a triangle of light-tinged dark framing the generous shape of Mrs Martin. Two scrupulously white china mugs were stretched out towards the dreamers. "Tom says it's the best time of the day, so up you get and we can see the lads come back in for breakfast." The pair sat up and took the cups that Mrs Martin was offering. The cold draught that swept around their shoulders made them instantly regret it. Too befuddled by sleep to talk, the two women silently sipped their coffee.

"Jaysus, what's that?" Mary knew before she asked the question. Down the wind came a great volley of heavy fire that seemed to fill the canvas-topped back of the wagon.

"Guns, and lots of 'em," replied Mrs Polley, "can they be ours?"

An awful, sickly feeling swept over both of them. They didn't know the lay of this position like they did their own up on the ridge, but they had a dreadful suspicion that the gunfire was far too heavy and persistent for anything that the Turks had in the Redoubts. As they struggled into bodices, skirts and boots, the canvas whipped aside again.

"Quick, girls, it's just like Tom said, Russ must be having a go at the forts and we shall see the most beautiful charge of the Eighth. Do get up, you'll miss it all, else" Mrs Martin was all a-twitter with excitement, just as Tom had told her she would be.

As the light improved, though, there was little to be seen from the camp and the vines that surrounded it. The guns pounded away and they could hear the brassy notes of the Brigade's bugles occasionally sounding one routine manoeuvre or another, but until a young, dismounted private led his horse up to the forge, nothing more was known. The blue-coated lad approached the women, busby under his arm, reins held lightly as his charger limped behind him.

"Now, Mrs Martin, my horse has thrown a shoe and, I think, split its hoof. I've been told to wait here until the farriers get back. There isn't a brew is there?"

"I'm sure we can find something for you, David Shields, there's plenty of firing, just as Corporal Martin said there would be. Are the Eighth to charge?"

The youngster smiled below his thin moustache. "I don't know about that, Mrs Martin, but we've just seen Johnny Turk 'oppit from Canrobert's Hill and I think some of the other Redoubts have already fallen."

"Well, you must be disappointed to be missing the charge that we're bound to make?" Mrs Martin was quite clear in her mind's eye of how events would unfold — but then, Tom had explained all.

"There's nowt to charge at the moment, Mrs M, just a bunch of fleeing Mussulmans and if our luck's how it normally is, there'll little beyond sore backs for the hosses and a soaking for us." Shields sauntered off to tether his chestnut.

Mrs Martin's coffee was famous throughout the Brigade. It wasn't that it was especially good, it was just the fact that it was always available — so the farriers' tents and wagons became a rendezvous not just for the 8th Hussars, but for almost anyone that was passing. Mrs Martin, of course, loved it for it not only gave her a chance to hear the latest gossip, it also allowed her to dignify her Tom to anyone that would listen. Now the three women sat around the fire, plaids firmly clasped against the chill of the early morning, their conversation drowned out by the booming of the guns.

The Heavy Cavalry Brigade's battery of horse artillery went hammering by on the road on the Causeway Heights above them. Half-heard commands brought the guns into action just a couple of hundred yards from the women and soon the din had taken on a new pitch. It was loud enough to swamp the noise of the scuttling Turks. Mary and Victoria Polley were gazing mutely into the flames of the cooking fire when Betty Martin swiftly rose to her feet, knocking over her neat little milking stool.

"Oi, you blaggard, what d'you think you're doing?"

From the middle of the surrounding vines a dowdy Turk had appeared, unarmed, blinking at the women, a British army blanket untidily under his arm. He was just sneaking into the other farriers' tent when she noticed him. Despite her girth, Betty could move like lightning. Grabbing the short sword that had been left sticking into the wooden chopping block, she threw herself at the unfortunate man, swiping him about the bottom and thighs with the flat of the blade. How Tom would have approved.

The Turk yelped like a girl, eyes swivelling, booty dropping from his arms whilst his feet skidded in the mud to get away from his ample assailant. But Betty had the better of him. Holding him by the collar she pasted him so hard with the blade that his yowls redoubled, loud enough to alert three of his companions. They burst from the brush, all spats, pantaloons and fezzes — the leader still had his musket and drew it up to club her.

162

Lethargy instantly gone, Mary and Mrs Polley launched themselves. Only a long spade came to Mary's hand whilst Mrs Polley went to the aid of her friend with nothing more frightening than her nails and her enraged visage. They were just too late to save Betty from a butt-stroke to her shoulder that sent her sprawling and allowed the first Turk to make good his escape. But Mary's dainty hands could be as cruel as her temper. Now they wielded the spade to good effect, banging the leading looter across the ear, making the metal sing. He dropped his musket, staggered, and with a strange oath stumbled off into the brush, hands clasped about his head. The third followed him, arms outstretched like a cartoon coward from one of the illustrated papers.

The roughest handling, though, was saved for the fourth marauder. Nails sank into his neck and cheek, he was slapped across both ears, his turban flying from his head. Mary had had time to recover and now she swept into the fray jabbing the hapless Turk's rump and back with the blade of the shovel, driving him towards the flailing, ranting berserker known as Victoria Polley. Like a shuttlecock the poor man cannoned off the two women, not knowing which of the two inflicted worse pain.

The sport might have continued indefinitely. The Turk was bawling so much, though, that Private Shields came hurrying to the rescue. The women's doughty performance thoroughly impressed the lad — as an act of brotherly sympathy he decided to use his fist rather than his sabre.

163

"Ladies, please; please stand aside and let me deal with the rogue!" Slaps and shovels were nothing compared to the punch that the muscular little trooper now delivered. Only last year Shields had walked off with a prize goose at Carlisle Fair when he'd floored a local bruiser; now his bemused and battered opponent got the same. A quick feint with the left distracted him before the cavalrymen floored him with a crushing hook just below the left ear. The Turk crashed into the mud, quite unconscious.

"That, girls, is how you deal with Johnny Turk." Shields pulled Betty to her feet whilst apparently addressing all of them. But his eyes lingered just on Mary.

"Good job you snuffed him out when you did, Mr Hussar, I was just about to measure the heathen for a tin hat." Mary's eyes danced with anger. Private Shields looked at the spade in her hands and the heave of her breast. He didn't know what to admire more — her husband's luck or his bravery.

"Will you keep up, Pegg, you fat little sod?" Sergeant Ormond was enjoying the young drummer's discomfiture.

"Ah'm doin' me best, Sar'nt . . ." Pegg puffed and heaved along between two of the other men who had fallen into step either side of him, pushed their arms behind his shoulders and below his cross-belts and relieved him of the weight of his rifle. Now the trio were just managing to stay with the rest of the running squad and in front of the cavalcade of mules. "Must 'ave been summat I ate, me guts is rotten."

"Just save yer breath, lad. Get 'im up to the front, you two." Sergeant Ormond, satisfied that Pegg wouldn't fall out by the side of the road and disgrace the company, put on a spurt, overtook the rest of the doubling men and joined Morgan at the front of the column.

"Pegg's all right, sir, just a bit blown." Sergeant and officer were breathing deeply but evenly, the sweat starting to soak into their socks and cap-bands, both of them in prime, physical condition. "Don't know 'ow 'e manages to keep that blubber on 'im, I don't, the rest of the lads 'ave got less fat on 'em than a butcher's pencil."

"Aye, you're right, Sar'nt Ormond, my clothes are falling off me." As they shuffled down into the depths of the valley it became harder for Morgan to see how the situation was developing. "Look there, are that Scotch lot shaking out to fight?"

About quarter of a mile away on a low hillock in front of a village, Morgan could see a kilted regiment moving from column into file, ready to form a defensive line on the forward slope of the high ground. Just as he was wondering what to do, a gunner subaltern whom he thought he knew came cantering towards them on a handsome chestnut.

"Hey, hold hard . . ." Morgan flagged the young officer down, ". . . what the devil's going on, d'you know?"

The gunner was clearly not pleased to be stopped by some plodding infantryman, but he, too, thought he recognized Morgan and pulled his horse to a stop.

"God alone knows." He fought to control his mount as it scraped and pawed the gravel. "But we've seen Russian cavalry just up on that skyline yonder . . ." he pointed to a dip in the Causeway Heights about a mile away, ". . . Lord Lucan's bloody cavalry are nowhere to be seen and, if they decide to advance, there's not a blind thing between them and Balaklava except our guns and the Ninety-Third Highlanders over there in front of Kadikoi."

Morgan swiftly pulled his glass from his pocket, tried to control his breathing and looked in the direction that the Gunner was pointing. The roofs of Kadikoi were just visible from where they were and he could now see the tall feathered bonnets of the Scotsmen settling into battle formation and, he assumed, waiting for orders to load.

"What d'you suggest we do?" Morgan asked.

"Why would I know?" said the gunner. "The battery captain has sent me off to get more shell. You're Ninety-Fifth, aren't you? If I were you I'd get over to those Scotties and stiffen them up a bit, they're as green as grass and could do with your help, though those mules will be a bloody nuisance in a fight . . . good luck," before he spurred his horse hard up the slope of the road.

It took no more than a few minutes to run the men over to the waiting 93rd — the Highlanders seemed strangely clean and smart as Morgan and his scruffy band approached. Most of the Scotsmen were tall and brawny, their height exaggerated by their billowing bonnets, the whiteness of their leather equipment and

166

spats giving them a solid, parade-ground appearance and without their greatcoats, the red of their coatees was bright against the dull autumn landscape. Morgan realized that it was easier for them to maintain these standards, living in huts close to the re-supply point of the harbour and so far untouched by any serious fighting, but he was still uncomfortable as his score of men and mules scuttled past, with torn coats, muddy trousers and unwashed faces, only their weapons and eyes bright and ready.

"Sergeant-Major, Lieutenant Morgan and a party of Grenadiers of the Ninety-Fifth at your Commanding Officer's disposal."

As the disreputable gang had scurried along the rear of the 93rd's ranks, Morgan hadn't been able to grab the attention of any of their officers to announce his presence and receive their orders. Only the Highlanders' senior non-commissioned officer could be distracted from the battle that was obviously about to unfold and even he was deeply perplexed by the prospect of dealing with an officer from a strange regiment. Tartaned, broad and ginger, his beard bursting out above his gold-laced collar, the Sergeant-Major eyed Morgan distastefully for a moment before bringing his hand up to the diced band of his cap.

"Will you be so kind as to take your men to yon flank, sir . . ." he said, pointing down to the right of the 93rd's firing line, about eighty paces away, ". . . report to Number Six Company, please . . . an' dinna leave those untidy bloody asses here, sir, if ye don't mind." As if the sweaty, grubby appearance of the men of the

167

95th wasn't bad enough in front of these pristine Scotsmen, two of their mules began to piss in unison, great puddles of steaming yellow liquid gathering just behind the 93rd's Colour Party.

With a perfunctory nod, Number Six Company's captain showed Morgan where to form his men telling him merely to, "obey his orders". But he could be forgiven any shortness for no sooner had Morgan fallen his men into two ranks than he saw exactly what was holding everyone's attention.

"There they are, sir, the bleeders." Sergeant Ormond had immediately spotted the Russian cavalry hovering in a tree line on the near horizon about eight hundred yards in front of them. As they watched, a handful of men in light-blue coats and dark shakoes leaked forward, followed immediately by more, most walking, some trotting slowly down the slope towards them, nothing standing in their way except the odd ditch and vineyard. Steadily they gained pace.

"There must be three hundred on 'em, sir . . ." Sergeant Ormond had quartered his target off, just as the manual advised, counted them and then multiplied by four, getting a remarkably accurate estimate, ". . . at about eight hundred paces."

"Five hundred . . . ready." To their left, the 93rd had already loaded: now the estimated range was being passed down to the men. Six hundred feather bonnets dipped and fingers tinkered, carefully adjusting the ramped iron sights.

"That's bollocks, sir . . ." Ormond turned urgently to Morgan.

"Aye, you're right. Ignore that, Ninety-Fifth; load in your own time, six hundred, await my order." They rammed and fitted their caps mechanically, deftly flicking their sights forward like the veterans they had unconsciously become.

"Present!" the Scotsmen flung their rifles into the aim, pulled their butts hard into the shoulder and blinked down their sights.

"They'll hit fuck-all like that, sir," said Ormond, just as the horsemen broke into a slow canter.

"Fire!" Every rifle bucked, kicking up dust and twigs well in front of the Russian hussars, but emptying not a saddle.

"Reload!" The order echoed amongst the Scotsmen as Morgan's party held their rifles at the waist.

"What d'you think, Sergeant Ormond?" Morgan guessed the Russians were now vulnerable.

"Aye, sir, 'bout right, but aim at the nags' knees, you lot," Ormond advised the men, as casually as if he were at the races rather than the battlefield.

"Present . . . aim low . . . fire!" Quite out of kilter with their hosts, the 95th's handful of rifles banged out, sending half a dozen Russians reeling from their saddles whilst a quiet chuckle ran down the grimy English line.

The Russians slowed to a walk — it was the wrong thing to do, for the horsemen concertina'd together, just as the troop of Horse Artillery that had come pounding-up to support the 93rd, wheeled into action. All six guns warmed their barrels with roundshot that whistled over the heads of the Russians, before they

169

smoothly switched to shell, sending furious, black bursts spitting above the hussars' heads.

"Reload . . . five hundred, ready." Now Morgan was back in step with the 93rd who had been going rigidly through their drills just to their left.

The Russians were now milling about, sandwiched between two small vineyards and harassed by the guns. With increasing urgency the leaders were turning their horses about, shrill bugle calls trying to tell the men at the rear what their commanders wanted them to do. Slowly, the mass of horsemen began to creep back up the hill, the way they had come as the shells burst above.

"Present . . ." Every rifle came to the aim.

"They're a bit more than five hundred now, lads, aim at the very furthest buggers from you," Ormond bellowed above the bangs of the guns.

"Fire!" But the 93rd seemed to have misjudged things again.

"Bloody-hell, sir, 'oo taught these Jocks their musketry?" Ormond was convinced that the few rounds of the 95th had flown true, whilst the Scotsmen's bullets had, once again, fallen short. But who hit what hardly mattered, for under the grinding of the guns the Russians were now in full retreat up and over the ridge. Meanwhile, the Highlanders cheered themselves hoarse, stamping their spats and raising their bonnets high on the muzzles of their rifles. Morgan wished that all victories could be as bloodless as this one.

The next chapter of the drama unfolded gently. Mogan told his men to brew tea and smoke and clean their weapons, whilst further along the slope the 93rd did much the same. From time to time, pairs of enemy horsemen would appear in the woods from which the hussars had sprung earlier, dithering, looking through telescopes at the slender line of British until an artillery round sent them skittering away.

"That last lot weren't too bad, sir, but if they send one of them great bunches of Cossacks and some guns, we'll be pushed to 'old 'em off." Sergeant Ormond voiced Morgan's exact fears.

"You're right, Sar'nt Ormond, but look there, are those our cavalry moving towards us?" Through the bushes and vines there were glimpses of scarlet coats and flashes as the sun caught the brass helmets of the regiments of General Scarlett's Brigade of Heavy Cavalry.

"They are, sir . . ." Pegg had been nosing around making tea in the background and now he cut in, ". . . see there, them's the Scots Greys, wearing the furry 'ats. Mind you, Mister Raglan wants to send us more guns up 'ere, not donkey-wallopers."

"Just get that tea in the officer's hand, Pegg. We'll let you know when Lord Raglan's got a place for you on his Staff." Ormond withered the lad.

The Heavy Brigade had obviously been split in two by its commander, for whilst one column of horsemen disappeared from view amongst the scrub below them, a couple of squadrons were clearly visible, dismounted

171

amongst the vines beside their own tented camp on the gentle slope opposite them.

"I guess that'll be the Heavy Brigade's reserve hanging about the camp over there?" Morgan mused to Ormond.

"'Spose so, sir, General Scarlett won't want to keep all his eggs in one basket until he knows what Russ is about, will he sir?" Ormond had undone the top of his coat now that the sun was out whilst trying to clear the stem of his pipe with a slender twig.

"Where's that tea, Pegg? Mr Morgan and me are spittin' feathers" But just as Pegg wobbled an over-filled tin cup forward, Sergeant Ormond pushed his arm out, pointing excitedly. "Look, sir, look yonder," Sergeant Ormond had seen what Morgan had feared — a mass of horsemen were probing over the ridge in exactly the same spot that the last group had appeared.

Morgan said nothing at first. His lips just silently counted the files of light-blue and grey-clad lancers and hussars that were trotting slowly down over the rough-ploughed, chalky slope. But where just a few hundred had been turned back by gun and rifle fire less than an hour ago, there were now many more.

"Christ love us, there must be two thousand of them, Sar'nt Ormond, why aren't the Heavy Brigade turning to cut into them?"

"Probably can't see 'em yet, sir, it's clear to us here, but you know how broken the ground is and, besides, them trees on the ridgeline will give a lot of cover."

Morgan pondered what Ormond had said, knowing that he was right and that he'd exposed his own callowness. He quickly focused his telescope and then it was obvious that neither body of cavalry, probably no more than three-quarters of a mile apart, had seen the other. Russians and British trotted on in happy ignorance of each other.

The early morning mist had all but cleared now and the air was still. Then Morgan saw the leading files of cavalry slow and come to an uncertain halt, the lines of horsemen bunching into each other before the Greys and the Inniskilling Dragoons slowly turned and began to face the enemy. He could see mounted officers and NCOs shouting and pointing, shaking the regiments out, dressing the troops into the proper formation to attack. One little knot of four pecked about in front — Morgan could only suppose that it included their commander, Brigadier-General Scarlett. As he watched, a bugler next to Scarlett raised his instrument to his lips and a few seconds later the unfamiliar cavalry call "prepare to attack" reached their ears.

"'E's not going to tek that lot on just with what there is down there, is 'e?" Sergeant Ormond and the rest of the group were now on their feet, tea forgotten, shading their eyes, straining to see. He spoke quietly, incredulous at what was about to happen.

"They'll be all right, Sar'nt, one of them's worth ten of Russ." Pegg's normal disdain for the cavalry had suddenly evaporated.

"Don't be a knob, Pegg, or are you now a dragoon as well as a master bleedin' gunner?" Ormond had had

173

quite enough of Pegg for one morning. "There's only a couple of hundred of our lads that are ready to attack, the rest of the Brigade's strung out to buggery an' they'll have to go at 'em up hill. If Russ spurs on, the Heavies'll be cut to slices."

"S'pose you're right, Sarge," Pegg conceded.

The Russians gained speed. The dense block of horses and riders swept downhill heading straight for the Scots Greys and Inniskilling Dragoons. Both regiments calmly continued their preparations — the watery sun glittered on a couple of hundred straight, steel blades as they sang from their scabbards. On their flanks the 4th and 5th Dragoon Guards — black and bay horses — tried to make up time over the difficult, vine-obstructed ground. But when it seemed that the unstoppable Russian mass would simply gallop and trample the Heavies into the ground, the inexplicable happened.

"They've stopped, sir, the daft, serf bastards have just stopped dead!"

"What can they be at, Ormond?"

So sudden was the enemy's halt that the rattle of bits, snaffles and bridles carried up to the ridge. Morgan saw panic in the leading Russians. Although their peaks obscured their eyes and the thick, grey, caped coats reminded Morgan of so many pouter pigeons, there could be no mistaking the urgent commands and the hurried fumbling for swords and pistols.

But if the Russians were ruffled, the Heavies were not. The regiments were still far from ready when the

174

"Charge" was sounded. There was no mistaking it and Morgan thought he could see a frown on the NCOs' faces whose backs were still to the enemy and whose precious dressing was not yet complete. There it was again — insistent, compelling, the urgent bugle notes that should have set the two dragoon regiments off like greyhounds. But Morgan could only see one group of men advancing — Brigadier-General Scarlett and his half-dozen Staff cantering up hill as hard as they could, clods flying from their hooves, sabres above their heads, shoulders set and tense, ready for the butchery. They were yards in front of the rest of the Brigade and as they drove into the face of the enemy column, sword hands falling and chopping to both left and right, the Russian flanks curved round them, closing, enveloping, cutting the handful off.

In seconds they were surrounded. Morgan was intent upon the flailing clutch of men whose destruction could only be seconds away. But then a shock wave swept through the Russian cavalry, sending horses and riders crashing into one another, packing the whole mass even more tightly together so that cut and thrust could hardly be delivered, chargers wedged so firmly that they could barely move.

Morgan had been watching Scarlett's group so closely that he had missed the pounding arrival of the Greys and Inniskillings. The two regiments had cannoned into the inert face of the enemy horsemen, arriving no faster than a trot, but using all their weight and momentum. Some of the static, distracted Russians had been knocked over bodily by their onslaught, and

175

now possessed, desperate men in scarlet hacked and beat at their foes, all line and dressing lost.

A slight twist of his lens brought the morass into sharp focus. The British were demented, chopping in all directions with their heavy sabres. The Russians recoiled, alarmed, appalled by such brutal force. The hard-learnt lesson that a thrust was always better than a cut was instantly forgotten in the press of bodies, scabbard-blunted blades bouncing off the Russians' caped shoulders. One man, though, brought his sword far back over his head, slicing down with all his strength, rising in his stirrups to give the blow extra weight. The steel caught an enemy dragoon square on the crown of the shako, driving down through leather, hair, skull and flesh so hard that the victim fell from the saddle cut almost to the jaw. Blood sprayed crazily; the dead man took the sword with him, almost unseating his executioner.

So tight was the mêlée, so fighting mad were the British that Morgan saw one thickset Inniskilling whirl his sword around his head — the "moulinet" as it was known — catching not a Russian but a friend with the back of his blade. The wounded man threw his hands to his head but he was lost to sight as smoke fanned across the scene. As sword arms tired of the hacking or sabres were lost, both sides used their pistols — pushing the barrels hard against their enemies' chests and faces before they fired.

Bangs, thumps, yells and ringing sword-swipes reached up to the ridge as the next two regiments swept into the fight. One after another the 4th and 5th

Dragoon Guards drove into the Russians' flanks. A strange, low, moaning cheer filled the valley as the Irish 5th crashed home, many simply punching the Russian horsemen with the steel hilts of their sabres.

One trooper barged his horse so hard into an enemy hussar that he overbalanced with the shock of the collision, whilst swiping wildly with his sabre. The blow was badly aimed, for his frightened, bruised horse had jerked him off target. The blade twinkled and fell, but it skidded off the Russian's sleeve, doing no more damage than cutting his reins and leaving the attacker sprawling over his horse's neck.

The rest of the duel owed nothing to the fencing master. The dragoon dropped his sword, caught hold of his enemy's coat and bridle to stop himself from falling under the stamping hooves, then slowly clawed and grabbed himself upright. The Irishman grasped and pinioned the Russian, preventing him from getting to his pistols whilst both the horses bumped together, harnessed by their riders' embrace. Finally, he drew his head back, smashing the Russian on the bridge of the nose with his forehead — a blow perfected in brawls from the Curragh to Kandahar.

Like a great, shivering jelly, the Russian host started to give way. Even though their attackers were less than half their number, the British were starting to get the better of them. Then the last cheering, shouting regiment thrust home, the Royals' helmets and swords flashing in the morning sun as they drove into the Russians' flank. Morgan saw one hussar drop his reins and sword to shield his head, before both hands were severed by a sweeping, slicing blow.

Harder and harder the red regiments pushed, joined now by the petulant crack of shellfire. Slowly, gradually at first and then ever more quickly the enemy broke and cantered away towards the shelter of the ridge. The Heavies pursued for a short way, swords falling briskly, pistols cracking, before Scarlett pulled them up, giving the artillery all the space they needed to send them on their way.

"Look at the bastards go, sir," Sergeant Ormond's voice was thick with excitement.

Along the ridge almost two thousand cavalry fled, their horses' tails streaming like flags of surrender. The riders hunched over their reins, swords trailing from their wrist knots, pistols and carbines abandoned. They disappeared across the ridge so much faster than they had appeared.

"They're running all right, but why doesn't Lord Cardigan and the Light Brigade finish the job?" From Kadikoi, Morgan could just see the commander and the Staff of the flower of Britain's army in the Crimea — the Light Cavalry Brigade — sitting high on the Causeway Heights. From that point, Morgan guessed, Cardigan would have been able to see the Russian cavalry fleeing, almost broken into the North Valley with their backs to his Brigade. There they sat, hardly touched by war, Cardigan's regiments now with the chance to turn a defeat into an utter rout. But no, feuds, stupidity and arrogance — at which Morgan and his lads could only guess — robbed the Allies of a quick, decisive victory.

Where the ground was pocked and churned by hooves and shells lay the fruits of the Heavy Brigade's work. Flies buzzed over spurred and booted bundles: a few moaned and moved, whilst a score of horses limped or stood stock still, cropping the meagre grass, waiting faithfully for their silent masters' commands.

"Those Heavies will be pleased with themselves, won't they?" Mrs Martin mirrored her Tom's sense of rivalry, but the other two women could barely tell the difference between the mounted regiments, let alone the Brigades.

They'd seen a trickle of their own wounded dragoons and a handful of ragged Russian prisoners being shooed towards the Heavy Brigade camp next door, but of the Light Brigade there was no news. Betty could identify the various regimental bugle calls in the distance, but it was hard to see anything from the slopes below the Causeway Ridge.

"Ladies, I've had enough. First heathen Turks come romping through 'ere, now the bloody — oh, do excuse me — the wretched Heavy Brigade take all the glory to themselves. Still, Tom says Lord Cardigan knows his job and if there's real work to do then the Light Brigade will do it. Copper to a guinea our boys will be at the Muscovites soon enough. If that's the case I want to see it and the surgeon will want us to hand, any road. What say you that we ride off and find the Eighth?" In her enthusiasm Betty Martin hadn't

179

noticed that if nurses were needed then her precious Tom would be in greater danger.

"I don't know, Mrs Martin. We ought to be getting back to our own lot up yonder, the surgeon will be asking after us and his medicines." Mrs Polley's face was no prettier when creased by responsibility.

"No, come on, now. We've missed one good do, we can't have the regiment saying that Victoria Polley and Mary Keenan were shy, can we?" As usual, Mary's view prevailed. Led by Betty on her pony the hospital wagon and its ill-matched Amazons set off up the low ridge.

And there they sat for two or more hours. The guns thundered on, some Guardsmen and Rifles hung disconsolately around a nearby empty Redoubt occasionally trying their hands with long-distance rifle shots at the Russians but nothing conclusive happened. Meanwhile, both of the cavalry Brigades manoeuvred back and forth over the ridge, the Heavies looking almost as good as new and the Light untouched.

"Russ has got very bold all of a sudden, hasn't he?" Mary shaded her eyes against the morning's gentle sun. "Why doesn't Himself do something about it?"

From the handful of trees where they had placed their wagon, the women could see right down the north part of the valley and along the line of Redoubts. On the other side of the saucer of ground, hills rose gently up to what was called the Fedioukine Heights and on these they could see Russian guns and horses. Below them a dark mass of riders swirled and eddied at the far end of the chalky, tree-studded valley whilst the further Redoubts were now firmly in the hands of Russian

180

infantry. Whilst all this was going on, about a quarter of a mile behind the women the Light Brigade had trotted into the north valley to be greeted by long shots from the enemy guns. Then, to prevent any casualties, they had immediately withdrawn and now stood by their horses under the distant eyes of the commander-in-chief on the ridge above.

"Bold's not the word, cheeky more like. Everywhere's crawling with them, but they won't dare venture towards Balaklava again, mark my words." Betty's opinion had to be worth more than the other girls' — she was an NCO's wife after all.

"If Mr Raglan wants them forts back, though, they'll have to attack from the other side of the ridge . . ." Betty stabbed her finger to the south, though the lie of the ground made it invisible to them, ". . . they'll get support from our guns there. It's no good the Light Brigade hanging about here, there's Russians on all three sides and more guns than a Turk's got lice."

"Ah, now we shall see something, Mrs Keenan." Betty Martin had realized that the group in the distance were the Staff around Lord Lucan at the head of the Cavalry Division. Arms and telescopes were being waved frantically and she recognized the bugle notes that called all commanders together to receive orders.

"Aye, d'you suppose that that's your head man in the red pants?" Mary had spotted Cardigan in his 11th Hussar uniform as he trotted forward to speak to the officers commanding the five Light Brigade regiments.

"It is, he must be about to move the Brigade back into the south valley." Betty had seen that the only sensible, sheltered route for Cardigan's troops lay back over the ridge into the south valley where they would be screened from the host of enemy guns and horse.

"Why then, Mrs Martin, are they starting to deploy into line?" Mrs Polley was at a loss.

"I cannot say, Mrs Polley, you are correct, though, for they seem to be facing quite the wrong way."

Betty Martin was certainly right. Just out of gunshot, the first line of the Light Brigade — 11th Hussars, 17th Lancers and 13th Light Dragoons — were turning, moving to get into a long, thin line abreast of each other. Dust spiralled under the hundreds of trotting, stamping hooves almost hiding the fur busbies and cherry overalls of the 11th, the waving red and white lance pennons of the 17th and the sombre blue jackets and black shakoes of the 13th. To their rear the other two regiments, the 4th Light Dragoons and Tom Martin's own 8th Hussars were forming into a second, supporting line.

"Aye, but don't worry, they'll just be sorting theirs'en out before hopping off over the ridge." But all the confidence had drained from Mrs Martin's voice.

"You must be right, Mrs Martin, but those guns over yonder will get them unless they wheel away sharply." Mary pointed towards the closest Russian battery up on the Fedioukine hills opposite them. They had seen the enemy's horses dragging the winking brass guns into position, now they menaced the whole of the north valley and, unless the Light Cavalry Brigade turned away quickly over the ridge where the women sat, they would soon have a target.

But there was no sign of this. Now the whole Brigade — nearly seven hundred horsemen — had closed up making a bold, confident sight as they formed first into two lines, then three as the 17th Lancers fell back. Bugles sounded, ranks were dressed as peace-time perfect as possible and then one of those strange silences fell upon the field. It was quiet enough for the women to half-hear shouted commands and then the steely shriek of hundreds of sabres being drawn.

"Why are they getting their swords out, Mrs Martin?"

"Well, Mrs Polley, I expect that they're just getting ready for anything that might lie over the ridge. We'll get a good view of 'em in a minute when they wheel past us. Yes, there it is: d'you hear that, it's the 'Walk-march' ". Betty's ear recognized the initial call to the Brigade and then the repeated bugle commands down the regiments.

The horsemen jibbed forward. Angry shouts were clear to the women as the NCOs — never happy — tried to get them just-so, facing straight down the north valley. Then came the next call, "Trot-march". Raggedly, the pace increased across the regiments, the front of the Brigade coming almost level with the women as they watched.

"They'll turn now, girls, you see if they don't . . ." but Betty's confidence had gone, ". . . we'll get a grand sight of Tom and the Eighth, they'll be closest to us."

Then the guns started. The battery on the Fedioukine fired, a rifle regiment volleyed from the other flank along the Causeway Heights, and guns

183

belched from the captured Redoubts. Smoke tongued and fanned across the valley, a breathless cheer echoed from the five regiments and the horses picked up speed.

"Mother of God, they're not going to turn at all . . ." Mary said what they were all thinking but had been too amazed to say, ". . . they're goin' straight down the goddamn valley — why?"

A single rider dashed from the lines of horses, spurring hard towards Cardigan and his bugler in front of the Brigade. One of the first shells exploded right above him though, the splinters lancing into his soft flesh. The women watched — horrified — as his dead body rode on until his thigh muscles gave way and he toppled from the saddle.

"They must have seen something down there at the bottom of the valley, but I'm damned if I know what it is . . ." Mrs Polley could see no more in the gathering smoke and dust than anyone else. "The officers must know what they were doing, mustn't they?" The hooves drummed harder, the "Charge" was quite distinct and the last clear detail that the women saw were dipping pennons as the lances came down for the kill.

"Quick, you two, over here, it's our Tom." Mrs Betty Martin, her cheeks wet with tears, waved wildly to Mary and Mrs Polley.

It had all been over in minutes. From their position on the ridge the women had seen almost nothing as the Light Brigade had charged home. From the Brigade's left, right and front artillery and riflemen had fired incessantly as Mrs Martin had rung her hands so anxiously. During lulls in the gunfire the trio had heard yelling and the clash of steel on steel. Just visible to them along the ridgeline were a regiment of the enemy's Rifles who cheered even as they fired and loaded.

Then, as quickly as the noise reached a crescendo it died. The guns ceased as if they had nothing more to fire at.

"Where has the Brigade gone, Mrs Martin?" Mrs Polley asked Betty the very question she dreaded. As the firing had died away they had expected to see the regiments come wheeling back out of the smoke, enemies vanquished. But from where they sat all the women could see were odd pairs of men, some galloping hard, some trotting — clearly wounded — and a handful on foot heading back up the valley away from danger.

"The good Lord knows, Mrs Polley . . ." A determined fatalism had crept into Mrs Martin's voice, ". . . but I'm not sitting here if we can be of help. Come on, we must find the Eighth and the doctor."

Betty and her pony led the rattling wagon off down the dusty, bush-studded slope. Soon, knots of horsemen came walking and stumbling past them. Two Lancers dismounted when they came to the women. Both men, sensing that they were now out of danger, took cloth from their saddlebags and began to dab at their horses' wounds. One of the roans snorted and threw up its head whilst its rider tried to sooth it. The other stood quite still, just trembling, as the bloody lint was wiped down a bullet gash in its shoulder.

"Lads, where are the Eighth, were they engaged?" Mrs Martin spoke quite firmly.

"They were, missus. They came in behind us once we'd made the serfs run for it. We saw a few of 'em trying to get out the way of some Cossacks that we'd just had to see off. There's a few back there." He pointed showily, making quite sure that Betty could see the blood on his white, leather gauntlet.

"Did they do well, were many hurt?"

"Don't know, love, but their surgeon was hard behind our own. Is your man with them?" The troopers both looked up from their horses.

"Aye, Farrier-Corporal Tom Martin, d'you know him, is he all right?"

"No, I don't, but I hope he's not hurt. God bless you, missus." The lancers walked off, leading their damaged mounts as gently as they could. Betty dug her heels in hard.

The stream of survivors increased. Mary noticed how most of the men were unwounded but so few now had horses. All looked ashen, shocked — busbies and shakoes abandoned and most had lost their swords. A couple were still in the saddle, but most horses were bleeding from wounds or limping badly.

"Mrs Martin, Tom's over by those trees, an orderly's with him." A clutch of uninjured 8th Hussars, came trotting down the gentle, grassy slope, the Sergeant reining his horse in to speak to her.

"Is he badly hurt, Sergeant Lloyd?" Betty bobbed a greeting but her lips were shaking, her dread almost overwhelming her good manners.

186

"He's still with us, but he was pulled from his saddle and they say two of the rogues cut him badly. Forgive me, but we must get on." No victor's smile came from Sergeant Lloyd, just concern. As he cantered to catch up with his men, Mary noticed how the seam of his short blue jacket had split down the back of his sword arm.

"Oh, dear God above!" Betty wailed, all decorum gone. Forgetting her companions, she kicked hard at her horse forcing him into a trot over the banks and furrows.

By the time Mary and Mrs Polley drew up in the wagon, Betty already had Tom in her arms. His head lolled in her lap, eyes closed, a great slick of blood oozing from a swelling on top of his head, matting his hair. Another gash had taken away his earlobe and opened a cut along his jaw. He moved — just — and babbled something from his semi-consciousness.

"I know, my love, I know, we'll soon have you right." Betty pressed her cheek against his forehead, petting and shushing him, oblivious to the great smear of Tom's blood on her face and the gore that spattered her bodice.

"Ladies, look lively, will you? Let's get him into the wagon and up to Mr Noakes, it's not far." One of the 8th's hospital orderlies felt for the farrier's pulse with one hand, pointing back down the valley towards their own surgeon.

The 95th wives had been hardened at the Alma. The cavalry battle, though, had left many with brutal, scything wounds that bled horribly. The surgeon had his own wagon and apothecary's chest with him and was busily sowing a flap of skin back onto the shoulder of a young lance-corporal. The man sat on a stool, jaw clamped, fists locked together and eyes screwed shut as the suture needle pricked either side of the wound before the thread was drawn through and tied off. Fourteen times the surgeon tacked the skin, a neat crescent of black stitches reaching down towards a tattoo of an arrow-pierced heart. Each time his orderly snipped the thread and dabbed the wound with spirits.

"How came you by this, Corporal Shutt?"

"I cut at a Cossack's head, sir, he parried, I came back on guard and then the damn fool, instead o' cutting back at my head like he ought, sliced me across the shoulder, fuckin' idiot." The young corporal disapproved of any move that had not been taught in the Depot.

As the surgeon finished his embroidery Tom Martin was lifted down from Mary's wagon. The orderly and Betty moved his softly moaning body off the tailgate, supporting him under knee and shoulder, daubing themselves liberally in the process.

"Right, get him over here onto the table. Penrose, get a mirror." The surgeon had only one assistant left. "Ladies, have you done any nursing?"

"Sir, we're 95th wives and were at the Alma and have been at the siege daily. Mr Fergusson's our surgeon." Mary's confidence was obvious.

"Fergusson, yes, a fine man and if you were at the Alma you'll shift very well. Place the man on his belly . . . does anyone know who he is?" The doctor thought he knew everyone of his regimental flock, but the blood and pallor made the man unrecognizable.

"Mr Noakes, sir, it's our Tom off the farriers." The surgeon stared, Betty was almost as bloody as her husband.

"Oh, Mrs Martin, I'm sorry for it, but it's good that you're here with him. You'll find razors and soap in the wagon, ladies, would one of you get his jacket off, if you please?"

Mrs Polley had already started to strip off Tom's tightly buttoned jacket, whilst Mary had run for hot water. Just as Noakes said, brushes, a bar of yellow soap and six folded razors were in one of the drawers in his wagon and in no time she was lathering the blood-caked hair around the wound. When Glassdrumman was quiet she had occasionally shaved Tony Morgan — now she drew the razor over Corporal Martin's gouged scalp with no less care or love. The clotted hair fell away from the blade exposing milk-white skin and a bruised, bloody swatch from which a ragged edge of bone emerged. As Mary shaved, so Mrs Polley dabbed and blotted.

"This isn't as bad as it looks, Mrs Martin." The surgeon might have reassured Betty, but the cut was as nasty as anything that Mary had seen before. A sabre had been swung at Corporal Martin from above, cutting through the scalp and bone like a knife half-taking the top off a boiled egg. Less than an inch of bruised skin held the flap in place and as the surgeon's fingers probed carefully down, lifting the edge of bone, shiny grey matter peeped out from below.

"Penrose, reflect some light from the mirror, can't you? You, madam, hold this skin back . . ." Mary clamped the flesh, ". . . and please get me some common dressing forceps, my dear." Mrs Polley guessed and luckily produced the right instrument from the surgeon's box.

"Damn me, the skull's been cut right through. Get a scalpel, madam, and whilst I grip and probe the bone, you'll see the skin move above it. Cut gently until I tell you to stop." Mary did just as she was told. Carefully she slit down into the skin whilst Noakes coaxed the fragment of bone through the opening that she had made, Mrs Polley wiping away the blood.

"See here, ladies, we'll have to take some matter with the bone, but I fancy that the dura mater is sound." The two women nodded, none the wiser. "Here, Mrs Martin, a curio for you and your husband." Noakes drew his apron over the fragment of bone, cleaning it of blood and scraps of tissue — it looked like a piece of bleached orange peel. "In years to come, you'll shake that bit of bone in Corporal Martin's face and tell him not to lose his head . . . ha!"

The surgeon was clearly enjoying himself rather more than Mrs Martin.

"Sir, will Tom be all right?" Betty Martin gazed mesmerized at the bony souvenir and her broken, butchered husband.

"Well, he's had a bad blow to this bit of the cerebral hemisphere." Noakes pointed to the top, left part of the shaven skull.

"Cerebral hemisphere . . ." parroted Mary and Mrs Polley blankly.

"We think that part of the brain controls speech; I guess that he might be a bit slurred — but then you'll be used to that when's he's drink taken, won't you . . . ha!" Betty Martin was too contorted with dread to notice Noakes's plodding wit.

The surgeon felt no need to try to replace the piece of skull — the women, wide-eyed, nodded their agreement — and Tom was swabbed, plastered and bandaged before being carried away. The last that Mary and Mrs Polley saw of Betty was her walking next to the stretcher hand-in-unconscious-hand with her Tom.

Morgan reckoned the day had gone well enough. True, they were trudging back up to their camp along a different route now that the Russians had taken a fort or two on the Causeway Heights and they had none of the stores that they'd been sent to get, but they'd been in a battle that none of the rest of the regiment had, hadn't they? He'd also seen a grand cavalry charge for the first time in his life and none of his men or mules had a scratch on them. He was just thinking how he would avoid Carmichael's inevitable anger when the click of approaching hooves drove his thoughts away.

"Well, it's Morgan, ain't it, I've remembered you now, we met in Portsmouth." It was the Horse Gunner subaltern whom he'd met on the road that morning — he knew he'd met him before. "Did those Scotsmen want your help?"

"Want our help? Why, they couldn't have managed without us . . ." Morgan was blustering, trying to cover for his lack of poise when they had seen each other just a few hours ago, but the gunner wasn't listening.

"Terrible news, ain't it?" He'd brought his tired horse to a halt and was talking down to Morgan from his saddle as the men gathered round, alerted by the note in his voice. "The whole of the wretched Light Brigade's been thrown away. There's hardly a man and not a single horse left standing and Lord Raglan's going to sack both Lucan and Cardigan, they say." The group of infantrymen stood gawping at the Horse Gunner like so many children, mouths open, groping to understand the news. "Well, I must get on, see you on some other blasted heath, I daresay," and the gunner shook Morgan's hand distractedly before clattering away.

"A whole Brigade gone, Sar'nt Ormond." As they continued their plod towards home, Morgan still couldn't quite grasp what he'd been told. "Seemed like we gave them a thrashing to me, not the other way round."

"Aye sir, well, we did, just shows how little you can see of a battle though, don't it, sir, even if you reckon you've been right in the thick of it. But the 'ole Light Cavalry Brigade gone, sir, that's really bad."

Pegg was just within earshot. "Serves 'em right: what's left can come an' do some proper soldiering with us, says I."

CHAPTER
SEVEN

Little Inkermann

"So where did you and your little gang get to today?" Carmichael reproached Morgan.

Back in the company's camp on the ridge, Morgan had been trying to explain to Colour-Sergeant McGucken why his carrying party had returned from Balaklava empty handed when Carmichael appeared. McGucken had understood, but the acting company Commander wanted a proper explanation for this apparent dereliction, so Morgan had been led off to the gloomy interior of Carmichael's tent out of earshot of the troops.

"We were well on our way down towards the port when the firing started. The road was full of troops and guns and Russ was all over the place. So we went and joined in." Morgan was already guilty enough that he'd failed to bring back the mail and rum upon which the Company's morale rested and that McGucken would have to explain his incompetence to everyone — he didn't need Carmichael's rebukes as well.

"What do you mean, 'went and joined in'? Who told you to do that?"

"Well no one, Carmichael, but it can't have been wrong to fight, can it?" Morgan was genuinely puzzled.

"Fight? Listening too much to the non-commissioned officers again and sticking your nose into other folks' business, more like — you've hardly used a round. You're becoming far too close to the men, Morgan, they take advantage of your slackness and now you've failed to bring back their letters and grog, the only pleasures they have. You need to understand them better: they're simple creatures with simple needs who'll follow a gentleman to the ends of the earth but mock anyone who tries to lick up to them." Carmichael had obviously been building up to this lecture for some time.

In the half-light of the cluttered tent Morgan stood silently, trying to control his anger. He'd done his best to be respectful and loyal to Carmichael, even after the troops had started, quite openly, to make fun of his cowardice at the Alma and the fact that he dodged trench and picket duty.

"Do you realize how badly this will go down with the men and that poor old McGucken will now have to flog down into Balaklava to pick up all the stores that you were meant to get?" Carmichael continued, icily.

Poor old McGucken, thought Morgan. Had Carmichael no idea how much he was despised by his own Colour-Sergeant? Why, McGucken had broken every unwritten rule of loyalty and military protocol to discuss a senior officer with a junior one and he knew how McGucken did his best to suppress the men's derision towards their company commander. He longed

194

to tell Carmicahel all this, to spit his contempt right in his face, but he knew that an outright row would only result in his being moved to somewhere else in the regiment under a cloud, leaving the men at Carmichael's mercy. He stood there silently clenching his fists.

"And another thing. The surgeon sent Mrs Polley and Mrs Keenan to get medical supplies from Balaklava. Like your party they were very late back and had completely failed to do as they were asked. They may only be wives, but they belong to this company as surely as any soldier and I won't have them out of order. You wouldn't know what might have detained the lovely Mary Keenan would you, Morgan?"

Morgan felt that even in the murk Carmichael could see him colouring. "I haven't the least idea, Carmichael. I haven't seen Mary . . . er, Mrs Keenan, all day. Have you any idea just what's gone on and how much ground the enemy has taken? And the whole Light Cavalry Brigade's been destroyed just when we'd driven the Russians back. With blockheads like this in command we'll be lucky if we're the ones that don't end up under siege."

"So, Morgan, you now think you know better than generals like Lord Raglan and sir George Cathcart, do you?"

"Yes, yes . . . I know Cathcart's your damned uncle, but your smart connections don't cut it with me or, 'poor old McGucken' come to that!" Morgan could control himself no longer, though he instantly regretted his outburst.

Carmichael was furious. "Don't try to change the subject: be warned, Morgan, keep your hands off your former, so-called maid. She may be your servant's wife, but she ain't your property any more to do with as you please." Seething but guilty, Morgan knew that he had been bettered. "Now get back to the Company and prepare to take our pickets out before last light, we're to relieve the 41st. I'm giving you an extra duty to give you time to think about how an officer should conduct himself — Sar'nt Whaley will brief you. Any questions?"

"No, sir." Morgan saluted stiffly before slapping the canvas tent door out of his way.

By the time he'd gathered his glass, pistol and the coat that he'd left to dry, he was late. Trying not to run, Morgan reached the assembled picket as they gaggled around the tents, Drummer Pegg the centre of attention. Unnoticed, he caught the lad in a spirited reenactment of the day's fighting.

"It was like that . . ." Pegg brought his drumstick down over an imaginary Cossack's head, ". . . General Scarlett cut the bugger's skull in two, he did, blood and brains all over the . . ."

"Party, party, 'shun!" Sergeant Whaley brought the sixty or so men to attention once he'd snatched himself away from Pegg's impromptu theatrics.

"Beg your pardon, sir, but we was waiting on you. Just hearing what you and young Pegg had seen today, sounds like a grand do." Sergeant Whaley was typical of the regiment's senior NCOs. Reliable, unimaginative, just a few inches over five foot and tempered by his young life in a Sheffield slum, he was as hard as a bit of his local steel. Whilst the men knew that any corner-cutting would be dealt with by a fast-moving fist, he was essentially kind, at twenty-six the father of three children and devoted to them. Now he stood rigidly at the salute, trussed up in coat, cap, belts, bayonet, ammunition, pouches and water-bottle ready for the long night watch on the hillside.

The party shuffled back into three ranks. Laden like their Sergeant, the troops also carried bundles of kindling, strapped to their cross-belts in as soldierly a manner as possible in order to avoid Lieutenant Carmichael's ire. Pegg had his drum slung on his shoulders, and was cradling the picket's most precious possession, an earthenware rum bottle.

"I'll tell you all about it on the way up to Shell Hill, Sar'nt Whaley. Do I need to inspect the men, or have you done it?"

"All done, sir. Rafferty somehow got a skin-full last night, but he's all right now and I've made him take on extra water." Even here in a wind-blasted, tented camp several miles from what could be termed civilization and under the noses of the enemy, the troops could be depended upon to seek, find and guzzle the least drop of alcohol.

"Good, well done. If you're happy that you've checked that every round's dry and that their cap-pouches are full, let's be gone." Morgan could see that Whaley had done a good job for him. The black fury that he'd felt earlier began to seep away, it was so much better to be amongst the men.

"Sir! Party, shoulder arms, left turn, by the centre, quick march." Whaley barked, muddy, worn boots stamped and the new picket set off through the tents and guy ropes of what passed for home for the half-mile trudge up to the oak- and brush-clad slopes of Shell Hill.

The enemy would be close by. The last six weeks of marching, watching, digging, cooking and the occasional ghastly fright had taken their toll of the men. Permanently tired, sometimes dry but always hungry, a dull fatalism had crept over them — they'd resigned themselves to whatever fate had in store. Morgan knew them all now and trusted them to do their duty, but they were a very different lot from the keen, sprightly bunch of lads who had left England just a few months ago.

Whaley and the young officer swung easily along by the side of the column. "What exactly happened today at Balaklava, sir?" Whaley asked, for the infantry on siege and picket duty had heard nothing except rumour — and highly-coloured rumour at that.

Morgan told him how the threat to the port had been defeated — despite the Highlanders' dreadful marksmanship — how Pegg's mock swordplay wasn't so far from the truth and the needless sacrifice of most of the Allies' cavalry.

"But the real problem, Sar'nt Whaley, is the fact that all those Redoubts are now in Russian hands. We won't be able to walk directly to and from the port humping all that gear without getting shot at. Now there'll be miles extra to go just to keep out of harm's way and, I have no need to tell you, the men are on their uppers already."

"Aye, sir, they are. Have you seen the sick list? It's bad an' the other companies are mostly worse-off."

"I know it's bad, but is Mr Carmichael fully aware of it?"

"S'pect so, sir, but it don't seem to register." Whaley shot a sideways glance at Morgan to see how his disloyalty would be received.

"All right, Whaley, I'll make sure that I speak to him after my next round of the hospital . . ." Morgan's terse reply gave the NCO the answer he was looking for, ". . . but the Russians have done better today than we realize and I'm sure they'll want to have another go either down at the port or up here. So, Sar'nt Whaley, let there be no dozing or arsing about tonight."

"Right, sir, I'll keep an eye and a half on Rafferty."

The hands of his watch must have been set in treacle. Every time he got back to the light of one of the fires and pulled at its chain to check, time had almost stood still. Morgan had spent all night tramping up to the outer pickets, speaking with this pair of lads, plodding a bit further, having a chat with that lot, confirming that the bushes casting dark shadows, ". . . there, sir, there, can't you see?" were not a set of Muscovites bent on murder before coming back to rest by the fire. But how the time

199

dragged. Church bells had been pealing all night in Sevastopol to celebrate the victory at Balaklava and when Sergeant Whaley had thrust a cup of coffee into his dozing hand just before dawn stand-to, they were ringing louder than ever.

"All quiet, Sar'nt Whaley?" Asked Morgan, only half-awake.

"Aye, sir, just them bloody bells a-going all night. Nowt else to report, I had to relieve Pierce — least, he had to relieve hissen, got terrible shits he has. New picket will be up shortly."

"It's Sunday, Sar'nt Whaley — Russ must be delighted with a victory, no wonder they're ringing. Is that the new picket coming?"

Through the dark scrub a file of men could be heard approaching. Boots scraped, equipment slapped against legs, there was the odd, subdued cough and whispered challenges as they reached the outer pickets.

"Hello, sir. I've got sixty-two for you from Number Three Company." McGucken's teeth flashed in the firelight. Knowing that Morgan had been condemned to another sleepless spell on the hillside, he'd come to collect the men of his own Company and guide them back to camp.

"Hello, Colour-Sar'nt, we've had a grand night here. All's well, though they're busy down in Sevastopol."

"Aye, sir, them bells could get on your tits, though, couldn't they? Mr Carmichael done his rounds, has he?"

"No: well, if he has he was mighty stealthy about it. What are these Three Company boys like?"

"No bad, sir, they did all right at the Alma, when all their officers was down. You'll know most of the NCOs."

"Off with you, then, Colour-Sar'nt — get our lads back for breakfast. These boys and I'll keep the Tsar at bay whilst you lot slumber." Morgan smiled back at McGucken.

With just a few easy instructions, the burly Scotsman gathered the Grenadiers around him and set off down the scrubby hill into the first light of dawn.

"Mr Morgan's goin' to be fit for fuck-all with another night up on the 'ill there, Colour-Sar'nt." Sergeant Whaley was bone-tired himself — he could only pity Morgan.

"Aye, Mick, but at least you know that if Mr Morgan's on duty the job will be done right." McGucken was hard to please; Sergeant Whaley had never heard him being so generous with his praise. "He did well at the Alma and the lads trust him. Wish I could say the same for Mr Carmichael."

Sergeant Whaley wasn't used to being taken into the Colour-Sergeant's confidence like this. He probed no further, ticking off in his mind the thousand jobs that he had to do before he could get his boots off and climb into his blankets.

As Morgan watched them go, one man hung back just a few paces and, hoping he hadn't been seen, drained the last few drops from the rum jar. Even in that light Morgan recognized his short, round form.

"Can you hear that, sir?" As with most of the rest of the Number Three Company men, Morgan recognized the speaker's face but didn't know his name. Now one young lad cupped his gloved hand to his ear, opened his mouth to amplify the sound and listened intently.

"No, I can't hear a damn thing." Morgan was jaded after another broken night and impatient with the freshness of men he hardly knew. "What d'you think it is? I'm sorry, I don't know your name."

"Yarrow, sir. There, listen, can you not hear harness and horses?" The other sentry strained hard into the breeze, all three men breathing as lightly as possible, trying to catch the slightest noise.

The new picket had arrived, been posted and eaten a meagre breakfast before Morgan had rolled himself in his blankets and dozed a little. Now it was late morning on a cool, sunlit, late October day that, for once, was dry. But with a snatch of sleep and a cup of red-hot coffee straight from the watchfire warming his stomach, Morgan began to feel semi-human again. There wasn't much that could be called beautiful on the slopes of Shell Hill, but as the oak and brush that dotted his view began to turn brown and the wind caught their leaves in the gentle sunlight, he was reminded of the hills near home where they ran down to the sea. Now he didn't need some recruit from another, half-tried company jumping at shadows, ruining what should be a quiet morning. Only last week the 30th's pickets had started firing at nothing — the whole of the 2nd Division had stood-to and there was a dreadful fuss — Carmichael was just waiting for him to preside over a mistake like that.

"Yarrow, you're away with the fairies." Morgan had done his best to humour the boy, played the dutiful, interested officer, but he could hear nothing. "Still, I'd rather have you alert than . . ."

"Fuck sake, look there!" The other sentry, standing just behind Morgan, yelled, raised' his rifle to his shoulder and instantly fired.

The muzzle was only inches from the young officer's ear when it exploded deafeningly. Morgan ducked away, head ringing, cursing the man for an inexperienced fool when Yarrow fired as well, the smoke from both weapons fanning back into their faces and obscuring everything just when they needed a clear view.

But there they were. No more than seventy paces away, half-hidden by the brush and bushes was a great phalanx of pasty-faced, mustachioed, silent troops. For a fraction of a second Morgan thought they were British for they wore the same, grey greatcoats — perhaps a stray company, badly lost. But there was red at their collars and their cross-belts were polished black and now at least a hundred of them just stood and gazed at the three Englishmen. One man had fallen to Yarrow's bullet — a couple pawed at him with looks of surprise on their faces — but the rest dithered, musket barrels and bayonets shining dully.

"Jaysus! Russians, bloody thousands," said Morgan, ". . . reload, quick!"

"Said summat was up," replied Yarrow dryly whilst both sentries calmly rammed fresh rounds into their rifles.

"You get back and get the rest of the picket now, Yarrow and I will hold them," Morgan pushed his telescope into a deep coat pocket and hauled at his leather pistol holster.

"No need, sir." The nameless soldier carelessly spat a twist of cartridge paper whilst answering Morgan. "The lads are coming now, look there."

The two rounds must have been fired just as the main body of the picket were standing-to, for up ran two dozen or so men, all strapped and belted and ready for the fight. But the NCOs had them well in hand, for none fired — despite the closeness of the enemy infantry — as they scrambled up to form a firing line. Their job was to buy time for the guns and the mass of the 2nd Division, three-quarters of a mile behind them on Home Ridge, to stand-to and ready themselves to counter-attack. The Sergeant and corporal at their head had reacted well and quickly but they were clearly delighted to see Morgan — an officer — who would take command and the responsibility that went with it.

"Well done, lads, up here, swift now." The Russians had stalled and if Morgan could put a volley into them they might just fall back and give him time to think of something else.

But as the first of the men arrived blown and puffing next to him, a Russian officer came barging through the ranks opposite, waving his sword. He planted himself in front of his supine command, turned, yelled and set off

204

at a sprint towards the English. For a second the enemy didn't respond, then the spell was broken. With a harsh, high-pitched yell, their faces creased, the whole mob came rolling forward, bayonets levelled, one or two firing as they ran, the grey tidal wave sweeping down the slope.

"No, don't wait, for God's sake get into line and make ready." Morgan instinctively knew that there was only one thing for it. If the troops did as they were trained to do — every other man firing before falling back covered by his mate — all would be lost, for every bullet was needed now.

"Ready . . . aim low . . . wait for my word." The men scrambled into a rough, ragged line amongst the bushes, some kneeling, some standing, all gasping to get their breath, the smell of sweat and last night's rum all around them. One man jerked backwards crashing into the branches that, for a second, supported him before he slithered to the ground. He was ignored as butts were cuddled hard against cheeks, wavering barrels curbed and steadied.

Morgan aimed his pistol just below the cross-belts of the leading Russian, an NCO judging by the way that he was shouting and pushing the others on. At fifty yards he could see every button on their uniforms and, quite detached, he noticed how the skirts of their flapping coats were hooked up at the waist to make movement easier.

"Fire!" All around him the heavy rifles banged and kicked, every man's shoulder jerked backwards with the recoil, as if pulled by some invisible string. Instantly they were enveloped by greasy, grey powder-smoke, but none came from his Tranter. His father's present sat mute in his hand, the trigger unmoving and the hammer jammed solid.

Pulling his sword from its damp-swollen, leather scabbard, Morgan pushed through the smoke. "Come on, get at them!" He launched himself into a patch of clearer ground, his boots scrabbling on the grass and grit. If he could blunt the enemy and break their momentum, his men might just survive.

As the smoke cleared they could see the effect of their volley. At point-blank range the Minié bullets had ripped into the enemy infantry, bowling over a dozen or more and leaving others dazed, holding their wounds or hopping and limping to the rear. Most had stopped, stunned by the fire, but others came on hard down the slope, whooping and yelling. It was just like a ruck at school except for the steel — and the fear. He knew raw, physical contact with other men on the playing field and in the ring, but this was different. It was the same sensation that he had had with that young skirmisher at the Alma — the desperation in his scratches and blows before his head was broken open by McGucken. Here it was again, screaming, spitting hate, no rugby ball or gloved hands now, just death or survival.

They met at a run. Morgan dreaded the hesitation that had nearly cost him his life at the Alma — a hesitation born of a cultured, Christian society — a hesitation that had no place on the battlefield. But it had gone, all his weight and strength were behind his sword as he thrust at his enemy's belly. With a heavy, awkward parry, though, the Russian slammed his musket down, catching the sabre on the socket of his bayonet, both blades skidding into the earth as their owners cannoned into each other, the shock sending them reeling back.

All around men crowded into each other. Bitter, lethal contests with butts, barrels and bayonets eddied over the hillside, bushes trodden under foot, twigs and branches snapping, the moans of the wounded harsh above the grim silence of the contestants.

Winded, Morgan sucked for breath. The Russian's mouth dropped open, his eyes round with fear and indecision, his feet rooted to the ground. With that clumsy, over-arm swipe that he knew was wrong from the moment it was launched, Morgan chopped at his enemy's head. Shocked as he was, the boy had all the time in the world to bring his musket up to guard himself — the blade rang on the barrel, sparks flew as it snapped in two.

There was no time to think. Morgan punched hard at the lad with hilt of the broken sword, swinging his shoulder behind the blow exactly as he would in the ring. But just as the punch connected, something glittered across Morgan's chest, ripping at his coat, cross belt and cape, throwing him off balance, making him stagger, barge, half-fall into one of his own men in the mêlée.

A furious Russian NCO now had Morgan on the end of his musket and bayonet just as surely as a gaffed salmon. The long, thin, spike of a blade had missed his body by fractions of an inch but now it was firmly snagged in his clothes and the wide leather of his sword-belt. The more the Russian tried to wrench his weapon free, the more he pulled Morgan with him: the more he pulled the more they both cursed. The pair windmilled and swung through the other fights, smoke in their nostrils, Morgan almost pulled off his feet by his enemy's frenzied tugs.

In the chaos the stub of his sword had gone. Morgan reached for his jammed pistol as a club, but as his clothes tented out in front of him as the Russian tried to free his blade yet again, all he could find was his telescope. He had just enough sense to hang back as the NCO pulled again, launching himself as the Russian jerked, hammering at his enemy's head with the brass tube as their chests thumped together. As they fell, so Morgan struck. There was no weight to his telescope, but he beat time and again at his enemy until his palm was numb. Under the rain of blows the Russian finally gave in, dropped his musket and shied off up the hill with the rest of his running troops.

Then all was quiet. Morgan looked around him in the brush. A few of his men sprawled on the ground, but bleeding, crawling, torn Russians were everywhere. The clutch of 95th puffed and wheezed, some reloaded but most just stared in disbelief as the scrub swallowed up the great mass of their foes.

"Fuck me, sir, you showed that Russ how to fight. You'll have to send back to one o' them smart London shops for a new glass, though, sir." A freckled, stubbly boy, cap right on the back of his head, greasy hair jutting out, grinned at him. "It'll cost you a bob or two."

Morgan's buckled telescope was still in his hand, the lens shattered, a smear of blood over its leather sheath. It was a good one — it had cost three guineas. He dropped it to the ground next to an equally buckled man and, trembling uncontrollably, tried to pull the bayonet from his clothes.

The guns thumped and the Russians broke. The pickets and Morgan had done their job — some said they had done it too well. By fighting so stubbornly and so far forward they had prevented their own guns on Home Ridge from getting into action sooner, but really it made little difference. Six Russian battalions had come forward with the guns that Yarrow's sharp ears had heard under the command of a colonel, but when he fell to a British nine-pounder, all the steam went out of the attack and it collapsed.

So Morgan sat on a sandbag amongst their own artillery as the shells cracked and clawed at the enemy. Two British battalions whooped across the saddle up to Shell Hill, driving all before them and he was more than content to let them get on with it. He'd drunk half his flask of brandy on watch last night, sharing a bit with the men, now he gulped greedily at the rest. Twice, now, he'd grappled hand-to-hand with Russians, smelt their breath, felt their spittle on his face and seen their eyes as scared as his own. Would he have to do this again? Could he take it? Then a small, warm thought came to him — what was it that soldier from Three Company had said — "You showed that Russ how to fight" wasn't it? He smiled to himself and emptied his flask.

The hillside opposite was dotted with Russian dead and wounded, but his own men had got off lightly. A handful of stretchers bobbed back towards the regimental hospital — he ought to go and visit the injured before finding Carmichael and reporting to him, he would need to know how many men were down. Strange, though, he'd not seen Carmichael since their argument the day before — perhaps he'd just not noticed him in the chaos of the fight.

"Mrs Polley, I'm glad to see you. How many of our boys are here?" A wisp of hair had escaped the iron clutches of her bun, now she brushed a wrist across her forehead, turned and bobbed a curtsey to Tony Morgan.

"Why, sir, it's good to see you too, sir." She was bandaging the hand of a Russian who sat, quite bemused on a wooden stool looking about him at the inside of the big hospital marquee, oblivious to any pain. "Less than a dozen all told, sir, two of our Grenadiers, Tommy Baxter and young George Clarke — but they're all right. Word to the wise, Mr Morgan, sir, the Sergeant-Major caught one. Might be a good move to wish him well, he's yonder," she pointed with her bony chin to a trestle bed in the corner, then, dropping her voice, "just don't ask where he's wounded," then much louder and staccato "now hold still, Tsar Nicholas, we'll soon have you mended." But the Russian looked no better informed.

The regiment's senior non-commissioned officer, Sergeant-Major Roger O'Connor, lay face down on the straw-filled mattress. At forty-four his curling hair and beard were starting to grey, lines of pain etched the corners of his closed eyes, his bottom stuck up below a blanket, supported by a pillow. His scarlet coat, muddy trousers and sword hung on a peg beside the bed, whilst a pair of shockingly dirty feet hung out over the end of the mattress. With only an issue shirt on, though, the imposing, muscular man had lost none of his authority.

"Sar'nt-Major, it's me, Mr Morgan; how are you?"

"Fine, sir, I've never been better, so I haven't." The big, Belfast man rose on his elbows, opened his eyes, grimaced and almost smiled through the pain.

"A good fight today, wasn't it, and I see we've got more prisoners than we can feed." Morgan tried not to ask the obvious question.

"I'm not sure that Mrs O'Connor will be as pleased as we are with it, but they call that the fortunes of war, sir, don't they?" O'Connor half-joked, "I hear you did well today, sir, though you'll be needing a new sword and glass. Keep your thieving, Orange hands off mine, sir."

They both laughed. But how could the Sergeant-Major already know about his scrimmage — his palm was still tingling — and could that awkward, bruising tussle really reflect well on him?

"Sir, the commanding officer's well pleased with things and will want to speak to you." The last time that Major Hume had spoken to Morgan had been when

211

he'd torn a strip off him at the Alma for shooting a Russian rifleman. He'd avoided him ever since. "But, sir, what officer's up with your company? I've just seen Mr Carmichael and there's only the pair of you now, ain't there?" Even in his pain, O'Connor was still the Sergeant-Major, always worried for his flock.

"I didn't know he was here, Mr O'Connor, I must find him." Morgan was instantly suspicious. Why had Carmichael left the Grenadiers when he was the only officer with them? Or was he trying to find fault with Morgan again?

He stopped to see the company's wounded. Both had been grazed by shot and would return to duty soon enough, but neither had seen Carmichael.

"He wasn't with us when we leathered them Muscovites today, sir. Jock . . . er, Colour-Sar'nt McGucken was in charge," added the youngster, Clarke. He wandered back to Mrs Polley who was sticking plaster on yet another Russian.

"Oh yes, sir, he was here just before you arrived. He's always here in the hospital, most attentive to his duties he is . . . well, attentive, anyway," she added flicking him a glance.

"So where is he now?"

"Why should I know, sir?" Mrs Polley busied herself about her patient, hesitated then added, "Mithering poor Mrs Keenan at the wagon, I shouldn't wonder."

Morgan caught the note in Mrs Polley's voice straightaway. Carmichael had never made any secrecy of his lust for Mary and now, as acting company commander, he would have every opportunity to visit the sick and wounded in the regimental hospital daily. Morgan was only too aware of his own frailties to expect anything better from Carmichael — a check on exactly what his elder and better was doing was in order, he thought.

Whilst he'd been in the hospital tent, though, he'd become aware of the din of voices nearby. A noisy crowd had gathered by the horse lines and now, as he left the tent, there were fifty or so men jostling in a circle, talking excitedly, one strident voice dominating the others, shouting a litany that Morgan couldn't quite hear.

"Harry 'Otspur, what's the odds? 'Oo fancies Sevastopol Sam?" A big private with a bandaged hand — Morgan thought he recognized him as a Light Company man — had a sheaf of notes in his good hand. He was standing on a straw bail, part of a ring made from the horses' bedding. There was no formality here, not even a hint that the men recognized an officer, for the excitement was running too high. Morgan pushed through a gap in the bodies to see two men crouched in the straw circle, both holding cock-birds tightly so that they couldn't flap their wings. The birds had their necks outstretched, beaks straining, as the men pushed them at each other, tauntingly. The cocks clucked horrid little rasps of hate, their legs drooping below where their sharpened, iron spurs shone.

"Five bob on Hotspur, please." Morgan dug in his pocket for the few coins he kept on him. He'd always wondered how sensible this was when he remembered the boy from the 7th at the Alma who had been struck by coins propelled from another's pocket by a roundshot, but he needed some money, if only to chance his arm like this when the opportunity arose.

"Hello there, sir. Five bob on Harry's beak it is, three-to-one, note it down, Jem." The bandaged private had to yell above the rumpus to his partner. "Check their gaffs, handlers," he called to the men in the ring, who tugged at the spurs' leather bindings, making sure that the two-inch-long spikes were secure, ". . . and loose!"

Both birds fluttered onto the ring's floor, wings outstretched, beaks trembling and eyes alight. The crowd fell silent, the birds circled and circled again.

"Chicken, they're bloody chicken," "Get at 'im, can't yer." "Must be a Turkey," the crowd was impatient until both cock-birds flew at each other, all feathers, wings and furious, black eyes. They clung in mid-air, inches above the ground, scratching, pecking for a few seconds before falling back to the floor. As Sam flapped and steadied himself, a cascade of grain fell from his crop where a spur had caught him. The seeds rolled across the ring, Hotspur's backers cheering with delight, until Sam came back on guard, apparently oblivious to the wound.

Again the birds flew, again they clashed and scratched before dropping back, but this time Sam staggered. At first his wings flopped down as spots of blood dripped to the floor, then up came his beak to face his opponent, clucking his defiance.

214

"He's a game 'un," ". . . plucky bugger," yelled the delighted mob, as the birds dashed together again. Now Sam stayed down; his wings flapped weakly, his head dipped and touched the grit as Hotspur strutted onto his body, pecking briefly at his neck before opening his wings, throwing his head back and crowing for all that he was worth.

Both birds' supporters were delighted with the display. Win or lose, they'd had a grand time, now they clamoured for their money or began to drift away, Sam's owner finishing the bird with a quick twist of its neck.

"'Old 'ard, you lot, 'ere you are, sir, fifteen bob an' yer stake, that's a quid . . ." the Light Company man trickled florins and crowns into Morgan's hand, ". . . not quite enough for a new glass, sir, but better than a bang on the bonce."

How on earth did the men know about his telescope, thought Morgan, but even as he turned away from the soldiers, pocketing his winnings, there stood Carmichael. "Morgan, what are you doing here, cock-fighting?" Carmichael was poised, he'd obviously been watching Morgan for some time. "Besides that, you know the sport's illegal, not to mention the crime of taking money off the men; I've told you before about getting too familiar with them." Carmichael's sally rocked Morgan back.

"But I can overlook all that; what I can't understand is why you're down here when it's almost time for stand-to." Carmichael was calm, almost conversational in his accusations. "Your place is on Shell Hill with the men, not trying to curry favour with them down here."

For an instant Morgan faltered, for Carmichael was right in everything he said, but suddenly the man's utter hypocrisy was too much for him. "Goddamn you Carmichael, why aren't *you* with the company? You duck every fight, you neglect the men and now you're here sniffing round someone else's wife — and one of your own soldiers' at that." He just reined himself in, "If I didn't think it's what you'd want, I'd kick your lights out here and now." Morgan's chest was thrust out, his fists clenched, he'd come forward on the balls of his feet almost like one of the game-cocks.

"Thank you, Morgan, that's quite enough of that." To his credit, Carmichael showed no fear. "Remember where you are, who I am and who Mrs Keenan is. Now, visit the wounded and sick and report back to me after stand-down. Do I make myself clear?"

"You do, sir," Morgan fought to control himself.

"Good. I could break you for this, Morgan, and don't forget it. You're on borrowed time from now on." Carmichael turned on his heel, tucked his sword up under his arm and strode calmly away.

Morgan trembled with anger. He knew that he'd gone red with fury and that his last sentence or two had been thick with emotion, but he'd failed to notice Mary deep amongst the ponies; she had heard every word.

"Mother of God, Tony, was that wise?" Mary instantly dropped any formality. She bit her lip, looking towards Carmichael's back.

"It had to be said, Mary, I can take no more of that gutless prig. I spend my time covering for him — he despises the men, you know."

"And they just hate him, Tony. Here, I've a wee drop of rum in the back somewhere, jump up for a minute." Morgan hauled himself over the tailboard, pulling the canvas down behind him. Immediately the back of the wagon seemed warm, cosy and private, everything that a ditch on Shell Hill or his wretched, bleak tent wasn't.

Mary'd lit a lantern; now it gently dappled her. She settled herself on one of the litters, smoothed her hair, made absolutely no attempt to find any rum and looked him straight in the eye.

Hypocrisy — it wasn't a word that crossed Tony's mind in the next few minutes. He fell on her lips, their hands tore at each other's buttons whilst all that Morgan could think of was his horrid, coarse beard and the grime in every pore and the lice that were in all his clothes — but Mary didn't notice for she was as hungry as he was. The exhaustion, worry, loneliness, brutality and fear of the last weeks melted as their limbs twined round each other. The same hands that had beaten at a Russian just hours before now gently stroked and probed. With a moan they lost themselves in each other, all horror, hate and dread forgotten for the moment.

"Tony, I'm so in love with you." Mary lay on top of him just as she had at Glassdrumman.

"As I am with you, my darling girl." They had always known it, but it had never been said. Now Tony

217

smothered her hair, her lips, her neck, her breasts with kisses.

"Darling, you have to know it. Bloody Carmichael's always round me, but tonight he had some news. Poor James is quite recovered. He's on the next draft back from Turkey and he's to be a Sergeant — it's for what both of you did at the Alma." Mary stroked at his hair and cheek, smoothing the whiskers back as she always had, her eyes fixed on his.

"So Mr Morgan, sir, you know what we have — and it's something that Sergeant James Keenan and I will never have — and I can't live without you."

CHAPTER
EIGHT

Eve of Inkermann

"Right, together now, lift." All four men grunted as they took the weight of the stretcher and its corpse.

The early November morning was crisp, just cold enough to nip the men's bare hands on the wooden stretcher and to leave their breath hanging in the air. The grey blanket that covered the dead man had been tied off with coarse, straw-coloured string at ankles, waist and head, the whole bundle now sparkling with frost in the weak sunlight. The body and those of two other men had lain outside the regimental hospital tents overnight — the cold only adding to the stiffness of rigor mortis — all three victims of a combination of exhaustion and cholera which was never far away. As the carrying party lifted Private Thompson onto the stretcher he was unbending, rigid in his blanket, hard to handle and deathly cold. Now he bounced and bobbed on the pregnant canvas as the stretcher party shuffled towards the regiment's makeshift cemetery.

"You're an 'eavy bugger, you, Tommo . . ." Drummer Pegg talked to unlistening ears, ". . . you always was selfish, bet you told Jock McGucken specially to put me on your burial detail."

219

Pegg was several inches shorter than the other three, so a greater proportion of the dead weight fell upon his podgy arms. He had to use both hands on his corner of the litter, puffing and blowing with effort to match the taller, older men as they plodded slowly over the rough turf and grit.

"Steady now, watch where you're putting your feet." The great-coated, muffled group staggered over an uneven, frost-slippery bank where the limey soil broke through the grass. The senior soldier leading the party had done this many times before, but even his experience wasn't enough to avoid the inevitable.

"Ow . . . Bollocks." It had to be Pegg who slipped. As he picked forwards with his load, his feet suddenly went from under him, his thigh struck a stone, his elbow banged into the soil before the stretcher's handle thumped him squarely in the centre of the chest. The others were pulled down in a welter of limbs and curses, as cold, stiff Tommo first bundled over Pegg before bouncing off down the slope. As it rolled so the parcel came untied. The string undid itself at waist and then head, allowing rigid arms to poke out like oars, eventually halting its crazy progress against a line of tussocks.

"Right, let's get 'im — and, Pegg can do the poor sod back up for falling when I told you not to." The older man tried to make light of the tasteless accident, but they all felt the indignity of their friend Tommo's last journey. The daily exposure to death and injury left them all numb to it — the handling and burial of bodies was seen as a simple part of mortality — but few

220

had been robbed of their humanity. Here was a friend, a messmate from Dublin and Weedon, a man who had faced danger well and who could be trusted to stay awake at a lonely post and share his rations and tobacco.

More than just that, his death took away another pair of hands, making those posts lonelier and the burden of work even heavier. Now they were stuck with the tedious, arduous task of their friend's disposal. A nuisance he might have become — his final act being to deprive them of sleep and rest — but Tommo still didn't deserve to be chucked down a bank by a feckless boy.

"Come on Tommo, it was an accident, stop looking at me like that." Thompson's face now stuck clear of the blanket, a yellow, waxy mask that had lost all tone and definition, its skin folding back over teeth and cheekbones. Pegg had rolled him over in the grass and was doing his best to pretend that he was blind to the older men's resentment.

"Just get him done up again, Pegg, let's not keep the priest waiting any more." The senior soldier crossed himself, speaking with quiet contempt.

The stretcher was held on its side on a piece of level ground before Thompson was pushed back onto the canvas in a too-often practised way before the party trudged back up the slope.

"Don't drop the poor bastard again, let's get him in the ground, respectable-like." The senior soldier chided them over the next half-mile.

Another Catholic was to be buried. As the Grenadiers drew close to the grave, three men from Number Two Company stood talking to the priest. In front of them lay a further packaged body: their rifles were piled in a triangle behind, whilst their shovels and picks had been respectfully secreted in some brush. The breeze ruffled the hair of their bare heads as they twisted their woollen caps in their hands.

The priest was a stark contrast. His black and white vestments stood out against the low bushes and the drab, grey coats of the men. His beretta looked almost tailor-shop new, perhaps due to the ribbons that held it firmly in place on his head against the Crimean wind. He smiled and nodded as the party approached, the sun winking off the tiny round lenses of his spectacles.

"Hello, lads, another customer? Who is he, boys — you're sure he's one of ours?" Father Mountford was one of the few dozen Roman Catholic priests who had volunteered to accompany the forces to the East. Only Anglican and Church of Scotland padres were provided for the spiritual comfort of the troops, despite the large number of Catholics who were serving. Housed at Brigade Headquarters, Mountford on his little pony — that now cropped the meagre grass well away from the lines of wooden crosses — had become a familiar sight to the regiments.

Normally just in sombre black, his legs squeezed into the latest India-rubber wading boots, a simple shooting cap covering his head, he could be seen well forward in the trenches or with the pickets. His greatest delight was to break two sets of rules. Without fail he could be depended upon to produce a neat silver flask and offer it (when away from prying officer or NCOs' eyes) to the men. From his other pocket he would conjure one of the latest American Colt revolvers. What God's view would have been of his firing on fellow Christians had yet to be put to the test — but the men loved it.

"Right, lads, two of you jump down and catch hold of your friends. I fear it's so much quicker to dig a double and the lads won't mind each other's company will they?" It might have been a routine pauper's funeral anywhere — the novelty for the priest in scenes like this had evaporated long ago.

One of the Number Two Company men scrambled into the wide hole, whilst Pegg had to have a bony finger pushed into the small of his back before he realized that he had much ground to make up. Both long woollen parcels were passed down with as much reverence as possible, before the other, taller soldier levered himself out of the grave with ease, brushing the soil from the waist and skirts of his coat. Stumpy Pegg tried the same, failed and found himself slithering back down the fresh-dug earthy wall where his boots came to rest on Thompson's chest and shoulder. Sheepishly, he looked up into the appalled faces of his companions.

"For the love of God, boy, catch hold." The senior soldier and one of the others grabbed Pegg's wrists and pulled him with such exasperated force from the hole that the drummer wondered if he was ever going to stop.

"There's no need to pull me fucking arms off, is there?" Pegg was shocked by the force.

223

"Eh, watch your language in front of the priest!" A lance-corporal in charge of the other party spat furiously at Pegg. The boy had run out of credit.

The priest prayed and intoned. He had a small thurible with him that he swung with gusto whilst one of the soldiers held his prayer book open for him at the right page. Pegg stood a little way apart, not because he detected a less than benign atmosphere, but out of simple suspicion for anything parish. Father Mountford's lips were uttering the oddest of noises, he was swinging a strange, smelly thing whilst everyone else crossed themselves as if it were the second coming. Mercifully, Pegg didn't have long to wait in the cold before the shovels were at work, spooning the chill, loose soil onto the bodies until a wide, browny-white mound was all that remained.

Wooden crosses made from ration boxes had been carefully painted with the men's name and regiment, "Fidelis Usque Ad Mortem" below the inscription. One man banged the cross into the frosty spoil with the flat of his shovel blade whilst another crouched, holding it erect, eyes closed against the flying grit.

"Right, lads, fall in." The group shuffled into a straight line, replaced their caps and took their dressing under the corporal's direction. "Thank you very much, Father. That was, er . . . very nice," the NCO stuttered, before, with much greater confidence, "May I have your leave to carry on, sir, please?" as his hand snapped to the brim of his cap as smartly as if they were all back in the barrack-yard.

"You may, Corporal. God bless you all, keep safe," replied the priest, returning the salute with a darted blessing.

There were mumbles of "God go with you, Father" as the group separated into its two parts and moved off.

The four Grenadiers stepped as fast as they could to warm themselves. They were quiet, wrapped in their thoughts until Pegg broke the silence.

"Fancy poor old Tommo having to have all that foreign lingo said over him."

It took at least two days before the swelling round his left eye subsided. The young drummer was almost as hurt by the fact that no one seemed the least surprised by his bruises.

"Bloody end's come loose again. 'Oo made the thing anyway?" Private Almond cursed in flat, Thirsk vowels. "'Old it steady, Pegg, an' I'll do the bleedin' twine up again."

Night was falling. The two soldiers stood by the edge of the regiment's tented camp waiting to go forward into the trenches with thirty others — half of the depleted Grenadier Company. A physically hard, tedious and probably dangerous night lay ahead as they moved equipment down into the forward positions and then filled sandbags and gabions with soil. Slowly the trench lines crept forward towards Sevastopol, but each yard of digging had to be protected from the Russians' fire by awkward, heavy kit that had to come from somewhere.

They'd spent the afternoon weaving gabions. A pile of eight-foot-long willow branches, still green and springy — that was the only thing that prevented them from becoming instant firewood for the troops — had been magicked-up by the quartermaster and the troops had set to. Weaving was a skill taught to all recruits, many of them from rural backgrounds already being familiar with it, but it was seldom practised until it was needed.

For weeks now the soldiers had spent every available moment producing these vast baskets, taller than a man and three times as wide, until they had become fast and proficient at it. But the difficult bits were the finishing touches where the end branches were bound by that universal, rough Army twine that needed deft, careful fingers and clever knotting. The troops were good at the brutish business of bending and notching branches, but the skilful bits still, occasionally, defeated them. The end product was surprisingly light and could be quite easily rolled into position before being filled with packed, protective earth. But the most frustrating sight was one that came unbound on the move, leaving its cursing handlers with a ragged, tatty rim that needed instant, time-consuming attention — and always in the dark.

"Dunno, doesn't matter who made it, just get the bastard fixed." Pegg held the twine in place with a grubby thumb as Almond tightened and knotted. "Who's taking us up the line tonight, anyway, d'you know? They say we're to relieve some Frogs."

"Aye, that's right. Probably Paddy Morgan or Tom Whaley, Jock McGucken's been on two nights in a row and he's about done." The company was now so short of officers and senior NCOs that even the privates were noticing the uneven workload.

"It's them Zouaves from Bony's Div. S'if you can rob some brandy off of them, Pegg, they call it Cog-nack. They might swap some for a bit of pork if you've got any left."

The French-Algerian soldiers contained a surprising number of English-speakers and seemed to get on well with the British troops. They were older than most of their allies and with endless experience of the campaigns in North Africa. Almond, Pegg and the others admired their cheerfulness and resilience though pitied them the vast red pantaloons and white spats that they wore, to which mud clung like glue. But through their platoons and companies ran an *élan* and derring-do that was attractive but which meant that they took more risks and casualties than their comrades from the French regiments of the Line. They also had a reputation for being impatient and sloppy in defence.

"Why's it always my bleedin' pork what's got to be swapped?" moaned Pegg, "What's wrong with yours?"

"I ain't got any left, that's what's wrong with mine, you twot," bickered Almond. "Can't you ever . . ."

"Shut your grids, you pair," Corporal Cahill muttered before bellowing, "Detail, detail, 'shun!" Bringing silence to the whole group as they stamped to attention.

It was almost completely dark by now. The men looked like nothing more than featureless bundles of coats, caps and belts, set about with shovels, picks and back-breaking gear. At least they had been spared the weight of their rifles and ammunition, each man carrying no more personal kit than some rations, a water-bottle and a bayonet.

Corporal Cahill had done well to spot the tall, slender figure of the company Commander, Richard Carmichael, as he loped through the dusk. His soft, peaked cap perched on his now luxuriant hair, a cheroot glowing at his bearded lips, he'd pulled the cape of his greatcoat back from his neck to allow his woollen muffler to sit comfortably but rakishly forward. The party hadn't expected such an august figure to lead them up to the trenches: they stiffened with expectation as he spoke.

"So, Corporal Cahill, who's in charge?"

"Dunno, yet, sir, we're waiting for one o' the sergeants or Mr Morgan, sir . . . or is it yourself?" The quietest of snorts came from the men when Cahill made this suggestion, his Irishness disguising any mockery.

"Well, bejabers, Corporal Cahill, I don't yet know who's taking you and these broths of boys up the line." Carmichael appeared not to have noticed Cahill's sally and had lapsed into one of his music-hall brogues. "Just wait here a wee while an' I'll see what's holding your mysterious leader up, so I will."

"Knob!" an anonymous Irish voice said quite clearly from the dark, faceless group.

228

"Who said that?" spat the officer, instantly English.

"Said what, sir?" replied Cahill, as Dublin-broad as possible.

Just as Carmichael hesitated, trying to decide whether this was a confrontation that he could hope to win or not, Sergeant Whaley came bustling up through the line of tents.

"Evenin' sir," the squat senior NCO slapped his rifle sling in salute as he crashed his boots together loud enough for the Russians to hear it in Sevastopol.

"Good evening, Sar'nt Whaley, you're late." This was an easier way for Carmichael to re-establish his authority.

"Not according to the Colour-Sar'nt's watch, sir, it's just that Corporal Cahill's a bit early, like the good man he is, sir." The answer came back with the impervious confidence that seasoned NCOs reserve for officers whom they despise. There was nothing insubordinate in what he said, just sweet reasoned, disdain.

"Now, excuse me, sir, but I don't want to be late for them Froggy Zouaves, we'll get the Company a bad name." Again, there was no room for Carmichael to manoeuvre. "Pick up your monkeys and parrots, lads, get them bloody gabions up 'ere at the front an' control the things. Right, coom-on then."

Sergeant Whaley's Sheffield calm lent another dimension to the troops' glee. The party had been lethargic, sullen even at the prospect of yet another sleepless night in the trenches, but now they set off with a silent chuckle in their throats.

★ ★ ★

229

Sevastopol was quiet that night. The odd gun snapped at the main French works as they pushed their trenches forward towards the Flag-Staff Bastion, but up on the Left Attack they were being treated to little except for an occasional star-shell. So short-handed had disease and casualties left the 2nd Division that some of the crucial digging details had to be done by French troops — a fact that offended the officers' pride but delighted the men. Not only were the cocky French having to do donkey work for the British, but they patently hated it. There had been some ugly scenes between the 47th and the French 6th Light Infantry in October during a trench relief and since then the French had tried to use only colonial troops with whom the British had much greater rapport.

Now the party picked slowly forward in the dark. The big gabions wheeled along without mishap other than getting stuck in some brush just as the first, shallow part of the trenches was approached. Much to everyone's surprise a vast Zouave corporal, their guide, was waiting at exactly the appointed spot at exactly the appointed time. Slumped full-length at the mouth of the first diggings, the hairy hood of his woollen cape pulled up over his head, his arms folded around his rifle, an enormous pair of nailed boots stuck out below his muddy leggings. His beard rose and fell rhythmically as he snored, patchy moonlight shining off his tanned, beak-like nose.

"*Alors, Frog, sacré-bleu,*" Sergeant Whaley did his best to wake the great Algerian by voice alone, "*. . . allez-vous, cognack ici.*" His repertoire was soon

230

exhausted. A quick tap with the toe of his boot on the sole of the Zouave's *chaussure* did the job, though, and the man awoke with a start.

"Oh, hello, are you the detail of the Ninety-Fifth that's to relieve my gang?" Perfect, public-school English came from the Zouave who was instantly awake and cheerful. It took Sergeant Whaley a second or two to recover from the disappointment of not being able to display more of his *patois*.

"Where the 'ell are you from, Corporal?"

"Algiers, of course, Sergeant." The Anglo-Frenchman stretched his arms, pulled his hood back and rose easily to his feet, giving a little stamp to restore the circulation. "It's a chilly one tonight, Sergeant. Now, some of your colleagues seem to have chosen a narrow bit of the trench to catch up on their sleep. With all this junk you're having to carry, may I suggest that we move overground, above the trench? *Les Russes* are on best behaviour tonight and it'll be so much quicker. Might be a bit of a squeeze when we get forward, we took a prisoner earlier and the boys are having fun with him."

Sergeant Whaley yielded his authority at once to the Zouave's officer-like confidence whilst his imagination was aflame with sympathy for the Russian prisoner. What on earth was a digging party doing taking prisoners? Didn't these savages have enough to do scraping holes for the British without prowling round terrifying decent Christians? And what could a bunch like this mean by "having a bit of fun" with the prisoner? They'd all heard about this lot. A picture of

231

the Russian pinned to the ground with bayonets whilst his captors shrieked and danced about him in the firelight brandishing their knives leapt into Whaley's mind. Worse still, suppose poor old Russ had been strapped over one of those big water butts that the Frogs used and had been . . . the idea was too awful even for his hardened imagination.

The party crept forward in a long, clumsy line over the rough-dug rear of the trench. The gabions were having to be carried now as they tried to be as silent as possible, but boots still scraped pebbles, shovel blades — despite their hessian coverings — still rang against bits of equipment and men coughed continually. As star-shells fizzed into the sky, sending shadows darting crazily from every twig and branch, so they threw themselves to the ground. There they paused, hoping that it wasn't their crashing progress that had attracted the enemy's attention, waited for darkness to return before hauling themselves to their feet, brushing the soil from their clothes and hoisting their ever-heavier gear for the next few yards of halting progress. They passed a group of Sappers who, just as the Zouave said, had unaccountably chosen to choke the trench with their slumbering forms — they didn't like to disturb them — before moving on.

Then, from the darker line of the trench just to their front; "*Halte, arrêtez-vous! Qui passe?*" An invisible sentry's challenge saw them all sink to a crouch, equipment rested on the ground in the darkness. Their guide slunk forward, gabbled in French, and then returned to the waiting line.

"Right, Sergeant, we're in the right place. I suggest that your men jump down into the trench now, we're only a short distance from the head of the sap." The Zouave pointed over the rim of the trench that, in the moonless dark, looked bottomless.

Gingerly, the men slithered over the edge, not quite knowing how deep it was, carefully dragging their gear and tools after them. Pegg and Almond rolled their gabion along the lip and when they found that the trench only came up to their waists, they shouldered the big basket, holding it firm against their cheeks. But there was a price to pay for their close contact with the soil.

"Christ, what's that stink?" Variations of Almond's hoarse, affronted whisper were being repeated up and down the working party.

"What d'you think it is? It's shite — it's in me hair and all over me coat." Pegg — naturally — had been affected more than anyone else. "Them dirty Frogs 'ave been turdin' all over the back of the trench . . ." The gabion had smeared its way through the Frenchmen's muck before coming to rest against the lad's collar and neck, ". . . an' it's in me lug. They've got no bleedin' discipline that foreign lot, ain't they never 'eard of latrines?" Pegg scraped at his ear with a fingernail, making little retching noises as many of the others swore and rubbed at the tails of their coats with hanks of grass, merely spreading the ordure more evenly.

Sergeant Whaley knew none of this. At the head of the column he angrily but silently beckoned his muttering party forward, increasingly aware that to his front he could hear subdued laughter mixed with the metallic rasps of picks and shovels. Out of the darkness loomed a row of empty gabions on their sides — this was obviously the drop-off point that the Zouaves had chosen for all their defensive stores. Big piles of sandbags and wooden staves showed gloomily in the dark but amidst all this equipment and draped half-in, half-out of the shallow trench were several dark figures, giggling noisily.

"Ah, they've got the prisoner." The Zouave guide pointed to a shrunken figure in the middle of a knot of Frenchmen.

Whaley expected the worst. He could just see the man's bare head and full moustache above a red coat-collar: he lolled back, eyes closed and mouth half open. Had they tortured him unconscious? Worse, had these barbarians buggered him to death? Sergeant Whaley's imagination was soon allowed to rest, though, for the air was stiff with "cog-nack" fumes.

"They're all lashed to the gills, ain't they?" Whaley's years of service had left him an expert in detecting drunkenness, but a skinfull this close to the enemy was a new one.

"Well lubricated, shall we say, Sergeant? It seemed only right to give the prisoner a share of the victors' spoils and what's the harm?" The big Zouave seemed to take it all in his stride — so who was Whaley to object?

The handover between the two groups was just as informal — mercifully, the Russians didn't interfere. Sergeant Whaley had expected the stylized pattern of one British unit relieving another — work would cease

234

quietly, the newly arrived party would post its own sentries whilst the others were pulled in, then both groups would stand-to for ten minutes, listening intently for an enemy approach, before the outgoing detail would steal away as silently as possible. Only when they were completely clear would work start again.

But this wasn't the Zouaves' way. At the word of an NCO, tools were downed with a clang, weapons picked up, the prisoner half-pushed and half-carried forward and before you could say "Prince Napoleon", the whole saturnine mob had bustled away without even the 95th's sentries being properly posted. Whaley couldn't swear to it, but as the tail of the column merged into the darkness of the trench, he thought he saw the flicker of a pipe being lit. Just let any of his lot cut capers like that.

Routine eventually returned. For such a forward position things were surprisingly quiet, with Sevastopol's guns only occasionally booming and the Allies' almost completely silent. A bomb-ketch in the harbour lofted a solitary round high over their heads at one point, lighting up the other Russian ships and the walls of the forts on the north bank of the straits with a harsh, yellow-white flash. As it crashed home far behind the lines, they all hoped that some Staff officer's rest had been ruined.

They had been told to lay a line of gabions and sandbags on the enemy-facing side of the sap that the Zouaves had dug. Once the bullet-proof screen was in place, the gunner and Sapper officers would be able to come up just as daylight allowed the enemy's positions to be seen and ranges judged accurately. If the officers worked quickly and well, they could survey and then place the markers for a new gun position before the enemy realized exactly what was going on and fired on them. Then, with the precise work done, the infantry could dig the new position under the cover of darkness, hoping against hope that the Russians would not raid them whilst they were working nor bombard them accurately enough to destroy what they had done. Now it required fast, hard digging and alert sentries.

"Keep the bugger up, can't you, son?" Pegg was meant to be holding open the throat of a half-filled sandbag for Almond to shovel in the spoil, but a coughing sentry in the darkness at the front of the position had distracted him.

"Sorry, I thought I 'eard some fuckin' Russian out there," like the rest of the troops, Pegg was happy enough not to be encumbered with rifle and ammunition when they were carrying heavy loads up to the trenches, yet he missed the familiar weight of his weapons when danger loomed. Now the earth leaked out of the bag as Pegg let its hessian sides go slack as Almond's laden shovel came forward in the dark.

"No, it's just Dan-bloody-Shearman — he can't get rid of that cough, he can't. He's a fuckin' liability on sentry, he is." Almond had dropped his voice at the very mention of Russians.

"The officers say that the Russians won't just sit in 'Polan' let us batter at them," Pegg replied quietly. "Mr Morgan reckons that they'll have a go at us soon, that

that sortie of theirs the other day after they took a shy at Ballyklava was meant to be some sort of warm-up for a big attack."

"Fuckin' expensive warm-up; they lost 'undreds of dead an' wounded an' we had more prisoners than we could 'andle, 'n they fucked off when we gave 'em a shamrock or two." Almond had picked-up the strange, Irish phrase for taking the bayonet to the enemy.

"Aye, I know, but you saw the dead — they was all carryin' digging tools. Jock McGucken says they was going to tek Shell 'ill, an' dig a Redoubt up there that would scupper our Div's guns during an assault." Pegg tinkered with the mouth of the sandbag.

Almond paused for a while, "You think they've got the balls for it?"

"Balls for it? Didn't you hear what 'appened to Paddy Morgan last week? He had a right bloody tussle with hundreds of the fuckers: broke 'is sword, ran out o' shot and had to thump 'em with 'is glass 'e did." Pegg was happy to embroider the tale of his officer's bravery. "I tell yer, if Russ comes mob-'anded next time, you'd best know 'ow to swim."

Almond scraped another shovel-full of earth into the now open bag, "Right, it's full enough, young 'un, tamp it down."

Pegg lifted the almost full bag to waist height, his cheeks billowing with the effort, before letting it thump down to the floor of the trench. He repeated it four times, settling and packing the earth, making it so much more resistant to splinters and bullets. At thirty-odd pounds, a full bag was heavy and awkward,

237

the rough sacking being almost impossible to handle in gloves so that the men's bare hands were soon sore and chapped.

"Well, if Russ wants a fight, he can 'ave some more of what we gave 'im at the Alma an' at Ballyklava — 'e dint like that did he?" Almond had heard enough of the drummer's black predictions.

With all his strength, Pegg lumped the porky sack up into the triangular space on the front of the trench where two gabions met. At this point the baskets offered almost no protection at all and the gap had to be filled with sandbags which, in turn, had to be thumped down firmly.

"Coom 'ere, then, I'll steady you." The trench was only three feet deep, but Almond held Pegg's waist and the cuff of his coat as the boy climbed high onto the piled column of sandbags between the basketwork.

"Bastard things," Pegg grunted in the dark as, perched precariously on one foot he stamped the bags down with all his weight.

"Not too much, Pegg, you'll split the damn' thing." Almond held onto the lad as his iron-tipped boot thumped against sacking that contained the packed earth.

"I do love jumping up an' down like a cock in front of Russ and havin' dirty Frogs as allies," Pegg was blowing hard as he leaped down into the trench before returning to the muck in his ear, "Why, I'd do it for free, let alone tenpence a night." The men hadn't been impressed by the additional field pay that had just been announced.

"Aye, and we're to 'ave a medal an' all, I just 'ope they give us a new coat to stick it on." Almond pulled at the threadbare elbow of his greatcoat where the scarlet of his coatee was peeping through.

"Want, want, want, that's all I ever 'ear from you, Almond. You should just be glad of the chance to serve 'er Majesty under the inspiring leadership of that quim Mr-bleedin-Carmichael."

The banter flowed almost as readily as the two men sweated — British soldiers happy in their work.

The night seemed endless. A flurry of shells arrived in the first murk of dawn and had all of them cringing in the bottom of the freshly-cut trench but, other than that, the dark hours were uneventful. Sapper officers had peered through telescopes and looked intently at charts, the contents of the earthern rum jar had been splashed into cups, sweat had cooled below their coats and boots been emptied of loose earth before their relief arrived. A smaller party of the 30th, fully armed and equipped, had come up to hold the trench and do a little sniping and harassment work during daylight hours before the grimy 95th had been allowed to hobble back down the trench.

"Right, check yer digging tools and personal kit." Sergeant Whaley had led the party back down the deeper trench line until they were out of the enemy's reach before parading them for a perfunctory inspection. "Any o' you buggers lost owt?" The rum had left them light-headed, sulky and unresponsive in the early morning light. Eyes red-rimmed with lack of sleep, hands sore with gritty blisters and shoulders aching from picking, digging and lifting the cloying soil, all they wanted to do was to get back to their muddy blankets. But Whaley was a tartar, there would be no corner-cutting with him.

"No, Sar'nt" the group mumbled as they half-heartedly checked their belts and haversacks.

"This got broke, Sar'nt." Private Swann held up a snapped pick-helve, the broken hickory showing clean and white against the grime on the outside of the shaft.

"No it didn't 'get broke', Jimmy-bleedin-Swann, you busted it yersen, being bloody clumsy, didn't you?" Swann's face fell as Whaley's anger showed.

Why did the men always have to try to avoid responsibility for misfortunes, the sergeant wondered? Swann had just come out of the depot before they left Weedon, a decent enough boy straight from the plough somewhere up near Ashby and the pick-axe had "got broke" through his honest endeavour, not through some piece of vandalism. So why couldn't the youngster just say that? But Whaley was too tired to torture him further.

"Right, son, just hand it in to the colour-sergeant's stores when we get back an' draw a new'un. If you cop one out of the dead lads' kits and don't need to sign for another, so much the better." Despite the organized chaos of the siege work and the wholesale damage to men and equipment, the old army mentality stuck. Kit had to be accounted for, but if a dead man's gear could be pilfered and paperwork avoided, then Whaley was happy.

"Owt else?"

"Yes, Sar'nt, me water-bottle's been robbed." Horn had cast about desperately during Swann's pick-axe saga, wondering why he couldn't feel the comforting weight at his hip.

"No, Horn, the trench-fuckin-fairy hasn't been flittin' up an' down all night just looking for lonely little water-bottles that are a long way from home and taken it into her safe-keeping — yer've bleedin' lost it. Christ-on-a-crutch, half you lot should be at your Mum's tit — if I left you alone for a day you'd be naked, the way you chuck yer kit away."

Horn coloured visibly under Whaley's tirade, his head hung slightly over the collar of his coatee that had been torn by a bullet at the Alma.

"Get a bleedin' new'un. I've a good mind to send you back to look for it, Horn, 'cept that the Thirtieth'll rip the piss out on us. Now fall in the lot on yer an' let's get 'ome." No one else dared to admit to further losses. The soiled, scruffy little party pushed into their ranks, thumped dully to attention and, at Whaley's word, stumped off back to camp.

"I dunno how we'll ever get this muck out of us clothes." As they marched along, Pegg looked in dismay at the brown, orangey stain on the rump of his coat to which grit and bits of grass stuck obstinately.

"We'll just 'ave to wash it and rub it with flannelette." The rolls of off-white cloth issued to the troops specifically for cleaning the locks and bores of their rifles had a thousand illicit uses. "Anyway, Pegg,

241

you should be used to it, you're always in the shit,"
Almond's predictable joke raised some titters from the
others. "Mek sure you've got all that Froggy filth off yer
hands before you eat, son — me guts have only just
settled down after I had the runs last week an' you
don't want the same." Almond spoke matter-of-factly
about a complaint that struck at the troops incessantly.

"I've still got some in me lug" Pegg whittled at his
ear with a little finger.

"Well, now you know what it's like for us having to
listen to the shite you normally talk!" This got one of
the other soldiers a better laugh.

"Did you rob any of that cog-nack off of the Zouaves
like I told you to, son?" There were only a few years
between them, but Almond always played the old
soldier when talking to the young drummer. "Stick
some o' that into the soup an' it won't half brace it up."

The men had become deadly bored with the
monotonous rations. Ship's biscuit was only occasionally relieved with bread baked down in Balaklava, green
coffee beans were now being issued that the soldiers
had to roast themselves, whilst salt pork was almost
universal. Some had tried horse-flesh — but whilst it
was said to be palatable, few dared to eat meat from an
animal that had collapsed through disease or
exhaustion. The fact that the French couldn't get
enough of it made the dish even more suspect to most
of the men. A real favourite, though, were the endless
variations of soup that the amateur cooks conjured up.
Stock thickened with biscuit and flavoured with wild
herbs or nettles could be warmed over a brazier on

picket or in the trenches and made a welcome, warming distraction and Almond's exotic idea of flavouring it further with brandy was an instant success.

"No, I didn't have time to, besides, there was only that big bugger who spoke English." Pegg's recent beating had left him unusually keen to please the others, but he'd quite forgotten to try his luck with the Zouaves. "There's them French guns yonder, d'you think Mick Whaley will let us go an' see what's what?"

Pegg scampered up to the sergeant who was setting the pace at the front of the column. "Sarge, is it all right if I nip over to see what I can get off of them Frogs?" Whaley looked Pegg over. Other than his personal kit, he was carrying nothing of value that the French could steal and he did have a reputation as an expert scrounger.

"All right, youth, but if you do get yer hands on any grog, don't drink it yersen, we'll all want a swat."

The drummer trotted away as the party swung on its way to camp with Whaley instantly regretting his decision. The problem was that Pegg would almost certainly extract something alcoholic from the French and the sergeant knew that the temptation to neck the lot there and then would probably be too much for him. Only two weeks ago, a youngster from the Light Company had been found very dead in a ditch with an empty rum bottle beside him and his corporal had been bust down to private for lack of supervision.

But the lad was intent upon restoring his good name. An unexpected treat courtesy of Drummer Pegg would set the record right, so he straightened his belts and cap, rubbed a grubby hand over his wispy excuse for a beard to rid it of any imagined grime and strode confidently up to the French sentry at the edge of the gun park. Since the Russian sortie against the Inkermann position, the French had kept two of their field pieces ready for instant action on this exposed flank. The guns were hooked-up and ready to move with their ammunition caissons, the great, black muzzles of both nine-pounders peering menacingly from beneath their canvas covers. The horses had been tethered nearby where they slept standing up or chewed noiselessly at their nose-bags, great, lazy eyes swivelling towards the visitor. But this was all the interest that Pegg provoked, for the crews were wrapped in their blankets, tousled heads and beards just visible below the oilskin sheets that were pulled over them.

"Bong-jour, mong-sewer. Avez vous any cog-nack?" The Frenchman looked bemusedly at Pegg, merely cocking an eyebrow and muttering *"Bonjour"* in return.

"Votre chef, is he ici? Je needs to speak to him tray vite."

"*Comment?*" The Frenchman knitted his brow, wondered at the smell and shifted his carbine that was slung muzzle-down against the wet. "*Le chef est la.*" He pointed towards a row of sleeping bodies behind an ammunition caisson.

"Mercy-buckets, mon ami, I'll just have a look around." Pegg could hardly believe the sentry's *sangfroid*. He'd be damned if he'd let a wandering Frog scout about his lines looking for loot — still, that was

244

his ally's problem, not his, and these sort of opportunities didn't come his way every day.

The Frenchmen had obviously had a sleepless night judging by the snores in the early morning light. Their breakfast fires had been doused but were still just smoking and over by two horses that were tethered separately was a miniature folding table and two leather-seated chairs. In the middle of the table were a silver pepper and salt set and a brown glass bottle — the precious "cog-nack" — set for the battery's officers, Pegg had no doubt. On the other side of a fodder wagon a French orderly washed plates and cutlery in a bucket of water, his uniform covered with a grimy white apron. He was the only person other than the sentry who was awake, but, fortunately for Pegg, his chores absorbed him. With a quick look to see that no other eyes were upon him, the lad palmed the cruets, pushing them deep into his left coat pocket — his mum would be the talk of Wirksworth with those on her table — before sliding the bottle home on the other hip. Trying to move silently, making sure that his boots scuffed no stones, Pegg did his best to saunter back towards the sentry.

"Couldn't find votre chef, mon ami," he grinned, "but it don't matter, got what I came for, mercy tray bien." Pegg nodded vigorously, flipped the French gunner a faux salute and added in quieter tones, "That'll teach you to turd on the back of your trenches, you dozy twat," before walking away, a study in nonchalance.

No challenge followed, no harsh cry in French. The sentry just shrugged at the malodorous figure as it scuttled away, pulling his arms tight around him to keep the damp and cold at bay, whilst wandering up and down his beat trying to conquer his weariness.

"Come on, you lot, get up for pity's sake." It was an hour and a half before daybreak, time to rouse the men for the military ritual of stand-to when everyone, no matter how exhausted, dragged themselves from their blankets, put on their wet equipment and shuffled to their battle positions. Morgan had watched the Sergeants whacking the side panels of the bell-tents with their canes, heard their familiar oaths and heard the occupants coughing and cursing sleepily inside. But, despite Sergeant Ormond's calumny concerning the occupants' parentage, in one canvas pyramid no one moved,

"Devil take you, get up!" Morgan yelled through the fabric, before unlacing the door flap and peering into the blackness inside. Four inert forms lay there, still in their blankets, a warm, smoky fug filling the place. "Here, you help me with this lot." Morgan, half-in, half-out of the door yelled to a dark, passing form, for he knew immediately what had happened.

A zinc bucket, a quarter-full of still-smouldering charcoal, stood in the middle of the tent floor. One of the soldiers had, obviously, brought it inside hoping to warm the place and dry the men's clothes, despite the warnings that they had been given that the embers would eat the oxygen and might poison them.

"Richardson, get that one outside, quickly now." Morgan dragged one of the recumbent forms by his armpits, as his companion, a nineteen-year-old from Leicester, took another by the ankles and pulled for all he was worth. In a welter of damp wool and rumpled greatcoats, the rescuers soon had the four bodies outside in the chilly air, fanning hard at their faces, pinching their cheeks, trying to detect vital signs in the dark. Three of them soon flickered back to life, trying to sit up in the soaking grass in their shirtsleeves and socks, coughing, moaning gently and holding their heads. But Prince, an older man who had re-enlisted after service as a corporal in India, wouldn't respond.

"Here, Richardson, push Prince's lungs when I tell you." Finn, the groom, had once told Morgan how to revive a drowned man and, whilst he'd never had to do such a thing, he supposed it was worth a try now. Holding Prince's nose, Morgan crouched over him, clapped his lips to his patient's and blew gently, wagging his hand to Richardson to show when he should push.

"Bloody hell sir, the bugger's alive." The pair of them had massaged and blown for what seemed like an age, but now Prince's chest was falling and rising by itself, then his eyes blinked open and he coughed as Morgan sat him up.

Unnoticed in the dark, Sergeant Ormond had realized there was a crisis; now he stooped over the litter of spluttering bodies. "Damn me, Prince, I know you want yer rank back, but you don't 'ave to kiss Mr Morgan, you know!"

Despite the four men who had to report sick, stand-to went as normal. Now the half of the Grenadier Company that had been allowed a night in their beds were plying their weapons with oil and rag whilst their breakfasts were prepared by every fourth man.

Satisfied that nothing more had gone wrong, that no more of his boys had "woken up dead" as McGucken would have it, Morgan walked over to the central, kitchen fires where the other half of the Company, who were coming from the trenches, were having their meals prepared for them. And there were other attractions — the duty cook this morning was Mary Keenan.

"Well, what culinary delight d'ye have for us this morning, Mrs Keenan?" Morgan pulled his muffler right up around his ears, smiled only with his eyes whilst the troops were around and just happened to brush the sleeve of his coat against Mary's bare forearm.

The girl stirred gently at the big, oval, soot-stained cooking pot. The fire crackled and spat below it, Mary shifting her position around the iron tripod to avoid the shifting, wafting smoke.

"Well, I like to think it's what Cain and Abel would o' called a 'mess of pottage', Mr Morgan, sir." Mary didn't catch his eye, but her arm lingered against his.

"Well, it's a mess, anyway." Morgan liked this joke a little more every time he heard it. "Bacon-rind, biscuit, oats borrowed from some idle matelot's saddlebags an' as much potato as Mrs Polley could find, your honour. It may not be much, but Ma and Da would have been glad of it back in the famine and this lot'll swallow it rightly." She nodded towards Whaley's party that had just arrived in camp.

Mary couldn't resist a dig at him: she never missed the opportunity to underline the difference between them, but her arm continued to brush against him at every turn of the ladle. Any retort would just invite a sharper one from her, so Morgan said nothing, savoured the smell of wood-smoke and cooking and realized how odd it was not to be bone-weary.

"Now, sir, Mrs Keenan, that smells like a bit o' all right." Sergeant Whaley, exhaustion temporarily at bay, grinned at the pair of them even as his fingers touched his cap in salute. "Is it almost ready, love? The lads are on their chinstraps an' need to turn in. What is it? It smells grand."

"Aye, Sergeant Whaley, give it ten minutes to warm right through, though. It's one of my specials, the Frogs would call it *bouillon d'intestin*." The Sergeant frowned blankly. "Mrs Polley's got some stew ready, yonder, I should get the lads over there first." Mary's scrawny friend poked industriously at another steaming cauldron.

"Corporal Parsons, leave the weapons for now. Get the lads over to Mrs Polley, snap's ready." The sergeant threw his voice over to the gaggle of men without effort. He would hang back until all of them were fed, though he might just take a bit of soup to tide him over.

"How was it, Sar'nt Whaley, lose anyone?" Morgan held his hands to the cooking fire.

"No, sir, dead quiet. Relieved some Zouaves 'oo were a right bunch, and the Thirtieth took us off. I'm a bit worried about young . . ." Before Whaley could finish his sentence there was an exaggerated stamp behind them as Drummer Pegg thumped to attention before throwing Morgan a magnificent, quivering salute.

"Morning, sir, everyone." The boy beamed, his bruised eye now yellowing fast. "I got some cog-nack off of the Frogs, like you wanted, Sar'nt."

Sergeant Whaley would rather not have the boy telling an officer that he had given orders to loot their allies — and, anyway, he hadn't. There was no point in saying anything, though, he was just glad that Pegg was back and apparently sober.

"I'll stick it in the soup, sir." Before the cook or anyone else could remonstrate, Pegg had whipped the cork from the bottle and up-ended it over the pot. "By God, sir, that'll put lead in yer pencil."

Mary almost smiled at Morgan.

"Don't put the 'ole bloody lot in, son, save a swat for us, can't you?" Whaley watched longingly as the pale brown liquid splashed into the soup. But it was too late, the bottle had been emptied.

"Right, then, it's hot enough, here's a wee taste for you, John Whaley." Mary's ladle found a bit of meat and some oats and a half-inch of broth before she passed it, steaming hot across to the sergeant. Pegg watched delightedly. It was his skill, his daring that had added such piquancy to the soup. Not only that, but the first to taste it would be his Sergeant and his officer. Whaley blew carefully at the tin ladle's bowl. First he sniffed its richness, then just dipped his tongue in the liquor to make sure that he wouldn't burn himself, before he threw back his head and drained the lot.

"Oh, Jesus Mary," Whaley half-choked and cursed as he spat the liquid across the grass, ". . . that's vinegar, not bleedin' cog-nack, you silly little bastard!"

CHAPTER
NINE

Dawn at Inkermann

He was a funny little man. Pennefather, the Brigade's pugnacious, blasphemous commanding general held his spurs to his horse's flanks as he trotted up the scrubby slopes of Shell Hill to visit Morgan and the 95th's pickets. In his wake followed a trail of other horsemen, Major Hume the commanding officer, McDonald newly promoted to captain and filling the post of adjutant that the Alma had left vacant, an aide and — more expensively mounted than any of them — Richard Carmichael. Even at seventy yards Pennefather's Tipperary tongue could be heard lashing incessantly through the cool, afternoon breeze, questioning, probing, seeking answers to which he listened intently.

Carmichael had briefed Morgan and the senior NCOs of his Company the night before about Brigadier-General Pennefather's visit. "And I don't want any idleness or smart answers when the General asks a question. You all know what he's like, he'll look in the men's pouches, check weapons for rust, see that they know the order of the day — be generally bloody meddlesome."

Taken a leaf out of your book, then thought Morgan.

"Just make sure the men agree with everything he says and don't croak about the rations or how much sleep they're getting. Right, I trust that's clear. The commanding officer and adjutant will be with him — it's important for the company that this goes well."

Important for Richard-wretched-Carmichael's career, more like, but Morgan kept his thoughts to himself.

The 95th had seen much more of their brigadier lately and he was gaining a reputation as a hard, brave man who spoke directly to the troops in language they understood. Not for him the detachment of the Staff nor the distant feudalism of the gentrified officers who clustered through this army. Morgan guessed that a glassy, brainless reply from the men would irritate their fiery little Irish general more than anything else and, besides, the troops weren't like that any more, for the doltish, thoughtless obedience of peacetime was long gone. In its place was a self-possession and confidence that had been forged in battle. If the soldiers were spoken to honestly by a senior officer they would reply in the same currency — and there wasn't a damn thing that Lieutenant-bloody-Carmichael could do about it.

The horses were reined in, blowing gently, just as they reached the gritty clearing where McGucken and Morgan waited. "Bloody hell, sir, the commanding officer and adjutant haven't got their greatcoats on. Mr Carmichael did say that we were to be in cold-weather dress, didn't he?" McGucken fretted.

"Yes, he did, but he's got his coat on and a face like a dose of pox — don't worry about it." Morgan smiled inwardly at Carmichael's evident discomfort.

But Pennefather swung down cheerily enough from the saddle, wrapped in a sheepskin *poshteen* that proclaimed his earlier hard campaigning in India. Both waiting men took a stiff pace forward before snapping to the position of attention, Morgan bringing his hand to his cap, McGucken slapping the sling of his rifle.

"Sir, Colour-Sergeant McGucken and Lieutenant Morgan, commanding the forward pickets of the 95th's Grenadier Company, sir." Morgan went through the ritual.

"Yes, yes, goddamn you. Stop all that barrack-yard clap-trap, I know you lot right enough. How are you, Colour-Sergeant?"

Pennefather grinned and reached out to shake McGucken's hand. The Scot fumbled with his weapon before stretching a mittened hand, slick with rifle oil, towards Pennefather, a surprised smile showing through his beard.

"Fine, sir, and yerself?" That a brigadier-general would bother with just a senior NCO was remarkable — Carmichael's frown deepened.

"I'm prime, thank you, but what scrapes have you been letting Mr Morgan get into?" Pennefather reached towards the young officer's bayonet-torn coat, pushing his fingers through the rents and waggling them.

"The moths have been at him, sir, I'm always having to grip him about his turnout." A genuine ripple of laughter spread through the group, though it didn't quite reach Carmichael.

"Moths be damned, lead more like: what is it about the Ninety-Fifth, you're like magnets to the bloody stuff? Look at Hume and McDonald, more sieves than soldiers." The commanding officer and adjutant glowed with pleasure as the general drew attention to their flirtations with death. Daylight showed through a shot-hole in Hume's epaulette whilst stuck in the whistle-holder on McDonald's cross-belts was a Russian bullet. Morgan hadn't seen him since the day after the Alma when the Scot had been showing off the saucer-sized bruise on his chest that the round had caused.

Without taking his eyes off Morgan and McGucken, Pennefather gently smoothed the hairs that grew around a new, livid scar on his own horse's flank before handing the reins to his aide. "Now I've heard all about you testing the thickness of the Muscovites' skulls with your glass a few days ago, young Mr Morgan of Cork. Tell me what you think Russ will do next." Pennefather was smaller, older, grizzled against the subaltern's youth and vitality, but there was an immediate empathy between the two Irishmen.

"Well, sir, I believe they'll have another go up here at Inkermann. We saw 'em off when they last tried it, but that was only a reconnaissance and now they know how we'll react next time. The problem is that if they come up on the blind side of Shell Hill we won't see them until it's too late and if they get enough guns up they could silence ours over yonder . . ." Morgan indicated the main British positions on Home Ridge three-quarters of a mile away, ". . . quick as you like."

"You're right, of course. Russ had six guns up here in no time the other day and the ground is so broken down there that he's got any number of covered routes to advance up once he's out of Sevastopol." Pennefather peered at the deep, scrubby ravines flanked by great, craggy ridges that led up from the Tchernaya valley below them. "And the rumour is that reinforcements are on their way from the interior of Russia. Any signs?"

"Last night's picket reported large flocks of sheep and shepherds on the heights opposite, sir." Carmichael, neatly dressed and with no sign of battle on his clothes or equipment, cut in quickly rather than let Morgan — his so valiant junior — monopolize the General. He pointed across to the area of St Clement's monastery on the other, Russian-held side of the valley.

"When did you get to know this?" Pennefather rounded on Carmichael, instantly cross.

"This m . . . morning, sir, when the night picket made their report," Carmichael stammered.

"Well, that's hours ago, I need to know these things faster, Carmichael. Large flocks mean large numbers of troops on the move and if they're on that side of the valley they won't have come out of Sevastopol, will they? They'll be coming from the north, just where any reinforcements will be approaching from. You've got to be quicker with the passage of intelligence like this." Carmichael wished he hadn't spoken. "Go on, young Morgan, what else?"

Conscious of his audience, Morgan tried to be as unassuming as he could. "Sir, the few defences that we have over at the Sandbag Battery," Morgan looked towards a disused two-gun battery, invisible in the scrub, ". . . and the Barrier," he pointed below them to a loose, stone breastwork that dominated the Post Road snaking out of the steep Quarry Ravine, ". . . can't see each other, let alone support one another with fire. We haven't got enough men or guns to hold this flank against a determined attack. Should we not dig more positions and get the French to lend a hand?"

There was an embarrassed silence. How would the General receive this subaltern's heretical suggestion that the British should be helped out by the French? No one came to Morgan's aid whilst they waited to see which way Pennefather would jump.

"You have a point, Morgan." The sighs of relief from colonel, adjutant and company commander were almost audible. "But the problem is that the whole focus is upon getting those goddamn trenches and parallels close enough to the town for an assault to take place before the fucking weather gets any worse. If I suggest to milords that we should take time off from worming away towards Sevastopol in order to make things safer up here, I'll be counting blankets back in Horse Guards quicker than kiss yer arse."

Predictable chuckles greeted this.

"Why not use some of those Turks that are loafing around in Balaklava to do the donkey work, sir?" Carmichael tried to make up some lost ground.

"Because, Carmichael, as you so rightly point out, they're bloody idle. It takes as many of our boys to supervise the useless gits as there are of them. Didn't you see how they ran the other day from the Redoubts

257

on the Causeway?" Even Morgan winced for Carmichael.

The tension was broken by a soldier who slipped quietly through the brush before coming to a startled attention in front of so many officers and horses. To McGucken's relief he was tolerably smart, his weapons freshly oiled.

"Go on, boy, ignore us, say what you've come to say." Pennefather put the man at his ease.

"Your honour, I've been sent by Sar'nt Whaley to tell Mr Morgan that them flocks of sheep are a-moving and that a couple of what look like commissariat wagons have been seen with them." The soldier reported confidently and well.

"Where was you born, son?" Pennefather asked.

"Dublin, sir." The soldier looked surprised and pleased to be asked such a question by a general.

"Dublin, eh, what about ye?"

"Doin' rightly, your honour."

"That's good work, my boy." Pennefather deliberately made the man feel that it was his efforts and his alone that had brought such crucial news to his attention. "I reckon that something's brewing, Hume and that young Morgan here may not be too far from the mark. Fetch my horse, will you, I must get back to Division and tell them all." Pennefather pushed his boot into the stirrup, threw his leg over the saddle with practised grace and, gathering his reins, continued, "You've got as good a pack of hounds here as any in the Army, Hume, but try not to let the likes of Morgan be so damned bold, will you? We'll be needing every bloody man in the near future if I'm not mistaken. You've done well, good luck to you all." The general and his aide spurred away through the brush with the 95th standing rigidly at the salute.

"Well done, the Grenadier Company." The commanding officer was obviously pleased with the way the visit had gone and, despite Carmichael's earlier hamfistedness, the news that had sent Pennefather away in such a lather. "Please tell Sar'nt Whaley that he's done well and let me know at once if you see anything more of interest." Hume and his Adjutant reined their horses around and trotted off on a path through the shoulder-high scrub.

Carmichael dismounted, holding his thoroughbred's bridle in his right hand whilst gently stroking its nose with his left. "Thank you, Colour-Sar'nt. If you'd like to get back to the men I just need to have a word with Mr Morgan here before I come and inspect the pickets."

McGucken hesitated for a split second, knowing quite well what was coming. But it wasn't his place — the mutual loathing of the two subalterns was officer-business and nothing to do with him. With a "sir" and a stamp, McGucken turned about and made off.

"So, Morgan, you've quite made your number with friend Pennefather, haven't you? You had to wear your heroically torn coat — it doesn't impress the men you know, they expect an officer to be above such behaviour."

Morgan was taken aback by the venom in Carmichael's words. "But it's the only one I've got and the damn thing's not been off my back since it got ripped — you told us to be in our coats." Morgan was immediately cross with himself for being so defensive. Pennefather had picked him out in front of the commanding officer, whilst Carmichael had looked an ass. Why didn't he just say so?

"Now get back on duty and try to behave like a proper officer should."

One day, Richard Carmichael, I'll show you what being an officer's really about, thought Morgan, but all that he could manage was, "Very good, sir," before he trudged back to the men and another sleep-starved night.

"Where in God's name d'you suppose they've got to, Sar'nt Ormond?" Morgan whispered.

Once the thick, sticky fog had taken hold just after darkness fell, the order had been given by the duty field officer to pull the pickets back from their forward positions on Shell Hill to their rallying points on the lower slopes.

"Buggered if I know, sir. I posted 'em hereabouts, but it all looks the same in this dark and shit, don't it?" There was a real note of concern in the normally stolid Sergeant's voice.

Morgan had passed the order on to his NCOs and in dribs and drabs the men had come wandering back in to form a shorter line of sentries that was easier to control but which could not foil an enemy sally as

260

quickly. Eventually, they had all returned except for Little and Shaw, an old hand and a younger man, who had been posted within spitting distance of where the Russian sentries normally stood. After Ormond and a corporal had blundered around for an hour or more in the cloying fog, and still returned empty-handed, Morgan realized that he would have to lead the search himself.

The story of the picket of the 55th who had been silently overpowered by the Russians loomed large in both men's imaginations. On a stormy night a few weeks earlier, fresh sentries had looked in vain for the men whom they were to replace. At first light they discovered nothing more than crushed grass, broken twigs and one slightly blood-stained belt. No shots or cries had been heard and so the legend of wraith-like Cossacks who stalked their prey with nothing more than wickedly sharp knives had been born. The story had its uses when it came to keeping exhausted lads alert on sentry, but now those Cossacks seemed awfully real and frighteningly close.

Each bush seemed to take on human form as the pair tried to stick to the little goat tracks in the brush, the fog weaving in and around the branches as silently as the imaginary Cossacks. The damp would almost certainly have got to the charges in Morgan's pistol and Ormond's rifle, making both utterly unreliable, so they picked their way slowly forward, sword and bayonet outstretched.

"Blanket," hissed Ormond into the fog and dark, hoping to hear "pillow" as the answer to his challenge.

261

There was almost always an irony in the daily-changing password that was designated and issued by Divisional headquarters. Usually it revolved around food, drink or women but today the joker who thought it up had decided to concentrate on another commodity that was in short supply — comfort. There was nothing but silence in the drifting fog . . . or was there?

"Listen, Ormond, can you hear something?" whispered Morgan.

"Yes, sir, I thought I did, that's why I chall . . ."

"Hush . . . there!" Morgan cut Ormond off for out of the stillness and the slight rustling of the leaves came a strange, rasping noise as if someone or something was fighting for breath.

"I can't mek it out, sir, we'll 'ave to get closer."

The officer agreed with a slight nod and the pair eased forward as gently as possible trying, in the dark, to stop twigs from whipping noisily back across their path.

Then they found them. Little and Shaw lay at their feet, face down and quite still, rifles below their bodies pointing towards the Cossacks. In the dark it was almost impossible to see what had happened to them until that curious, choking noise came again from young Shaw's throat as both men's backs rose and fell rhythmically.

"They're fast a-bleedin-sleep, sir, I don't believe it this close to the enemy." Ormond whispered his outrage.

"Wake the stupid bastards up, Sar'nt Ormond. Take their names and get them on report tomorrow morning. The commanding officer will have to deal with this." Morgan was furious, not just with the utter stupidity of what the men had done, but also with the seriousness of the offence and the disgrace that it would bring.

"Mr Morgan, sir, can I mek a suggestion that ain't exactly right but might be better for everyone?" The snoring continued as Ormond made his case. "If we report this we'll lose two men for weeks whilst they serve their sentence or recover from the lash. Usually, they're fair to middling good an' we can't afford to be any more short-handed. Besides, the company will lose its name. You know how much is being asked o' these boys — just walk away a few paces, sir, an' let me sort it out."

Morgan could see Ormond's arguments perfectly. Too much was being demanded of the men who, as they would put it themselves, were permanently, "chin-strapped". They rarely got more than a few hours' sleep, the food was hardly enough to sustain them whilst the physical work and danger were remorseless. Yet if these two men were taken away for field punishment the strain would be all the greater for the others. Besides, hadn't he found himself pecking like a hen just the other night? But if the other soldiers found out that he'd been soft on these two then . . . well, he just didn't know, but it was a risk he was willing to take. He nodded almost imperceptibly to Ormond and walked off a distance into the bushes.

There were muffled oaths and curses as Ormond kicked both men awake. Angry mutterings followed answered by plaintive whispers. Morgan heard a fist meeting flesh, a slight cry, then another thump. There was silence for a moment then a few more angry, inaudible words before the trio pushed their way towards him through the foliage.

"Found 'em, sir. Their relief must have missed their way an' these two didn't want to leave their posts to go a-lookin' for them." Ormond's story might have been more plausible had Shaw not been holding his coat-cuff to his nose.

"Anything else?" The brigade commander's worries about enemy movements were at the front of Morgan's mind. McGucken had questioned all of the men as they came back down the hill about what they had seen or heard, now Morgan demanded to know every detail.

"Not really, sir. There's more than the usual din from the church bells in 'Pol — just like there was before the last sortie — but they're always clanging the bastards, an' it don't signify. No, it's the wagons that a couple of the full-screws thought they heard that worry me." McGucken wasn't normally worried by anything.

"You heard what the general said about enemy reinforcements. Tell me again what the NCOs thought they heard, please." Morgan pressed his Colour-Sergeant.

"Well, sir, both Corporals James and Cleary said that they heard heavy wagons or maybe guns moving towards the town on the other side of Shell Hill. Nothing they ain't heard before, but they was worried when the major pulled the pickets in 'cos we can't hear

264

nothing from this far down the slope." McGucken voiced Morgan's own fears.

Morgan understood why the duty field officer — today Major Grant from the 41st — wanted to shorten his picket line in the fog, but he'd never forget the last time that the Russians had crept up unseen over this same piece of ground.

"Well, there's nothing else for it, Colour-Sergeant, I'll have to go and take a look for myself. Find me someone as an escort, please."

"Do you 'ave to, sir . . . all right, but just don't get yerself killed, Mr Carmichael would never forgive me — he wants to keep that pleasure for himself." McGucken smiled; "I'll send young Pegg with you, you'll be too busy looking after him to find extra drama, but you've only got a bit more than an hour before stand-to, so don't fanny about, sir."

So it was that for the second time in a couple of hours, Morgan found himself stalking his way forward through the foggy, dripping leaves of Shell Hill. But instead of a trusted NCO beside him, this time he had only Drummer Pegg. The boy's rifle and bayonet were almost as long as he was tall and he held the weapon so firmly that his knuckles showed white. With eyes darting madly and pink tongue hard at work on his downy lips, all Pegg's normal bluster seemed to have left him.

"So what do we do if we do see any o' them Cossacks, sir?" It was the second time Pegg had asked.

"They won't be Cossacks, Pegg, just ordinary old Muscovites like the ones we thrashed at the Alma. Fire at their bellies or give 'em a few inches of steel if they get that close and then run like the devil back to the Company — I won't be far behind." But even the homely description of the enemy did little to steady Pegg.

On they crept; Pegg's nervousness so infected Morgan that every time the lad jumped at the swirling fog, so did he. Eventually the slope flattened out as they reached the hill's crest and Morgan beckoned to Pegg to flop carefully down and listen. Both men lay prone, mouths open to amplify any noise. At first it was hard to hear anything beyond the distant bells in the town, and Morgan's attention began to drift. He wondered where Mary was now and if she gave him even a thought. Her last words to him when he'd been with her in the back of the hospital cart — "It's all or nothing" — were as clear now as they had been when she said them, yet he doubted that she appreciated exactly what they meant. How was an officer — and a Protestant one at that — meant to give up everything for a soldier's wife? And that was another problem, how the hell was he going to manage when James Keenan — Sergeant James Keenan if you please — came back to the company? Quite apart from anything else, was he going to survive the fighting and . . .

"Sir, can you hear that?" Pegg suddenly hissed. The boy had been a parody of attentiveness ever since they'd arrived, mouth wide, hands cupped behind his ears just as he had been taught in training. He'd constantly twisted his head back and forth, his hands making him look like an ill-kempt fieldmouse, until

266

he'd heard the noise. "Wheels, sir, lots of 'em down in the valley." He'd heard just what the others had. Morgan pulled himself from his reverie, listened hard for a moment then he, too, picked up the incessant rumble. Satisfied at last, he led the boy back down the hill just as the first glimmer of dawn lit the fog.

But Morgan's urgent, flapping hand and tense shoulders soon had Pegg sinking to a crouch, rifle at the ready. The officer had sensed them before Pegg was even aware of any danger. Yards away and just visible were two, grey, great-coated figures, their soft caps and weapons just discernible. They were muttering to each other, unaware that they were being watched.

"They're ours, sir, reckon its Ben Jenkins and Johnny Peat." The boy's lips were inches away from Morgan's ear. They certainly looked like their own people, but what were they doing this far forward when the pickets had been withdrawn? Perhaps McGucken had sent a couple of lads to look for them — but had they been gone that long?

"Blanket," Morgan challenged, just loud enough to be heard by the pair. Both stiffened, shrank down in the brush and turned towards them.

"Hey Ben, Johnny Peat, it's us." Pegg spoke quite clearly and rose up to make himself obvious in the murk — it was almost the last thing he did. Two stabs of flame lit the mist accompanied by guttural shouts

"Fire, Pegg for pity's sake." The lad brought his rifle to the shoulder and squeezed the trigger, but nothing happened except the pop of the percussion cap. "Go, boy, I'll hold them." Pegg dashed downhill — he didn't need to be told twice. Out of the corner of his eye he saw Morgan throwing himself at the enemy, his sword slashing in the mist. He ran as hard as the branches would let him until some inkling of duty pulled him to a halt. If he arrived back in the company without his officer he would never live it down, so he turned about, trying to control his breathing and steady his heaving bayonet.

He didn't have long to wait. Crashing trough the bushes behind him came Morgan.

"Over here, sir." The young officer swerved hard in his direction, gasping for breath. In the half-light Pegg could just see the crimson stain on Morgan's blade.

"Have I done something to upset Jenkins and Peat? And when did they learn Russian? Never, in the name of all that's holy, do that to me again, Pegg."

"No, sir, sorry, sir." The drummer's eyes were round with fear. "I think I can hear the company just over there, sir."

"I hope you're right, boy, and it's not some more of your mates from Moscow!"

Close at hand, through the wisping mist, came the coughs and scuffles of several men and Morgan could just pick out the start of the earthy bank that his company used as a rallying point. But this was the most dangerous part of the whole patrol. Just before the night picket handed over to the day picket, all the troops would be roused, alert and ready to fight, each weapon pointing in the very direction from which the pair were now coming. The men were jumpy for they had picked up the officers' and NCOs' worries and on top of this the recent firing suggested that Russians were nearby — fingers would be itching to pull triggers.

"Now Pegg, just let me do this, will you — no more bloody shouting out or any of that damned malarkey that nearly got you plugged when you'd been out shooting rabbits: remember?"

How could Pegg forget it. He was still due a flogging for that scrape — he nodded sheepishly.

"Get down on your belly, boy, and do as you're told." Morgan lay down next to the drummer before raising himself up on his arms and bellowing, "Blanket! as loudly as he could into the fog before instantly dropping flat in the coarse grass."

The tension in the sudden silence to their front was palpable. Murmurings and coughing ceased, there was a pause and then, in broad Nottingham, "'Oo the fuck is it? Get 'ere with yer 'ands 'oop."

Both of them rose from the ground, arms held high and walked towards the disembodied voice.

"I think you mean, 'pillow', don't you, Carlton," Morgan chided as he stared down the muzzle of a rifle that emerged from the gloom.

"Oh aye, sorry, sir." The soldier lowered his weapon, grinning with relief at his officer. "We was on the lookout for you, sir, 'ave you got that young twat Pegg with you, we 'eard firing?"

Pegg, damp and bedraggled followed behind, "I'll give you, "twat", John-bleedin-Carlton, next time you come whining round me for a hot brew." All Pegg's bravado had returned now that danger was past.

"Stow it you two. Where's the Colour-Sergeant, Carlton?"

"Yonder, sir," Carlton nodded towards the next thicket, "day picket's just arrived, Forty-Seventh int it?"

Morgan moved through the gloom, half-seeing his own troops who were still silently scanning their front. One of their own guides had led the new picket of the 47th with a subaltern at their head, up to McGucken. Now a knot of figures stood talking quietly.

"Och, sir, was that you hangin' away? You didn't manage to get Pegg shot, did ye?" McGucken was clearly relieved to see his officer in one piece.

"No, it was them banging at us, I fear. I slashed one of 'em," Morgan saw how the 47th's officer cocked an eyebrow at him and immediately regretted mentioning it, "but Pegg's rifle missed fire, we'll need to draw all of the charges when we get in."

"Aye, sir, I was just tellin' Mr . . . sorry, sir, it was Mr Jocelyn wasn't it — that it'll be hard as hell to keep their firelocks dry in all this . . ."

As if to prove McGucken wrong there was a rifle shot not ten feet away followed by a yelp. Before anyone could react one of the 95th's Grenadiers came trailing tendrils of fog, towing another, his face screwed up in pain, weapon and cap missing.

"It's Strawson, Colour-Sergeant, his rifle just went off by itself." To underline the point, the soldier thrust Strawson's hand forward for inspection, a ragged, oozing hole showed white with bone splinters just behind his thumb, whilst his palm was black with powder burns.

"Strawson, you stupid bastard, how many times 'ave you been told never to put your hand over the muzzle. Get it dressed, someone." McGucken knew at once that Strawson would never return to duty. Such an accident was bad enough, but the fact that it happened in front of another regiment was doubly galling.

"Listen, Jocelyn," Morgan knew the 47th officer a little from card schools in Varna and he was keen to distract him from this embarrassment. "Russ is busy again and he's got his pickets well forward. We heard heavy traffic all night in the valley and I fancy that the reinforcements that've been talked about may have arrived. But it'll be hard to know anything until this fog lifts."

"Fine, Morgan, thank you. You just get your boy with a hole in his paw back to hospital, the Forty-Seventh can handle things."

He'd always suspected that Jocelyn was a supercilious clown — now he knew it.

Morgan left the men starting the laborious process of drawing charges. As he returned to his tent looking for dry clothes and something hot to drink, the Sergeants had been attaching steel corkscrew-like, "worms" to the end of the troops' ramrods, before pushing them down the barrels and twisting the teeth of the harder metal into the soft lead of the bullet. But the rifling of the Minié made this a tricky operation and with only four worms amongst the sixty-odd men, it would take time to get every rifle clear, dry and ready to be reloaded.

271

"Thank you, Peters." He'd only just been given a new orderly. A small, slightly timid, older Lancashire man, Peters had twisted an ankle at the Alma. What he lacked in confidence, though, he made up for in the way that he looked after his officer. A scalding mug of hot chocolate had been waiting for him: now he sipped at it whilst pulling off his cap, his sword-belt and pistol.

"Jaysus, that's good and hot, Peters, you made it yourself?"

"Aye, sir, I did. Now, gimme your cutlery and pistol, sir, an' I'll get 'em oiled." Peters limped to reach the weapons.

"Thank you, deal with the sword first, if you please." But as Peters drew the blade from its scabbard and looked at the crusted blood, his face fell, but before either could say anything a spatter of firing was just audible on the dawn breeze.

"D'ye hear that Peters?"

"Aye, sir, it'll just be the new pickets blazin' away at nowt. You know how green most of the other regiments are." But there was another rattle in the distance. "If they don't give over soon, though, sir, we'll all be turned out again an' your chocolate will get cold. Best drink up."

Morgan had to smile to himself. So, Jocelyn and the 47th could handle it could they? They'd probably seen a lonely Russian scout and now the whole of the picket line was turning good powder to smoke and hot air.

"I don't know how you get that chocolate so hot, there wouldn't be a drop of milk would there?" Morgan had just handed his mug back to his servant when a gut-wrenching noise shattered his complacency — with a screeching brrr a heavy gunshot flew past the tent. "Christ, Russ must have got guns up on Shell Hill — we've been caught bare-arsed for a second time."

Another shot ricocheted off the ground so close to the tent that grit and dirt were hurled against the canvas.

"Give me my belt, Peters." Morgan grabbed it from his servant who was as white as the tent's canvas, but getting it round his waist was a different matter. His hands shook: time after time he tried to fit the snake buckle; he only succeeded in getting it done up by devoting every bit of his attention to it and shutting out the cracking gunfire. *Christ, I can't let the men see me in this state.* He was appalled by the weakness in his legs and the churning of his stomach. Thank God that Peters was there for he had to control himself in front of him. At last he had all his equipment on and he turned to leave the tent.

"'ere, sir, it's a bit cooler now." The servant passed him the remains of the hot chocolate whilst Morgan wished that he could say the same for himself.

"Thank you, Peters, but I need this more." In one practised movement he grabbed his silver hip-flask that had just been refilled with brandy and pulled heavily at it. Then he realized what he'd said. Did he really "need" it? Certainly, its fire calmed him and his hands were steadier — but he dreaded the men smelling it on his breath.

Almost as if stepping out into sheeting rain, Morgan hunched as he left the flap of his tent. No sooner was

273

he outside than there was a mighty crash from a tent close by — its canvas flew apart, spewing the contents and a crazily-twisted trombone skipped to a halt a few feet away from him.

That'll cost us a king's ransom, he thought inconsequentially. The band's instruments — bought out of the officers' pockets — had been stored all together and now lay ploughed and broken by a roundshot.

"Will you be back for your dinner, sir?" asked Peters shakily.

I doubt I'll be alive by dinner time, thought Morgan as he rushed towards the men's lines.

There, all was chaos. In the early, foggy light the troops ran to gather up their kit and clothes. Most were still attending to their weapons when the firing started, but some had stripped down to shirtsleeves whilst others were hopping about trying to get their sodden boots back on. Everyone except McGucken was struggling into their belts and equipment as shot after shot bounded through the lines of tents. Only the colour-sergeant was ready. In truth, he'd been too busy supervising rifle cleaning and breakfast after he returned from duty to look after his own needs, but that didn't matter now. Like a slab of Scottish granite he strode amongst the men, encouraging here, admonishing there, issuing clear orders that restored the men's confidence.

"What d'you think, Colour-Sar'nt?" Morgan asked as he galloped up.

274

"Just like we said, sir, Russ saw that we'd done fuck-all after the last set-to an' now he's crept up in the mist and got a brace o' batteries up there at least. I counted two volleys o' twelve, sir, did you?"

Morgan marvelled at the man. Whilst he'd been worrying about the smell on his breath and whether he'd see dinner time, McGucken had been counting the enemy's guns as calmly as if he'd been on a field day at Chobham.

"God's teeth, sir, there's another battery." More balls skipped through the gloom, though this time further off to their left, followed by a ripple of bangs. How McGucken could count them was quite beyond Morgan.

"They're firing blind through this fog, sir, but they're making good practise."

"Indeed, they'd have got the range last time they fooled us," Morgan replied ruefully.

"We've only got about half the old charges drawn, sir. Permission to break cartridge?" In emergencies, rather than drawing the rounds with worms and ramrods, the NCOs would use the combination tools that they carried to unscrew the nipples at the breeches of the men's rifles before pouring dry powder from a new cartridge over the damp charge. Then the nipples would be replaced before the rifle was re-cocked, a percussion cap fitted and fired. The theory was that the fresh powder would detonate the old charge and clear the barrel. Most of the time it worked, but the random discharges, especially in these confused circumstances, were dangerous and very unsettling.

"Yes, of course, get on with it, Colour-Sar'nt, and lie the men down, they'll be less vulnerable." Morgan could see that the process had already started, but McGucken had wanted to cover himself. As the ranks formed up and fell flat in rough lines, the occasional shot was already being fired into the heavens as rifles were cleared.

"What in God's name's going on, Morgan?" In the din he'd not noticed the rattle of the hospital wagon and the hooves of horses. Mary and Mrs Polley had come trotting up to their battle positions with Carmichael in close attendance. Mary stood up in the cab, scanning the mist. As she saw Morgan, the frown left her face, a half-formed wave dying even before she raised her hand.

Carmichael swung down from the saddle of his gelding and passed his reins to the women, his face a combination of dislike and fear. In fresh, dry clothes the company commander was a stark contrast to the rest of them. As he approached, another Grenadier fired his rifle into the air to clear it, the sharp crack making him duck.

"Take that man's name, Colour-Sar'nt." He was visibly angry.

"Sir, we've having to clear the weapons by firing them." McGucken was just as cross.

"Why, and who gave you permission to waste cartridges like this?" Even in the surrounding cacophony the two men's furious voices carried to the troops around them.

Morgan could see the men turning curious, worried faces to listen and watch. He knew how unsettling a scene like this amongst their leaders would be for the men who were frightened enough already, but before he could intervene, McGucken took matters into his own hands.

"If you'd been up on the hill with us last night instead of chasing quim around the hospital lines, then you'd fuckin' well know why we're clearing the weapons, Mr Carmichael, sir!"

Nearby soldiers became intensely interested in the fog as the Colour-Sergeant spat his reply.

Morgan watched Carmichael closely. It was one thing for him to be insubordinate to Carmichael — although he'd been placed at the head of the company they were still the same rank — but for an NCO to speak to an officer like this was completely unacceptable. Already he was calculating which sergeant would take over once McGucken was sent to the rear under arrest — but to his amazement Carmichael folded like a pricked blister.

All his overweening self-confidence suddenly disappeared; he seemed to shrink physically as he silently admitted defeat.

"I s . . . see, Colour-Sergeant, you should have explained." His authority had gone: now he could hardly be heard above the gunfire.

The adjutant's arrival could not have been more timely. Like a cameo part in their own, domestic drama, McDonald cantered up on his charger, studiedly relaxed and apparently indifferent to the firing. "Carmichael, good morning to you. Would you oblige me and double your company up to the battalion's right, as fast as you like?" The Scot tightened his reins to stop his horses from fidgeting nervously. "Seems like we were right, Russ has tried the same trick again but this time mob-handed," he yelled against the noise.

We? thought Morgan. He could only remember one lonely voice — his — pointing out the vulnerabilities of the Inkermann flank to the Brigade commander.

"Attend to the commanding officer once you're formed-up, if you please, and listen out for his bugler, if you can hear anything at all in this *bourrach*."

"Sir" replied Carmichael meekly as the adjutant rode away.

With a few crisp commands McGucken had the company on its feet, faced to the left and doubling away up the slope of the hill, rifles "trailed" parallel to the ground. To the men's right trotted the two officers and Pegg as their bugler. Morgan watched Carmichael's back as they ran. The confrontation with the colour-sergeant had changed everything — for whilst Carmichael had always been able to depend on the regulation loyalty of the men, after the last scene he could never command his company's respect again. Despite everything that had happened, Morgan had a sneaking sympathy for his brother officer.

The 95th were well in-hand. The Grenadiers were the last company to form up with the rest of the battalion behind the British gun positions on Home Ridge.

There, as the mist roiled around him and the Russian balls skipped and bounced Major Hume sat on Charley, his charger, waiting for his company commanders.

"Ah, Carmichael, glad the Grenadiers are with us. Now, gentlemen." A shell cracked blackly overhead, hot iron splinters kicking the dirt up all around Charley's hooves, yet Hume was unruffled. "There are rather more Muscovites than we might have hoped for and we're the only reserve that general Pennefather has. The three companies of the Left Wing are to move off immediately to reinforce the left flank. I'll command the Right Wing: we're to remain here with the guns until the general orders us forrard. Colours stay with me, Grenadiers to take the right of the line. Any questions?"

The six officers knelt in the grass and brush, notebooks and pencils (sharpened at both ends as they had been taught) ready, looking up to their commander. Things couldn't have been clearer: they had practised operations by Wings many times — the difference was that after the Alma and the last Russian sortie none of them was under the least illusion about the blood and death that hovered about them and their scruffy, exhausted, much-loved men. Carmichael swallowed heavily.

Almost immediately the Left Wing was ordered to reinforce the breastwork they called The Barrier. Brisk musketry could be heard from there through the mist, but the three companies moved off without a backward glance leaving Major Hume's wing of the 95th lying down amidst the flying metal and grit, awaiting orders. This really wasn't the best place for infantry to wait. Whilst there was some cover from the sandbag and gabion positions of the Division's artillery, the flashes of the British guns were obvious, even in the fog, and the Russians concentrated their fire upon them. A cocktail of roundshot and shrapnel bounced and burst all about, wounding and killing gunners and infantry alike.

Morgan hated this inaction more than anything. Looking around him he could see how all the others pressed their bodies into the ground more earnestly than they ever had with a woman, yet none seemed to shake like he did. He felt as if everyone knew that the ground trembled not with the guns but with his terror. To his front a nine-pounder crew went about their business. The gun crashed regularly as it replied to the half-seen Russian flashes on Shell Hill opposite, each belch of smoke thickening the mist. But in an instant the rhythm of the gun-team collapsed. A thump and spray of dirt saw two gunners clutching at their faces whilst a third jerked, kicked and twitched on the ground, a bubbling choke coming from his mouth. A fraction of a second before he had been a husky, muscled lad, sweating as he swabbed and rammed at the gun's bore. Then the round had caught him on the right hip, just as he was turning, almost cutting him in two, throwing the remains to the ground. Morgan saw the great smear of blood on the grass between two piles of torn cloth and flesh and he noticed how the boy's eyes, even with injuries like this, blinked for a few seconds before death arrived.

"Come on, you." Morgan grabbed the men either side of him by their cross-belts and pushed them up towards the gun. But their surprise subsided as soon as they realized that they were being made to do something useful rather than just wait for death. "Get up to the gun — lend a hand with the ammunition." Both soldiers slung their rifles and ran over to the lance-bombardier who was preparing rounds and charges at the limber. Morgan lifted the long, wooden rammer from besides the dead gun-number and reported to the bombardier in charge. "Just tell me what to do, Bombardier, I've got a bit of an idea." Morgan could see how wise Major Hume had been in insisting that all officers knew something about gunnery.

"Right, sir." The NCO looked a bit bemused at the events of the last few minutes, but the wallop of another passing ball soon reminded him of reality. "Just poke the next round down the bore when it's offered; push it right home, sir."

Two flushed, whiskery gunners came trotting up, looking surprised to see infantrymen at the gun-line but clearly glad of the help. One placed a cotton bag of gunpowder — the charge — just inside the muzzle before the other pressed the black, glistening ball and wooden *sabot* on top of it.

"Righto, sir, ram as 'ard as you please." The smooth tempo of the team had gone, but with an awkward grunt Morgan thrust the stave down the barrel until it could go no further. "Now, sir, get yer sponge wet there," the gunner pointed to a bucket full of oily water and the young officer dipped the woollen "sponge" that was attached to the other end of the ram into it, ". . . now just stand clear whilst we fire."

As soon as the charge was home, the bombardier stuck a metal pin down the touch-hole to expose the charge before fitting a copper initiator on the end of a lanyard. Now he squinted down the barrel towards the enemy, twitched the elevation wheel minutely before hopping to one side and dropping his hand, the signal for the lanyard to be snatched tight. A fizz at the breech was instantly followed by the gun's great bark as the recoil pushed it back several feet.

"Come on then, help to get her back in position," the bombardier chaffed at the infantrymen good-humouredly, ". . . and sponge her, sir, if you please." Morgan pushed the soggy wool down the barrel knowing how important it was to extinguish any smouldering bits of lint before fresh powder was introduced. "Well done, you lot, we'll make gunners o' you yet." The Bombardier was humouring them as they bumbled around the gun position. But whilst their efforts were better than nothing they simply couldn't compare to a properly trained and practised crew.

It could have been minutes or it could have been hours. Morgan seemed to be ramming and sponging for ever, twirling the great Staff around him as men dashed about with powder and shot and shrapnel rained down. Eventually a gunner officer came puffing up with three new men.

"You've done well here, we're much obliged to you." The man was dismounted and very flushed. Judging by the mud all over his legs and back, he'd already had excitements of his own.

"I'm damned if I can count the enemy's guns, can you?" To Morgan it was now just one long ripple of fire.

"Not accurately, there's too many of them now — at least fifty or sixty."

"Dear God, that many? I hope Pennefather's got some more reinforcements a-coming." Morgan was genuinely surprised by the gunner's estimate — ten times more guns than the enemy's last sally.

"Don't think so. Seems that they've held Russ over there," he pointed to the left of the fog-shrouded field, ". . . but I've just come from the Sandbag Battery — the Muscovites are over it thicker than fleas on a dog. My guess is that you'll be needed down there soon enough." He gave a worried little smile; "Hope your pouches are full."

Indeed: the idea that the Russians were already in one of their main defences and that three depleted companies of the 95th were all the reserves that remained chilled Morgan. He reached for his flask.

CHAPTER
TEN

The Sandbag Battery

"Pegg, go on picket, Pegg, get the brew on, Pegg, duty-bloody-bugler — is it the only bastard name they know?" The four of them loped down a sheep-track in the brush towards the shouts and firing, the chubby drummer hard on his officer's heels.

"I can take any amount of misery from the Russians, Pegg, but your moaning murders me — will you please hold your tongue?" Morgan was hollow with fatigue, hunger and fear. He'd also had quite enough of Pegg for one day. "Wait, get down you two." Pegg and Carlton squatted in the bushes beside the track, weapons ready, whilst Morgan walked back past them to speak to Sergeant Ormond.

"Just like the Alma again, sir, thee and me." The NCOs grinned a solid, reassuring grin. Now he waited to see what the officer would tell him to do.

As the company on the extreme right, the Grenadiers had been told by the adjutant to send a patrol out to the flank and investigate the situation at the Sandbag Battery. With Carmichael commanding there hadn't been much choice about who would lead it. So Morgan, with the gunner's words that the Muscovites were "thicker than fleas on a dog" at the front of his mind and a sinking stomach, had taken the duty bugler — Pegg — and the trusted Sergeant Ormond and Private Carlton to find out exactly how bad things were. As they left Home Ridge there had been shouts and shots, volleys of high-pitched cracks from the rifles of the 41st and the flat boom of Russian muskets to guide them through the fog.

But as they got closer, the firing died down to just an occasional bang. Things seemed to be under control until, when they were even nearer, they could hear the low rumble of grunts and curses, the clash of metal on metal, ragged cheers and a great collective gasp and thump of bodies more like a rugby scrum than a fight.

"Why's all the firing stopped, Sar'nt Ormond?" Morgan found himself whispering despite the noise all around them.

"Dunno, sir. Must be at each other with the steel. They're only just ahead, sir, want me to go an' 'ave a look?"

Morgan's eyes narrowed. Had he given the impression of hanging back, of being "sticky" as the current *argot* had it? "No, thank you, Sar'nt Ormond." The Sergeant wouldn't think that of him, would he? Not after all they'd been through together, surely? Perhaps he'd smelt the Dutch courage on his breath. As he moved to the front of the patrol he cupped his hand to his mouth and nose and breathed out to check: he had. Pulling his pistol out with all the confidence he could muster, Morgan said, "Follow me," and pushed the branches to one side as the bestial, furious noise grew louder.

There, just where the ground fell away to a much steeper slope and the brush grew less thickly, was the Sandbag Battery. Thirty feet wide and twelve feet high, it had been designed with embrasures for two heavy guns. Morgan could remember the sweat of helping to build the thing and everyone's bemusement when no guns were ever placed there (Carmichael had warbled some damn nonsense about its being built "just in case the Russ placed guns on the other side of the valley"), but it did have its uses. Anyone who had been on picket on that flank had been grateful for its shelter and the bogus reassurance that the hessian and earth walls gave. Still, it served no tactical purpose that he could see.

The gunner had been right: the enemy was bitterly determined to take the battery. A few on both sides tried to reload their weapons, but most, just as Ormond had thought, were at it hand-to-hand, toe-to-toe. There seemed to be no more than a couple of dozen of the 41st on the home side of the battery, though there must have been more, for Morgan could see both Colours in their great varnished leather cases — they bobbed about in the hands of their ensigns like two big, black rockets. The rest of the 41st stood like a wall stabbing, clubbing, butting any Russian who dared to jump into an embrasure or to sweep around the side.

The Muscovites swarmed like wasps, their bayonets clashing on the barrels and blades of the defenders who resisted madly. There were a handful of dead or wounded within the Battery and as Morgan watched a young Russian leapt from the top of the wall, lost his footing and was seized by his belts by one of the 41st who tripped him to the ground. Another held him still with a boot on his chest before deliberately, slowly, positioning his bayonet on the side of the boy's neck before jabbing it firmly through the flesh and arteries as the blood spurted from his nose and mouth as from a slaughtered sheep.

The British just sucked for breath and swore, the occasional word coming from the NCOs, whilst their enemies yelled as they rolled forward. Then to the left the Colour party was suddenly in trouble. A mob of snarling Russians dashed forward at the subalterns and their escorts, bayonets levelled and Morgan saw one Colour grabbed by a Russian, but the ensign clung to the pike with both hands and the struggle developed into a tug-of-war between the two of them. The pair circled and jerked until a Colour-Sergeant stepped in with his rifle-butt — just as McGucken had done at the Alma. The Russian fell back, clutching his face, whilst still more flooded into the ruck.

"Come on, lads, we can't let Russ take British Colours," Morgan beckoned with his pistol whilst Pegg and Carlton looked on blankly.

"No, sir, this ain't our fight." One of Sergeant Ormond's arms was thrust restrainingly across the young officer's chest. "Besides, look there."

A clutch of silent 41st charged to save their own honour. An officer led, slashing the head of a Russian corporal with his sabre. The enemy fell back from the

287

onslaught, both Colours were lifted up high as around them bayonets found their mark and rifles rose and fell, with the distinctive thump of brass butt-plates meeting fragile, yielding flesh. On the edge of the mêlée, Morgan saw one soldier pull a bayonet twisted at right angles from a Russian stomach — he hurled the now useless weapon away but still kicked viciously as the man went down. In moments the threat had evaporated. A blanket of Russians lay moaning or still amongst their foes. In the tangle of limbs one hand was raised up, its fingers slowly opening and closing.

"Sir . . . sir, we know enough now," Morgan was transfixed by the carnage, but Ormond pulled him away, ". . . if we don't get our lot up here damn quick, the Forty-First will be overrun."

"You're right, Sar'nt Ormond," Morgan replied, ". . . lead on." Whilst he lingered watching the fight, the NCO and men needed no more encouragement and set off uphill as fast as they could on the path through the thicket. In no time Morgan was alone and he found himself running to catch up with them. He'd just caught sight of Carlton's cross-belts when a bugle, invisible in the brush, blared a few dozen yards in front of them. It was distinct, each note well formed but it sounded a call that none of them had ever heard before. Ormond brought the two privates up short as Morgan puffed-up behind. Now, despite the artillery overhead, Ormond also whispered:

"Whose was that call, sir?" British units started each bugle signal with a few bars unique to them. "Never 'eard it before."

"I don't know, it's new to me, too." The urgent notes came again, just to their front. "Might be reinforcements from another Division . . . push on, but be careful." Morgan was caught between an overwhelming desire to get back to the comparative safety of his own battalion as fast as possible and the need for stealth, but no sooner had they started off again than Ormond stopped, Pegg and Carlton bumping into him.

Morgan just had time to see a clutch of figures on the path a few yards in front of him. As he stared over his own men's shoulders, one of the strangers turned to look at him, the green at his collar and the black cross-belts instantly recognizable as no regiment he knew.

"Russians — fire for God's sake!" Why did he have to keep tripping over the enemy at such close quarters, he wondered; it never seemed to happen to any of the other officers. But the thought was snatched away as all three of his men fired almost as one.

It was good shooting. Three greatcoated figures sprawled beside the track whilst the others scrambled away into the woods, hastened on their way by a round from Morgan's pistol.

The British ran forward.

"I got that fucker, din't I?" Pegg pulled the forage cap from his dying victim and stuffed it in his pocket, whilst Carlton merely looked down sadly at his torn, broken man. Ormond's bullet, though, had only wounded the third Russian, a younger soldier who lay on his back, kicking at the earth, pushing himself away from the British, uncertain whether to pray for mercy with both hands or to keep one clapped to his heavily bleeding ear.

"*Nyet, spaceba, nyet!*" A bugle trailed from one of the boy's black belts and as Sergeant Ormond raised his bayonet to finish the job he shrieked, "*Christos, Christos, nyet!*"

Now it was Morgan's turn for restraint. "No, Sar'nt Ormond, don't. Take him prisoner."

"Aye, yer right, sir." The blood-lust had instantly gone from the Sergeant. "Stop buggerin' about you two an' reload. Come on then Russ, on yer feet." The boy jumped up and, propelled by an almost playful jab from Ormond's blade, skittered up the path, blood soaking into his collar.

As they reached the 95th, the companies were already preparing to move. Morgan told Sergeant Ormond and Carlton to return to the ranks as he and the prisoner escorted by Pegg playing the victor for all that he was worth, went in search of medical aid and the adjutant.

"Here, tell him to hold this on his ear," Mary passed a wad of bandage to Pegg, pointing to the Russian, ". . . I'll deal with him when we've dressed our own lads."

All softness had gone from the girl as she knelt next to an unconscious man whose shoulder was gashed and bleeding hard. The enemy's artillery had taken a toll of the men as they waited. Most had been wounded by splinters and they all sat or sprawled, some moaning quietly but most just pale, shocked and silent. To one side lay a half-dozen men whose shoulder-capes had been pulled over their faces. Their dead fingers were still curled as if around their now absent weapons.

"Mary, are we about to move? D'you know where to?" Morgan saw the same hands that he had kissed tearing and knotting the dressings expertly.

"How should I know, Mr Morgan, sir, I'm not the commanding officer, am I?" The answer came back hot and tart. "They say there's to be a general attack with the Guards to retake the Battery. Have you just been there?"

"I have, though I saw no Guards — plenty of Russ, though." He immediately regretted the last phrase.

All Mary's toughness vanished. "Mother of God, Tony, be careful." The great brown eyes blinked with fear whilst a blood-stained hand no bigger than a child's rested on his arm. He desperately wanted to kiss her.

But, "Have you seen Major Hume?" was all he could say.

"Aye, over there." That same hand pointed through the mist as another ball flashed overhead.

He ran through the strangers of Number Five Company who were picking themselves up, pulling down their coats and belts and settling their equipment before he came to Hume and his adjutant, McDonald. The major was already in the saddle, the adjutant just mounting.

"Ah, you're back, Morgan, what news?" Hume looked down enquiringly.

"Sir, the Forty-First were just about holding on to the Battery when we saw them, but there's not many of them. The enemy are doing their damndest to take it and on the way back we bumped into a group of light infantry who'd got some way up the hill behind us." He tried to be as brief as possible.

Hume and McDonald exchanged glances. "'Some way': can't you be more exact, boy?" Hume frowned.

"Sir, about three hundred yards I would say and that must be five and twenty minutes ago, now."

"Right, the Guards are supposed to be forming-up somewhere hereabouts, we're to protect their left flank." Hume paused for a moment before adding, "D'you think you can guide us?"

Morgan's stomach tightened; he licked his lips. "I can, sir."

Morgan led the stuttering column back down the same paths. Anxious to find the Guards and not to lead the whole Wing in the wrong direction, he pressed on hard through the bushes, only to be told by Ormond.

"Hold hard, sir, you're losing them."

The column had concertina'd behind him. He'd quite forgotten that one man could move three times faster than a column in thick country, especially when visibility was so poor. To help him find his way, though, incessant ripples of firing were now echoing from the Battery again with redoubled shrieks and cheering. Clearly, fresh troops had already arrived to prop up the defenders.

Almost before he knew it, Morgan burst into a clearing some way to the rear of the Battery. The fog was less dense and he found himself amidst a group of bearded, bearskinned Guardsmen, all intent on the fight to their front. In the middle of them, surrounded by a group of other horsemen and easily recognizable as a member of the Royal Family, was the Guards' divisional commander, the Duke of Cambridge. Despite his jowls and whiskered face, at thirty-five he was by far the youngest of the major-generals and he'd done well at the Alma. Now he stood in his stirrups, tugged at his forage cap then settled himself back in his saddle. Just off to his left stood the Grenadier Guards' Colour party. Like everyone else, their flags had remained furled in their cases, the escort clustering round the subalterns trying to find comfort together as the musketry, artillery and yelling rose in another crescendo. More of the 95th followed Morgan and soon a group of them stood, waiting for their officer to tell them what to do.

One of the Duke's party spurred his horse over to Morgan. "Who are you?" The young officer in the blue frock coat and cocked hat of the Staff struggled to make himself heard. "How many of you are there?"

"Sir, Mr Morgan, I'm guiding a Wing of the Ninety-Fifth, we've been told to support you."

"Good, we need it. Can you get your commander up here to speak to the duke?" His horse jibbed at another storm of fire in the Battery.

"Sir," Morgan broke away, leaving Ormond to collect the men, and dashed back up the path, bumping straight into a very pale Carmichael. At the mention of the Duke's name, though, he brightened and insisted that he be taken straight to His Royal Highness.

293

"Good: Carmichael, was it? I'm damn worried about our left. Get your commanding officer to form up over there," the duke pointed to a gap in the trees someway to the left of the Battery, ". . . but impress upon him that he must stay on the high ground, there's too many Muscovites to go chasing down into the glens. Is that clear?"

The proximity of blue-blood was almost too much for Carmichael. "Yes, Your Highness, Sir George Cathcart's Division is also on its way — he's my uncle." But this nicety went unremarked by the duke who merely nodded into the din before walking his horse back to the rest of his party.

For a moment it seemed as though Carmichael had become his old self again, his confidence and arrogance had returned. He told Morgan where to gather the Company and in which direction they were to face before haring back up the path to find Hume and to pass the duke's orders on to him.

"Bet that's the last we've seen on 'im, sir." Sergeant Ormond waited till Carmichael was out of sight.

"I'm surprised at your lack of charity, Sar'nt Ormond," replied Morgan, "if a royal duke's here, I can guarantee Mr Carmichael will be back."

About half the company had arrived and were being shaken out into line by the NCOs as another wave of attackers crashed against the Guardsmen holding the Battery. Not fifty yards in front of them British and Russian dashed and stabbed at each other, the defenders' bearskins bobbing in the fog and powder smoke. More and more of the enemy were climbing

294

onto the flat top of the Battery's wall, firing down into those inside whilst others lapped around its flank, threatening to engulf the ever shrinking band within.

"This is a fuckin' mess ain't it, sir?" Colour-Sergeant McGucken had been marking the rear of the company's column, now he flopped down in the grass beside Morgan, a bead of sweat slowly running down his forehead.

"Aye, Colour-Sar'nt, it is. Have you seen Mr Carmichael? D'you know what he wants us to do?"

"No, sir, he was going in the wrong direction last time I saw 'im — just for a change. We'd better do something about this though, sir, or the Guards'll be done for."

He was right, the Battery would fall unless they acted. Morgan knew that Major Hume would expect to use all three companies together, but the situation was dire and Carmichael had told him nothing of what the duke wanted. As he tried to decide what to do, more Guardsmen were falling; as he dithered his men turned tense faces towards him expecting orders. His hand went for his flask but fell away.

"Right, Colour-Sergeant, get them on their feet." The decision made, he instantly felt better.

The NCOs had been expecting this and in a flash the men of the company were up, settling their equipment and, even before he could give the order, reaching towards their left hips.

"Fix bayonets!" He'd had the same sensation at the Alma when he'd told the men to load with live ammunition. How many times had he given the same

295

order on the barrack yard, never dreaming that, one day, he would say it in earnest? But now the order was being repeated down the line and sixty or so long, thin slivers of steel sang from their scabbards and clicked home over the rifles' muzzles.

"Prepare to advance." Again, the command was repeated by the NCOs. The bayonets came down level with the men's waists. Some made sure that their rifles were cocked and that their percussion caps were firmly in place and ready to fire, but most just stared at the insanity into which they were about to plunge.

"Advance." The line belched forward, Morgan sighting along his sword-blade at a Russian's cross belts. Where was that indecision now? He had no need for a pull at his flask or, indeed, anything except the sweet release of action.

"Charge!" The men had been forcing the pace as they closed with the Battery. They stumbled into a run through the long grass; a primeval, animal growl arose that Morgan had never heard before from these boys.

The Russians hadn't seen them coming. Exhausted Guardsmen were barged aside as the 95th hit their enemies like a wall. Some aimed and fired at point-blank range, the heavy bullets throwing the Russians to the ground, but most went in with the bayonet.

Morgan saw that it was a fresh enemy unit: they had white belts and red collars and cap bands and they looked older than the others that he had seen this close. All had tanned faces, luxuriant moustaches, their boots were caked in mud and they fought with a determination that was new to him.

McGucken was where the company colour-sergeant should be, just to the officer's right and rear. Now he pounced on one of the enemy who parried his blade but who then stumbled until his back was against the sandbag wall. McGucken feinted with his bayonet, the Russian floundered with his and almost lost his balance as he tripped over the casualties on the ground. Too late, for the burly NCO's blade flashed low at his foe's stomach, before it skidded off the double thickness of serge greatcoat and lodged deeply in a sandbag. The force of the thrust had the two men pressed almost face-to-face, their weapons useless. But McGucken's "Glasgow kiss" ended things. His head came back before snapping forward onto the bridge of the serf's nose. Even in this din Morgan heard the bone splinter. The man's knees buckled just as surely as many others had on Sauchiehall Street.

All this left the colour-sergeant exposed, though. Another Russian lifted his musket and bayonet ready for a deadly thrust into McGucken's back, but Morgan was there. He struck in exactly the same way that he would with an uppercut with his right, except that his hand now held his sword. Every ounce of his strength was behind the thirty inches of steel that met the Russian's throat just below the jaw. Morgan saw the point go in, a dab of blood and his foe almost left the ground as the blade jarred heavily against his backbone. The musket fell with its owner, whose body slipped

297

smoothly off Morgan's sword. Morgan had never killed at such close quarters before — he felt nothing.

"Thank you, sir, a pretty stroke. Bastard almost had . . ."

Before he could finish his thanks, though, another attacker dashed at them through the press of struggling bodies. He threw his musket up within inches of them, there was a scorching flash and concussion, but through the gout of smoke McGucken skewered the man through the cheeks. His long blade caught his enemy just in front of his right ear, banged his head hard against the bags where it stuck, spitting the Russian firmly. Then one of the Colour-Sergeant's boots came up, stamped hard against the man's ribs and held him there as the gory blade was withdrawn. The Russian sagged unconscious onto the growing pile of bodies at the base of the wall.

"Go for their throats and faces, boys, not their bellies." McGucken had seen how the Russian coats could be proof against their bayonets, yet he also knew that the men would instinctively attack the stomach as they had been taught.

Heeding his words, a Guardsman fighting alongside threw his whole weight behind a thrust just as his enemy did the same. The British blow caught the Russian in the eye, the blade sinking its whole eighteen inches in the man's face and emerging from just behind the right ear, bits of spongy grey matter sticking to the steel. At the same time, the Russian had struck just as hard but low. Morgan saw how the shaft of the weapon went straight through the Guardsman's body, its point ripping his coat in the small of the back, staining the off-white leather of his belts red with blood. Both men gasped, the Russian's head tilted sharply back, transfixed, the Englishman slowly toppling backwards. They fell away from each other, their weapons exchanged in death.

The 95th's arrival had helped to staunch the flood of Russians on the left. Now Morgan's men, having driven the enemy back to a respectful distance with the bayonet, started a rapid fire from the flank that tore into the enemy's column. Just a few yards to the right, though, the enemy pressed forward against the wall of the Battery as densely as ever. The Guards had been in action for an eternity now, almost all their cartridges had gone and many of their bayonets were bent or broken — now they fought with anything that came to hand.

"Sir, give me a hand will you?" Their own men were busy blazing away at the Russians, so McGucken was searching the pouches of the dead and wounded for cartridges. He'd taken off his cap and was filling it with the paper tubes: Morgan did the same. They pushed forward into the mass of Guardsmen, thrusting rounds and percussion caps into filthy, blood-stained hands.

What he saw at the Battery's wall was to stay with him for ever. A tall Grenadier Guards officer stood on top of the stacked bags cheering for all he was worth. Like some ancient warrior he was hurling stones and boulders onto the heads of the Russians below, more brickbats being passed up to him by the sea of bearskins. Every so often a braver head would appear

299

over the wall to be kicked squarely in the face by one of the officer's boots.

So that's what Eton teaches you, thought Morgan.

All the time shots and a rain of stones, branches, sods — anything that came to hand — whistled past this hero, but nothing touched him until a brick found its mark. The thrower was invisible to Morgan on the other side of the wall, but his aim was true, catching the officer full in the face and sending him staggering back, tripping and falling into the tumult.

A great shout went up from the defenders for their captain, whose bloody face was just visible being wiped by one of their bandsmen. Then from the crowd came another young officer. He straightened his great fur cap, took a cheroot from between his lips and bawled, "We must clear these rascals. Who's with me?" Pistol in hand, he climbed up and into the embrasure, paused, fired two shots and leapt into the thronging enemy.

But the British troops hesitated. Screams and shots came invisibly from beyond the wall, but still no one moved. Morgan pushed the cartridges he was carrying into the pockets of his coat, grabbed a rifle and bayonet from the ground and elbowed through the mob to the embrasure.

"Come-on, then, I thought you were the Queen's favourites . . ." Even in this chaos the taunt stung the Guardsmen, ". . . aren't you going to follow your officer?" Turning, he clambered up through the gap in the hessian sacks, jumping down onto the rough ground and bodies beyond.

300

He braced himself for the pack that must attack him, but they already had another target. At least half a dozen Russians jabbed and stabbed at the young Guards officer who was now slumped against the bags. Bayonets rose and fell, piercing the man's chest, face and neck endlessly. Each thrust pushed another gasp from his dead lungs, though his damp cheroot stuck to his bottom lip, wobbling with each stab. Morgan saw how the officer must have thrown up his arms to shield himself from the blows; one of his assailants' blades had pierced his forearm right through and now the Russian was trying to drag it clear. The more the attacker tugged at the blade the more the Guardsman's arm and torso followed like some ghastly marionette.

But the Russian was easy meat. Morgan had never attacked anything fiercer than sacks of straw before with a bayonet and he was surprised how little resistance he met as the needle-sharp steel met the nape of the man's neck. The weight of the rifle made it easier and he tried not to dig the blade too deeply in case it stuck. The man dropped his own weapon and sagged to his knees, his hands scratching at the air, all fight gone from him.

Despite his caution, the dying man took Morgan's blade and rifle with him, just as he had feared. But, with a quick stamp from his boot against the back of his victim's neck and a sharp pull, the bayonet came clear — just in the nick of time. An expressionless Muscovite stopped prodding the Guards officer and whirled at him, his musket ready to strike. With a silent prayer, Morgan fell to one knee and squeezed the trigger. To his relief the rifle jerked back against his thigh, the round hitting his enemy and passing straight through his body to wing another behind him who hobbled away squealing.

Then they were with him. Guardsmen enraged by the slaughter of their officer, a shabby, almost blown bunch of his own men with Sergeant Ormond at their head then, also puffing hard, McGucken. It was difficult to judge how long this contest lasted. No one fired as both sides hacked and clubbed at each other. At first the Russians held their own until McGucken and two giant Guardsmen decided the matter with their rifle-butts. It was too much for the enemy who fled over the plateau into the bushes below.

"Come on, sir, we've got 'em beat," Ormond beckoned the group off the ledge in pursuit.

"No, there's not enough of us, fall back into the Battery." Morgan was suddenly exhausted. All around him the men panted for breath, one or two pulling at their water-bottles.

"Damn that, yous scunners, who said you could drink? Reload, get the cartridges from the dead and clean the fouling off yer locks, sharp now." McGucken's anger pulled the men away from their own needs, corks being swiftly, guiltily pushed back into their big blue-painted canteens.

Morgan looked around at the horror. The ground was a sheet of bodies, a few moaning in pain, others in silent agony. Many just lay still, torn with bullets or pierced by long, deep wounds, some with faces that had been beaten to a bruised, bluish jelly by butts, boots or bricks.

"Will you look at that, sir?" McGucken lifted up his right arm, peering at the sleeve — the exertions of the fight had been too much for the seams, the scarlet of his coatee peeping out from below the grey serge of his greatcoat. "That's cheap, bloody, Army contractors for you."

"Sir, sir, it's the recall." Pegg was searching amongst the dead not, for once, for booty, but for a bayonet to replace his bent one.

In the relative calm, behind the Battery wall the mixed battalions of Guards and reinforcements from other Line regiments were being re-grouped by their non-commissioned officers, names being called and answered by the living — just silence from the dead and wounded. They were shouting to make themselves heard above the continuing thunder of the artillery and each other's voices, but clear above the noise the distinctive bugling was repeated. The preliminary bars of the 95th's own call came before the usual notes of the "recall".

"There, sir, off to the left, they want us back." Pegg had blown the same sequence often enough himself and there was no mistaking its urgency. So, the knot of 95th shuffled off from in front of the Battery's walls, some limping, some supporting others whilst comrades took letters, rings and other personal belongings from the dead.

"Where the devil have you been, Morgan?" Waiting well to the rear, behind a bank of Guardsmen was Richard Carmichael — he'd kept well within earshot of His Royal Highness. A few of the Grenadier Company had listened to his commands and stayed close to him: now they looked down, shamefaced as their battle-weary comrades trailed back.

"His Royal Highness and the Guards' Colours have been in grave danger." Carmichael was bellowing, not just in an attempt to re-establish his own authority, but also, Morgan suspected, to let the duke know how devoted he was.

"You think you command this goddamn company, well you don't," Carmichael was furious. A fleck of spit landed on Morgan's cheek. Fastidiously, he wiped it away with a hand covered in Russian blood. *You're so bloody scared, aren't you?* thought Morgan, as he stood silently to attention — there was chaos enough already and he wasn't going to add to it by open insubordination.

"Mr Carmichael." They had both been so distracted by their hatred that neither had seen the commanding officer trotting up through the gloom. He shouted down from his saddle. "Be so kind as to move your Company up to the right of Number Five; as quick as you can."

"But sir, His Royal Highness the duke wants us to stay here and help to protect his flank . . ."

And it's a damn sight safer here, thought Morgan.

"Thank you, Mr Carmichael, that's exactly what I intend to do and I'll be grateful if you remember that I command this battalion, not you." Morgan smiled inwardly at Major Hume's words — it was as if he had just heard their own altercation. Now Hume's normal urbanity had quite gone and there was no mistaking the ice in his voice: the soldiers looked away in embarrassment.

McGucken and the other non-commissioned officers sorted the Grenadier Company out as quickly as they could before doubling them a couple of hundred yards through the fog to join the other two companies. Captain McDonald was good at his job. He'd sited the Wing at the top of a steep ravine down which a great mob of Russians had retreated after their last assault on the Battery. Now words of command and drumbeats could be heard through the fog and gunfire and it was clear that any new attempt would come from here, plodding up the slope before falling on the Guards' left. But the Russian guns on Shell Hill couldn't plunge their fire into the depths of the ravine where the 95th's adjutant had put them. Other than for the occasional shrapnel round, they were as safe as anywhere on this death-stalked field could be.

Numbers Four and Five Companies stood easy, rubbing wet off their weapons, adjusting their equipment or smoking their pipes as nonchalantly as the constant symphony of death all around them would allow. Morgan half-expected a cheer from them when the Grenadiers came trotting up. It wasn't to be, though, for the rest of the Wing had yet to be blooded in this fight and they all but ignored his men. But then, the other companies always thought that the Grenadiers

305

— the 95th's own elite — were a mite too pleased with themselves: "gallus", as McGucken would say. *A hero's seldom honoured in his own land*, he thought to himself, mangling the Bible ruefully.

"Now then, Pegg, our kid." As the right-marker of Five Company stood Frank Luff, the lock of his rifle tucked snugly under his elbow to keep it dry, a pipe that refused to light between his yellow teeth.

"Eh up, Luffy, youth. Fine old pickle this — meks the Alma look easy, don't it?" Most of the other troops had wiped their bayonet blades clean after the last fight — but not Pegg. Casually he let Luff get an eyeful of the gore before he asked. "'Eard from yer Mam yet? Did she get Pete's bit of hair an' your letter?" The two friends had hardly seen each other since Frank's brother had been killed in September.

"Aye she did. 'Ad a couple o' pages from 'er since. 'Ardly mentioned Pete, just reckoned that 'e'd be in an 'appier place now an' told me to take care of meself." Pegg wished he hadn't asked — things were dire enough without reminding Luff of his mother's misery and constant worry. "I reckon that means she's taking it really bad."

"Aye, well, Frank you'll be all right, Number Five never does any o' the rough stuff, does it?" Pegg continued clumsily, looking at the depleted, threadbare ranks of his mate's Company, knowing that he was talking nonsense.

But before Frankie Luff could riposte, a lance-corporal and private of the Grenadier Company came bustling along the ranks pulling a pony that had wooden barrels strapped to both of its flanks. "'Ere you are lads, tek ten apiece." Pegg reached into the tub and pulled a fistful of cartridges from it, hardly counting them before dropping them into his pocket. Luff held out his hand. "You an' Number 5 don't need 'em, you ain't fired a shot all day," Pegg — all solicitude gone — was now at his cockiest, ". . . it's only the boys who do the scrapping that need more shot."

"No good anyway." Luff said quietly, dropping his hand. "Ain't right for our weapons, they're for the forty-two pattern."

Pegg pulled a cartridge out and looked at the round ball at the end of the paper. They were for the old, smooth-bored muskets that most of Cathcart's 4th Division still had and were no use at all with the Minié rifles. The stray horse had obviously been grabbed by some enterprising soul without first checking what it carried.

"If you were with 'Fighting Five' you'd know about these things, Pegg, my son," said Luff smiling gleefully.

There was no wind at all. Where the three companies stood at the top of the ravine the mist thickened, reducing any sight that the men might have of their enemy's advance and, at the same time, hiding the middle of the line from its ends. The troops waited in three ranks, fidgeting, tense as the noise of the Russians drew closer. Their bugles were shrill and clear, the drums less distinct at first as the slopes sent their rattle echoing back, then more sonorous, beating the time of the slow, deliberate advance up the slope.

Closer they came, closer, invisible in the mist, until the clink of equipment and scraping of boots on the earth could be heard clearly, menacingly. The 95th were silent, ears cocked, taking shallow, quiet sips of air — ready for whatever the fog hid. Then Morgan saw them. The haze cleared a little no more than a hundred yards to their front, showing a great mass of infantry, ten, fifteen times the number of the men who waited for them, shoulder-to-shoulder, trudging up the slope.

The front rank's bayonets were levelled but the columns behind had theirs raised up like some great metal porcupine. At intervals came the drummers, their sticks rising, falling in time with each other, beating that same, rolling tattoo on their polished brass drums that Morgan remembered so well from the Alma. Above their white cross-belts every mustachioed face seemed identical whilst their soft, red-banded caps were worn straight and level. They even marched in step up the uneven glen. Morgan thought of the barrack square — no amount of drill and shouting could reduce British troops to this sort of mindless obedience. The great, unstoppable, steel-tipped wave came slowly on, holy flags and icons bobbing above their heads, sombre priests marching with them.

"At one hundred yards, ready." The command from the centre was repeated down the line, floating through the fog. Rifles were thrown up to waist height: out of habit, the men looked down to adjust their sights, though there was no need — a round had yet to be fired at long distance in these conditions. Hammers were drawn back to "full-cock", forefingers checking

308

that the percussion cap was still in place on the nipple before returning to the right of the trigger-guard.

"Preee . . . sent." The non-commissioned officers prolonged the syllables and one hundred and fifty rifles flew to the shoulder. Morgan looked around at the screwed-up faces. Some cuddled their cheeks more comfortably against their butts, here and there startlingly pink tongues wetted dry lips whilst everywhere fingers caressed triggers.

He stole a glimpse along the ranks at Carmichael, his company commander. Standing, quite properly, at the centre and rear of the Grenadiers, he gawped over their shoulders, as pale as the chalky soil. At the last word of command he'd raised his sword: Morgan swore that he could see the blade shaking.

"Fire!" must have been shouted though he didn't hear it. The rifles crashed out in a great ripple, a swathe of powder-smoke darting down the glen, hiding everything.

"Reload!" he yelled, as right hands groped for pouches. All down the line men spat twists of paper away from the cartridges they had bitten open before ramrods were pulled from the wooden furniture below the barrels. Then, just as iron pushed lead down rifled steel, the enemy answered.

No volley came, just the cracks of rifles. The blunt columns of enemy infantry were surrounded by a cloud of nimble sharpshooters — the 95th already knew to their cost how lethal they could be. After the Alma, the men had picked up any number of pointed, thimble-like rounds as souvenirs — now just the same lead hornets sang around them.

"Fucking hell, can't you be more . . ." Pegg bit off his curse as Frank Luff banged into him. The lack of numbers meant that Pegg was having to wield a rifle rather than confining himself to a bugle. He'd fired at the same time as Luff to his left, then the pair of them had engaged in an undeclared race to reload faster than the other. Pegg was just ahead — he'd returned his ramrod to its holders and was just fumbling for another percussion cap when Luff quite spoilt his rhythm. But before he could utter another word, Pegg saw the top of Frank's skull: it was cracked and oozing like some giant, too-softly boiled egg after the strike of the spoon. A rifle round had struck him high on the forehead, the bone distorting the lead and sending it furrowing through the thin shell. Even as he staggered he was dead.

That'll be another lock of 'air for Frank's mam, thought Pegg dispassionately as his friend jerked convulsively at his feet.

"Preee . . . sent!" Came down the line again, then, "Fire!" as the rifles bruised shoulders once more. This time, though, a gust of wind wiped smoke and fog away from their front. Mechanically they reloaded, but the Russians had stalled. Their rear ranks hesitated — a few tried to clamber over the bullet-torn bodies in front of them, but most just stood there staring as the British muzzles came up for a third time. Officers waved swords, sergeants and corporals urged the men forward but as the Russians faltered so the 95th ached to be at them. There were no drums or bugle calls, no preparatory orders, just the simple, single, delicious word, "Charge!" that started with one voice somewhere in the fog and then was on everyone's lips. Bayonets were already fixed, rifles reloaded and like hounds off the leash, the line bounded forward.

"No, damn you, stand still. The duke has told us to stay where we are." But Carmichael commanded deaf men and no respect.

McGucken looked to Morgan — Morgan looked to McGucken. "Charge" — that word was so easy to say: Carmichael was so easy to ignore — and that's just what they did, leaping down the slope after the men in a murderous catharsis.

A spatter of shots felled one or two of the 95th, but the sight of even a few dozen wild-men shouting, spitting to be at them was too much. The ranks in front turned to run but they were held in the funnel of the gulley by those behind. A cry went up from the Russians, a low moan from the British as the two sides met. Morgan saw at least half a dozen Russians lie down shamming death, whilst others fell to their knees, hands raised up in supplication bellowing the now familiar, "Christos, Christos!" The quicker-thinking ones even held up crosses and icons to ward off their attackers.

A handful resisted bravely, but didn't last long. The other two companies had a point to prove to the battle-stained Grenadiers and fell-to with a will, lunging deep into the flesh of those who stood at bay, felling others with shots from the waist, whilst the crazy, cheering pack hurtled down the slope.

"Leave him, Almond, get after the others." Morgan saw how the young soldier's bayonet rose up starkly, aiming for the back of an unarmed Russian. Blood already stained the leg and skirts of the man's greatcoat — he was no threat. Almond did as he was told, lowered his weapon and caught the fugitive by the belts instead, throwing him to the ground before a kick from his muddy boot curled the man up.

"We're driving them, sir." Morgan remembered how Almond had fallen out of the march to the Alma, utterly exhausted: how they'd all envied his pasty Thirsk face as Mary had poured water down his throat. That same boy now stood before him grinning, lips grimed with powder, blood on his bayonet blade, his whole frame alive with vim and warlike confidence. How these lads had changed — the ones that were still breathing.

Sliding, skittering over the wet grass and grit came Hume and McDonald his adjutant still in the saddle — just. Even as he watched, though, the commanding officer's horse stumbled badly on the slope, Hume being almost thrown over Charley's head. It was too much for both horses and riders and they dismounted before the broken slope did it for them, taking pistols from their saddle-holsters and looping their reins over their arms.

"Morgan, where's Carmichael?" McDonald had lost his spectacles. He squinted hard.

312

"I don't know, sir, last seen just as we charged." Morgan fought for breath; he could confess his casuistry later.

"I ain't seen him either — can't see anything now. Is he struck? If you can find him in this damn haar, tell him to rally on us at the bottom of the slope. He's to go no further than the level ground." McDonald led his horse back into the fog to tell the other company commanders the same, Morgan assumed.

But to rally the men he would have to catch-up with them. Their victors' cries were now ahead of him in the fog, and he stumbled as fast as the ground would let him. Dead and wounded Russians littered the earth, marking the Grenadiers' path and off to one side, using the mist to shield themselves, sneaked an unarmed party of the enemy, intent upon getting back to their own regiments. He let them alone. Then booming through the mist came the unmistakable tones of Colour-Sergeant McGucken.

"Hod yerselves there. Yous two, stop there, God rot you." He'd read the battle better than anyone else, instinctively obeying orders that he had never heard. The men were now tired, they'd slaked their thirst for blood and needed to be taken in hand before they overreached themselves. The Russians had run, for sure, but there were plenty more lurking in the folded ground, re-grouping for the next assault. "Ah, there you are, sir, thought you'd gone back to keep Mr Carmichael company." McGucken grinned at Morgan before breaking off to chivvy the men who'd stayed together.

"The adjutant said we're to rally on the rest of the Wing, about here, Colour-Sergeant. D'you see anyone else?" Twenty or so of their own men were there and a few from the other companies, but there was no sign of the main body.

"No one, sir . . . Pegg, stop fannying about before I put the toe of my boot up yer arse." The drummer was going through the haversacks of the dead and dying Russians, taking the flat, round loaves of black bread that they all carried and impaling them on his bayonet as a snack for later. "Get those damn things off yer blade, we ain't finished yet. The rest of you, search pouches, re-distribute ammunition and caps: an' get water whilst yer at it."

Pegg, for once, did as he was told, but as he turned over a dead Russian to get at his canteen, he noticed a great, scaly-pink scar running up the man's neck. "Bloody hell, sir, this 'un's seen some fighting before. We did for 'im, though, din't we?"

"Aye, Pegg, these are veteran troops; probably picked that up from the Turks," replied Morgan.

"Pegg, stop distractin' the officer." McGucken's snap was meant as much for Morgan as for the drummer, but just as some calm was returning a hail of balls swept over them from behind. They all ducked into the brush.

"There's the answer, Colour-Sar'nt, I guess that's Number Five Company giving us a wee salute." Morgan tried to sound nonchalant. Mercifully, no one had been hurt and at least they now knew that the rest of the Wing were behind and above them.

"Got to be Five, sir, their shooting's shite," Pegg offered helpfully, peeping from behind a stout tree trunk.

"You two," Morgan spoke to a couple of lads who had attached themselves to his band, "go and tell your mates to save their powder for the Muscovites. We'll join them directly."

The pair set off into the fog, hooting and hallooing to identify themselves in the thickets. But there was another sputter of shots and in a flash, they were back, one without his hat, both wide-eyed.

"Sir, that ain't Number Five." Morgan's bladder tightened — he knew what they were going to say. "It's Russ, sir, dozens o' the fuckers."

What was he to do? The charge had cleared all of their enemies — hadn't it? The field was theirs, wasn't it? "Fucking dozens" of Russians had no right to be behind him and obviously ready to cut them off, had they? More to the point, now that the attack was spent, who was there to tell him what to do, what decision to take? He looked at his men. All of their exhausted eyes, even those of the battle-wise corporals and sergeants, were turned on him, expecting a decision. He reloaded to buy himself some time and as McGucken approached he pulled out his flask and offered it to him.

"No, sir, thank you, I don't need that and . . ." the colour-sergeant's voice dropped, ". . . neither do you." Morgan was ashamed of himself as he put it away, but the big Scot's very presence helped him.

315

"Right, we're going back up the hill to find the rest of the regiment." He was surprised by how confident he could make his voice sound. "Get into single file, try to avoid these goddamn Muscovites, use the fog. All loaded and got some shot?" The men nodded. Where they'd been noisy, clamorous in victory they were now quiet, shrunken in greatcoats that seemed too big. They all looked to him, suddenly conscious that the riotous charge had gone sour and that they were in a tight corner.

"Colour-Sergeant, bring up the rear if you please."

And with McGucken's grave "sir," the band set off uphill, weapons forward and eyes scanning the bushes for their enemies.

They didn't have far to go. Morgan heard the characteristic metallic clinks and jangles and the animal noise of a group of men no more than two hundred paces up the slope. Through the bushes he could just see a host of Russians milling about, looking to their muskets and pouches, with authoritative voices rising up from time to time. They were obviously forming up for another attempt on the Battery — but with a slice of luck they might just be able to get past them before they realized who they were. He raised his hand to halt the column, took off his cap and stuffed it away, silently signalling to the rest to do the same, for other than their head-gear, the two sides looked remarkably similar in their long grey coats and belts. He'd heard that the Guards had tried this trick when they were in a similar fix — it had worked for them.

They had to stick to the goat track, to do anything else would look damned odd, but it meant that they would pass within yards of the nearest Russian. If they were challenged those at the front could buy some time whilst the others ran past and away — so why hadn't he checked the priming in his revolver, he wondered?

On they crept trying not to scuff the path. The Russians were just a few yards in front obviously being briefed by an NCO: they had gone quiet, their butts were rested on the ground, looking towards a speaker invisible in the undergrowth, completely attentive.

They were squat and broad. They had long, soft leather boots beneath their coats, the skirts of which were hooked up in the same awkward way that Morgan had seen before. The British inched onwards, Morgan quietly putting his rifle over his shoulder in order to look less menacing. Just six feet away something caught the closest Russian's attention and he turned to look at the approaching strangers. How do Russians greet each other casually, he wondered? There was nothing else for it, he raised his righty thumb, mumbled "Tsar Nicholai," with a scowl and strode past. To his amazement, his enemy returned the salute with barely a glance — he'd obviously stumbled on some manual *lingua franca* — before turning back to his superior. But would the rest of the column get away with it too?

On they climbed, puffing up the slope. Morgan's shoulder-blades itched and his scrotum was as tight as a padre's purse — he expected a ball to thump into him at any moment. A hundred paces clear, though, he halted the column and gathered them around him in a clearing. McGucken was the last man in — he looked completely unflustered.

"Get yer headdress on, yous." Whilst the young officer sighed with relief his colour-sergeant attended to the men's dress and turnout — the important things in life.

The noise from the Battery had decreased. They were close enough to hear words of command and the occasional shot, but there was a lull as the Russians prepared for the next bout. A series of thumps suggested more heavy guns firing in reply to the enemy from Home Ridge, but as the echo died away, Morgan could hear horses' hooves on the track behind them. The party stiffened, McGucken put his finger to his lips, signalled to one of the men to come with him, and as the rider drew near they both jumped out, rifles raised.

The adjutant was as quick as the two men. His horse shied, frightened by the sudden movement in the thick brush, but even with his eyes screwed tight, McDonald's pistol was up and covering them. Happily, neither fired.

"What are you doing frightening good Presbyterians, Colour-Sar'nt?" Both sides lowered their weapons, grinning in relief.

"Sir, Mr Morgan's leading us back up to the Battery." McGucken reached forward to stroke Sam's neck. "Where's the rest of the Wing, sir?"

"Scattered to blazes, McGucken, and there's a gap a mile wide between the Battery and the Barrier with not a soul to plug it. Russ will be through there and up to our main position like shit through a goose unless more reinforcements have arrived. Have you seen any, Morgan?"

"No, sir, but the slope's crawling with Muscovites, you'll have noticed them."

"No, Major Hume's ordered me off to find extra men, ain't seen a creature 'til McGucken decided to have some sport with me."

Myopia could have its advantages, thought Morgan.

"Right, rally on the Battery, Morgan. Try to find the rest of the Grenadiers — and get your cap on, where d'you think you are?" Without waiting for a reply, McDonald spurred his horse into a trot, bending low over his saddle to avoid the branches.

Quickly they were back on the track, facing back up the hill towards the Battery. They thought nothing of the shots and yells up ahead until Sam came cantering back down the narrow track towards them, from exactly the point that he and McDonald had disappeared from view. Now the horse's nostrils flared and his eyes rolled in fear, for his saddle was empty. One of the men caught him by the bridle, soothing him, tickling his nose under the broad, regimental-yellow band. The leather of the saddle had been grazed by a ball, the rough edges showing light brown and new, a smear of blood below it.

There was no discussion. Their adjutant was clearly in trouble and Morgan set off up the steep, sloping track with his men scuttling behind him, swiftly breaking through the brush into a saucer-shaped clearing. In the middle was a circle of Russians, grunting primitively, stabbing and pushing at something on the ground. Amongst their jostling legs, Morgan could just see McDonald's feet and spurs jerking, half-formed shrieks coming from his throat as the steel pierced him time and again.

Then a handful of men bundled urgently into the clearing, Sergeant Ormond amongst them. Morgan knew that whilst the enemy were distracted, if they volleyed then charged home they might beat them, but just as he paused to let a few more men come up, a great burst of firing broke out in the bush immediately behind him. Muskets boomed, strange voices yelled, a few rifles cracked in reply before a yowling cheer — that they had all heard too often before — broke the mist. Through the chaos, Morgan could just hear McGucken's gravelly voice telling the men to fall back on him.

The Adjutant must have ridden right into a Russian regiment that was forming-up to attack: he's probably too short-sighted to realize and he's paid the price, thought Morgan. *And now I've led my lads straight into the same mess.* Certainly, the enemy were assaulting the middle and rear of Morgan's strung out command with unusual speed but typical ferocity.

"Come on, sir," Sergeant Ormond was dragging him away by his sleeve from the bloody mêlée around Captain McDonald's body, ". . . we can't do anything for the adjutant now: we need to help Jock McGucken. 'E's back down the track somewhere."

They took no time to organize. Morgan and Ormond pushed their handful into a tight wedge using every inch of the track's breadth. "Right, lads, shout like hell, stay with me." And they hurled themselves down the slope to where McGucken had last been seen and where the crashing of bodies and weapons was almost completely hidden by the smoke and mist.

Sergeant Ormond just beat Morgan to the first man. The Russian was ready to plunge his bayonet down into one of their men who cringed, wounded, on the side of the track, his arms thrown up in front of his face. Fired from the hip at no range, Ormond's bullet caught the man just below the armpit, throwing him bodily into the bushes and killing him instantly. His musket whisked from his hands before it trembled, muzzle down, impaling the earth.

The next target that Morgan chose was getting the better of a fight with one of the Five Company boys. The Russian, an NCO, was parrying and thrusting the lad down the track, gradually wearing him away before he went for the final, fatal thrust. Intent on the duel, he dodged and ducked, unaware of Morgan, presenting nothing but thick coat and belts or a bony ribcage in which a blade would stick. So, he tried a trick that he'd seen at the Battery. Darting in quickly he pricked his target in the shoulder, giving him no more that an inch or so of steel, but enough to bring him — with a curse — face-to-face. Then there was no contest. With one straight thrust, the officer ran the Russian through the throat — he wobbled, threw his hands up to the blade, blood running from his mouth as he fell to his knees and then onto his face as Morgan pulled the bayonet away in one clean movement. But still he resisted. As he writhed his hands reached out and caught at Morgan's ankles, before one sharp blow to the skull with the butt finished him.

"He's hit, sir, colour-sar'nt's hit!"

In the press of bodies, smoke and thrashing limbs, several voices yelled to him from the back of the column. He pushed down the track, swerving out of one Russian's way before another swung round to confront him. The shouts continued, but this enemy had no intention of letting him pass. He stood there, four-square, just like an opponent in the ring except that fourteen inches of steel glittered at his belly. He was no older than Morgan, but a dark moustache fell over his upper lip — it was wet with sweat. He thrust, the officer drew back. He came on again with a stamp and a feint straight from the drill-book, his eyes holding Morgan's — blue, confident and experienced beyond his years. Morgan had intended to save his single round for an emergency, but he had no time to fence with this creature, so Morgan whipped his rifle straight up into his opponent's face and pulled the trigger. But only the percussion cap popped — nothing else: his charge was wet.

Then everything blurred. The Muscovite lunged hard, Morgan tried to pull his belly away from the darting steel, but stumbled, watching the metal jab into the inside of his thigh — there was no pain, the point bursting through his trousers. He could recall thrashing limbs and shouts as they both rolled in the dirt, tepid sunshine through the mist, a canopy of leaves and the Russian's musket jarring and tearing his thigh with

322

each roll until the bayonet finally broke off in the wound. Big, florid Private Carlton was suddenly there. He babbled Nottingham nonsense about "settling that bastard's hash," and ". . . lucky 'e din't get yer nads, sir" before he dragged the cooling, dripping Muscovite away.

Next, Sergeant Ormond and Drummer Pegg were looking down at him, pulling at his arms, getting him on his legs that collapsed below him and telling him, "It's nowt, sir nowt at all," whilst he mumbled about the colour-sergeant and they exchanged glances and told him, "not to worry about nothing," and to "'op on 'ere, sir and hold tight to us necks," before jogging him up the track sitting on a musket that they held between them.

He remembered the next bit much more clearly, though. As he bounced on the steel barrel his thigh began to hurt — perhaps it was that that cleared his mind — and when they came to the edge of the Battery, there was Carmichael. He ranted at all three of them — yes, ranted was the word — making no attempt to control himself in front of the men. He wanted to know why he'd been disobeyed, why no one had stayed with him to guard His Royal Highness and how many men had, "been thrown away"? He wouldn't listen to either Sergeant Ormond's or Morgan's pleas to get some men together to go and look for the colour-sergeant. Oh no, Richard-cowardly-bloody-Carmichael was going to stay just where he was safest and the devil take McGucken.

The last memory stayed with him for the rest of his life. The three of them glared at Carmichael with silent contempt. Drummer Pegg had said nothing: then he hawked — as only soldiers can — turned his head and spat. And there it sat, green and sticky, right on the toe of the officer's boot.

"You little guttersnipe . . ." yelped Carmichael, ". . . I'll . . ."

But Carmichael never finished his sentence for Ormond and Pegg were already stumbling away with Morgan between them.

CHAPTER
ELEVEN

Wounded

Now Morgan was lying down, the pain was a little eased. Pegg and Sergeant Ormond had dropped him off their makeshift litter at the saucer-shaped dip in the ground that was serving as the collecting point for the wounded. It was sheltered by a bit of a herdsman's wall, but the Russian artillery rounds still shivered through the air so closely overhead that Morgan felt that he could reach up and touch them. Occasionally, one skidded just the other side of the stone barrier, showering the rapidly growing bunch of wounded with grit, adding to their pain and fear.

His sergeant and drummer had propped him against the bank, Pegg pulling his flask and pipe out of the folds of his coat for him before telling him that he'd ". . . be right as rain an' back in the thick of it in no time, sir," before scuttling back to the Company and the butchery of the Sandbag Battery. In a curious act of kindness, the boy had pressed a chunk of rindy cheese into his hand before he left. Morgan had no doubt that it had come from deep in some Muscovite's haversack and it was made no more appetising by the blot of blood on one of its corners. Still, it was a kind thought.

"Here, your honour, is it a light you're wanting?" A grimy hand reached a glowing, stumpy, clay pipe across the body that separated them. Amongst the groans of the many wounded and distracted by his own pain, Morgan had barely noticed the others around him. To his left lay a man with the shoulder-cape of his coat draped over his face. The toes of his worn, muddy boots touched each other, very still. But peering over him was a great, round, whiskery face that could have been any age from fifteen to thirty. His hair was thinning — and had clearly been self-trimmed with a razor. He beamed with pleasure.

"I'm sorry, I don't know you, man, but a light for this goddamn thing would be perfect." Morgan had been looking half-heartedly at his new clay pipe since Pegg had left a few minutes earlier. He'd bought a dozen at a tobacconist's in Portsmouth before they left England and this was one of the last to survive.

"I'm Corporal Patrick McEntee, your honour, Light Company, Thirtieth. Got mixed up with your lot and them Guards down at the Battery, so I did, now look at me."

Morgan puffed at his pipe, holding the soldier's hot bowl upside down against his own tobacco. "Where were you struck, Corporal McEntee — and where are you from? You sound like a Corkman?"

"Right up the arse, but one hoop does the job rightly, I don't need another! And you're dead-on, I'm from Leap, sir — you?"

"Skibbereen, Corporal . . ." Morgan's pipe was going now and he spoke between mouthfuls of smoke,

". . . just up the road. Looks like there's another one of our neighbours come to join the party."

Amongst the shrieks of shells and the groans of the wounded came the scrape of nailed boots in the dirt and the clash of pails. Dr Fergusson, one of the Regiment's assistant surgeons, came ducking down through the mist, a slim box of instruments in his hand and Mrs Mary Keenan on his tail. Both were crouched almost double seeking the cover of the wall, the girl weighed down with two buckets of slopping, red-tinged water, her eyes flaring wide with worry when she recognized the wounded officer.

"Oh, so it's you, Morgan. I was told we had another officer casualty, buggering about as usual, I dare say, and getting yourself into mischief."

"Look after this corporal first, won't you Doctor?" Morgan asked.

"Don't worry about me, Doctor, both my bumholes are fine and numb. See to the young gentleman first, sir." Pleased with another base joke, McEntee leered over the neighbouring corpse, fascinated by whatever voodoo the surgeon was about to perform on Morgan.

"All right, that's enough of the courtesies, you two, Mrs Keenan isn't impressed. Now, how came you to break this bayonet off, Morgan, it won't make it's extraction any easier, you know." Fergusson held both ends of the blade between his fingers, gently waggling them and peering into the ragged, bloody cloth of Morgan's trousers.

"I'm so sorry, Doctor, I'll try to bear that in mind next time I'm wrestling a Muscovite." He managed the

quip through clenched teeth, but Mary gave no sign of
hearing above the noise of the guns.

"Hmm, quite so. Now, Mrs Keenan, oblige me by
putting a swab either side of the wound, . . . that's
right." Even through his pain, Morgan could feel how
Mary's hands trembled. As the surgeon placed one
palm against his thigh and grasped the broken end of
the steel with what looked like a pair of plumber's
pliers, she stared deeply into his eyes.

"'Ere you are, sir, get a tot of that down yerself, whilst
I slip yer pants off."

Morgan took a deep pull at the tin cup full of navy
rum as the orderly rummaged around his waist looking
for the buttons that would release his overalls. He was
lying on the same blanket in which he'd been wrapped
as he clung to the back of a mule all the way down to
Balaklava. The pain of the bayonet blade's extraction
had been deadened with grog and this had made the
first mile or so bearable, then the effects had started to
wear off, the jolting of the animal hurting his leg until
by the time that he half-hopped and was half-lifted up
the gangway onto the hospital ship he was in agony
again. Now some sort of well-scrubbed sailor,
maddeningly cheerful and brimming with banter was
intent upon pulling his trousers down.

"What on earth are you doing, man?" Through the
rum and pain Morgan knew that his question was
unreasonable — the matelot obviously knew his
business — but he asked it anyway.

"Just 'avin a look at yer todger, sir, you're in the hands of the Navy now, an' you know what we're like. No, sir, only joshing . . ." the orderly's voice lost its jokiness, a soft edge of concern showing through, "I need to get a look at yer wound so that the surgeon knows which of you officers to deal with first."

The candle-lit deck was fast filling up with injured officers of all ranks and regiments. Opposite Morgan was a captain of the Rifle Brigade whose lower jaw had been shattered by a musket ball, his breath bubbling past the remnants of his tongue though he was completely conscious, his eyes dull with pain. Meanwhile, soldiers of all three battalions of the Guards streamed onto the deck, tenderly carrying their officers in blankets or on stretchers, setting them down beside each other before filing respectfully away.

Morgan looked hard at these young gods and the way in which their soldiers handled them. They were just ripped and bloody flesh like every other officer in the room yet he knew that if he asked who they were, most would be titled, sons of noble families and products of the great schools. Their commissions would have cost twice what his had and whilst they all had conventional military ranks, the Guards also had more elevated "regimental" ranks that meant that even a junior officer was referred to as "major" or perhaps "colonel". Many officers resented this false division, but Morgan had always been rather awed by their whole arcane structure and the fierce loyalty that even the lowliest Guardsman seemed to show his officers, wondering how it might work in battle. Well, now he had seen these men fighting like tigers, standing shoulder-to-shoulder not just with their own men but with his as well, scarcely noticing the blue blood that they shed. Eventually there were half a dozen Guards officers, all lying quietly in their pain, one dying within minutes, a rusty stain dripping onto the teak through the wool of the blanket that stuck to him.

Morgan recognized a gunner officer whom he had first met on the hunting field in Northamptonshire. "Miller, is that you?" Morgan put as much confidence into his voice as he could muster.

"Yes, who's that?" the gunner replied shading his eyes against the candle-light and squinting across the decking.

"Tony Morgan of the Ninety-Fifth, we met hunting in Weedon, remember? What's happened to you?"

"God blind me, it's Paddy Morgan! Your lot's had a hard day, ain't they? Goddamn shell hit my horse in the belly on Home Ridge, just as we was unlimbering. Next thing I knew I was below her, leg busted like a shot hare, and here I am before I got a chance to put a round at Russ."

So the conversations rebounded back and forth across the deck, tales of death, pain and lucky escapes the only thing that each officer had in common was that none had the slightest idea of the real progress of the battle. All had snapshots, all had vignettes, some more encouraging than others, but the smoke, mist and undergrowth had served to make the usual chaos of combat utterly impenetrable.

330

The hours passed. Morgan emptied his flask, took as much rum as the bumptious orderly would let him and dozed. In the evening the naval surgeon at last arrived.

"Now, Mr . . . Morgan of the . . . Ninety-Fifth," the surgeon read the paper label that the orderly had painstakingly written and attached to his coat's lapel, ". . . puncture wound . . . right upper thigh, through and through," he read on. "Let's have a look." Morgan had lain for hours with his soaking coat pulled up around his waist, his muddy, bloody trousers rumpled round his knees above his filthy boots, showing the cream skin of his well-muscled thighs and his once white now grey embarrassingly yellowed drawers. Two great scuts of gauze were taped either side of his limb, their snowiness now blotched red. Gently, the surgeon pulled the dressings away looked at the oozing holes for an instant and then smoothed them back in place. "Got any movement in the toes of your right foot, young 'un?"

"Yes, sir, a little," Morgan replied.

"Good. The muscle's been ripped badly on the outer side of the thigh, but as long as we can prevent mortification, you'll be as good as new in six months."

"Six months?" Morgan knew that he was expected to protest.

"Well, five if you're sensible. Where's home? Because that's where you're going."

"County Cork, sir; but what of the battle?"

"Cork, eh? Keep out of the saddle as long as you can." The surgeon scratched at a purple-coloured form with his pencil. "The battle? We — well, you and the

331

loons you command — have won a famous victory — as they say. The goddamn Frogs turned up late and are trying to take the credit, but they reckon that eight thousand of our men have licked fifty thousand Russians and ninety-odd guns. Trouble is, I'm told we've lost the flower of our army — not that I'd describe you and these thugs . . ." the surgeon pointed to the broken, blanket-wrapped men who lined the bulkheads, ". . . as delicate blossoms. It's said that you'll all get a special star for today's heroics — and so you should. And promotion will be good, too. Half the bloody brigadier-generals are dead, I've been stitching colonels all day, there's hardly a major without a hole in him and look at this sorry lot . . ." the surgeon pointed with a jerk of his chin to his torn customers, ". . . most of them will never soldier again — they'll have to sell out. So, if you want a free step or two up the ladder, get better then get back. We're going to need men like you: the Tsar and his boys ain't going to make it easy."

At that moment a return to the inferno he'd just left was the last thing that Morgan wanted, promotion or not.

The Black Sea was mercifully calm. The three-day voyage passed fitfully in unconsciousness and throbbing pain as the months of exhaustion and pressure sloughed off him and there was little to remember about his fellow travellers, either, for they were just as torpid as he. Every day the orderlies told him of burials at sea — the wounded troops on the lower decks seemed to be dying by the dozen — but all that Morgan was fit for were sleep, rum and food.

He wished that Scutari was just as forgettable. He and the rest of the wounded officers were stretchered ashore, put in cots in one of the wards of the big local barracks and nagged to distraction by a series of ill-humoured young women. In the Crimea they had heard and read much of this marvellous corps of volunteer nurses who made life so much better and healthier than anything that the military medical system could achieve, but Morgan saw no marvels. Whilst the ward was clean enough, the bedding and food were acceptable and the doctors were courteous if heavily overworked, the privies were just unspeakable. Hopping with the help of another, he dreaded his trips to what the naval orderlies called "the heads". The plumbing was totally inadequate for the amount of sewage and the rags with which they cleaned themselves, so the filth overflowed leaving his felt hospital slippers soaked and disgusting.

The coven of harridans seemed incapable of sorting this mess out. Instead, they churned about frowning mightily, throwing open windows that were better shut against November's winds, carrying sheaves of paper but never a bandage or nip of rum. Their idea of therapy was turmoil rather than rest.

His luck improved, though. After less than a week of this Turkish torture, and now as "ambulant" — as the medical men would say — as two crutches would allow him to be, Morgan found himself on another ship and bound for England. Arriving first in a cabin with just two berths, he chose the one by the scuttle, throwing down what few bits and pieces he'd kept or managed to acquire in hospital and easing himself onto the thin mattress. Then a din erupted in the companionway outside, before the door of the cabin banged open and a hospital orderly, struggling at one end of a litter, barged in.

"Oh, sorry, sir, dint know anyone was 'ere," the man grunted under his burden, easing the stretcher through the narrow door as carefully as he could.

"Who the devil's that?" A great, Scots, bad-tempered roar rose from the recumbent form, wagging beard and jumbled hair above a stout, blanket-covered frame, arms waving.

"Anthony Morgan, Ninety-Fifth's Grenadiers, and who the devil's that?" he yelled back: he wasn't going to be bawled at by anyone any more.

There was no reply at first. Between the beard and the thatch of hair winked a pair of spectacles, two eyes wide open with surprise stared back at him as the new arrival levered himself up onto his elbows. "Morgan, God save us all, I'll be damned — and don't speak to your adjutant like that!"

"Christ, McDonald, I saw you killed dead in that God-awful clearing below the Battery — the Muscovites were making you look like a fucking colander — I'm sorry we left . . ."

"Don't bother yourself, man, I've got eighteen stab wounds and a shot-hole in me: the surgeon reckoned I'd give Saint Sebastian a run for his money . . ." both officers and the two orderlies laughed at this, ". . . and if it hadn't been for Patrick Murphy — you know him, used to be right-marker of Number Six Company — who went at 'em bald-headed, there'd be another captain's commission up for grabs."

So the voyage passed. They were nicknamed the "Pin-Cushions" by the other officers, but both men improved as rest, food and sea air took effect, Morgan soon mastering his crutches and soon helping his chunky companion to get out of bed, then slowly to shuffle round the deck, getting a little stronger and more mobile as each day passed. They managed to piece together as much as they knew about the great battle, the fortunes of their own men and officers and, from the newspapers that arrived only a few days out of date, a list of dead and wounded. But both of them quickly tired of the hackneyed joke about vacancies caused by death and wounds and how much money this would save them. Instead, as the numbers mounted showing how ploughed-up the regiments had been, they just thanked God to be alive and relatively whole.

Just before they touched Malta the surgeons allowed Morgan down to the orlop to see the men for the first time. They lay on palliasses on the broad decks, scuttles open when the swell allowed it, as clean and comfortable as possible. A clutch of 95th had gathered in one corner, by far the most cheerful of whom were two men who had lost a leg apiece. Morgan visited daily, jumping down the gangways with increasing speed, to read extracts from the papers to them. Mr William Russell's accounts of the war in *The Times* were always greeted with great mirth, for his lurid prose and its focus on generals and admirals had little in common with the experience of the infantry.

Their favourite diversion, though, was *Punch*. The men crowed with pleasure at the magazine's ruthless pursuit of certain generals — the martinet sir George Brown in particular — and regiments like the 46th that had been foolish enough to catch the editor's eye. Next to Punch they adored the serialization of *Hard Times* in Charles Dickens's own *Household Words*, listening intently to the convolutions of his story whilst puffing at their pipes. Although Morgan knew most by sight, none was from his company, but young Conaughton — who had lost two fingers from his left hand — swore that he'd seen Colour-Sergeant McGucken, alive and swearing hard, being loaded onto another hospital ship.

Morgan scarcely dared hope that McGucken had survived that ghastly mêlée in the brush. He thought back to how the burly Scot had bandaged his hands and encouraged him before regimental boxing back in Weedon; how he'd beaten that damned rifleman off him at the Alma; how he'd supported his every decision on picket and in the trenches; how he'd protected the men — and him — from that swine Carmichael and how he'd fought like a lion at the Battery. It was a strange thing, but despite the huge social gulf that separated the Glasgow tough and the Cork gentleman, Morgan had no better friend. As long as they lived they would always be "sir" and "Colour-Sergeant" to each other, but whatever the titles suggested, they were as equal and close as any brothers.

"Goddamn you, Finn." Morgan grinned at the groom as he limped back into the tack-room in Glassdrumman and threw himself down in the big cracked leather chair, the stuffing of which was just beginning to stick out from both arms. "You've hardened poor Daisy's mouth good style with your great clumsy cavalry ways."

The chestnut mare had just been bought by Billy Morgan before Tony went to the Crimea and he'd never ridden her. So now he'd taken her for a canter over the meadows below the house and found her slow to respond to the bit — a sure sign that his father had spent more time astride her rather than the gentle, careful Finn.

"Clumsy cavalry, is it, yer honour?" Finn retorted. He was rubbing some dubbin into a bit of age stiffened, leather tack whilst he spoke. "If the papers are to be believed, yous was damn glad o' the Light and Heavy brigades at Balaklavy. Showed them Muscovites how to fight didn't we, so?"

"Fight! The bloody donkey-walloping cavalry?" Morgan bellowed in mock outrage. "They don't know the meaning o' the word. Why, there's only one thing that puts Russ in his place and that's a bit of Birmingham steel with one of the old 95th on the end of it!"

"Spoken like a true flat-foot infantryman, all due respect to ye." Finn crowed in response, "Always the

337

bloody same you lot was, whenever there was fight out in the Punjab, the cavalry had to save the day."

Morgan thought back to one of the last times that he and Finn had been together here in the tack-room. Then the rubicund Colonel Kemp and Finn had relived the glories of slaughtering Sikhs back in the Forties — Morgan could still remember how their faces glowed over the tales of death and destruction. He wondered, as the years passed, if time would soften the memories that haunted him at the moment? When he was as old as Kemp, would he remember the suffering and misery with a rosy affection?

"But, sir, the papers tell us what a dreadful fix you're in out there." Finn dropped the *craic* as quickly as Morgan had started it. "Bad rations, no warm clothes and too few men to do the job. Is it true that the Frogs have had to take over most of the British siege lines — and will Austria get involved like *The Times* keeps saying she ought to?" Finn may only have been a groom and an ex-lancer, but he was nobody's fool, thought Morgan.

"Why ask me, Finn? I'm just an infantry subaltern who's more interested in rum rations and sentry rosters than the bloody politics. Why, I scarce saw a Frog the whole time I was out there — all the buggers did, as far as I could see, was fart away on their trumpets and then claim that they won Inkermann for us when they did nothing worth telling." Morgan realized that he was in danger of lapsing into a caricature of himself. "But yes, you're right about the tents, the food and the sheer amount of work that we have to do with not enough troops." He added more thoughtfully, "Mind you, it must have been much worse after I left, what with the storms and the cold that the papers tell us about. As for the Austrians, God knows. If you listened to all the shaves around camp last November, you'd have thought that the Tsar's lads were ready to chuck in the towel, but it didn't seem like that at Inkermann, I can tell you. They fought like very devils, they did, and reckon that we'll need every pair of willing hands if we're going to take Sevastopol this year. So, Austrians, Italians, Froggies — the more the bloody merrier, I say, and if it saves my boys from getting their cocks shot-off, then I'm all for it."

Finn had seen how the young officer was when he got home not long before Christmas. The whole household had expected him to be full of vim and vigour, wounded but glamorously so, brimming with tales of blood and thunder. Instead they'd found him quiet, almost dejected, painfully thin and endlessly tired, obviously glad to be home but irked and frustrated by his injury. Now he was short-tempered where he'd always been full of fun with the servants and even the blue-eyed Jeanie Brennan — who'd quite fancied her chances now that Mary was out of the way — had found the young master ". . . really not himself, so he's not."

"Jesus, Finn, the Crimea's bloody ghastly — it's not the fighting so much — it's just the ceaseless pressure of having to put a good face on everything for the sake of the men and pretend that it's all going to be one, great glorious victory." Despite all sorts of kind

339

enquiries from all sorts of kind people, Morgan hadn't felt ready to talk to anyone about the real face of the war since he'd got home almost three months ago, "Some of the bastards that pretend to be officers, you know, Finn, all puffed-up with self importance until the lead begins to fly and then where are they? Bloody skulking miles to the rear."

"Sure, your honour, we had an officer just like that in the Sixteenth." But as Finn charged off down one of his Sikh Wars byeways, Morgan's attention wandered.

He couldn't admit to Finn the paralysing fear that he sometimes felt — he could hardly admit it to himself, but all the marks were there, especially the terrible dreams. No matter how much brandy he'd had to keep the night horrors away, still they came back, some nameless, horrid, shapeless thing stalking him through brush and braes. Whatever this malign presence was, it meant him a great deal of harm and the hours between three and five were usually spent in jumpy, nervous dread of . . . of what? His lowest point came when he woke cold and wet with piss. It happened only a handful of times, Seamus his valet stripping the bed personally but never mentioning it.

All this made Morgan a poor suitor for Maude Hawtrey. Their first meeting after his return was at church on Christmas Eve, she dressed in dark-red velvet, hat and veil, he in his best coat and an odd, leather slipper on his bloated foot. Maude charmed, almost gushed in her chilly way, asking him if he would come to her family's Winter Ball in January — it was for the soldiers' charity after all — before she was overcome with embarrassment when she realized her gaffe. He was polite, he was courteous, but try as he might he could put no gallantry or real warmth into his answers. What on earth did he now have in common with people like that — gentle, decent folk for sure — when his mind and soul were still at the war?

Meanwhile, the newspapers never rested from lambasting the conduct of the war. He'd half-expected that the pasting given to the Russians at Inkermann would mean that the Allies could push even harder at a weakened Sevastopol, taking the city before the worst of the winter weather set in. But no, the opposite was true. A dreadful storm soon after the battle had destroyed quantities of siege stores, ammunition was scanty, no one had thought about getting reinforcements out to the Crimea in meaningful numbers and the men were woefully short of decent rations and proper clothing. *Punch* made him smile. There was one cartoon of a tattered Guardsman and a bearded, pipe-smoking, tramp from the Line discussing things as a storm whipped around their threadbare uniforms.

"Well, Jack! Here's good news from home. We're to have a medal," said the Guardsman,

"That's very kind. Maybe one of these days we'll have a coat to stick it on?" answered the other ruefully.

Each day came more news of dwindling numbers caused not by battle but by disease, hunger and incompetence with every sign that the garrison of Sevastopol was snug and smug inside its walls. As he read of his friends' and the regiment's hardships, he struggled to understand his own feelings. He was

warm, comfortable and, above all, no one was shooting
at him here in Glassdrumman; he was a certified hero
with holes in him to prove it; even if he were burning to
return, his wounds prevented it; he'd done more than
most; and, anyway, by the time he'd be fit for duty,
Sevastopol must have fallen. But if everything were so
damned rosy, why was he so damned wretched?

". . . an' you know, your honour, we never did find
out who ordered 'right-about' that morning." Finn had
been sabreing Sikhs again. "You haven't heard a word
I've said, have you, your honour? Come on, here's your
stick, your father will be expecting you for dinner."
Finn helped Morgan to his feet, clapped his walking
stick in his hand and shook his head slowly to himself
as the young officer hobbled back into the main house.

Morgan's mood wasn't helped by the next day's
paper. In yet another account of Inkermann, it claimed
that Richard Carmichael had been one of the few
officers of the 95th left standing at the end of the day.
Indeed, it said that he'd even temporarily been in
command of the whole Regiment, ". . . marching at
their head from the field of honour." Further hot coals
were heaped upon him when he read in the *Gazette*
section that one "RLM Carmichael, Lt, 95th Regt,"
had been appointed, "Captain without purchase," and
was posted as, "Assistant Quartermaster General, 2nd
Division."

That scrub, that yellow creature was not only
promoted, but he'd been moved away from the
regiment and danger as a smooth-arsed Staff officer.
What a damn disgrace. The only fly in Carmichael's

342

over-flowing pot of ointment, though, was that his uncle, sir George Cathcart — or whatever relation the fellow was — was no longer in a position to give his nephew a leg-up: the Muscovites had seen to that. Even so, it was still a damn disgrace. He was miserable because he felt guilty — guilty of abandoning his men. He couldn't loaf here whilst the boys — and Mary too — had to endure this sort of injustice in the Crimea.

"March is a bit early in the year for this, ain't it, Father?" Tony Morgan hadn't liked to refuse the invitation to shoot seals, for it was something very special to the old man.

Last season his sea-trout had been ravaged by the gluttonous things, now he'd cull them as early as possible to stop it happening again. But why March, when the waves romped into Bantry Bay from the Atlantic and the spray flew even well inshore? And why had Billy insisted that his water bailiff should wait for them on dry land, leaving just the pair of them to handle the boat, the rifles, the gaffs and all the other gear, especially when his leg was still so stiff?

After twenty minutes' hard rowing they nosed into something approaching calm. More than a hundred paces away, several fat, flippery forms lay high on the rocks, their short dappled fur making them hard to see.

"There's a gang of them yonder, Father." Tony knew that Billy's eyesight would never make them out at this distance, but he wouldn't admit it, ". . . d'you want me to load the rifles?"

"Ah, yes, I can see the brutes." Father lied, shading his eyes against the non-existent winter sun. "No, wait you, we need to do some straight talking before anything else."

Tony had expected as much. Since he'd got home, Father had made several attempts to corner him, all of which he'd avoided with one excuse or another. The old man had never been much of a mentor to him, even after his mother died, and their private conversations were normally brisk, businesslike affairs where money, horses or careers were discussed — nothing more intimate. But this was obviously going to be different, that's why he'd brought him to a place where there was no escape and no one could eavesdrop on them.

"Son, I know all about Mary, have done since the first night you tupped her — bloody awful row the pair of you made. That was fine — well, not fine exactly, but you know what I mean. But she was little Mary Cade then, our chambermaid and if she'd found herself eating for two or generally cut up rough, then I could have dealt with it — heaven knows that sort of thing was quite usual in my day."

Tony pulled gently at his oar, keeping the boat straight and trying to avoid Billy's eye.

"But now she's Mrs Mary Keenan, married to your one-time batman from just up the road here. Now he's a sergeant, promoted for bravery at the Alma — it's been all over the papers — Keenan's a bloody hero in these parts and we've known his family since before the first famine." Tony could see that this was going to be difficult. "And what of my own gallant boy? Fucking

344

one of his own men's wives — one of the men who depend upon him for every bit of leadership they can get, who depend upon my son to keep him and a host of others alive." Billy fixed him with a stony eye. "Don't deny it, boy, the servants write to each other you know. And I'm quite aware that the silly mare married Keenan just to follow you out there without telling you a thing. It's not just the scandal hereabouts if this gets out, son — I can live with that — it's what you're doing to a Papist couple who deserve better from the likes of us."

"But, Father . . ." Tony tried to reply.

"No, lad, don't waste your breath, 'love' be buggered. You may think that at the moment but it wouldn't work. The Romans won't let their people divorce, so what sort of a life could you have with the girl? You couldn't stay in these parts and the army would crucify you for what you'd done to a non-commissioned type." Billy was unrelenting.

"But . . ." Tony tried again.

"No, son. Marry the Hawtrey girl, she's a wee cracker. Forget Mary: let her and James Keenan get on with their lives. There, it had to be said, now I'll say no more about it unless I find that you've disobeyed me. Do we understand each other?" Billy reached forward and touched his son's knee in a rare gesture of affection.

Tony had no words to answer his father. He had no strength to argue his case — he just nodded his agreement.

"Good, then, that's settled. Take my oar and get us up close, I'll load these rifles."

But that doesn't settle it at all. Does father really think that a few peppery words from him will put the whole thing straight? He's absolutely right about the family's place here in Cork, especially amongst the Catholic people and the example that we're all expected to set them; and I know that I'm risking the army's wrath, but he can't understand what Mary and I have found with each other? thought Tony.

"Gently now, boy, turn the boat carefully." Billy had got his eye on a basking seal on a rock about fifty paces off. As the boat came round, he slowly lowered himself in the stern, resting his double-barrelled rifle on the tiller housing.

And if he thinks that I'm going to shackle myself to that frigid Maude just to keep his Protestant . . . Then some reflex threw Tony from his seat, leaving him cringing in the bilges at the unexpected, mighty bang.

"What the hell's got into you boy?" An angry Billy had to grip the gunwale of the boat as it rocked with Tony's sudden movement. It was quite clear what had got into Tony. The young officer was pale, lying as flat as he could on the boards, making the smallest possible target of himself. "By God, son, that war's hurt you worse than just that hole in your leg, ain't it?" Murmured his father to himself.

It didn't take much to persuade the medical board in Fermoy. Tony had been called for a review of his injury in late March and by gritting his teeth and

346

concentrating every bit of strength he had, he managed the rudimentary tests that the doctors set him. He confessed to still needing a stick, but when they asked him if he felt capable of training duties at the reinforcement depot in Malta, he couldn't agree quickly enough. The surgeon-colonel in charge made the kindly suggestion that he should take another week's leave, ". . . just to let the leg settle a bit," and to ". . . kiss the girls goodbye," the latter phrase accompanied by a horrid wink, but Tony insisted that he could be up and off in two days.

"Just like the bloody army, so it is. No bloody notice, no consideration for your personal affairs at all, just rips your honour away on a bloody whim." Finn had watched Morgan's mounting frustration and had guessed that he would use the medical board's verdict as an excuse to get away from Glassdrumman. But he went along with the pretence. "You've made yourself too bloody valuable, sir. Still, there it is, the army'll post you in a rush just to keep you hangin' about in some fly-blown hole of a place."

Morgan's self-imposed crisis was ideal. He escaped from his father without more discussion; Maude was staying with friends in Roscommon so all she got were a few, breezy lines; and there was no time for a leaving party, just a simple supper and a skin-full with Finn.

"Look, sir, be careful, can't you?" Finn was as fragile as Morgan in the half-light of All Fools' Day morning as they mounted the jaunty and set out for the station. "I can just see the next time we'll meet you off the train

— you'll be wearin' an oak box." Finn shook the reins, starting the mare into a steady trot.

"You're talking balls, Finn. I'm just being sent back to train recruits, that's all. The war'll be over before I get back and, anyway, even if I do rejoin the regiment and they're still fighting, there'll be no heroics, believe me."

"'Course I believe you, sir, like there was no heroics with you an' young Keenan at the Alma, like you didn't break your glass on some t'ick Russian skull . . ." Finn's words touched Morgan, ". . . an' like there was no heroics that got you that wounded leg. Just have a care, sir, we need you here in one piece." The older man's face was creased with concern as they pulled up at the station.

The train was on time. Their headaches prevented any more talk, but as Morgan swung his bags up into the carriage before climbing stiffly aboard himself, Finn reached for his hand; "an' we need that young Mary back too, your honour, by your side where she belongs."

Was that really what the servants thought? wondered Morgan. If Finn was right and the ordinary folk could see the rightness of the match, couldn't Mary and he overcome all of the objections that his father and others would put in their way? A warm tingle of hope crept down Morgan's spine.

Naturally, Finn was right. Malta was a fly-blown hole of a place and there was as much hanging about as you wanted. Morgan's duties were simple enough, he oversaw the drilling and physical training of the recruits who came through the reinforcement depot and taught both the instructors and the men the intricacies of the '53 Pattern Enfield rifle that was gradually replacing the Minié.

Long days in the brassy sun were spent stomping up and down the sandy ranges that looked out into the Mediterranean, trying to stop the men from flinching in anticipation of the rifle's kick and to teach them how to judge range with some accuracy. The technical side was absorbing enough, showing the men how to lay-off for wind, how to indicate targets to one another and other battlefield wrinkles — at least, it was absorbing the first couple of times, but he chafed to be back with the regiment.

Morgan's greatest distraction and pleasure was Pat, a brindled Staffordshire that had cost him five guineas from Billy Acton of the 77th who, like him, was recovering from a wound sustained at Inkermann,

"He's a grand ratter, look at him," claimed Acton.

If Pat's scars on nose and lips and the absence of a left eye made him a "grand ratter", then, by the same token, Acton and he with their limps and shiny scars must have been grand soldiers — Morgan wasn't convinced. But Pat's first time in action against a horde of furry vermin that were driven out of a grain store just below the camp by a pair of ferrets, changed Morgan's mind.

"Will you look at that," Morgan had seldom seen the like, ". . . that's extraordinary."

349

As the ferrets — the property of Private Styles, the camp commander's batman — slunk down the entrance to the rats' holes in the big, dusty barn, so a sea of scurrying shapes came pouring out of the other side of a wooden partition wall. Here waited Pat, his stump of a tail going hard, muscles bunched, quivering with anticipation. To kill one rat at a time was quite normal — Morgan remembered how impressed he'd been with the soldiers' Jack Russells back in Weedon — but two was nothing short of splendid. At almost every pass, Pat gulped one into the depths of his jaws and nipped another with his front teeth. A quick shake, a burst of blood and the dead animals arced through the air before landing with a dull thump on the packed-earth floor of the barn.

"Damn me, twenty-two in under two minutes, Styles, amazing." Morgan had his hunter in hand, stabbing at the second hand as accurately as he could.

"Aye, sir, but Pat had to chase under them bales for five or so." Styles had seen how a stack of straw had provided convenient, if temporary, cover for some of Pat's quarry. "If he'd been in a proper ring you could shave a couple of seconds off for each rat. What d'you pay for 'im if you don't mind me askin'?"

"Five guineas off Captain Acton; what d'you think?"

"Good deal, sir . . ." Styles answered, whistling his admiration, ". . . mek you a king's ransom in 'Pol."

Morgan held the dog by the collar as Styles recovered his ferrets — Pat was straining to be at the creatures, his front paws off the ground as his back legs scrabbled to get a grip in the dirt. The battered terrier would have dealt with his ferret allies in exactly the same way as he'd killed the rats, given half a chance. Morgan pulled a handful of straw from a nearby bale and wiped the vermins' blood from Pat's muzzle and flank as the dog's stump of a tail wagged appreciatively.

The officer's mind turned to Sevastopol and the savage fighting that lay ahead. The Allies had been on the verge of storming the place in November, but the Russians had not only blunted their ambitions by attacking at Inkermann, they seemed to have emerged from the winter bolder and stronger than those who were meant to be besieging them. Somehow, he doubted that he would leave the place with a king's ransom — he probably wouldn't leave it at all. He shivered, despite the heat of the day.

May started with the trickle of reinforcements turning into a steady stream as recruiting and training in Britain at last began to be organized properly. Despite the wholly predictable complaints from the regiments in the Crimea who were receiving the new drafts (they were too young, too green, too awkward, two left feet — in other words they were just callow), the men looked pretty good to Morgan. There were no weaklings that he could see and they all seemed keen to taste the fighting. Perhaps more importantly, a leavening of men who had now recovered from their wounds was beginning to come through. They were worth their weight in gold, reinforcing the instructors' words with lessons learnt the hard way in the field.

351

The seventh of May was Morgan's birthday and as he woke that morning he wondered what lay ahead in his twenty-fifth year. It started well. Late the night before a new draft had arrived; Morgan had been dimly aware of crunching boots and muted commands as they marched up from the quayside and were shown to their bed-spaces, cookhouse and armoury. On the way to his morning swim he passed the Sergeants' Mess where breakfast had just started.

"Sir, Mr Morgan, sir, it is you, ain't it?" A rasping Scots bass came from deep within, its owner invisible but instantly recognizable by his voice.

Morgan stopped, delighted. "Is that Colour-Sergeant McGucken? Show yourself for pity's sake!"

The big man pushed past the tables and his guzzling comrades, launching himself from the darkness of the room out into the glare of the spring sunshine. He stood on the cinder path for a moment grinning, just as barrel-chested and bursting with life as when Morgan had seen him last. His strapped overalls clung to his legs and he looked as though he had been poured into his new scarlet shell-jacket, the gold-lace chevrons gleaming on his arm.

"Damn me, sir . . ." the two men wrung each other's hands, ". . . there was no need to dress." Besides McGucken, Morgan looked distinctly shabby in his shorts and singlet, a towel draped around his neck. "I heard you'd taken a bad 'un, sir . . ." the Colour-Sergeant looked down at the red, livid scar on his subaltern's thigh, ". . . coming to look for me, they said. More than Mr Carmichael did."

Morgan's smile faded as he recalled Carmichael's behaviour. "Didn't get very far, though, did I? What happened to you?"

"Well, sir, I got a belt on the skull from a Russian butt that laid me out cold 'til the next morning when two of our orderlies found me. D'you know, the clowns, had the damned cheek to lift me up a couple o' feet before a-droppin' me just to see whether I was dead — meanwhile the bloody Russians are giving their men anaes-fucking-thetics, talk about the march of medical science. There's too much to tell you just now, sir, you go and have a bath — and don't forget to wash behind your ears. Are you free for a swally or two in our Mess tonight?"

Morgan was, indeed, free that evening — he was free every evening in sociable Malta. Then, he'd just got the men settled-in to a gentle morning's practise on moving targets when one of the commandant's clerks arrived on a pony, leading another.

"Sir, Major James's compliments, an' could you report to him at your earliest convenience, if you please? Brought an 'orse for you."

"Thank you, Hallam, I will. Good of you to bring the pony. Am I in trouble, d'you know?" Morgan had always liked the clerk, an educated soldier of the 55th who'd had a shin smashed at the Alma, hobbled terribly and who was now only fit for light duties. Hallam, in turn, had responded to Morgan's interest in him — that's why he'd brought the mount, to spare the young officer's leg.

"No, sir, get away. Your lot's had some bad casualties in the trenches, officers an' all, an' I think the Major's going to ask you if you think you're up to taking a draft over. Don't let on I told you, sir."

Major James of the 30th commanded the Depot Battalion on Malta that trained and despatched reinforcements to all the regiments of the 2nd Division. He was fifty and florid and whilst many men much older than he were serving well and gallantly in the Crimea, peaceful Malta tested him to the hilt.

"Ah Morgan, how's the leg?" James's eyes watered like those of a much older man.

"Much better, sir, good of you to ask." Morgan saluted smartly before removing his cap and shifting his weight off his right leg and onto his walking stick.

"I'll come straight to the point, the Ninety-Fifth are less than three hundred effectives and another dozen or so have been killed and injured during a bad session in the trenches last week. A captain and subaltern are hit . . ."

"D'you know who, sir?" interrupted Morgan, hoping it was no one he knew well but also seeing a chance for himself.

"No, 'fraid not. But it means that I'm going to send all twenty-three . . ." James checked his figures, ". . . yes, twenty-three of the Ninety-Fifth that are here at the moment with you at their head. Here's a boon, the regiment wants you back to command your old Company — you're a Grenadier by the look of you — and you'll fill a captain's vacancy without purchase if you choose."

354

"Sir, I'll bloody swim there if you want me to!" Both men laughed at Morgan's genuine delight.

"I have to say, though, I wish they'd get a bloody move-on and take Sevastopol." Major James made it sound as though the slowness of the campaign had been intended to inconvenience him personally, to keep him away from grouse moor and trout stream. "Look here . . ." James put on a pair of spectacles, shook another of Willaim Russell's dispatches in *The Times* in Morgan's face, ". . . they reckon that there's tens of thousands of fresh French troops in the Crimea now and that our regiments are looking much better now that reinforcements are arriving — mind you, that's the only bloody thanks I'll get, from the papers, not from our Staff — and that if we looked as though Sevastopol would be assaulted soon, then the Austrians would weigh in on our side and Russ would have to give in, they should put me in charge," said James, removing his spectacles.

"I'm sure we'd be very glad to have you with us," flattered Morgan. "Just one thing, sir; Colour-Sar'nt McGucken's just out from England — he's from my company and has been with me all the way through — can I take him with me?"

"Just arrived, you say . . . not yet on my lists. But, if he's well enough; daresay the Ninety-Fifth need every man they can get, but it'll play the devil with my books. Still, take him anyway. You leave on tomorrow evening's tide, I suspect you'll be on the *Bristol*. Good luck, boy, thank you for all you've done here; I'll write to your commanding officer and express my thanks, now don't

get killed and for pity's sake, look after those lads."
James smiled kindly as Morgan saluted and faced
about, burning to tell McGucken the news.

The "swally or two" multiplied many times over,
especially when Morgan revealed that it was his
birthday. A lame Sergeant from the 55th and another
from the 20th with a great, scaly furrow through his left
eyebrow joined them whilst the Tsar's men were put to
flight time and again.

McGucken was delighted with the young officer's
news, declaring himself ". . . fit to take Moscow wi' one
hand tied behind me," before excusing himself briefly
to tell his orderly to get his kit together. Then he was
back, laughing with savage mirth at the account of
Pegg's gobbing on Carmichael's boots, in turn telling
Morgan what little reliable news he had of the regiment
whilst refilling the glasses and revelling in the fact that
they were to be together again.

"Mind you, sir, Mick Whaley — who's been filling in
for me these last months — is due promotion to
another company and I hear good things of young
Sergeant Keenan. You know he's stayed with the
Grenadiers, don't you, sir?" McGucken looked across
the top of his glass, eyes narrowed quizzically.

"I do, and I'm right glad of it," replied Morgan.

"Are you, sir? You know you'll have to settle that little
business of yours pretty fucking quick now you're to be
in charge, don't you, sir?"

"I'm not sure I fully understand you, Colour-
Sergeant," Morgan was almost convincing.

"Yes you do, sir. We all turned a blind eye with Sergeant Keenan away an' everyone distracted by that arse Carmichael, but it won't answer now." McGucken fixed him with a glare every bit as uncompromising as his father's. "I know what went on back in Ireland, but do yourself and us all a favour an' drop the lassie, sir. She's Keenan's now an' we need a company commander that the men can look up to."

Morgan was getting used to such advice, not that he liked it. He drained his glass and nodded, it was so much easier than trying to argue.

"By God, sir, you've a drooth on you, ain't you?" McGucken had watched as Morgan's glass was emptied much too quickly for his liking. "an' that's another thing, sir, please stop drinking so bloody much."

CHAPTER
TWELVE

The Raid

Balaklava stank so much worse in the spring than it had in the winter. The harbour was just as crowded with ships and people, the water just as foul as Morgan remembered it, but the smell was now indescribable. Things weren't helped by having to hang around on deck for more than two hours whilst the Captain found a berth as the putrid, scummy water lapped around them.

"I see Peters is waiting for you there, sir, I'll march the draft up to the new camp, d'you know where it is?" McGucken had got the replacements packed and ready to disembark in plenty of time. Now they sat about the deck in their new red jackets and caps, their blankets rolled neatly on top of freshly-issued knapsacks, well-blacked boots and whitened belts, just as if they were about to go on parade.

Morgan looked at them as they read, played cards and smoked, basking in the sunshine on the freshly cleaned-decks. There were some old hands amongst them who'd recovered from wounds or disease, but they were mostly lads straight from the slums who'd been drawn to the war either through a sense of adventure or for the bounty if they were already serving in the militia. They were terribly young and new — just like he and the others had been before their first taste of war.

"I don't, Colour-Sar'nt. Come ashore with me and Peters will tell us, I've no doubt." The pair stumbled down an uncomfortably steep gang-plank, Pat the dog at their heels, to find Morgan's servant waiting with three ponies, two to ride and one for the baggage.

"Hello, Captain Morgan, sir, hello Colour-Sar'nt, welcome back, you've brought the sun wi' you." Peters smiled at both of them, saluting as smartly as the multitude of reins would let him whilst emphasizing Morgan's new rank.

"Hello, Peters . . ." Morgan shook his hand, ". . . quieter than when we saw each other last."

The officer remembered how his batman had quavered after him in his flat Preston accent demanding to know what time he would be back for dinner as the balls skipped about their tents on that foggy, Inkermann morning.

"Yes, sir, but it don't 'alf pong 'ere don't it? I'll just go an' get yer kit an' yours, Colour-Sar'nt?" Smaller and thinner than most soldiers, Peters was muddy but as smartly dressed as could be expected on campaign.

He was certainly a contrast to half a dozen hairy things in dun-coloured smocks and greasy belts who came hooting and laughing down the quay, puffing at pipes, trousers and boots crusted with mud, rifles slung anyhow. They gaggled past Morgan and McGucken, ignoring them completely.

"Stand still, yous!" McGucken had been unusually placid on the trip from Malta. When one of the new men had got dreadfully drunk in Scutari, he'd been almost paternal to him; when, during an inspection, he'd found rust on a rifle-lock he'd all but laughed it off; but this was too much. Even in the clamour of the harbour his voice petrified the party. "Who's in charge of you clowns?" All McGucken's professional senses were outraged by this mob. He threw his chin out pugnaciously, positively brandishing the gold-lace chevrons and flag on his arms.

"Me, Colours . . ." A muddy wretch had pulled himself to a semblance of the position of attention but wasn't allowed to finish.

"'Colours' . . . 'Colours' . . . I'll give you bloody 'Colours', it's Colour-Sergeant to the like of yous." McGucken bristled; "Marines, I guess, though you wouldn't fuckin' know it! How dare you pass an officer without saluting? Now get into a squad and try to look like soldiers — well, Marines anyway."

The humbled little gang shuffled into two ranks and their non-commissioned officer wobbled a compliment before marching them off as quickly as possible to get out of McGucken's range.

"Christ, Colour-Sergeant, if even the Royals have got into a state like that, maybe everything the papers have been saying is true." Morgan looked about the harbour. Certainly, there was plenty of evidence here of the chaos that the broadsheets had been reporting.

"I'll ride up to the regiment and make sure they're expecting you, gennelmen," said McGucken before he saluted and rode away.

Peters and Morgan mounted and set off across the muddy quay, the baggage pony trotting quietly behind.

With Pat across his master's saddle-bow, they rode out of the harbour past great piles of stores and ammunition. Bales of clothing, tents and blankets lay soaked by rain and grimed with mud whilst they passed at least three commissariat wagons that had been abandoned in ditches beside the road.

"There ain't much wrong with that wagon, Peters, nothing that a wheelwright couldn't put straight, anyway." They both looked down at a cart with a broken rear wheel.

"There in't, sir, it's just that no one seems to bother with things like they used to. Truth is, sir, this road ain't too bad now that the sun's dried it out, but in t'winter it were feet deep in mud. Made gettin' things repaired very difficult an' people just gave up, like."

Morgan could see what his batman meant as they wound out of the valley, up the Col Road and onto the great, flat Sapoune plateau. Horse and mule skeletons peeped from the earth, here and there piles of shapeless canvas had been abandoned, there were broken bottles everywhere that threatened to cut their horses' hooves and litter blew about promiscuously. Most tellingly, though, every living horse that they saw was badly out of condition. Charabancs full of navvies were pulled by wretched, thin nags and even the mounts of a patrol of the 4th Light Dragoons had dull, patchy coats and gnawed tails.

Peters prattled about the winter; how in January the regiment had been down to one officer and a hundred and fifty men, the rest all sick or injured; how Russ seemed as "happy as a corn-fed rat" and as cocky as ever; and how the reinforcements were "nowt but kids an' soft as grease". Morgan let it all drift over him, shivering slightly when he heard the first boom of the heavy siege pieces, before getting used to the irregular drumming of the guns and the replies of the Russians from besieged Sevastopol.

They meandered past the regiment's old camp near Inkermann — the French had now taken over that sector as the British were too weak to man it — and on to the lines of new wooden huts that the 95th had just occupied.

"Well, Peters, this looks a damn sight better than those leaky old tents." The huts were so new that the troops hadn't yet been able to dirty the paint-work and, in any event, the regiment was still so below strength that many of them weren't occupied.

"They're grand, sir, but we needed them four months ago, not now that the weather's improved. Any road, I've boxed-up Captain Davidson-Smith's kit an' sent it 'ome an' you get the whole hut for yourself now, sir."

As they trotted past the guard-room, two young soldiers passed, bringing their rifles to the shoulder and tapping their slings in unison. In their caps sat the brass badge of the Grenadier Company.

"Hello, you two . . ." Morgan recognized neither, but he grinned down at them, trying to ingrain their faces on his memory, ". . . what are your names, lads? I'm your new Company Commander, Captain Morgan."

"Cooper, sir."

"Langham, sir." They flickered their eyes up to meet Morgan's, but with no smile, no enthusiasm.

There was something about them that worried Morgan. In most circumstances he would have dismounted and spoken to any soldier, no matter whether they were his or not, but they had both radiated such a lack of interest in him that he thought better of it. Were these two undergoing punishment and in some sort of sulk, or did they reflect the attitude of the whole company? The last thing he and McGucken needed in the fighting that lay ahead was listlessness like this.

"'Ere you are, sir . . ." Peters showed him into his spartan accommodation, ". . . adjutant says how the commanding officer would like to see you soonest, sir. I'll get some hot water for you to wash, then I'll show you to t'orderly room."

Morgan had thought long and hard about the responsibilities of commanding a company. Now he would be in charge, there would be no one to turn to in the heat of battle and all those men would look to him and him alone for leadership and inspiration. But until he'd met those two lads on his way into camp the reality had been very distant. Pensively, he scraped some of the mud and horse muck off his boots whilst the guns rattled the glass in the windows of his hut.

★　★　★

"Have a seat, Morgan, I'm extremely glad to have you back." After last year's battles and the trials of the winter, Major Hume might have confidently expected promotion to lieutenant-colonel, but no, he had to content himself with flattering mentions in his superiors' dispatches and the fact that he was still drawing breath. Now he sat as trim and spry as Morgan remembered him, his hair and beard showing just a tinge of grey, but his eyes as alive as ever. "Sorry I had to pull you back from Malta before your leg's fully recovered, but Davidson-Smith's getting himself wounded gave me no choice: anyway, I'd sooner see you have that captaincy than anyone else, you deserve it." Hume wasted not a word.

"The regiment's being reinforced slowly but we're still less than four hundred strong: despite this, Brigade expect us to cover the duties of a battalion twice the size. That means that trench duty comes round incessantly and the men are suffering."

Hume paused, sucking a pencil briefly before he continued. "You won't recognize the Grenadier Company — what there are of them. Sergeant Whaley has done wonders acting as Davidson-Smith's colour-sergeant, but he's to be moved on promotion and McGucken is perfect to support you when we assault Sevastopol — and that must be soon. And you're not to breathe a word of it, but he's been put up for a Distinguished Conduct Medal for Inkermann." Hume watched Morgan's reaction.

"The thing that worries me about the Grenadiers, though, is their morale. You remember how they were

364

last year, even after Eddington was killed and then that fool Carmichael took over?"

How could Morgan forget that happy bunch? How could he forget the bonds of shared experience, danger and hardship, the willing sacrifice and selflessness of almost every man? Seeing those two Grenadiers earlier had made him wonder: would he and McGucken be able to recreate all that?

"Well, they've been ridden hard and they've taken more than their share of casualties and they're . . . they're tired and just off form. There's some good non-commissioned officers — Sergeant Keenan's doing particularly well — but things aren't quite right. They're in the line at the moment under, God help us, young Parkinson. You and McGucken can take them over tonight after dark: take your reinforcements with you, they might as well be blooded." Hume had no more time for pleasantries. "Oh, one more thing Morgan, I want the company to push the Russians out of some forward positions they've established, here." He pointed to a spot on the map spread out on the desk in front of him. "The adjutant and I will come up to brief you the day after tomorrow. Now please go to work and get a grip of the Grenadiers."

How could he have wanted to be back here? As the four reinforcements followed him, McGucken at their backs, through the flashes and bangs that decorated the darkness, Morgan wondered at his own eagerness. The pull he took at his flask as he waited outside his hut and allowed his eyes to adapt to the night had helped, but

365

when the guide at the start of the parallel challenged, "Carrot," he jumped visibly.

"Stick . . ." he replied, ". . . officer and five Grenadiers, Ninety-Fifth."

"Eh-up, sir, it's me." A round form emerged from the dark, a furry jerkin over his greatcoat, despite the spring night.

Morgan didn't recognize the guide at all — but there was something about the blunt accent, something about the familiar mix of onions and rum on his breath.

"Pegg, is that you?"

"Lance-Corporal Pegg, if you don't mind, Captain Morgan, sir."

"Lance-Corporal Pegg" mused Morgan. "Well, things had come to a pass if eighteen-year-olds were wearing tapes. Still, the boy had more experience than most and he was doing his duty when many weren't."

"Did you bring that grog I asked you for, sir?" grinned Pegg.

But before Morgan could reply, McGucken broke in, whispering coarsely in the gloom, "Corporal Pegg, shut yer grid an' just get us to the Company, will you?"

"Hello, Colour-Sar'nt, it's wonderful to see you too. Coom on, then, sap gets a bit deeper round the corner, then it's about five 'undred yards. We'll 'ave to pass through Number Three Company on the way, but Russ ain't close 'til we gets up to our position. Can you keep these kids from doing any harm to theirsens, Colour-Sar'nt?" said Pegg.

Morgan wondered at the lad's confidence and his sneering tone with the reinforcements, most of whom

366

were older than he was, but he was soon distracted by a howitzer shell that whirred way overhead. Its fiery fuse showed clear in the night sky, yet it was all he could do not to duck down into a corner of the trench — Pegg, meanwhile, just ignored it.

They wove and ducked, jumped over water-filled sumps, had their nostrils filled with the smell of sweat, cooking and shit, froze when star-shells fizzed above them, pushed past the sleepers on the fire-step whilst trying not to wake them and snagged their clothes on every revetment, post and nail they passed before they came to their own company. Like the neighbours in Number Three Company, most of the Grenadiers were fast asleep, wrapped in blankets and oilskin sheets, every tenth man alert on sentry, peering over the parapet at the Russian lines, their breath hanging in the moonlight.

Pegg took the party up to the dugout that served as company headquarters. A larger pit had been excavated in the side of the trench that faced the enemy with earth-packed gabions placed in a semi-circle around the lip. In the middle of the floor a miniature brazier glowed red, throwing a soft light onto the three figures who were clustered around it. One man was tinkering with a kettle, the other two were sitting on ammunition boxes trying to read a document by the beams of a storm lantern. All three wore greatcoats, the skirts of which had been roughly hewn off to prevent the mud from clinging there. Morgan had already noticed that the men who had been through the worst of the winter months clung to these threadbare coats like a badge of honour, despite new ones being available. But then, he remembered how proud he'd been of his own bayonet-torn coat last year — and how it had rankled with Carmichael.

"'Scuse me, gennelmen, got Captain Morgan, Colour-Sar'nt McGucken an' an 'atful o' new 'uns for you." Pegg had to speak up to make himself heard above a sudden burst of firing over in the western French sector.

Sergeant Whaley was instantly on his feet, the light reflecting off his smiling face.

"Bloody 'ell, sir, Jock, we're right glad to see you."

The first grey of dawn was showing before Morgan felt more comfortable about the layout of his new command. Ten days had passed since Davidson-Smith had disappeared, moaning, on a stretcher during which nineteen-year-old Ensign Parkinson, the ink not yet dry on the cheque that had bought his commission, had nominally been in command. The boy had done his best, taking the company out of the line, going through all the tedious administration and carrying parties that consumed their "rest" period before bringing them back into the same stretch of trenches the day before. In reality, though, the experienced but increasingly weary Sergeant Whaley had been in charge. The strain showed: thank God he had McGucken.

Parkinson ran him round the trenches all night, showing him the new traverses that they had dug the last time the company had been there, the place where Davidson-Smith had been struck by a splinter, the

368

feeding areas, the collection point for digging tools and other gear — in short, all the paraphernalia of trench warfare that hadn't changed one iota since he'd experienced it last: even the wet sandbags stank just the same.

"Thank you, Parkinson, that all looks very satisfactory . . ." lied Morgan. It all looked very like it did almost half a year ago when he'd last seen it, ". . . though we don't seem to have got very much closer to Sevastopol, have we?"

"Difficult to say, I haven't been here very long. We improve the trenches as much as we can, but Russ is very active with both his guns and his raiding parties and it's my impression that we're sitting back a bit and letting the French do most of the work," replied the ensign.

Morgan had certainly noticed that very few of the troops or wagons moving behind the lines were British, most of them were French and a few of the latest nation to join the Alliance — the Sardinians. Whilst he had been in Malta, Morgan had seen how the papers had been lamenting Britain's inability to send more than a handful of reinforcements to the Crimea whilst French troops were flooding in and that seemed to be the truth.

"If you just listen to the French guns, Captain Morgan, you can hear how much more firing they do than our batteries and, it's got to be admitted, the Frogs have got all of the major Russian fortifications now as their responsibility except for the Redan." Parkinson must have thought about things much more clearly than Morgan did before he was wounded. "The problem is keeping the men interested. The old hands are awfully tired and don't want to take risks — I don't blame them — but they don't set the best of examples to the new'uns."

"Well what d'you expect? If you'd been through Alma and Inkermann you'd feel that you'd done more than enough," snapped Morgan, immediately realizing how defensive he must have sounded.

"Oh no, quite . . . quite . . ." Parkinson was taken aback by the rebuke, ". . . I don't mean any disrespect to the senior men, but it would be a lot easier if we had a full Company, if we had more men to share the work and the danger a bit more evenly and the Staff would let us get a bloody move-on rather than just hanging about making mud pies all day and night."

"Aye, I see your point . . ." Morgan regretted his outburst, ". . . but I wonder if we'll have the same conversation when you've been out here a while and seen more of Russ?"

"I have no doubt you're right, sir, and I'm keen to find out. If you want to know the truth, whilst it's a fine thing to have someone like you in charge of the company, I would have loved more time in command of it myself."

Morgan smiled at the lad's earnest enthusiasm, but two things worried him. First, Parkinson was very vague about exactly where the Russian rifle pits and trenches were and, secondly, the youngster knew none of the names of the sentries they met. Most of the men were trussed up in their blankets, snoring on the fire-step or in shallow dugouts, but when Parkinson spoke to a sentry there was no warmth. He merely wanted to know that the soldier was alert, could remember the password and was conscious of any patrols that were out, but he made no attempt to find out things about the man, to help pass the long hours of his duty, to talk of home or women or blacken the name of another regiment.

In return, the men were short and slightly sulky with the young officer. They answered his questions with just a "sir", or the briefest of explanations and when Morgan spoke to them — and he found that he knew only one or two — they were barrack-formal with him, standing stiffly to attention, barely meeting his eye. For everyone's sake, things would have to change.

Blinking with lack of sleep, Morgan watched his men stand-to. As blankets were shaken and packed away, damp greatcoats buttoned up before belts were pulled on over the top, oily rags taken from pouches and quickly rubbed over rifle barrels, they were brisk and thorough enough. As ammunition was checked, slings tightened and, just before they stepped up to the parapet, bayonets fixed, they were businesslike and commendably quiet, but there was none of the whispered chaffing, the suppressed, familiar quips and muffled laughter that he would have expected. The men were flat, efficient but without any spark: obedient but with no spirit.

The dawn inched up. Gradually, the dark forms took on shape and features, the shuffling, gently stamping, quietly coughing bundles becoming individual men.

They all kept their caps and heads just below the top of the sandbags, mittened hands held their rifles carefully, making sure that no bayonet tips showed above the top of the parapet to serve as an aiming mark for a lobbed grenade. As soon as they stood-down and returned to breakfast in the headquarters dugout, Sergeant Whaley briefed them about the new skills that the enemy had developed whilst McGucken and Morgan had been away,

"Russ has got these grenades he bloody juggles wi' — nasty, round, metal things just like a small shell, an' glass ones that go off with a real bang. He uses them close up when 'e's in the trench with you: stuns, but they don't throw any splinters out — safer for the attacker." Sergeant Whaley's picture of the Russians diverting themselves by scampering about the English trenches was new to both of them and rather daunting.

"Oh, aye, they've got right bold over the winter, the cheeky sods. They're usually after us rifles: the few they do 'ave ain't much good, so if they can cotch one of ours or a Frog's an' a pouch full of rounds, they're dead pleased. Trouble is, they're bloody good shots with 'em. Mr Parkinson will show you The Quarries in daylight, sir — stiff wi' Muscovites they are — an' they creep forward at night, dig themselves in an' snipe like buggery. We lost Parker two weeks ago like that. Right vexing they are." And there was worse.

"Watch out for the fougasses an' all, sir." Morgan was just familiar with the archaic term — they'd had a lecture from the sappers at Chatham once about them and petards as well, horrid devices that were designed to explode underfoot. "There's a little pop an' a short fizz when you step on 'em and then a flash and bang. They haven't done any harm yet, but Russ sticks 'em on likely approaches to his rifle pits an' they don't half put the shits up you when you're wandering about between the lines at night an' someone sets one off."

But this morning, the Russians were much more predictable. Just as the light improved enough for the enemy's artillery observers to see clearly, a shell exploded far too high over their heads and fifty yards short. Morgan looked up into the dawn-grey sky where a bruise of smoke was drifting down the wind. He could imagine the gunners now cutting a slightly longer fuse, adjusting the elevation of their barrels and carefully ramming home the next round.

"Right, boys, there's a wee 'good-morning' on its way. Just think o' them sandbags as a Weedon tart an' cuddle in tight." Morgan's mouth was dry: he tried to make light of the forthcoming ordeal, but the men were already taking what cover they could and those whose faces he could see looked uncomprehendingly at him. He'd forgotten, of course, that none of the new draft had been anywhere near their pre-war barracks in Northamptonshire, for they had all been trained at Aldershot. Here was another bond that had gone.

The next round was more accurate. It buried itself with a heavy thump and a great shower of grit just beyond the parados at the far end of the company's position. It failed to explode and an audible sigh of relief swept down the trench.

"If they're any bloody good, the next lot'll be right on top of us." Morgan knew he was telling the men nothing they hadn't worked out for themselves. Eyes were screwed tight shut, heads pulled down hard between hunched shoulders, bodies wedged between bags and gabions. "Keep down, lads."

The time dragged — the Russians would be making their final adjustments. A distant ripple of fire announced that the French were getting similar treatment, before half a dozen bangs — almost together except for one a fraction of a second later — came from much closer to them. Every man was counting the seconds as the rounds flew.

"For what we are about to receive may the Lord make us truly thankful." Someone had to say it — and it had to be Pegg.

Another wit just had time to say, "Amen", before the salvo arrived. Furious orange flashes frilled with coal-black smoke cracked about twenty feet above them, neatly straddling the trench, splinters and shrapnel balls kicking-up the soil like lethal rain. Morgan pushed himself hard against the wall of the trench. He'd pulled his unlit pipe from his mouth when the first, ranging round exploded: now its stem snapped in his tightly-clenched fist. He felt that horrible, itching contraction of his bladder as he waited for the cries of the wounded.

But none came. The Russians had made what the gunners would call "good practise", but the company, so far, had been lucky. It was almost a relief when the shells exploded, although waiting between salvoes was unbearable. When Morgan had last experienced such a bombardment, the men's dark humour helped to relieve the tension, but this new generation just huddled and shrank. Lance-Corporal Pegg's one quip had helped a little — but it was the only one he had.

Another batch of misery arrived and detonated, but, again, they all survived. A further dreadful lull had to be endured whilst Morgan searched vainly for words of encouragement and fought his desire to reach for his flask. The only thing that he could think of to say was that the enemy usually fired only three such harassing patterns — but he dare not say this to the men in case he was proved wrong. Then, just as he'd predicted to himself, the guns fired again, this time admirably together, and they all counted as destruction winged towards them.

Again, a wave of violent noise and the chemical smell of burnt powder enveloped them. But even as he pressed his cheek against a now warm sandbag, Morgan was aware of something different. A few yards to his right, just this side of where the trench bent away in a zig-zag, there was a giant thud, a scrape and an ominous fizz. How the round missed the cringing troops Morgan couldn't say; it had skipped off the front of the trench between two soldiers, playfully throwing a dozen sandbags about, before spinning merrily on the floor of the trench, its fuse spitting sparks and a jet of smoke.

Both men looked around white-faced, glimpsed the gyrating horror and threw themselves onto the earthy floor with a shout, shielding their heads with their

375

arms. But they were only a few feet from the thing: an exploding twelve-pound shell that close would injure or kill the pair of them. In the fraction of time that it took Morgan to absorb the scene, he realized that he was centre-stage in one of those heroic, naval paintings that hung on the walls at home: sputtering shell comes bounding aboard man-o'-war; barefoot tars recoil in terror, hands raised to protect themselves; quick-witted officer plucks it up as he might do a cricket ball on a summer's afternoon, before lobbing it casually over the side. Ship and sons-of-toil saved, young gallant shrugs it off as all part of a normal day's work.

But in the second that it took Morgan's brain to grasp all this and realize that he had to act, his body did nothing. He just stood there gaping, frozen, as inert as the shell was dangerous. Mercifully, others weren't. A stocky, older little man threw his rifle aside, grabbed a drinking-water pail that stood on a specially-cut ledge at the back of the trench and doused the ghastly thing as easily as if he were snuffing a kitchen candle. They all stood transfixed as the iron globe instantly stopped its dance, rocked a couple of times and then was still, a wisp of steam sighing gently from its unwinking, black fuse-hole.

"Holy God, man, well done . . ." Morgan stammered as the others lifted their ashen faces from the dirt, amazed to be unhurt, ". . . what's your name?"

"Cattray, sir." He was small for a Grenadier, deeply tanned below his beard and probably in his late twenties. Keeping below the parapet, Cattray tried to crouch yet still stiffen to attention, the empty pail swinging in his hand against the tatty skirts of his greatcoat.

"That was well done, Cattray: these two have got something to thank you for." Sheepishly the pair were lifting themselves up, brushing down their coats and reaching for their abandoned weapons. "Why don't I know you?"

"Transferred in from the Light Company, sir, when I got busted in January," Cattray said quietly. "Only joined the regiment just before we left Weedon."

"Where were you before, Cattray, and why were you reduced?" Morgan was surprised that he hadn't noticed this unusual man before.

"Eight years with the Saint Helena Regiment, sir. War was coming so I volunteered for this lot: wish I hadn't now." Cattray smiled ruefully, "I was a lance-corporal with a good conduct stripe. Captain Thomas took both of 'em off of me an' chucked me out o' his company just 'cos I got a bit lashed one night on picket. Most expensive grog I've ever 'ad: cost me eighteen pence a day, it did."

"Well, you've more than made up for that now, Cattray, we're glad to have you." Morgan replied. "That's just the sort of quick thinking I need."

"It was nowt, sir. You'll get used to the bangs and wallops after a while."

Get used to the bangs and wallops . . . get used . . . What on earth, Morgan wondered, did Cattray mean, *get used?* Didn't the man know that he'd been out here from the beginning? That he'd been at Alma? Didn't he know that he and McGucken had held the whole bloody show together at Inkermann? True, he'd missed the winter in the trenches but that hardly counted . . . or did it? Morgan began to realize that his company's collective memory was a short one, that only a handful of them had been together in last year's fighting and the common experience of most of his men was the cold misery of the trenches and impersonal little incidents like the one he had just experienced. It was as if nothing he'd done before counted and that this new set of men would need to be convinced just like the last lot did. Fine, if that was the case he'd find a way to do it.

Sleep, even in daylight with the odd shell whistling about, wasn't too hard if you were tired enough. Peters had his bed roll prepared and some food and drink in the pit where the officers and senior non-commissioned officers messed, and he soon fell into a deep, dreamless stupor. But he awoke confused. His shoulder was gently shaken before he opened his eyes to find a familiar face leering at him. How many times at Weedon or Glassdrumman had this been the first sight he'd seen in the morning, his former servant, James Keenan? But now he was no longer a servant: now he wore the three white worsted tapes of a sergeant, one of the most senior and trusted men in Morgan's command. And the fact that the face smiled at Morgan, that the eyes danced with pleasure at seeing him again suggested that he still didn't know the truth behind the relationship between the officer and Mary, his wife — thank God.

"Well, your honour, it's good to see you. Last time was on that goddamn hill full o' Russians." Keenan laughed. "Left it with a bit of a sore t'roat, so I did."

"You did that, Sergeant James Keenan." Morgan rolled from his blankets, grabbing the man by the hand. No matter how bad his conscience was about Mary, he was pleased to see his former servant. "I thought that sharpshooter at the Alma had killed you dead; let's have a look at the scar."

Keenan opened the hooks of his collar for the officer's inspection, showing a shiny, newly healed gash beside his windpipe. "It's not bad, sir, is it? An' they say you've got a good 'un too, let's see."

Quite forgetting himself and the dignity of their new positions, Morgan pulled his overalls down to show the purple dimples on both sides of his right thigh.

"Holy Jesus, sir, bit too close to himself for comfort, I'd say," said Keenan, pricking Morgan's conscience even further.

As they stood there, Morgan's pants about his ankles, Sergeant Keenan studying him closely, Peters walked round the sap's entrance, pulled aside the strip of canvas that served as a curtain and stopped dead, his face a picture, "Oh . . . oh, sorry sir, I . . ." The poor man was clearly appalled.

"Come here, Peters, an' look at the company commander's wounds: wonderful they are," said Keenan.

But the unblushing familiarity between the two Irishmen was too much for the Englishman, who just blanched and stammered, "Sir, commanding officer an' adjutant's coming up to see you," before fleeing the shocking scene.

Sergeant Ormond was their guide. Hume and the adjutant were hard on his heels and there was no time for anything more than a rapid "Good to have you back, sir," and a firm handshake before Ormond ushered the august pair into the Mess dugout.

"Hello, Morgan, Sergeant Keenan." Hume had that happy knack that so many officers lacked of being able to remember the men's names instantly. Not only that, his unruffled, frank manner and the way he looked you directly in the eye, made everyone feel that he knew them intimately and had the greatest trust in them.

Keenan responded with a vast grin, "Hello, your honours, grand to see you, I was just catching up on things with the captain, but I'll leave you all to it, now."

"No, don't go, Keenan. You know the Russian forward positions in front of The Quarries better than anyone, don't you? We'll need your help." Hume had done it again. Without really trying he'd made the freshly-promoted Sergeant Keenan feel as if he were the most important man in the world, upon whose sole advice his plan would rest.

The job was simple enough. The British were responsible for operations against the heavily defended earthwork known as the Great Redan. It bristled with guns slightly forward of Sevastopol, part of a chain of smaller and larger forts that could all cover the approaches that an assaulting party would have to take with carefully calculated and murderous fire.

But the Russians were masters of the defence. Between the Redan and the Malakoff — the main target of the French — lay some old diggings, the eponymous Quarries. Their steep sides made them difficult to reach with artillery, so the Russians massed infantry and light mortars there in order to break up any attacks that the British might make on the Redan. Indeed, this morning's bombardment had come from a particularly well-served mortar battery deeply ensconced there.

The Quarries' garrison also pushed out snipers — many by night, fewer, more skilful ones by day — into shallow pits, who would give warning of any attack that was forming up. At the same time, their sniping made life extremely dangerous and uncomfortable for the British opposite. Now, Major Hume had been warned that the Allies' attack on Sevastopol was imminent, and it was obvious that The Quarries and a series of other works across the British and French fronts would have to be cleared before any effective attack could be mounted. So, it came as no surprise when Brigade ordered him to clear the rifle pits in front and then hold them. Any prisoners who could be taken would, the Staff were sure, yield vital intelligence.

When the major had outlined the plan, the group — on Keenan's advice — crept up to a corner of one of the forward saps where it was sometimes possible to catch a glimpse of the enemy worming about.

"Just have a care here, your honours." Despite clear daylight and the frequent thump of guns, Keenan lowered his voice as the three officers carefully mounted the fire-step, slowly extending their telescopes as they did so.

"We can see Russ from here, but he knows it an' he'll be a-waiting for us to show ourselves. This is where Parker got it the other day." Sergeant Keenan pointed to a rosary and crucifix that were nailed to one of the revetments, crossing himself.

His caution had the desired effect. All three of them moved with Job-like patience, showing as little of themselves as possible. When it came to Morgan's turn, he swept the dun, chalk-streaked landscape with his glass, saw a few rocky outcrops that must have been The Quarries, but was really none the wiser.

"How many pits d'you reckon Russ has got out there, Sergeant Keenan?" Hume sat on the fire-step, a Sapper's chart spread out between himself and the adjutant, compass in his hand.

"Best guess would be a dozen or so, sir, but it's hard to tell." Morgan knew that Keenan had no accurate idea. He'd not yet had time to go on patrol himself, but every report about the enemy's activity was vague in the extreme. The only thing that was certain was that Russ was there and that any interference really upset him.

"So, Morgan, if we get Brigade to light things up with star-shells, I reckon you could roll the enemy up from over yonder . . ." Hume pointed over the parapet to the right with a pencil, ". . . take some of the bigger pits, hold them and then dig a sap back here so that you can link them to the main position. Will you be ready by tomorrow night? It'll all have to be very carefully timed and co-ordinated with the guns."

"I will, sir," Morgan wasn't at all sure that he would, but wasn't going to say so.

"Fine, you plan it, then tie it up with the adjutant. I should think twenty men and your best sergeant . . ." Hume looked meaningfully at Keenan, ". . . led by a subaltern would do it; but you must decide the details, Morgan."

"Thank you, sir: I'll lead it myself."

Ensign Parkinson was disappointed. The rumour, or "shave" as the men called it, that a raid was going to take place had been circulating for days and as they only officer present, Parkinson had assumed that he wouldn't just lead it, he would lead it to glory.

"There'll be plenty of other opportunities for you to get yourself killed, young Parkinson, and don't think I don't appreciate your pluck . . ." Had Morgan really heard himself calling another officer "young"? ". . . but I need to get the feel of the enemy's positions myself before we get involved in anything bigger. But, you've been out with the men longer than McGucken and me . . ." unconsciously, he was picking up some of Major Hume's tricks, ". . . and I'd like your advice on which ones to take."

The boy brightened as he sat in the dugout with his company commander and colour-sergeant. The fact that Sergeant Keenan would be second-in-command of the operation was already assumed and now they had to draw up the rest of the list. Under Parkinson's direction they picked reliable private soldiers and the non-commissioned officers who could be spared from other essential tasks and who weren't too tired.

"And you ought to take Corporal Pegg," Parkinson concluded, "he's damn good in a tight corner and handles the men well."

Morgan looked at McGucken who said nothing, merely raising an eyebrow, "Well, if you recommend him, Parkinson, that's fine by me." Morgan scribbled his name down, "I've told the men to wear their sea-smocks, sir — I'll get one for you," said McGucken.

The coarse, canvas smocks that were issued to the men when afloat to protect their uniforms from tar, had been dyed brown and were increasingly *de rigueur* for trench duty. Most other regiments wore them routinely, but in the formal 95th, it had been decreed that they would only be worn for special tasks.

"An' Sergeant Keenan's getting some clubs made for to cosh the poor bloody prisoners." That wasn't like McGucken, thought Morgan. He'd seen him despatch any number of Russians without any sign of remorse — now he was sympathizing with them. Perhaps his wound had mellowed him.

The day passed too quickly. By the time Morgan had scoured the ground again with his glass and talked to the four men who had patrolled there most recently, he was late for his meeting with the gunner subaltern who was waiting for him in the dugout. The man was impatient. What to Morgan was life or death, to the artilleryman was very routine, for all that these infantrymen wanted was enough light to let them see

384

the enemy's position once they had found the edge of it. There was no preparatory bombardment needed from his mortars, nor any protective fire once the job was complete — that would require careful timings and fussy fusing — it was just a simple, illumination job. Yet this jumpy-looking captain wanted to know every last detail.

"So you'll fire your first round once you see my green rocket, will you?" Morgan asked.

"Yes, as I said before, you'll have to judge it a bit cleverly because it'll take about twenty-five seconds for the star-shell to light up fully, then you'll get constant light for the next eight minutes." The gunner tried to be patient.

"It's vital that we don't have any of those patches of darkness halfway through the assault." Morgan was aware that he'd made the point before.

"No, of course not," the gunner said as breezily as he could, "but I can't absolutely guarantee the fuses: we do have some tricky ones occasionally. You should be all right, though."

Should be all right, though, thought Morgan to himself. It was fine for this base-rat sitting warming his hands on his mortars, drinking tea whilst he and the boys gave the enemy some target practice. But he mustn't show how worried he was. The last thing that Morgan wanted was a gang of gunners sniggering at stories of the reluctant 95th.

"They look fine, no damp or mildew there." The gunner threw a perfunctory, look over the two green signal rockets that the Quartermaster had provided. "Good luck, then."

Before they came into the trench system, Morgan had given careful orders: they'd rehearsed how they would fight through each enemy pit and how prisoners would be handled; how they would dig a link back to the company and which eight men would remain in the new position. Then bayonets had been taped tightly to muzzles to stop them rattling; digging tools were carefully secured and wrapped in hessian to prevent any scraping, whilst each man was dressed in his muddy-brown sea-smock, just a pouch, scabbard and water-bottle on his belt. McGucken had been there to oversee the issue of extra bandages and two spiking nails to everyone before hot broth and an extra tot of rum were issued. Then he watched them file off silently, wishing that he was going too.

By ten o'clock it was pitch-black. After the twists, turns and trips that any trench journey involved, the raiders had arrived at the point from which they were to leave the forward sap. Now they waited quietly, no moon showing and the guns unusually quiet.

"Sir, we need to check that no one's weapon is at half-cock." Keenan was clucking around the men quietly but purposefully. "We don't want a percussion cap falling-off just when we need it most."

"Yes, of course, Sergeant Keenan, get the non-commissioned officers to see to that, and get the men to draw socks over their boots now, if you please."

Keenan bustled off amongst the dark figures, whispering instructions to the corporals.

"Gi' it 'ere, you bloody crow." Just at Morgan's elbow Corporal Pegg berated a soldier in a venomous whisper, grabbing the man's weapon as he fumbled with the hammer. "an' hurry up getting them socks over yer boots, d'you want Russ to hear us before we've even started, you twat?"

Morgan wondered at Pegg. In a few minutes' time he might have to trust his life to the very man whom he had just humiliated — not a wise move. He'd speak to him about it later — if there was a later. Now he had no time for anything other than to crouch at the bottom of the trench and stare at his watch, dimly lit by the shrouded lantern that one of the corporals carried. Slowly the hands crept towards ten-past ten whilst Morgan imagined the gun crews, Hume, McGucken and the rest of the company waiting and listening for the first shot, the first yell. He wondered if the Russians were waiting as well.

Then it was time. As quietly as he could he levered himself onto the parapet, the men to left and right of him doing the same. There he crouched until all of them were out of the trench, then he beckoned them to stand, before the front twelve moved off, the second wave of eight — who were to hold the ground they took — just behind. The men stepped carefully whilst Morgan held his signal rocket ready, his fingers tight around its wire initiator. If the enemy fired first then he would launch the signal, but if they could get up to the rifle pits and silently overwhelm the sentries, then he would delay as long as possible.

The line moved quietly on. There was no light to flash on the levelled steel blades and the troops were silent in their muffled boots until, with a curse and a stifled cry one of the men on the left of the line fell headlong into a hole. For a second there was silence then all the devils in Moscow were let loose. Shouts and cries, Morgan crouching, confused, Keenan sprinting hard, the two men with clubs panting along behind. Then thumps, whimpers and more shouts before silence again.

"Got two of 'em, sir. Hennon stepped on one — teach 'em not to sleep on duty, won't it?" Keenan was exhilarated. His two bruisers supported one injured Russian between them whilst nudging another with a cudgel.

"Good, well done all of you. Take the prisoners back, you two: report to the Colour-Sergeant."

With a quiet "sir", the two men were away, but what to do now? Certainly, they'd stumbled over one trench, taken prisoners and, amazingly, remained undetected. But Morgan still had no idea where the other trenches were. The men lay or crouched, their pale faces just visible in the darkness, all looking to him for orders.

"Right, your honour, which way now?" Keenan whispered.

"I . . . I'm not . . . just wait and listen a moment, Sergeant Keenan." Morgan bought himself time.

It was a curious relief when a low, incomprehensible voice growled through the darkness. What it said, no one knew, but it was certainly a challenge that was repeated when there was no reply from the British. A second passed, two before Pegg piped up "Tsar Nicholas." It was an old trick but Pegg had seen it work before.

Not this time. The reply was a bang and a gout of flame that stained the eye, an angry shout, then nothing. The British sank to a crouch: more bellowed commands followed by more, tense silence.

Morgan looked about him, desperately wondering what to do whilst Keenan quivered with excitement beside him and said in a loud whisper, "Come on then, your honour let's get at 'em."

But before Morgan could make a decision there was another yell close at hand and a ripple of fire that sent one of the men sprawling in the dark, a metallic ring coming from his shovel.

"Shoot at 'em, boys, for Christ sake!" At last Morgan acted, but despite the preparations and rehearsals, he failed to tell only one half of the party to fire. As a result, the imprecise, panicky order caused everyone to fire blindly in the dark — and in an instant all the weapons were empty.

"Reload, then, quick as you can." Keenan whirled on the men, realizing the emergency. If half the men had held their fire — as they'd been trained to — they would be able to resist whatever the enemy's next move was. Now they were utterly vulnerable as each man grappled with ramrod and cartridge in the pitch-black.

"No, sir, wait . . ." But Keenan's plea was too late. Morgan had been fumbling with his rocket; pulling at the wire loop that would ignite it. Then, with a fan of flame and a mushroom of smoke, the giant firework fizzed into the sky until it burst high above, shedding a sinister green light over all of them.

Almost before the rocket reached its zenith there was an echoing bang from their own mortars and half a minute later the whole landscape was lit by a great, blazing ball that hung in the sky, dripping phosphorus. It was just as the gunners had promised, except that the wind carried the illumination behind Morgan's party, silhouetting them for the Russians who were now firing as hard as they could from their pits. Bullets whirred and buzzed, drying Morgan's throat in an instant, just as they always did. The men had gone to ground as the lead sang, making reloading almost impossible whilst a series of thumps and flashes came from deep inside The Quarries.

"Jaysus, sir, we don't need that fucking light . . ." Keenan didn't need to whisper now. They both looked into the sky as the star-shell fell at the end of its parabola. But, as its light began to fade, another round erupted just as brilliantly. "Can't we stop it, your honour?"

"No, we'll get continuous light now until . . ." But the end of Morgan's sentence was drowned out by the crashing arrival of the Russian mortar salvo that they had just heard being fired. Shells exploded across the top of the British lines, orange-yellow flashes ripping the night apart, momentarily brighter than the star-shells. There they crouched — a curtain of fire

390

cutting off their retreat, weapons useless and everything lighter than day.

"All we need now is a bloody counter-attack," Morgan yelled to Keenan as they both tried to press themselves into the earth.

And that's what they got. The enemy had, obviously, been expecting just such a raid by the British for they were out of their trenches and yelling in what seemed like seconds. In the juddering light, Morgan and his men could just see darting figures a hundred paces in front of them, rising, ducking and firing: a flurry of bullets whirred and cracked about them. Then to their right more shouts and stabs of flame — the enemy were skirmishing forward by half-companies, one half loading then firing whilst the other half moved.

Not that it made a damn bit of difference to the raiding party. All that they knew was that walls of disciplined lead were sweeping over them, pinning them to the ground whilst their enemies got closer and closer. Over to Morgan's left, the wounded man's moans rose and fell, but no one dared to go to help him.

"Sir, we can't just lie here," yelled Keenan, cheek flat against the earth, "what'll we do?"

Morgan didn't know — he could hardly think. The flickering light, the din of the artillery, the flying metal and the noise of the wounded were horribly confusing. In daylight it was all so much easier — your enemy was there in front of you, coming on like soldiers — that was how it was meant to be. Now they dodged and jumped in the dark, leaping from holes and dips, yelling like demons whilst his own, stupid, bloody artillery made it so much easier for them. He quivered with indecision.

"Your honour, come on, we must do something." Keenan was right. The first wave of Russians were close now, too close — he could see their long sword-bayonets gleaming in the light. To do nothing meant certain death: they must fight or run.

Then it was simple. What was it his father had said? These men needed ". . . every bit of leadership they could get", and he wasn't going to shame his family and the regiment and, more to the point, he was no Carmichael.

"Get up you lot . . ." Morgan rose, shouting above the racket, the hesitation, the trembling temporarily gone. He'd done all this before — the chaos of the Alma, that free-for-all on Shell Hell, then Inkermann: suddenly he didn't care if he survived; all that mattered were the men around him and the goddamn Muscovites. Shouting for the troops to follow, Morgan ran at the enemy, dragging his pistol from his belt.

"Jaysus, get after him lads!" Keenan bawled as Morgan's lonely, dark figure threw itself against the wave of riflemen.

The cloying spell of fear broke. Almost as one, the men were up and running after Morgan, bellowing, shrieking, falling on their many foes with such ferocity that the Russian line checked and faltered. The flickering monochrome of the star-shell reduced the whole scene to slabs of harsh light and lakes of deep shadow. Rifles banged as the two sides met, flames jabbing from muzzles. Then just an urgent torrent of grunts and bloody coughs as elbows jerked and butts pistoned quickly, brutally — bayonets flashing, sinking through coats and yielding flesh.

How many rounds did he have left in his revolver? Morgan didn't know — it had jumped in his hand several times as he ran madly at the Russians, but now he was at the centre of the mêlée with nothing else to defend him. What had Colonel Kemp said all those months ago at Glassdrumman when he'd been given the pistol? Something about waiting until you could touch your foe before firing — well, now was his chance to see whether the advice was sound.

A flat-capped serf was only feet away, the flickering light making his face look two-dimensional except for a great, black, snarling hole below his moustache. He came bounding forward then stopped and drew his rifle and long, broad blade back to strike — but just as he was about to thrust, Morgan punched his pistol forward, poking him hard under the chin with the barrel even as he pulled the trigger. The ball almost lifted the man off his feet. There was no colour in the spray of blood and brains that came from the back of his head, just a black geyser, his cap flying away into the dark. He fell with a clatter.

From the pushing, slashing crowd another man came at him. Morgan didn't wait this time, but raised the Tranter to fire right at the man's nose — but there was just an empty click. Happily, the Russian paused as he glimpsed eternity. For less than a second they stared at each other, Morgan's enemy not believing his luck, lowering his rifle, giving the young officer the chance he needed. As if he were handling a sabre, Morgan pulled the revolver back over his shoulder and swiped as hard as he could across his foe's face, the steel rammer opening a great, bloody gash through his eyebrow and cheek as he fell away.

Then it was just like that horrifying ruck when the enemy made their sortie last October. The Muscovites would come on full of piss and vinegar unless you went full tilt, meeting them toe-to-toe — then even a much smaller number might cow them and throw them back. As Morgan wheezed and panted in the dark, the Russians ran, leaving a litter of wounded. As the non-commissioned officers whipped the men in, Morgan half-stood, hands on his knees, lungs heaving just as he might at the Skibbereen Chase.

With no warning all went black — the last of the star-shells had expired and the night looked even darker to their unready eyes. Just seconds later, the Russian bombardment ceased and the men found themselves milling around, dazed by the unnatural quiet. As Morgan was gathering his wits and trying to decide what to do next, the enemy did the job for him. The charge had pushed back one half-company of riflemen, but not the other and they announced their presence by a searing volley that lit the night for a fraction of a second, the rounds whistling high and wide with no star-shell to help their aim.

"What now, your honour?" barked Keenan.

"Run, boys, just run!" It was the simplest order he ever gave in battle and certainly the most eagerly obeyed.

He jerked one arm of the wounded man over his shoulder whilst a faceless soldier did the same: then, stumbling and tripping, the three of them did their best to catch up with the rest who were going like hares. In the inky dark to his front a single voice boomed out, "Here, Grenadiers, here," in best Glasgow.

McGucken was guiding them back to their own lines whilst the lead still hummed overhead. Morgan was just conscious of a darker strip in the ground ahead from which black bundles emerged, one of which was frantically waving its arms and beckoning.

"That yous, sir? Last man?" McGucken bawled as the trio tripped over the bags on the parapet.

"Aye, Captain Morgan and two. Think we're the last. You seen Keenan?" He panted as they half-fell and slid down into the trench.

"Here your honour, all accounted for," a disembodied voice answered from the now crowded sap.

"Enemy front, Left Half-Company . . ." McGucken boomed to the rest of the Grenadiers who stood ready on the firestep, ". . . fire!" Half the rifles crashed right along the trench, spinning bullets into the face of the surging Russians. "Reload," ramrods rasped, "Right Half-Company . . . fire!"

His men blasted away at their foes whilst Morgan tried to wipe the blood from between his fingers. His whole body shook uncontrollably.

CHAPTER
THIRTEEN

Out of the Line

The hut smelt of new wood. Morgan was too tired to scrape the mud off his boots and stumped across the bare boards, leaving a trail of muck round each footstep. Belt, holster and sword were abandoned on a chair, his damp cap and coat draped over the back of it and his sea-smock pulled over his head before being dumped on the floor. The blankets on his truckle had been neatly folded back by Peters: now they sang like sirens, but not as loud as the bottle of brandy.

The spirit burnt his throat most agreeably whilst he fought to get his boots off before unbuttoning his tight red shell-jacket. As he spread out on the bed, sipping steadily, one great yellow-horned toe showed from his worn grey woollen socks. How Mother would have hated that, not to mention the lice that made him itch at armpits and crotch. How had the wretched things got back on him so quickly? Pat the terrier sat at the foot of Morgan's bed, scratching hard at his flank with a hind leg. Had he caught the damn things from the dog, Morgan wondered, or was this just some demonstration of misplaced, canine loyalty?

One man wounded wasn't too bad and two prisoners was better than any other company, but there was no getting away from the fact that he had failed to clear the rifle pits and hold that bit of ground. There was no getting away from the fact, either, that he'd dithered, that he'd buggered things up with that needless rocket. Had there been just a slight sneer on the 55th's company commander's face when they had handed over to them this morning? Morgan reached to refill his glass — he didn't even notice the mud on his trousers, now. And who cared if his clothes made the blankets wet — nothing could stop him from sleeping. Except the account of the raid that he would have to give to the commanding officer. But that was later.

There was a rap on the door. It opened immediately, daylight and the noise of the guns came flooding in. "Sir, just to tell you that we're all accounted for, men fed and bedded down." McGucken saluted in the doorway.

"Come in, Colour-Sergeant, how's Duffy?" Morgan rolled from his bed, conscious that he was half-undressed and in no fit state to be seen. He staggered as he stood.

"Steady, sir," McGucken reached out to catch him, but he recovered just in time.

"Sit down, man, d'you want a drink?" Morgan flopped back onto his bed as the dog ran to sniff the new arrival.

McGucken pushed the officer's kit from the chair almost contemptuously, before grabbing the seat, sitting down and staring at him, "Duffy's fine, sir." It

397

was only after Morgan had helped to carry Duffy back to their own lines that he had recognized him as his opponent from Regimental boxing in Weedon. "His shovel took most of the sting from that round and he's just bruised an' a bit cut." McGucken paused. "At least he's not half-cut like yous. What the fuck are you on, sir, you'll have to see Major Hume the moment he blows for you: you can't go lashed-up."

Morgan just stared at him.

"I know what you're thinkin' sir, but you did just fine. Sergeant Keenan told me how you led that charge — saved the day he said. Besides, we could never have held those positions even if we had taken them. Bloody stupid idea." It was clear that McGucken had already had a full account from Keenan.

"Yes, but I fannied around when the firing started like I've never done before . . ." Morgan was treading right over the line of rank and position now, ". . . and I fired that rocket when there was no need."

"An' you stopped the men from running an' tore into them Muscovites all by yourself, sir — the men are talking about nothing else an' Keenan reckons he owes you. Now get yer head down for a couple o' hours before you're called for."

Morgan was asleep almost before McGucken had finished. The Scotsman pulled a blanket up around his officer's shoulders — not that he would ever have told anyone.

Even through his exhaustion, Morgan was aware of the door opening and closing and Peters's furtive

398

movements. It was late afternoon when he was shaken awake.

"'Ere y'are, sir," Peters pressed a cup of sweet tea into his unreceptive hand. "Bloody guns, never give up, do they?" He pulled back the bit of canvas that served as a makeshift curtain and stared gloomily towards the siege lines, "commanding officer wants you within the hour, sir, done yer kit as best I can."

Morgan peeped from under his blankets at his clothes that his batman had laid out. His baggy spare trousers, the ones he'd bought from Eddington's effects after his death, would do and at least most of the mud had been scraped off his soaking boots whilst he slept.

"Thank you Peters, you saved my skin, again," Morgan mumbled through tea and sheets.

"'S all right, sir," Morgan just saw Peters tip the bottle of brandy, inspect its depleted contents and frown.

"Aye, bloody guns, they could give you an 'eadache, they could," he remarked, before bustling out.

Morgan did his best to keep out of the mud and manure as he hurried to the Orderly Room. He was concentrating so hard on the ruts and drying puddles that he would have missed Corporal Pegg's antics had it not been for the noise he was making.

Pegg, still muddy from the trenches, was shouting at two men who had their rifles above their heads, doubling for a few paces to the time that Pegg called out before, on his shrieked word of command, marking time, knees pumping. It was a sight that would have been common enough back in Weedon, but here? Certainly, on campaign, men received punishment for a number of offences, but they had to be serious and merited hard labour or even a stroke or two of the cat. Petty punishment like this was taboo. Pegg saw him, brought both men to a halt, ordered their arms and saluted.

"Good morning, sir." There was something slightly guilty in the way that Pegg spoke and the salute was over-punctilious. "Caught these two using sand to clean their barrels, I did, sir." Pegg offered an explanation before one was demanded.

"I see, right, you two, fall out, back to your duties." Morgan beckoned Pegg into the lee of a hut where they couldn't be seen. "Look, Corporal Pegg, I know that what they were doing was wrong, but at least they were trying to keep their weapons clean, weren't they? Would have been better to save punishment for when they'd not bothered to clean their rifles, wouldn't it?"

"Sir." Pegg was clearly unimpressed with Morgan's clemency.

"Well, don't you remember how Colour-Sergeant McGucken dealt with you and the rabbit-shooting drama before the Alma? Sure, you had a strip torn off you, but nothing else because he had a pretty damn good idea of what lay ahead. Treat the men better, Corporal Pegg: they need every bit of leadership that you and I can give them." That last bit of advice was in danger of being over-used, thought Morgan.

400

"Aye, sir, yer right." Pegg cocked his head a little as if weighing-up Morgan's words. "It's just that these sprogs can be so daft, sometimes."

"And that's just what we were saying about you not many months ago, Corporal-bloody-Pegg." Morgan smiled. "You've had no sleep yet after last night, have you? Get to your blankets now — and well done on the raid, by the way, Sergeant Keenan was talking very highly of you." Morgan lied — for he'd hardly spoken to Keenan — but it was a lie worth telling.

"Thank you, sir, you didn't do bad yersen."

The new adjutant was positively deferential to Morgan. There was none of the growling criticism that he would have had from McDonald about the length of his whiskers, lack of a sword knot or any of that peacetime rot. Instead, he was quickly ushered into Hume who was hunched over a chart of the trenches and parallels, making notes with a well-chewed pencil. His boots, spurs and trousers were covered in mud and his shell-jacket hung open: Morgan had no need to worry about his own appearance.

"Ah, Morgan . . ." There was a long, tense pause whilst Hume looked him over. He deserved whatever was coming for he'd failed to do what he was told — he braced himself. "Well done last night," said Hume, apparently without any sarcasm, "those prisoners are singing like good 'uns at Brigade, telling us all sorts of things about The Quarries."

Morgan sighed inwardly.

"Now look at this." Morgan joined Hume poring over his maps. "I know you know all this, but just humour me for a moment." There it was again, Hume putting his subordinate at ease, wrapping him in confidence. The major pointed out the series of earthworks and forts that were holding the besiegers of Sevastopol at bay.

"The key to the whole siege is the Malakoff; that, and the outer work, the Mamelon have got to be dealt with by the French. There's a whole series of lunettes and, of course the White Works just there," his pencil tapped the map, "but they're the Frogs' — I mean our gallant allies — problem. However, they won't succeed unless we can silence the bloody Redan . . ." Hume placed his finger very deliberately on the smaller fort off to the east of the Malakoff, ". . . and the Redan won't fall unless . . ." Morgan knew at once what was coming and that there was a place for him in the inevitable blood-letting, ". . . The Quarries are taken. Now, it seems that our Staff have a plan to mount a co-ordinated series of attacks with the Frogs to take all these outlying works simultaneously. You can see the sense of that." Morgan nodded slowly.

"But they've come up with some knuckle-headed idea to launch two columns of about six hundred apiece — one column from our Division and one from the Light Div — of mixed regiments, so that everyone gets a slice of the glory, I suppose. Obviously, it should be done by a couple of complete regiments from each Division, so much easier to command, but no, too many ministers' nephews wanting promotion, I guess. Now, this is where you come in."

More like, *This is where you go out in a box*, thought Morgan.

"You and your Grenadiers will be under Major Armstrong of the Forty-Ninth — you know him and the whole affair will be commanded by Colonel Shirley of the Eighty-Eighth. You won't have come across him, he wasn't out here during the rough stuff last year: frightful snob — he owns half of Birmingham."

Hume continued with more details about conferences that he would have to attend, reconaissances, special trench-fighting techniques that they would have to master, co-ordination with the artillery; everything, in fact, except the proposed date.

"Sir, when's all this planned for?" Morgan was already trying to draw up a mental time-table.

"Coming to that. I'll get you some reinforcements to bring you up to about seventy strong and you'll be left out of the line to train and prepare for the next two weeks or so — the other companies will hate you for it. So, you'll need to be ready by no later than about the sixth of June." Hume fixed him with his dark, pebble eyes, whilst Morgan tried not to quail too obviously.

"And Morgan, you'll need to keep this whole affair tighter than Scrooge: we don't need the Muscovites to be on the *qui vive*."

Private Duffy sat up perkily on his plank bed, a bandage around his shoulder.

"Hello, Duffy, how's the wound?" Morgan, head still spinning from lack of sleep and an overdose of Major Hume's instructions, had decided to visit their only casualty from last night's action.

"Eh up, sir." Duffy grinned at Morgan showing gums missing most of his front teeth. "Surgeon says it's a contusion, sir, me shovel took most of the power out o' the bullet." Duffy was delighted with the exotic word. "Worse thing is, sir, I lost me false 'uns: couldn't send a patrol out to find 'em for me could you?"

"Well, I never knew you was missing all that ivory, Duffy." Even when Morgan had inspected Duffy, he'd never noticed his teeth. "How do you bite off your cartridge paper?"

"With great fuckin' difficulty, sir. But I was all right until you loosened me last two in the ring back at Weedon, sir." Duffy grinned gappily — Morgan could almost feel his stinging punches. "Mind you, sir, I'll be all right for this big attack on The Quarries."

Morgan stiffened and tried to shush Duffy. "Keep your voice down, Duffy, there's a good man."

"No, sir, serious, one o' the Forty-Ninth lads was 'ere visiting, said 'is major was going to lead an assault in the next couple o' weeks — special training an' all." Duffy continued at full volume. Morgan wondered how the men learnt about these things so quickly.

"Now, Captain Morgan, sir, it's no good you sending your men to me half-kilt if you then try to talk the poor fellers to death." Mary Keenan had arrived silently behind Morgan. Now she stooped, tucked Duffy's bedclothes in, looking straight into the officer's eyes, betraying nothing. "Peter Duffy here's coming on fine, your honour, only a wee wound . . ."

"Contusion, Mrs Keenan," Duffy added quickly.

"Aye, contusion. Anyway, you'll need to excuse the Captain and myself, we have all the news from the Big House back home to discuss," and she turned on her heel, expecting Morgan to follow.

"Look, Duffy, for God's sake keep quiet about any attack, we don't want Russ to be waiting for us, do we?" Morgan was more than anxious to follow Mary, but he had to make Duffy hold his tongue.

"Aye, sir, all right, I'll keep me gob shut. Best not keep that a-waitin', sir," he added with a horrid wink as Mary's shapely bottom floated away.

The hut was just like Morgan's. Inside, though, it had been divided into four by blankets that hung from the cross-timbers, Mary's quarter, Morgan noticed immediately, being the one by the window and furthest from the draughty door. Both the Allies and the enemy had done their best to furnish the tiny space: a delicate Russian table stood in the centre of the floor — two camp chairs that looked French beside it; there was crockery that had certainly come from the baggage train they over-ran on the way to Balaklava and the issue bed was covered with a great Tartar coverlet. Thrust into the wooden walls were bayonets set at an angle, their sockets stuffed with candles whilst a sergeant's coat lay next to Mary's sewing basket. Three other wives and their husbands shared the place:

405

Morgan could only guess at some of the scenes that were played out in the tiny, blanket-walled rooms.

"Don't worry, you won't be embarrassed by anyone coming in, sir. The girls are all up at the main hospital and James is too damn busy patting his precious soldiers after last night's high-jinks to worry about me." There was no affection in Mary's voice, either for Morgan or, as far as he could see, for Keenan.

Morgan knew this was going to be difficult. It had been months since they'd seen each other and except for the news that he'd got from the servants in Glassdrumman, he had heard nothing. But whatever had happened before, things would have to change. Mary was no longer the biddable little jewel of the Morgan household whom he could toy with as he pleased. She was a sergeant's wife running a busy hospital, mixing with coarse men who were hardened by death and violence — and she was clearly flourishing.

And he was no longer a love-struck subaltern whose antics might be winked at. He commanded a company and, what's more, he commanded her cuckolded husband: he must leave her in no doubt about the fact that they couldn't continue together. Besides, everyone had told him to drop her — everyone except Finn the groom, that is: Finn who had taught him to ride, fish, shoot and drink — Finn who knew him better than anyone at home. What had he said? ". . . and mind you come home with Mary by your side — where she ought to be." Some damn nonsense like that.

406

"D'you still take sugar in your tay, Captain Morgan?" Morgan looked at her warming the pot and he knew that they were both thinking of those early mornings back at home when she would bring him his first cup of tea — and stay in his room just a little longer.

"I still do, Mary . . ."

"It's Mrs Keenan to you, Captain Morgan, sir." There was ice in her voice. "And how's everything at home? I had some nice letters from the servants, one from Finn who told me all about you, one from your father, even." Morgan knew that tart note in Mary's voice — it signalled danger.

"Yes, I have a wee packet of letters from home, most for you and a couple for your husband," Morgan tried to change tack, ". . . perhaps you could help him with them," but he couldn't have got it more wrong.

"Help him with them? How bloody dare you — are you suggesting that my husband is some sort of eejit that can't shift for himself? At least he hasn't been skulking at home with some pin-prick. Oh no, he was back here as soon as his poor neck was healed, standing alongside us as we froze our tits off with Russ laughing fit to bust down there in the town. And what did I hear of you? That quim Jeanie Brennan tells me that you're the grand man around Skib', squirin' Maude-bleedin'-Hawtrey whilst we all thought you'd never walk again." Mary's words were made all the more vicious by the steely control of her voice.

"An' here's me stuck with that great ox of a man who can think of nothing but his bloody soldiers. I bet he's

407

up there now wiping someone's hole rather than helping his wife. An' you come in here an' expect to lift me off some goddamn shelf whenever you wish, tickle me a bit an' then shove me back until I'm wanted again." Mary was blazing at him, chin thrust forward, fists clenched, every muscle tensed with anger. Christ, she was beautiful.

"Mary, it isn't like that, it can't be." Morgan was standing opposite her, staring into her great, chestnut eyes. Then the storm broke. Tears welled down her cheeks, her face collapsed and he found himself wrapping her in his arms, gently rocking her to and fro, all resolve gone as the sobs came long and low. "There, my darling, please don't cry."

"Oh Tony, you don't know what it's been like . . ."

But he could guess. Her language, her whole posture revealed her as a woman who had endured hardship, who'd had to fend for herself amongst men whose business was death, who'd slaved in some of the harshest conditions and who had plainly mastered it. Now she clung to him like she always had, not just his bed-mate but as his lover and friend. He'd dreamed of this moment in the past few months. The rational side of him knew that they must part, that it would be a kindness to Mary and Keenan. But he wasn't rational alone and hard in his bed at night; he wasn't rational when he was surrounded by comfortable, mannered folk who danced, laughed and ate, whose lives were no more dangerous than a fast chase after a fox. How could those soft, powdered women compare with this

408

girl? How could he ever hope to be happy with someone who didn't understand all this horror?

"Tony, please tell me that we're going to be all right," she clung to him, pressing her cheek against the buttons on his chest, ". . . you don't know how I've missed you whilst you've been away. The last time I saw you, you was bleedin' like Christ on his cross an' most of the lads that Dr Fergusson and I dressed at Inkermann didn't even make it to Turkey. Then I heard nothing at all from you." Mary paused, gulping her tears. "I know how difficult it's going to be, how people will talk and stand in our way. I know I've wronged poor, dear, simple James, but I can't go on like this for much longer. I need you, I can't live without you."

The guns rattled in the distance and they kissed. Mary's lashes were still full of great, salty tears that Morgan brushed away with his lips, kissing gently at first and then with increasing urgency down her ears to her neck, pushing aside her shawl and the cotton top of her dress and smothering her shoulders. She felt so small, so vulnerable in his arms as she struggled to undo the ladder of buttons on the front of his shell-jacket, eventually pulling it away and gently pushing Morgan back onto the bed. With practised ease, Mary lifted first one, then Morgan's other boot, undid the laces and pulled them off, getting hardly any mud on her hands as she did so.

"Jaysus, Tony, how can you go about like that?" Mary looked down at the dirt-rimed big toe that stuck through his worn, grey, wool sock, "I'll give you a damn good wash and darn that for you after."

" 'After' what, darling?" said Tony, cupping her breasts from behind with equally practised ease.

Then they were standing on the scrap of Turkish rug, unbuttoning, unfastening, undoing, until they were both quite naked. Mary pulled Tony on top of her on the bed, the planks complaining loudly. They probed, felt, licked and teased at each other seeking pleasure and comfort in each others' bodies, craving to be one.

Soon they were. Mary stretched her smooth, lithe legs around Tony's hard, muscled back as he pushed into her hungrily. Their passion swirled and rose, Tony losing himself in the love and sheer warmth of the intimacy.

"No, Tony, not yet, wait." Mary's arms had been clasped tightly round his neck, but now she was pushing him away, both palms flat against his shoulders. She wriggled free and in an instant was straddling him, her hair loose and cascading down over both of them. They could wait no longer. Neither cared if their moans were heard as they held each other tight, clasping, melting together into a moist warmth.

"You always have to be on top, in every way, don't you, darling?" Tony looked up into her smiling face, her great lazy eyes sated with love.

"Tony, I need you so much, please tell me that we'll . . ." But Mary was suddenly silent, quite still on top of Tony, listening.

A series of dull thuds came from just outside the door of the hut as someone kicked the mud and dung off their boots, then the door opened without ceremony, the blanket billowing gently as the wind

410

wafted in. Mary lay low on Tony, bottom in the air, finger on her lips, willing the intruder to be gone.

Feet scraped busily on the doormat: then there was silence as the newcomer detected others in the room beyond the hanging blankets.

"Mary, is that you? Are you there, hello?"

Tony looked through Mary's veil of hair as the blanket was moved to one side by an unknown hand. Then the pinched, wind-burnt face pushed through the folded cloth, the eyes bright, intelligent, taking in the situation at once.

"Oh, Mary dear, I'm so sorry to disturb you . . ." Mrs Polley paused, ". . . and Sergeant Keenan, how came you by those nasty scars?"

CHAPTER
FOURTEEN

The Quarries

"Now, you've got to keep a right sharp eye out for these bastards, lads." Sergeant Ormond had half the company round him, just to the rear of their huts. Dug into a soft piece of ground were three Russian fougasses, taken from in front of the enemy positions with the greatest of care during a patrol two days ago. "All you'll see is a glass tube lying just above the surface. They vary in length, some being as long as a good-sized cock, like these two, here . . ." he pointed to two crude glass tubes, about as thick as a finger, ". . . and some being much shorter, 'bout the length of Corporal Pegg's todger."

Gales of laughter from the men who were enjoying the period out of the line, despite the intensive training that they were getting.

"That's as maybe, Sergeant, but half Workswirth looks just like me." Pegg's reply drew just as good a laugh.

"Russ makes the tubes hissen, fills 'em with an acid that when you break it, leaks into a fulminate exploder at either end and sets off the charge. See 'ere . . ." Ormond used a long stick to point to a fougasse that had been disarmed and was lying exposed at the bottom of a shallow hole, ". . . this one's like most we've seen. Made out o' wood, probably two fists long and one wide, they're filled with about two pounds of normal detonating powder. Some 'ave been found with shot on top o' the charge, but we ain't seen any like that so far."

The men, soft field caps above tanned, bearded faces, brownish sea-smocks and blue-black trousers now always worn with the bottoms rolled up against the mud, listened intently. Ormond spoke softly so that all of them had to strain to learn facts that would save their lives.

"Now, obviously, the thing is set off by one of yer clumsy fuckin' boots catchin' it. If yer lucky, the charge will have gone damp and will sound more like this . . ." Lance-Corporal Carlton had been warned to expect this rib-tickler so he'd been brewing away and right on cue he let out a melodious, malodourous bubble that delighted the audience, ". . . than this." Just behind a bank a live fougasse had been sown with one of the men ready to detonate it by pulling a piece of string. There was a roar and a sheet of flame that made the troops mutter with awe.

"Party of the Sixty-Third trod on some the other day down by Green Hill: one killed, one lost a foot, one lad badly burnt. Not much you can do about them — especially at night — except keep yer eyes peeled and if you hear the fuse fizzing, get down. But, if you do find one, mark it using one of these sticks you'll be issued." The sergeant held up a two-foot-long piece of cut willow, one end sharpened, the other flying a pennon of white cleaning rag.

"He should be in Drury Lane, Ormond, not in the army." Ensign Parkinson was walking in the blowy, early June sunshine with Morgan, watching the men train. His cheeks had done their best to grow some whiskers, but the down emphasised rather than concealed his youth.

"Thank God he's not . . ." Morgan could have predicted the subaltern's cliché of admiration for stalwarts like Ormond, ". . . we need old hands more than ever. Will you just look at the men, they're nothing but boys."

And they were. Morgan remembered how callow even the old company had looked a year ago, but most of those men were a good two years older than these lads. But now they were gone. Morgan remembered how they were mown down at the Alma, cut to pieces at Inkermann, or simply spooned into a shallow pit, wasted with cholera and exhaustion.

"Yes, Captain, but they're good men — as you know — and the company's so much better since . . . well, since . . . recently." Parkinson blushed slightly as Morgan looked at him. Was he toad-eating, or was it a sincere compliment?

"We're lucky to have grand corporals and sergeants, Parkinson. Come and look at this." Morgan led the younger officer over to the other half of the company where Colour-Sergeant McGucken was just finishing off his lesson in gun-spiking.

414

All of the men were familiar with the long shafts of soft iron that were issued for raids and the like, but no one had yet had the chance to use one. Realizing that a demonstration would be invaluable, McGucken had sent a party down to Balaklava to acquire a number of gun barrels that had been worn-out by too much firing and were about to be scrapped. Mighty had been the moaning as they were humped back up the road to the 95th's camp, but now the heavy tubes were proving their worth.

"So, that's the easy bit." A spiking nail had been knocked smoothly into the touch-hole of one of the old guns with a mallet, making it impossible to fire.

"But unless you knock the bastard right home, Russ will come up and lever it free like this . . ." Just like an ordinary nail, the metal spike had a head on it that made it easier to knock in but, as sergeant Keenan now demonstrated, an entrenching tool could easily be pushed under the rim and used to lever it out.

"Thank you, Sar'nt Keenan. So, lads, the whole idea is to stop Russ being able to pepper us with the guns we've just overrun if a counter-attack drives us back again. So, think o' that sweet, wee Aldershot whore an' bang away 'til the nail's out of sight. An' if you lose your nail, use a bayonet instead . . ." Sergeant Keenan came forward to the next barrel that was lying on blocks in the grass, jammed a bayonet into the breech-end of the old gun, then stamped on its socket to drive it firmly into the soft aperture, ". . . then snap it off like this," knocking the bayonet at right angles with a hefty kick. This blow should have weakened the blade enough to allow it to be bent back and forth by hand a few times before it eventually broke leaving nothing but a stump that would be difficult to draw out of the touch-hole. In fact, even brawny Keenan's tugs made little impression at first, everyone laughing when they realized how unrealistic the task would be in the teeth of the enemy.

"So, lads, the lesson is, if even Sar'nt Keenan has difficulty in doing what the manual tells us to do, don't lose yer fuckin' spiking nail. Any questions?" McGucken recovered perfectly, as Keenan, red with exertion, finally got the steel to snap.

"By God, sir, I hope the good sergeant treats the succulent Mrs Keenan rather more gently than that." Ensign Parkinson was trying to gauge how far he could go with his company commander.

His reply was just a long, hard, silent stare.

"Bloody hell, sir, the Frogs are hittin' them hard, aren't they?" McGucken and Morgan watched, awestruck, as the French guns pummelled the Russian earthworks with an intensity that they had not seen before. As the company trained and the secret date for the attack drew near, everybody had noticed how the tempo of the guns had suddenly increased.

Until the day before, the fourth of June, there had been a steady, familiar rumble as both sides potted away at one another. Then, just as the garrison of Sevastopol were lolling in the sun of a particularly fine afternoon, the crescent of Allied guns that faced the town had erupted. Morgan hadn't been warned — nor

416

had anyone else as far as he could gather — as the usual drumming had stepped up to an incessant, mighty roar. Morgan had had to let McGucken know what the overall plan was, but when the bombardment had increased, there wasn't a man in the company who hadn't realized that the "shave" was true and what all the special training was about. Any attempts to hide future plans from the men had to be a complete waste of time, the only detail of which they were now unsure was whether the assault would be limited just to The Quarries or whether they would push into Sevastopol itself.

So, he and McGucken had set off to see what was happening for themselves. They'd trotted down the ravines on his pair of horses, followed by Pegg on one of the Quartermaster's screws to act as their messenger, then they'd hacked along the corduroy tracks that led up the steep banks towards the trenches, before stopping off at a vantage point on Green Hill. Morgan had worried that they might attract enemy fire, but as soon as they arrived to the rear of a battery of eighteen-pounders, he saw that the position was thick with other spectators. Now McGucken and Morgan had dismounted, handed their reins to Pegg and were scanning the earthwork well over to the left through their telescopes.

"They are, too, Colour-Sar'nt. The Malakoff's getting a leathering, but they're also pounding the Mamelon; look yonder." Morgan pointed at the fort that the Russians had thrown up in front of their main defensive position.

They couldn't see the pair of batteries that the French had dedicated to the destruction of the smaller position, but they were firing disciplined salvoes that arrived every three minutes or so, throwing up great gouts of earth and flame and a cloud of dust and smoke that hung in the sunny, windless air.

"Look carefully, sir, an' I reckon yous can see poor bastards getting chucked in the air every time the rounds land." McGucken might have been right. Each ripple of shells threw up black, solid lumps that arced away before falling into the dust and mayhem. But whether they were bodies or not hardly mattered, for the whole area was now just one shapeless mass of earth and broken gabions from which only occasional stabs of fire came in reply.

"Can't really tell what's happening up in The Quarries, sir." McGucken had balanced his glass on a sandbag parapet to steady it and was now crouching down behind the eyepiece, extending it gently to get a better focus.

"Well you won't see much up there . . ." Morgan mumbled in reply, tinkering with his own telescope, he'd paid almost ten pounds in Dublin for this new one, ". . . it's so much higher than we are and all the fire will be high-angle to get at the buggers down in the depths of the place. There's a hell of a racket going on, though and see how far our lads have got the parallels." They both studied the freshly-dug lines of trenches that were snaking closer and closer to their objective.

"Aye, if we jump off from the closest, I reckon it'll only be about three-hundred paces." McGucken was

418

right, but they were both thinking the same thing: unless there's supporting fire then three-hundred paces was more than enough distance to lose an entire company.

Impressed by the concentrated destruction and grimly satisfied with as much as they had gleaned about the forthcoming assault, the two men left their viewpoint, pushing past a few other infantrymen who were studying their own objectives and a host of others from the commissariat and Staff who had come just to be nosey.

Pegg was waiting for both of them a little way to the rear. "Jesus, sir, there's a right old din going on, ain't there, I 'ope it's all one way?" His hands covered his ears, purely for dramatic effect,

"Most of it is, Corporal Pegg. You seen anything from up here?" Morgan asked.

"Not really, sir. Whole bunch o' Frogs marched over that hillside yonder." Pegg pointed up to the left where the French gun-lines were deep in smoke. "Looked like them dirty Zouave buggers an' a brigade of Algerians. Can I borrow your nice new glass for a minute, please sir?"

"Aye, but be careful with it." Morgan handed over his precious telescope to Pegg whilst he and McGucken peered hard to try to make out where the French might be massing. By the time they looked back at Pegg he was scouring the parapets where they had both just been.

"What have yous seen, Corporal Pegg?" McGucken asked.

There was a pause for Pegg was concentrating hard. Eventually, "Would you look at that, Colour-Sar'nt. One of them blanket-stackers has brought his tart up with him from Ballyklava: she's got a prime arse on her."

"Now, lads, this'll be where Russ is concentrated. With a bit of luck the guns will have done the job for us and all we'll have to do is occupy the ground — but don't bet on it." Morgan pointed to the very centre of his sand-model of The Quarries — the Grenadier Company's target.

Until the night before, nobody had been told anything beyond the briefing that Morgan had received from Hume two weeks ago. The company had continued their lectures and weapon training whilst all the time listening to the increasing racket of the artillery and watching companies from other regiments in the 2nd Division going through similar routines, knowing full well that the attack must be imminent, but being told nothing beyond what they'd guessed.

Then it all happened at once. Just before lunch-time a runner had arrived direct from Brigade telling Morgan to report to Colonel Shirley for instructions and informing him where "specialist stores" could be picked up. As he trotted off to get his orders, McGucken plunged the company into a vortex of preparations, issues and inspections and when he returned two hours later, the previously orderly scene was like a wasps' nest that had been knocked from the eaves. Dry rations had arrived and were being dished

420

out, spiking nails and fougasse markers lay in bundles for each corporal's section, every man had been given an extra pouch of twenty rounds to be carried on their belts and a pile of coloured signal rockets was being divided up by Sergeant Ormond.

Now that the non-commissioned officers had done their work, Morgan assembled the company in front of the model of The Quarries faithfully made from sand by Sergeant Keenan and Peters. The pair had tried to pretend that the nine square yards of sand bordered by pegged lines of thick twine was simply one of Paddy Morgan's latest fads, but as they laboured with charts and diagrams, cut miniature trench lines and piled tiny hillocks, its real purpose was impossible to disguise. Troops going to and from the cookhouse would stop and offer advice and adjustments and in no time everyone knew precisely where they were to assault — but not when.

So, after an early supper, before the light faded, the men were assembled around three sides of the model, belching gently, most still sipping tea from their mugs, almost every man puffing at a pipe. They were relaxed but expectant, tense but eager to know when they would "jump the bags".

For almost an hour Morgan went through the French plan, routes, forming-up points, the tasks of the 49th's company that would be in front of them and the party of 55th who were behind, what to do with casualties and prisoners and where extra ammunition would come from. Most important of all, though, was the heart of the Russian position and its mortars.

"We'll get supporting fire from Major Armstrong's party and then launch ourselves from this part of the main sap . . ." Morgan pointed to a half-inch-deep squiggle in the sand, ". . . and once that's taken, boys, The Quarries will be ours. The Redan can be outflanked and then it's on your marks for the Sevastopol Steeplechase."

After so much concentration, the men laughed out loud, feeding off Morgan's confidence.

"Any questions?" But there was none. He looked round the ranks of faces as the light faded, keen, trusting, very different from the set of lads that McGucken and he had inherited just a few weeks ago. How many of them would be able to look each other in the eyes this time tomorrow, he wondered?

Well before dawn they were woken, fed and paraded, every man a jumble of sticks, stakes and shovels as the non-commissioned officers inspected them by the light of lanterns. As Morgan approached, each man was being made to jump up and down a few times to ensure that his equipment didn't rattle.

"Right, that'll do, listen-in." McGucken's voice penetrated even the crescendo of the guns. "Company, company, 'shun." The men banged their heels together, standing stiff as posts.

"Sir, one officer and sixty-three men of the Grenadier Company, Ninety-Fifth Regiment on parade, awaiting your orders." Even in his sea-smock and covered in kit, McGucken was magnificent.

"Thank you, Colour-Sergeant, fall the men into column of route, order of march as detailed." Morgan went through the ritual, turning stiffly to his left before marching to the flank of the company. Orders were bawled, the troops stamped and turned and the slab of men was converted into a thin, sinuous snake. "Right, lads, follow me," and with just one word of command from a corporal, all of them stepped out behind him.

Follow me thought Morgan as they started the mile and a half through the ravines that would lead to their assembly point. The cliffs towered either side of them as the dawn broke and he wondered what lay ahead and how he would manage. There could be no dithering this time, no indecision. Suddenly his mind flew back to his first taste of blood at the Alma, when he'd grappled with that foul-breathed rifleman near the riverbank. He remembered how the eyes of his men had seemed to bore into him, expecting him to lead. Now that tickle went up his spine again in just the same way.

By the time they'd cleared the Careening Ravine, climbed up the track to the rear of the last parallel, found the 49th and settled down in a fold in the ground, the guns were hammering harder than ever. Occasionally, a heavy round would skip over their position, or a shell burst off to a flank, tokens of the remaining Russian resistance from the Redan to their front. So, the soldiers were told to stay within the cover that the banks and sandbag lip provided, whilst McGucken, Ensign Parkinson and Morgan went forward to see what was what.

"The Frogs are in the Mamelon, ain't they, Colour-Sar'nt?" Parkinson's young eyes had picked a floating tricolour from the depths of smoke and dust that hung above the shattered earthwork to their left.

"Where . . . yes, I see it," Morgan had his glass on the scene of devastation as ripples of fire poured from the French guns into the Malakoff whilst, just discernible through the flying muck, columns of French infantry trotted up into the assault.

"I never seen gunfire like this, sir." McGucken was almost transfixed with professional interest. "See how our guns are punishing The Quarries and the Redan."

Certainly, the walls of the Great Redan, the ultimate target of the British, were punctured in any number of places whilst the shells and roundshot received hardly any reply from its garrison. Above The Quarries a great pall had spread suggesting, they all hoped, fires and damnation inside.

"No, Colour-Sar'nt, you're right. I hope it ain't bad luck to say it, but I think that we might be in for an easier ride than people expect. We may be told to bounce straight onto the Redan — Christ, I hope I'm right," but Morgan immediately regretted his optimism.

"Sir, Major Hume wants you back in the main position." In the gunfire, none of them had heard the young private who had been sent forward to announce the visitor. Morgan hadn't thought that his commanding officer might be present as the whole operation had been placed under the hand of another, but it was typical of the man. There he was, lying chatting above the noise with the men, the adjutant by his side, both puffing away at cheroots.

424

"Hello, sir, good to see you," Morgan had to shout to make himself heard above the cacophony. He slumped down on the ploughed ground next to Hume.

"Good to see you, too, Morgan. I've just been talking to Cattray here." Morgan wished that Hume had picked one of the more wholesome youngsters. "He tells me it's going to be a walk-over and that the Grenadiers are going to be in Sevastopol before the morning."

Morgan quickly revised his opinion of Cattray, "I'm sure he's right, sir. I see you've brought Father Mountford with you." Morgan looked across behind an embankment where the priest was busy administering the sacraments to the Catholic soldiers. His spectacles shone in the sunlight as his right thumb smeared at the foreheads of five men who knelt before him.

"I have: I'll leave him with you. I wasn't expecting the guns to have made as good a job as they have, the adjutant and I are going back to get the rest of the regiment in fighting trim, just in case they go on to the Redan." Hume had made just the same assessment that he had. "And Morgan, one more thing," Hume pulled him off to one side so that they couldn't be overheard, despite the noise. "You've made a damn fine start with the company. The whole Regiment will be watching you and your boys today, you know."

What did he mean? wondered Morgan. Hume was always courteous and a skilful leader, encouraging others by his own example — today he was positively gushing. In this tight-buttoned military society, no one bandied those sorts of sentiments about unless they were truly worried about you.

"Yes, sir, thank you." Even as Morgan whittled at these words, Hume was up, patting Private Cattray lightly on the calf and waving Father Mountford towards Morgan. The priest dumped himself down on the bank next to him.

"Just given some young lads of yours a bit of spiritual mettle," Mountford yelled, his black top-coat already wet with mud.

"Thank you, Father. The Protestants all went to the last church parade — it was thoughtless of me not to ask for your services."

"No matter, Morgan, they're now all as ready for what lies ahead as I can make them. That Sergeant Keenan is a grand man, ain't he?" Morgan had noticed Keenan in the row of communicants. "Had no idea that you knew him from home and that he's married to the lass that seems to run your hospital single-handed." Mountford sounded as if he was making small talk after Sunday Mass rather than shrieking under gunfire and Morgan warmed to him — until he spoilt it.

"Gather you know her as well?" Had the priest's eyes narrowed a little? What on earth had Keenan been saying? "Good luck, Morgan, the men think the world of you — and we all know what you've been through already." Mountford clasped his shoulder, his mouth close to Morgan's ear.

But Morgan was too bemused to reply, he simply nodded. He had visions of the cuckolded Keenan telling the priest not just about his officer's misdoings with his wife, but also about his cowardice. And why did he try to sugar the pill with all that, "the men think the world of you" and "we all know what you've been through", nonsense? Bloody priests.

What had Finn, the groom, said back in Ireland? Something about the army always being in an indecent rush just to keep you hanging about in one fly-blown hole of a place or another? That's just what had happened now. One minute they'd been waiting well to the rear, next a breathless guide from the 49th had arrived with a garbled message about the French moving faster than everyone expected, that the attack had been brought forward and, "Major Armstrong's compliments, sir, but the Ninety-Fifth had best get off of their fat arses."

So they had. They'd trotted as fast as they could in one long file up the winds, saps and traverses as the guns sang overhead until the guide had shown them where the 49th were, in the forward parallel just to their left front. Then, as Finn predicted, they hung about for an hour or more in shallow trenches where they only had room to crouch, where there was no water other than their own bottles and any movement attracted rifle fire from The Quarries just a couple of hundred paces up the slope from them. But this time it wasn't any old fly-blown hole of a place, it was a very frightening hole of a place indeed.

At least their own fire was overwhelming. Howitzer shells cracked above the target, mortar rounds plunged in incessantly and roundshot whirred flat over their

427

heads before bouncing and ploughing through the Russian embrasures. It was impressive, but so close that every man in the company clung to the earth walls of the trench, most with their eyes closed against the torment of noise.

Then, over to Morgan's left, there was a shout. "There, sir, yellow over green." Keenan yelled the link-man's warning down to Morgan. Arching up into the dusk were two rockets fired by Major Armstrong, the "make-ready" signal.

"Ball cartridge, load." Even before Morgan said it, the command was being passed up and down the trench, the men grappling with pouches, fumbling with ramrods as they half-crouched, half-sat in the shallow scrape. The signal not only warned the assaulting troops of all the companies, it also told the guns to lay-on one last concentration before the infantry sprang from the earth. Single shots were now indiscernible as one long shriek of hot metal bounded, stung and seared the target.

"Now, Duffy, it's the devil's own job ain't it?" To Morgan's left, Private Duffy was curled-up like a question-mark grappling with rifle and cartridge whilst desperately trying to keep his head below the parapet. Loading a rifle when standing upright was tricky enough; crouched like this it was close to impossible. Duffy was biting time and again at a cartridge, trying to rip open the paper, but failing. It was made no easier for him, Morgan noticed, by his violently trembling hands and his tight-shut eyes from which he peeped only when absolutely necessary. But when the officer spoke he answered well.

"Aye, sir, it's a right bitch trying to tear cartridge when you've got no front teeth."

Morgan squeezed past Duffy, smiled and patted him on the shoulder as he did so. "Well, I tell you what, Duffy, my lad, we gave each other a much worse time in the ring than this bunch of Muscovites up yonder will."

The soldier gave a gappy grin at this, but Morgan noticed how weak his own knees were as he crouched down amongst the troops. They laboured with ramrods and percussion caps as he bobbed his head above the parapet. The Quarries were now almost entirely obscured by slowly drifting smoke, but over to his left he just caught sight of a ripple of bayonet blades catching the last glimmers of the evening light. As he watched the next cry went up.

"Green over green, sir." He'd seen both rockets already and as they flew, figures scrambled from the dark scar of earth in front of them, pulling each other from the trench, wiping loose soil from their weapons.

As the 49th rose, so the artillery lifted. One lone gun fired late, the rest were as silent as they had been deafening. They heard a cheer from the 49th as they shook out, and then Morgan gave the command they all expected.

"Grenadiers, fix bayonets." Jesus, how the steely song made cold prickles canter up your spine.

"Prepare to move." The non-commissioned officers repeated the order along the sap as Morgan held his yellow rocket ready. This rocket — the same colour as

429

the regiment's cuff-facings — would tell the Staff that the second assault wave was about to move: a blue one shot up from the storming party of the Light Division over on his right. A quick check left and right showed him that the men were ready, then he pulled at the loop of the wire igniter. The trench was instantly filled with smoke as the rocket lifted.

"Jesus and Joseph but you love them fireworks, don't you, your honour?" Keenan chaffed him as they both coughed and blinked.

"Come on boys, let's be at 'em!" The men scrabbled and stumbled over the bags. "Check your pouches, form on me." A babel of cheers, encouragements and cursing swelled as they rose onto the open slope. Morgan's balls shrivelled to nothing as he pulled at a wooden stake, levering himself out of the trench and to the head of his company.

The line of men plodded along unevenly, weapons ready, sixty tongues licking one hundred and twenty lips, watching the 49th a hundred paces in front and the louring, smoky, broken defences of The Quarries.

Still no enemy fire. Their own guns had started again, pummelling the Redan and other forts, but in front of them there was no resistance. The 49th were slowly bunching, clambering and pushing their way up the mounds of shot-ploughed spoil, split sandbags and ruptured gabions, when the gathering dark was lit by a vivid flash and a spread-hand of flame. There were shouts of pain.

"All right, lads, it's only a fougasse . . ." Morgan heard Lance-Corporal Pegg quietly encouraging the same two boys whom he'd punished a few days ago, ". . . watch where yer stepping."

There was a spatter of rifle fire from inside The Quarries, a shouted cheer, then it was the 95th's turn to haul themselves into the earthwork. They were suddenly in the belly of the very monster that had hurled death at them for so many months — but how dangerous would its death throes be? Morgan pulled himself through a torn and scarred embrasure, grabbing the trunnions of a great naval gun whose muzzle had been gouged by their own fire. He saw bright, ragged gashes in the dull gun-metal of the barrel whilst three bundles of grey cloth lay scattered about. No faces or hands showed, just boots and coats torn by splinters, the coarse cloth wicking the dark blood away from the crew's death wounds.

Shattered trenches led everywhere. British and French fire had cratered the earth so thoroughly that scarcely a sandbag was in place or untorn. Splintered, broken gabions lay anyhow and there was hardly a plank or stake of the revetments that hadn't been knocked askew. It was almost dark now, but the light of burning stores showed bodies dotted here and there — Morgan noticed the dark belts of riflemen and the knotted scarves of sailors — mostly outside the entrance to dugouts and shelters. Shell splinters had done their scything worst, slashing and slicing at soft Russian flesh. Morgan guessed that they had been caught by the shells as the garrison pulled out and if they'd withdrawn without a fight then, as sure as the Pope lived in Rome, there would be a counter-attack.

"Get 'em into file, non-commissioned officers." The Company gaggled about, gawping at the destruction, one or two picking for loot, but the plan was to penetrate deep into the centre of the fort through the maze of trenches. The men responded to the barked orders, quickly forming into two thin ranks, crouching down and waiting to be led forward.

"Here's the guide, sir." McGucken waved through a lad from the 49th, just as three shells banged hard and high at the back of The Quarries, the first serious enemy fire they'd heard. They all shrank and ducked from the noise.

"Major Armstrong's compliments, sir, follow the route I'll show you, he's secured the left part of the main sap, but needs you up in support, sharpish." The lad coughed as thick, tarry smoke drifted across them all. Four more 49th soldiers, one with his head bandaged, another being supported by two comrades came shambling past.

"Dressing station's just being set-up over yon," Colour-Sergeant McGucken pointed the way for them, ". . . see there, by the Fifty-Fifth's leading troops."

As they bundled and tripped their way forward with only the light of the fires to guide them, more shells burst on the other side of The Quarries where shouts and bugle calls showed that the other column was making its way. Rifles stabbed in the night, there were flashes of grenades, but the Russians were being driven out.

All the training paid off. The men moved well and quietly, needing no more than the occasional word to

432

get them to respond quickly. Once they'd found the flank of the 49th and occupied their own stretch of trench, the troops were set to reversing the defences by piling sandbags and digging fire-steps at the back of the saps. Again, they'd been taught well, picks and shovels flying in the flame-lit dark.

"Colour-Sar'nt, this is too good to last. We need to find out what lies over that lip." Morgan and McGucken were standing looking over the back of a Russian trench towards ground that fell away steeply into the old diggings. "Can we get a patrol out to have a look?"

"We can, sir. If Russ boils up a counter-attack from there we'll get bugger-all warning and our flank will be in the air . . ." McGucken was just as uneasy as his Company Commander, ". . . so we might want to put a standing patrol there once we know what's going on."

"Prime idea. Who've you got for the patrol?" Morgan asked.

"Well, Mr Parkinson ought to lead it and, don't say no, sir . . ." in the dark McGucken's voice had automatically dropped to a needless whisper, ". . . but Corporal Pegg needs the experience as his second-in-command. I suggest that they take a reliable pair with them, if you please?"

"I agree, Mr Parkinson would never forgive me if he didn't go and Pegg's doing well, just make sure they all know the pass word and give them enough signal rockets — if they're not all pissed wet through and useless by now."

"Right, sir, come back in through this point when you're done." McGucken showed Ensign Parkinson through the sentry point and out into the dark. The men had put on greatcoats against the cold of the night and now edged up and over the parapet, Parkinson and his pistol outlined starkly for an instant as a Russian star-shell burst.

"Oh, ow, you clumsy fuck, be careful." One of the men had accidentally given Pegg's ample rump a "shamrock" as they clambered up the wooden ladder that the Russians used to get in and out of their deep trenches. His outraged whisper carried on the night air.

"Shhh, Corporal Pegg. Have a care, Cooper." Parkinson was almost quivering with excitement, his first night patrol in enemy territory.

"Good luck, sir, don't be all bloody night," whispered McGucken hoarsely as they slid away into the dark.

The Russian guns were beginning to respond. Shell and mortar fire was now falling at odd intervals all around The Quarries, whilst star-shells lit the night.

"This noise helps to cover us, Corporal Pegg," Parkinson muttered.

"Aye, sir, but Russ is ranging with those rounds, he'll be back to chuck us out if he can, I'll be bound."

"You're right, that's why Captain Morgan doesn't want us too far forward," the subaltern replied. "How about here?" The four men had slid over a shell-churned lip, falling out of sight of the company one hundred and fifty yards behind them. Parkinson had found a shelf in the old diggings where they could

434

look down onto the floor of The Quarries. As the light flickered and fled they all saw three abandoned medium mortars with a litter of dead horses and smashed wagons around them. "D'you think they've been spiked, Corporal Pegg?" The young officer had immediate visions of laying claim to the capture of three enemy mortars, why, there'd be a brevet in that . . .

"Shh, look there, sir." Pegg held Parkinson by the arm, slowly raising his hand in the gloom and pointing.

The young officer sat back on his haunches as both private soldiers stiffened and cautiously raised their weapons. Stealing quietly through a scatter of bushes came a handful of dark figures, short, blunt rifles at the ready.

"Skirmishers, sir . . ." Pegg rasped, ". . . main body probably behind. Got that fuckin' rocket to 'and?"

"I have, it's just here." The subaltern moved the long, wax-paper-covered light slowly from his belt and laid it carefully on the ground next to him. "Make ready, men, but don't fire unless I tell you." Parkinson would fire the rocket to alert the Company to the presence of the enemy, meanwhile, the hammers of their three rifles and that of his own pistol were thumbed gently back into the fully-cocked position.

A dozen skirmishers fanned out round the mortars, then turned in their direction and disappeared from sight as they began to climb up the slope.

"Right, sir, fire that bleedin' light an' let's fuck-off," Pegg whispered, as conscious as the rest of the group of

435

the Russians whom they could not now see and who would soon be between them and the company.

"No, not yet, Corporal Pegg. If that's just a patrol they don't know we're here and we can get some of them as they return. But if there's more coming we need to count them and let the captain know how many." Parkinson made his point as quietly as he could.

"Aye, sir, but we'll be bugger-all use if them Russians cut us off. There's bound to be more a'coming, let's get out of it whilst we can."

"No, Corporal, we'll just wait a moment," Parkinson whispered back firmly.

With a muttered, "Bloody officers," Pegg settled back down on the earth whilst both privates pretended not to have heard the altercation.

Both officer and NCO were soon proved right. Filing quietly onto the gritty, level ground below them came columns of Russian troops, grey coats and caps black in the shadows, muskets held upright, the light catching their bayonets whenever a star-shell burst. Whatever orders they received were covered by the noise of the guns firing on the Redan and the Malakoff, making the columns look like automata as they wheeled, formed and halted below the patrol. They stared down at the Russians, their featureless faces just showing as pale disks. As one, responding to some silent order, they jerked their weapons across their bodies, slid ramrods from beneath barrels and reached behind their hips for cartridges.

"Coom on, sir, you've seen enough, let's be off," Pegg urged as quietly as he could.

436

"Right, just let me count them," replied Parkinson.

"Sir, will you give over . . ." Corporal Pegg was almost at his wit's end, he'd had a bellyfull of skittering around in the dark surrounded by the enemy, ". . . there's fuckin' 'undreds on 'em, that's all the captain needs to know."

Infuriatingly, Parkinson delayed yet more, his finger tracing its way along the ranks, his lips counting silently.

"You're right, two companies, about one hundred and fifty, I'd say. Now, where's that light?" Parkinson groped around at his thigh in the dark.

"Here, sir, here, for pity's sake, just fire the sod."

Parkinson seized the big cardboard tube, pointed it skywards, firmly gripped the wire loop, pulled — and nothing happened.

"Damn, it's wet. Where's the other one?"

"How the fuck should I know, sir, you had it last." Pegg was bubbling with silent frustration — why did officers always have to do things the hard way? Couldn't this young gentleman see how perilous their position was? And now the silly little bastard had left their spare light behind. "Let's just get back to the company, sir, we can tell 'em what's cracking off."

"You're right, Corporal Pegg. Right, follow me, quietly now," and Parkinson slid off into the gloom, pistol at the ready.

The men trailed after the young officer towards the featureless pool of darkness; somewhere there was their trench line and the haven of the company. But they had hardly gone thirty yards before Parkinson stopped,

437

dropped to one knee and hunched over, trying to find their position against the constant flicker of the guns.

"Where d'you think our entry-point is, Corporal Pegg?" Parkinson whispered as the patrol closed around him.

It would be so much safer if they could come back into their trenches at the same point that they left them, for the sentries — always jumpy when so close to the enemy — would be expecting them and, in theory at least, so much less lethal to their own side. Pegg thought back to the endless narrow scrapes he and his mates had had courtesy of their people and shuddered: it didn't help him one jot, though, in picking out one bit of shadow from another.

"Over there, sir, I think." Pegg pointed confidently in the darkness, trying to hide his complete ignorance.

"Are you sure?" Parkinson rasped back. "When we left our trenches I lined up St Catherine's . . ." a black dome was just visible on Sevastopol's skyline, ". . . with a star in Orion's belt which must mean that it's more over there." The subaltern pointed in quite a different direction.

"Sir, I haven't a fuckin' clue where Onion's belt or even his bloody garters are. If you know, why don't you just say?" Pegg's voice rose in irritation, almost drowning out the nearby scrape of boots and soft words in the night.

Private Cooper's hand rose and grasped Pegg who was instantly silent. The debate was cut short as all four men sank lower in the grit and coarse grass, as two, shapeless figures were seen crouched between themselves

438

and the Company's lines, just visible in the light of a distant star-shell. Four barrels swung gently towards the Russians: two short rifles rose towards the British.

"*Skarjitii pajalsta?*" Whatever was being whispered, it wasn't in English.

Parkinson straightened his arm, pointing his pistol at their foes and yelled, "Fire!" The night lit up with the flash of his revolver.

The other three fired simultaneously, great tongues of flame spitting towards the Russians. One heavy Enfield bullet struck a Russian no more than ten paces away, the man groaning, throwing back his arms and falling as his weapon rattled to the ground. Even above their pumping hearts, the patrol could hear the thump of the other Russian's boots as he hared off. For an instant, they all looked at each other before the darkness was peppered with shots from every direction.

"Damn me, we're right in the middle of their bloody skirmishers," said Parkinson, hugging the earth.

"I told you fuckin' so, dint I, sir?" It was difficult to tell the difference between the terror and the triumph in Pegg's voice.

"Yes, all right. Listen, when I start firing, you lot just run back to the company as hard as you can and tell them I'm coming. Try not to get shot by our sentries. Any questions?" Parkinson reeled off his orders as the bullets continued to fly. "Go on, then, run!" Parkinson rose and snapped off a round from his pistol.

Ask him to compete in the regimental cross-country or to help to whip-in the officers' beagles and Pegg would puff, wheeze and cough his excuses, but when he was given an order that was very much more to his taste, he became an athlete of rare distinction. Both lean, fit private soldiers were hard pushed to keep up with their porky superior whose boots positively skipped over the rough ground, scabbard and water-bottle banging.

"Beef, beef," the three of them panted as they raced towards their own lines. "Pie!" bellowed by the company as every man tumbled into his battle position on the parapet as the rumpus grew in front of them.

The three of them dived and slid into the deep trench, Pegg barking his shins on the wooden revetments in his eagerness to get under cover.

"What have you done with Mr Parkinson, Corporal Pegg?" Colour-Sergeant McGucken towered over Pegg as he lay on the floor of the sap rubbing hard at his bruised limbs.

"'E's coverin' us in, Colour-Sergeant, 'e's just behind."

Instantly, McGucken was on the fire-step yelling, "Mr Parkinson, sir, over 'ere, sir, over 'ere."

A well-bred, breathless voice replied, "Here, Colour-Sar'nt," as bullets still ripped from the darkness. Then that sound. Once heard, never forgotten, the deep, bass thump of lead meeting flesh and no more hammering boots.

"Mr Parkinson, sir," McGucken shouted, but there was no reply except for a low, whimpering moan seventy or eighty paces in front of them.

"'E's bin 'it, Colour-Sar'nt, I know 'e 'as." Corporal Pegg had heard what everybody else had heard. "I'll go out an' get 'im, shall I?" There was more dread than determination in his voice.

"No, you bloody won't, Corporal Pegg, we'll lose you as well." McGucken groped for a flare on the lip of the trench, found one and launched it hissing into the sky. As it burst into light, they all saw, quite plainly, a group of jostling men clustered round a dark bundle in the grass, their butts and bayonets falling and jabbing at the object in a horrid frenzy.

A clutch of Grenadiers were quick enough to fire at the Russians before the light fizzled out, two, three, falling to the British bullets before the others sped back into lower ground and to safety. In the last, dying seconds of light, Pegg thought he saw Parkinson's arm reach briefly upwards to the sky before it fell across his torn chest.

"Right, Corporal Pegg, tell the company commander what 'appened." Once the company had been stood-down, sentries posted again and those that could had wrapped themselves in their blankets, McGucken had taken Corporal Pegg along to Morgan.

"Well, sir, we got oursen 'bout two 'undred paces out in front where the land drops away an' we just got settled down when a star-shell lit up this sort o' saucer-shaped bit o' ground. Right in the middle o' it was three mortars, all their 'orses dead . . ."

"Any idea what calibre, Corporal Pegg?" Morgan interrupted.

"Not really, sir, but decent siege pieces, sir, not them little fart-arse 'uns that they drag around on carts: big

441

wooden bases, 'bout three foot high an' bloody great bronze barrels — fourteen or mebbe eighteen inchers, I guess."

"Probably the bloody things that gave us such problems last time we were in the line, Colour-Sar'nt." Morgan took the pipe from his mouth, smoke trailing from his nose as the three of them huddled in a dugout cut into the side of the Russian trench. "What then?"

"Well, sir, we must 'ave crept up so sneaky that the Russian skirmishers 'oo was coming to poke around our position didn't know we was there. Anyway, whilst we was hunkered down with all these Muscovites milling about, couple o' companies of line infantry came up, shook out and made ready. That's when we took off, sir. Mr Parkinson an' me covered each other back, but 'e got 'it, sir, an' 'e's still out there." Pegg's inglorious retreat had quickly been re-ordered in his own mind.

"Yes, I know that Corporal Pegg, and I'm very sorry, we'll get him as soon as we can, but let me get this right, you reckon that there could be as many as two hundred Muscovites and three mortars ready to counter-attack, just a couple of hundred paces in front of us?" Morgan pressed the lad.

"Sir, that's about the size on it. I counted the Russ infantry like we've been learnt to — might be a few less than that, but they was preparin' to attack just when we saw them skirmishers off." Pegg could almost see the second chevron and the one and tuppence a day extra.

"Well done, Corporal Pegg. Thank you. Right, Colour-Sar'nt," Morgan pulled his watch from his

442

fob-pocket, "we've got about an hour before first light — that's when Russ will counter-attack, but we'll hit him before he can hit us. Start getting things ready, please, we attack at dawn."

CHAPTER
FIFTEEN

Victory

No shouted commands, no whistles, just the soft scrape of sixty men edging forward in the dawn. The long line had levered itself from the trench, shivering without their coats as the first hint of light showed in the east, guiding the Grenadiers towards their waiting foes. Morgan knew it was a gamble — if the Russians had stood-to for the last hour or so, ready to move at their officers' first words then they would meet far greater numbers and have to fight for their lives. But if most of the enemy infantry had been allowed to relax, to grab some sleep cuddled around their weapons, then they might just have the edge on them.

"Corporal Pegg, where d'you think those mortars are?" Pegg plodded along next to Morgan, supposedly acting as his guide.

"Somewhere over there, sir, beyond the lip." Pegg pointed into the pit of darkness that marked the area beyond the plateau, where the land sloped at first gently, then steeply down into the floor of The Quarries where no light had yet penetrated. Just visible, silhouetted against the pearl-grey sky was a mast, sticking up beyond the lip where the ground rose on the far side of The Quarries. At the top of it were two, black wooden fingers, both pointing towards the ground.

"D'you see that signal-mast yonder, Corporal Pegg? It's likely to be close to the gun-line, did you see it last night?" asked Morgan.

"Couldn't see anything in the dark, sir, except them mortars," Pegg replied.

"D'you think they've been spiked or not?" If the retreating Russians had dealt with their own guns then the situation wouldn't be so critical, but if they hadn't, three mortars firing right into the centre of the British attempt to take the rest of The Quarries could be disastrous. As Hume had said, this was the key to Sevastopol; so this attack must not fail.

"Dunno, sir, we didn't get down to 'em, but all the crews and beasts was lying dead alongside on 'em, hit by our guns." Pegg replied quietly.

On they walked, the grass swishing off their trousers, weapons ready, the light just catching the features of the men. Morgan looked round him: there was McGucken, striding out, beckoning urgently, silently for the line to kept as straight as if on parade, his face expressionless, as if death before breakfast was what he'd been bred to. Sergeant Keenan, over on his left, full of nervous energy, mouthing silently at the men, scampering about gently nudging one young lad forward into line whilst Sergeant Ormond stumped along solidly, bayonet outstretched, his lips set in a thin, hard line. Almond who'd all but died of cholera last year, Duffy the boxer, Cattray the old soldier, Cooper

445

who'd been with Ensign Parkinson when he'd been killed — boys whom hardship had turned into men. Morgan suddenly doubted his decision: he had decided to pitch these men against hugely superior forces, condemning them to another ordeal of blood and hurt.

And here was the evidence.

"The fuckin' bastards, sir," Pegg hissed at Morgan as he looked down at a hump of clothes in the grass, "that's out of order, that is."

The body was on its back, one arm thrown across its chest, the other pinioned by its own weight, the knees tucked up around the belly in one last attempt to ward off the agonizing blades. Its smock was blotched, blooms of rusty blood decorating the chest and stomach, but it was the face that was so shocking. The downy cheeks were smashed to a blue-jelly pulp, the nose banged flat and where the eyes should have been were two, swollen balloons of flesh, the lids gummed by dried blood. Even the sandy curls had been disfigured, for a flap of scalp had been scraped away by a rifle-butt, exposing the white, shiny skull. Where there had been a vibrant, handsome boy full of vim and energy, there was now just a bag of rag-dressed offal.

"Aye, poor Mr Parkinson — he went down fighting, though." Morgan was sickened, not by the ghastliness of the sight, but by the lack of mercy that it showed. He should have been accustomed to such things by now, he supposed — but he wasn't.

Two rifle shots just feet in front of him jerked Morgan back to the present. Against the early light, one of his men stood on the edge of the plateau, rifle in the

446

shoulder, a billow of smoke drifting away from his muzzle. The line paused, there was a fragment of silence, then, "Got 'im," from the man and a series of shouts left, right and, invisibly, from in front.

Morgan raced forward, Pegg behind him. As they came to the lip, a half-moon of earth had been eroded, leaving a natural shelter where wisps of wool showed that sheep normally gathered. The Russians had used it to collect the casualties from last night's fighting: two bodies were laid out carefully, arms crossed on their chests, their equipment and weapons piled beside them, whilst another man clung to his bandaged leg, his eyes wide with fright at the British troops topping the ground above him. A party had obviously been sent up in the dark to collect and dress them — now one of their escorts sprawled on the ground having come off worse in the exchange of fire. The improving light betrayed three more figures fleeing down the slope in front of them.

"Go on, knock 'em down!" Morgan shouted, all surprise having now been lost, as a crack near at hand, bowled a running rifleman over like a shot hare. But there was something odd about the other racing figures.

"No, stop!" Morgan pushed away another barrel that was just being raised into the aim.

Thin as a pencil, skirts and haversack flying with the urgency of her fear, ran a young Russian nurse, sprinting with every ounce of her strength: like Mary, he hoped, she was no mark for a bullet.

"What's that?" asked another voice nearby. A third figure pelted down the slope, dressed in a short black coat and long, sombre scarf; his muddy legs pumped almost as hard as his square beard wagged, sucking for breath.

"It's a priest, don't . . ." But Morgan was ignored as a rifle kicked and smoke drifted across in front of him.

The priest fell hard. He'd been struck squarely in the back by the ball: his face skidded into the dirt, he shrieked, he clutched at the soil as his conical black hat bounced away before he jerked and lay still.

Lance-Corporal Pegg lowered his rifle, wiping some imagined dirt off its long, walnut stock; "Teach the bastards to murder my officer, that will."

Now was the moment. Morgan hesitated, trying to see beyond the bodies of their victims, but surprise had been lost and the enemy would either be ready for them as the company pitched over the lip in the half-light, or caught unawares. There could be only one decision,

"Charge!" Yelled Morgan and all around him the corporals took up the command, the men raising a cheer as they launched themselves down the gritty slope. In an ecstasy of release, he bounded, tripped and ran to be at the front of the sweeping line as grass and mud flew from their boots. A rifle banged: one of his men fell and rolled as two figures rose from a clump of scrubby gorse and took to their heels a few yards in front of them.

Sergeant Keenan skidded to a halt just to Morgan's left, fell to a crouch and raised his rifle in one fluid movement, the butt no sooner touching his shoulder than the weapon cracked, gouted smoke and one of the Russians fell in a tangle of belts.

"Get the other bastard," shouted Keenan, and a crackle of bullets sent the second sentry sprawling.

"Come on, come on, lads." Morgan had to keep the momentum going as a trench line loomed out of the half-light almost at the bottom of the slope.

"Look yon, sir, we've caught the bastards napping." McGucken had seen what Morgan was hoping for.

The Russians had been curled at the bottom of the trench, wrapped in their blankets, hands thrust deep into the cuffs of their coats, caps pulled low over ears, seizing every bit of rest before their counter-attack. But the friend of instant sleep — the hall-mark of experienced infantry in any army — was now their enemy. Some groped for weapons primed the night before, one or two managed to draw their short swords, but most were too slow.

With a gasp of grim satisfaction, the company was upon them. Jumping from the parapet, kicking at faces and heads of those who stood or crouched, nailed boots landing hard on others who were still dozing, the men went to their brutal chore. Shots banged occasionally, but bayonets did most of the work, elbows and butts rising, falling like hammers as the breath was stabbed and pricked from Russian lungs all the way along the trench.

In an instant it was over. Morgan looked around as the men cleaned their blades on the blankets of their foes, or went through the pockets and haversacks of the dead.

"What d'you want us to do with these 'uns, sir?" Sergeant Ormond was hustling a trio of bruised, ragged prisoners between the earthy walls of the trench. This part of the defences was only three of four feet deep and Morgan turned to study his enemies.

"By God, I wonder they expect any mercy at all, Sergeant Ormond, after what they did to Mr Parkinson." They were all mature men, probably in their mid-twenties, mustachioed and with a couple of days' stubble, clasping their hands together around tiny crucifixes and beaded rosaries. Their coats hung loose, undone, whilst their eyes pleaded for mercy. "Send them back under escort of a couple of our wounded, if you please, Sar'nt . . ." But Morgan was cut short by the fizz of a green rocket and an almost simultaneous ripple of fire that sent them all to the floor of the trench.

"That's the rest of the buggers come to life, sir." McGucken expressed what they all knew. As the light improved, another dark trench-line could just be seen, from which muzzles spat and flickered. "An' there's yer mortars." Eyes just peeping above the sandbags, McGucken and Morgan could now see the three squat guns, two hundred yards away and in front of the second line of trenches. Their great bronze barrels, pointed at the sky whilst men leapt down from their big, wooden bases as rounds started to fly about them. Scared by the gunfire, eight horses in harness plunged and reared, hooves clawing as their drivers tried to control them.

"They've got them beasts hooked up to that mortar, by the looks of it . . ." McGucken jabbed a finger at the left-hand gun, ". . . trying to drag it round to fire on the other storming party, sir."

"Aye, Colour-Sergeant, that means that they can't have been spiked. If they get them into action, we'll never hold the place." Morgan's legs were wobbling again, all the vigour and decisiveness of a few minutes ago utterly gone.

"Right, you lot . . ." McGucken's voice galvanized four riflemen who were busily reloading next to him in the trench, ". . . two hundred, horses in open, two rounds on my order." But rather than adjusting their sights and crouching over the parapet into the aim, all four hesitated, looking at him blankly.

"Come on then, what's got into yous?" The men were clearly not going to obey the order.

"Colour-Sar'nt, I'll go an' get 'em, so I will," the nearest soldier answered in a deep brogue.

"Jesus save me from soft-hearted fuckin' Paddies . . ." McGucken never doubted his Irish soldiers' willingness to kill other men, but the slaughter of horses was different, ". . . I'll do the job meself," and rising from the crouch, he thumbed his sights forward, took careful aim and sent a bullet thumping into the leading horse.

The animal whinnied and fell instantly on its side, kicking hard, pulling the traces taut as the other horses bucked and tugged. One of the drivers ran for his life, dodging from the rounds behind a mortar base.

"Now do as you're told, for God's sake," and under McGucken's eye, the rifles spat, till every horse lay twitching in the dirt. Their reply was unexpected, though, as a great shower of canister shot ripped the dirt and grit up all along the parapet, whipping a puddle into foam and sending two of the soldiers into the bottom of the sap, cursing and clutching at wounds.

"What in the name of all that's holy was that, Colour-Sar'nt?" Morgan stooped low under the bags, almost face-to-face with McGucken who had done the same.

"They must have a wee gun sited to cover the mortar line, sir." McGucken and his officer raised their heads just far enough to see above the bags. "I saw its muzzle flash over by the base of that signal mast."

Morgan looked across the level ground to the next line of trenches that were now quiet as the garrison reloaded. The three mortars sat menacingly on their vast wooden bases whilst he saw a flick of movement amongst a line of gabions off to their left, just where the Colour-Sergeant was pointing.

"We've got to stop their counter-attack, Colour-Sar'nt and spike those goddamn mortars." Morgan licked his lips as a covey of bullets swept over them. "Tell Sergeant Keenan to get ten men together with spiking nails, they'll need covering fire from the rest of the company to keep the Muscovites' heads down yonder," he nodded towards the opposite trench line, ". . . and a party of five to storm your 'wee gun'."

"Very good, sir. We're doon to about thirty rounds a man, but I'll get Sergeant Ormond to redistribute what we've got." McGucken stared at Morgan. "I'll pick four men to take with me to nail that gun, if you please?"

What on earth did McGucken mean, thought Morgan? Who the hell did he think would take that gun — it was bloody dangerous and clearly the duty of an officer. Did McGucken suspect that he'd run out of pluck; had he detected his trembling hands and rubbery knees? And did he have some suspicion that he was sending Keenan off on some job that would get him conveniently killed?

"No, Colour-Sar'nt, you'll organize the covering fire and be ready to bring the company forward on my orders. I'll take the gun. Be ready in . . ." Morgan thought for a moment, ". . . twelve minutes, please."

"At your command, sir." Was it a look of relief that crossed McGucken's face? wondered Morgan. "I'll get Corporal Pegg, Duffy and Cattray ready for you."

Jesus, thought Morgan: Pegg — was McGucken determined to get him killed?

Half the company fired a volley and Sergeant Keenan's party leapt from the trench, taking advantage of the rolling smoke. Morgan watched intently from the top of the parapet.

"Right lads, just wait for that gun to fire and then we're at 'em." Morgan tensed, ready to move.

If McGucken was right about the position of the gun, Keenan's party would only be exposed for about half the distance that had to be covered before they were masked by the mortar bases. The volley and its smoke should help, but Morgan's group would have to depend on sprinting across the exposed ground only when the artillery piece was being reloaded — now they all prayed for cack-handed gunners.

Keenan's troops were almost in cover when the gun spoke again, throwing a great cloud of dust up around the runners at the rear, knocking two of them over. But then they were behind the high, solid wooden bases of the mortars, sheltering from bullets that clanged and whirred off their tilted bronze barrels.

"Come on, lads, follow me!" There it was again, thought Morgan, that "follow me" phrase that one day — perhaps today — would be his last.

The two hundred yards felt like a mile as three of men vied with each other to get into the cover of the left-hand mortar. As they ran, Keenan's lads were already firing steadily from the bases of the other two guns, one man, high up at a mortar breech, knocking a spiking nail firmly into its touch-hole with a vast mallet. Blown, their lungs aching for air, the men threw themselves down behind the bodies of the dead or dying draught horses or snuggled tightly against the mortar's woodwork.

"Corporal Pegg . . ." Two eyes, wide with fright, looked back at Morgan, ". . . see if you can spot that gun from your side of the mortar, I'll take a look from this side." Pegg nodded his understanding, whilst Morgan dropped onto all fours and inched round the angle of the base.

He'd expected a clear view towards the next trench line, about a hundred yards or so, hoping to get a glimpse of the gun somewhere below the signal mast. But all he saw was the terrified profile of a Russian

454

driver, just inches from him, who was crouching, eyes closed, terrified, with his back pressed against the wood. Morgan pulled himself back.

"Corporal Pegg . . ." Morgan tried not to shout too loud, for he didn't want to alert the Russian, even above the din of rifle fire, ". . . there's a bloody serf just round there." Morgan stabbed the air with his finger.

Pegg looked confused. "So what d'you want me to do about it, sir? Just shoot the sod."

Pegg was right, of course, but he flinched at the idea. Ridiculously, his mind went back to when his father had given him the Tranter that he now had in his hand, how Colonel Kemp had drooled over its lethal lines and how Amelia Smythe had told him to search his conscience before taking another man's life. So, Morgan thumbed back the hammer, scrabbled forward on his knees, rounded the timber corner, held the muzzle no more than six inches from the boy's temple and fired. The pistol jerked, the Russian fell sideways, the far side of his skull torn out, without ever realizing that Morgan was there. He glanced at the driver: as a red puddle spread under his twitching face, Morgan saw a wide, damp patch in the crotch of his trousers.

Then a twirling rammer caught his eye almost exactly where McGucken had said it would be. Two gabions framed a patch of shadow flanked by piles of sandbags, but he could just see frantic movement as, he guessed, the gun was being run out to fire again.

"Corporal Pegg, see that pair of gabions . . ." Morgan bellowed at Pegg, pointing urgently, ". . . fire between them, then be ready to attack."

455

"Aye, sir." Pegg — for once — cottoned-on quickly and the three rifles, all resting on the flanks of dead horses, barked together as the smell of singeing hair caught their nostrils.

Keenan's group sweated at the next mortar. The first had been spiked with no further casualties but now they were gambling with the courage of the crew of the gun. If the Russians braved the bullets that both Keenan's and Morgan's men were flinging at them, then the next discharge of grape would sweep the spiking party away, yet Morgan stood no chance of taking the gun unless he attacked whilst it was being reloaded.

So, they crouched, trembling, whilst Keenan's men sheltered behind the mortar's barrel, braced against the hail of shot. But as the British waited so did the Russians: they had no need to fire their gun until they had a target — Keenan and his spikers or Morgan and his stormers: whoever moved first would die.

"Ow, Jesus and Joseph!" One of the men in cover behind the next mortar yowled with pain as a musket ball caught him in the knee and sent him hopping into the open, both hands clasping his damaged leg. But no sooner had he straightened up with pain than a rifle bullet hit him in the cheek, throwing him to the open ground between Morgan's and Keenan's groups: there he lay, still and bleeding.

"What are we going to do, your honour?" Keenan yelled above the noise, pressed hard against the mortar fifteen yards away.

456

What indeed? Morgan could barely control his bowels, let alone think coolly. He'd committed both his and Keenan's groups to this hare-brained scheme, now he must get them out of it. To run back to the last line of trenches was possible, but it would leave them with the same dilemma of mortars that were still dangerous and the enemy in control of the field. No, the only choice was to attack, but would his legs obey him, let alone the men?

"Pegg, get every man reloaded." The young lance-corporal nodded, rolled on his back below the horse's balding belly and busied himself with a cartridge. "Sar'nt Keenan, when my party moves, fire as hard and fast as you can at those bastards yonder. Keep firing until you hear me shouting for you or I send a runner back with orders to bring your boys up: got it?" Sergeant Keenan, had to cock his hands behind his ears to hear above the noise, but he nodded his understanding. "Pegg, you ready?"

"Aye, sir," said Pegg with no confidence in his voice at all.

Morgan pulled a signal rocket from his haversack. If he could fire it parallel to the ground, straight into the gun's embrasure, he would get a trail of smoke that might give them some cover and, if it was a good shot it might cause the gunners to fire blindly into the cloud — if it wasn't damp and if he didn't get shot in the process. There were an awful lot of "ifs" and "mights" in that plan, thought Morgan.

He shuffled out of cover on both knees and aimed the cardboard tube straight at the distant embrasure. A bullet kicked up the dirt nearby as Morgan ripped the wire loop out of the initiator, but the rocket flew remarkably straight, sparks and smoke belching out behind it as it plunged firily into the gap. He paused; nothing happened except that the veil of smoke began to thin.

"Wait, lads, wait." Morgan looked at his men, crouched ready to leap over the dead horseflesh.

Then the gun fired. The air hummed as it was ripped around them, oak splinters flew from the mortar base and the barrel sang as balls gouged it.

"Come on!" Morgan was on his feet and running for his life. Those afternoons at school in the new spiked shoes that Mother had bought him, knees pumping round the track, lungs bursting: but there was no smoke in his face then, no pistol in his hand, no shrieking lads at his elbow and no one like this Russian who looked up at him as he leapt, chest heaving, onto the sandbag wall.

He dodged a jab from a rammer, fired his pistol straight into the man's neck and was then pushed down amongst the rest of the crew by Pegg's and the others' arrival. Rifles fired, butts flew into faces: one Russian struck out with a wooden trail spike, missing Cattray by an inch and got nine inches of slender steel poked hard into his liver. Then it was finished. The men all jostled together in the tiny, corpse-strewn space either side of the gun's carriage. They were blown, numbed by the sprint and the sudden violence — but alive.

"Some 'wee-gun' — it's a carronade." Morgan looked at the stumpy, iron barrel on its crude sea-carriage. "Re-load it; if we can turn it on the enemy, we'll even the odds a bit."

Whilst Pegg and Cattray tinkered with cartridge bags and shot, Morgan took Duffy with him up the trench towards the enemy infantry. For twenty yards the digging was shallow but straight, then it angled hard to the right. A bullet whined over Duffy's head.

"Bloody hell, sir, that was one of ours." The round had been fired by the company, doing their best to support the assault.

"Aye, keep down. Nothing personal, but they've got no idea where we are," said Morgan as they rounded the angle and looked straight down a long trench-line of sheltering Russian infantry.

"Dear God, fire and run, Duffy!" But the soldier didn't need his officer's order. Throwing his rifle straight into the shoulder he aimed at the nearest Russian, forgetting that he hadn't reloaded. Russian and Englishman looked at each other, then Duffy dropped his weapon and floored the leading Russian with a punch that would have decided matters if he'd used it in the ring at Weedon all those months ago. Another man tried his luck, this time with the bayonet, but Duffy swept the blade to one side and felled him with a right hook.

"Run, sir," and with a pair of bruised Muscovites blocking the trench behind them, they both turned tail.

Two more rifle bullets snapped past as they hurried back to Pegg and the carronade.

"The Company are firing at us, Pegg," Morgan was stumbling as fast as he could go back down the trench, ". . . and there's a whole lot of Musco . . ."

"Don't I bloody know it, sir . . ." Pegg was beckoning Morgan as hard as he could, ". . . get out the way, shall yer?" Pegg and Cattray had managed to manhandle the carronade up onto the back of the trench to cover a slight slope where the enemy could mass unseen — and that's exactly what they were now doing.

Morgan and Duffy's brawling had brought the Russians spilling out of their forward position determined to eject the British from their trenches: fifteen, twenty of them had tumbled into the saucer of land and were now trotting into the attack.

"Just get fuckin' down, both on yer." Pegg yelled, flapping his arms almost hysterically. Morgan needed no further persuasion. Duffy and he dashed themselves to the ground as Pegg touched off the gun, a sheet of iron fanning lethally above their heads.

If Pegg lacked maturity and morality he almost made up for it with flashes of common sense. He'd anticipated a counterattack and had the gumption to get the brutish, heavy carronade into a position to deal with it and now his handiwork lay sprawled in front of him. Even at Alma's charnel house or the abattoir of Inkermann, Morgan had never seen a single discharge cause such execution. Where there had been a score of husky Muscovites bent on their destruction there were now just mounds of bleeding flesh. The carronade was designed to clear ships' decks of boarding parties at very close range, the short, broad barrel allowing the

460

shot to spread wide and fast: that was precisely what it had done here. Men lay torn and ripped, some dead, most wounded, whimpering and calling for their mothers.

"Well done, Corporal Pegg." Morgan and the others stared at the appalling destruction. "Reload, there's plenty more where they came from," but no sooner had he spoken than another Enfield bullet whipped between them.

"Sir, our own lot'll have us away unless we let them know we're here," Cattray rasped as they all shrank under the lee of the Russian gabions.

Whenever there was a crisis, Morgan's mind flashed to the pictures at home. In the kitchen corridor at Glassdrumman there was a print of a young lion of his father's time, hoisting his scarlet coatee on a flagpole at some siege or other to show his comrades that he was king of the Froggie's castle — if it had worked then, it might work now. He peeled off his smock, ripped the scarlet jacket from his back and jumped across to the signal mast dressed only in a gaudy, regimental-yellow silk shirt that he'd bought for a joke in Scutari during a subaltern's spree — it was all that he had that was clean.

"Fuckin' 'ell, sir, our boys'll never shoot you in that . . ." Pegg shouted from the safety of the trench, ". . . they'll be laffin too 'ard."

As if to prove Pegg right, one of his own men's bullets chipped the signal-mast six feet above his head as Morgan struggled with the halyards.

"Aye, Corporal Pegg, remind me to order more musketry practise," said Morgan as the red coat at last ran up the pole. But if the coat stopped the British fire it had the opposite effect on the Russians, for as Morgan tied off the rope, shots flew at him from further up the trench sending him scuttling for cover.

"They're coming again, boys, be ready," and as if to confirm Morgan's words, two round black grenades about the size of cricket balls came arcing towards them. One bounced off the back of the emplacement and skipped away harmlessly, but the second landed perfectly amongst them.

"Geddown, sir!" Cattray pushed Morgan round an angle of the trench as the bomb exploded with a yellow flash, sending fragments whipping and whining around them all. Cattray was hurled bodily by the blast against the carronade's carriage, blood pouring from several jagged wounds in his back and thighs. His face lay flattened against the wood of the gun's base, both legs thrown heavily over Morgan's calves.

"Fire, Pegg, for God's sake!" shouted Morgan, pushing Cattray's dead weight off him and groping for his pistol.

Corporal Pegg was still reeling from the concussion of the grenade, but he stumbled towards the breech of their carronade, pulled its lanyard and produced another ear-tearing bang that flung canister blindly at the assaulting Russians. How effective it was none of them could tell, for the three survivors now sprawled at the bottom of the emplacement, tensed against the enemy who would appear over the lip of the trench at any moment. They all scrabbled to bring their weapons into the aim and as a clutch of Muscovites hung breathlessly above the defenders, they all fired, knocking the Russians back and out of sight.

"Right, lads, we've only our bayonets now . . ." said Morgan as he dropped his Tranter and picked up Cattray's rifle, ". . . remember what they did to Mr Parkinson, die hard!" The trio dragged themselves to their feet, steel pointing at the parapet ready for the end.

Then feet pounded and in an instant the trench was topped by ten, a dozen Russians led by an officer, panting, looming over them. But they paused, staring, the Muscovites at the defiant handful below them, the British at the last sight they would see. The officer raised his sword slowly, his men bringing their muskets carefully into the aim.

Like a vast scythe a volley cut into the enemy. Enfield balls thumped home, pitching the officer forward on top of them, catching the others in the head and shoulders, hurling them away and out of sight of Morgan, Pegg and Duffy. They ducked as another pulse of lead swept over their heads, the enemy officer twitching at their feet.

"It's the company, sir . . ." Pegg could hardly believe that he was still alive, ". . . Jock McGucken must be bringing them forward."

Indeed he was. In no time Colour-Sergeant McGucken was peering down at them, his rifle levelled across his belly, a broad smile on his powder-grimed lips.

"Why are you wearing that fuck-off shirt, sir?"

* * *

The Malakoff's and the Redan's guns still raged in the distance, but here in The Quarries it was quiet. The men went about their duty in a trance, their eyes dull and flat as they dug pits for the dead, cleaned their weapons or were simply overcome by the brain-numbing exhaustion that battle brings.

"And let me know how much ball we need . . ." Morgan, his gaudy shirt clinging to him in the breeze, was sitting on the lip of a trench alongside Sergeant Keenan, ". . . and get as many illumination and signal rockets as you can lay your hands on before dark; but you'll need to be sharp, everyone'll be after them and the quartermaster won't have brought up enough, that's one thing you can be certain of." He was rambling whilst trying desperately not to let his tiredness show.

"Aye, sir, I'll get all that lot sorted out." Keenan was wrestling with a notebook and blunt pencil. They'd accounted for all their dead but the non-commissioned officers were still trying to find out where the scattered wounded were; meanwhile they needed more ammunition for whatever lay ahead. Keenan's brow was furrowed as he struggled to add up the long column of figures. "And I'll see whether Doctor Fergusson has picked up Slater an' Rhodes. Sar'nt Ormond thinks that they made their own way back to the dressing station, but I'll check when I go back to the quartermaster, your honour."

From the trenches at the bottom of the hollow where they were sitting, the outer defences of The Quarries formed a shell-smashed horizon, only about two hundred and fifty paces away. The June sky was clear and blue, and against it figures shuffled into a little crowd where the doctor and his pair of nurses were doing their best to sort and dress the wounded. Mostly they were Russians, but one or two of their own men had been carried there by their comrades. At the same time, both Keenan and Morgan had noticed Mary's silhouette as she bandaged and dabbed at the injured.

"Yes, do that, and give my compliments to Doctor Fergusson and Mrs Keenan and thank them for what they're doing for the men." Morgan had seen how the doctor and his people had followed close — too close — behind the fighting. "But before you go, I must deal with Corporal Pegg, can you get him, please, Sar'nt Keenan?"

"I will, sir. It'll be about that priest, will it? That was an ugly business and the men are talking about it already. What're you going to do with him?"

"I don't know, yet: let's see what he's got to say for himself, shall we?"

Pegg was shouted for and in no time he was there. It was almost as if he'd been waiting to be called, expecting a fillip or some word of praise. The very moment he heard his name he'd pulled his smock tight, straightened his cap and pushed his pouch and bayonet well back on his hips. Now he broke into a few paces of a regulation march as he approached his company commander, snapping to a halt just by the sandbag wall where Morgan and Keenan waited. The smart little stamp would have impressed them all had it not come crashing down on the glass detonator of a fougasse that no one had seen.

On the ridge Mary and the others felt the bang before they heard it. A rolling thud echoed across the saucer of land and by the time that the doctor's party turned to look, a dirty cloud of dust and smoke hung over the very spot where the nurse's husband and lover had been.

"Mother of God," murmured Mary, hardly loud enough for anyone to hear. Then, in a garbled shriek, "Pass that satchel, will you, Mrs Polley?" Her hand was shaking as she reached across to snatch a bag of dressings from her companion. She'd never run so hard. Even at Inkermann as the splinters buzzed around her, she couldn't remember ever having dashed like that before, her boots skidding on the gravel slope, one hand grasping the satchel, the other pulling her skirt and petticoat high to free her legs.

By the time he'd gathered his wits and pushed himself out of the trench where the explosion had thrown him, Mary was beside Morgan. The yellow shirt was spattered with earth and grass, his ears sang, he could see nothing except the great flash that had imprinted itself on his eyeballs, but one glance told her that he was shocked and battered but not much else. He stumbled about trying to take in the scene.

Everything smelt of explosive, and by a blackened crater no more than twelve inches across lay the scorched form of Lance-Corporal Pegg. He twisted slowly, unconsciously, every bit of clothing up his right side charred by the flame that had briefly engulfed him.

466

"Here, Tony, help me sit him up can't you?" Mary only had time for Keenan. Now she was beside her husband, pushing and pulling him into a sitting position. "Here, jewel, take a wee sip, now." Keenan was semi-conscious, his beard, whiskers and hair had been singed into a frizzy, evil-smelling tangle whilst his face and hands were already blistered. Mary held a flask of spirits to his lips whilst Morgan, his own senses barely recovered, crouched behind the man, doing his best to support him. The liquor spilled from Keenan's cracked lips as he coughed.

"We've done too much of this, Captain Morgan." Mary gently held her husband's head, instantly reminding Tony of the Alma where the pair of them had first knelt round a torn James Keenan. "When are we going to be away from this hell?"

"Mary, my love, I don't know . . ." but their muttered conversation was never allowed to finish.

"All fart and no shit, lucky for you, sir." McGucken had been at the far end of the trench line checking weapons when he'd heard the bang. Grabbing a gaggle of men, he'd raced back to his company commander's position. "The charge was damp — must have been a 'partial' — how is he?" McGucken asked one of the regimental hospital orderlies who, breathless after he'd dashed to the scene, was dabbing at Pegg with a pad of lint.

"He'll be all right, Colour-Sar'nt. Won't 'ave to shave for a while, mind," replied the orderly.

"Aye, he only had a bit o' bum-fluff anyway," said McGucken without much sympathy in his voice. "How's your man, Mrs Keenan?"

"I've seen him worse, thank you, Mr McGucken," and she had. The burns were bad enough, but they were superficial and nothing like the great hole in his neck that had pumped blood so frighteningly at the Alma.

"Right, yous lot, get these two on the stretchers and get them up to Doctor Fergusson over there." McGucken pointed up to the skyline above. "Come on, then, they won't get any better with you lot gawpin' at 'em, move yerselves." The soldiers needed the rasp of the Colour-Sergeant's tongue to jolt them out of the torpor that battle brings.

The two stretchers bobbed away up the slope, one weary man on each corner and a pale girl fussing around the blanket that covered Sergeant Keenan. As the party left, Mary turned; "We've much to talk about, Tony." One hand rested on her husband's shoulder, but her eyes were full of love for Morgan. "You know where to find me."

"Stand up!" McGucken had seen the approaching horsemen long before Morgan, now he leapt to his feet and saluted. Company commander and colour-sergeant had been deep in discussion about the details of casualties, reinforcements, where the next rum ration would come from and a host of other things, absorbed in their own, battle-weary world, scarcely noticing as files of fresh troops tramped past. Only the noise of hooves close by distracted them.

"Well, young Morgan, you won't realize it just yet, but that was a prime bit of soldiering." Brigadier-General Pennefather and one of his Staff officers had trotted over from the marching ranks of the 2nd Division. "Those mortars were the key to the whole position: The Quarries are ours and now we're all set to go for the Redan."

Morgan, exhausted, hauled himself to his feet. "Thank you, sir, but it's these boys that have done it, not me." He nodded wanly towards a group of his men who were shovelling earth over Russian bodies collected at the bottom of a trench.

"And that's just what I hoped you'd say," Pennefather leaned on his saddle's pommel. "But you were at their head and . . ." he pointed towards the long files of fresh troops who were tramping towards the next battle, ". . . they all need every bit of leadership they can get."

Morgan smiled wryly to himself, that phrase seemed to be on everyone's lips at the moment.

"No, I reckon that you've turned the key that will unlock Sevastopol today: you've done the Ninety-Fifth proud, young Morgan . . ." Pennefather turned his horse back to his command, ". . . there'll be promotion in it."

"*Promotion*": *was that really what he wanted*, thought Morgan? Promotion meant more of this terror and pride, more of this doubt and triumph, didn't it? But promotion meant commanding more of the men

469

he'd learnt to love and respect, watching their simple faith in him and knowing that, whilst he drew breath, he could never betray them.

"Thank you, sir, I'll pass on your comments to the men." Morgan was too numb with exhaustion to think of anything more to say.

Morgan stiffened to attention as Pennefather rode away and as he did so, four of the boys stumbled past carrying a heavily-laden, grey blanket, the number 1124 inked on its edge. That was poor, dead Cattray: he'd had his last promotion.

Glossary

Adjutant: the commanding officer's principle staff officer, usually a captain

Aliwal: battle in the first Sikh War, January 1846, where the 16th Lancers, Finn's old regiment, won the day

Battalion: an infantry unit of about seven to eight hundred men commanded by a lieutenant-colonel. Confusingly, the term can be synonymous with "regiment", thus, 95th Regiment of Foot that was only one battalion strong in the Crimea

Bourrach: Gaelic for a mess

Bore: the inside of a weapon's barrel

Brevet: an honorary rank, given as a reward that carried extra pay but no authority

Brigade: in the Crimea, a British brigade consisted of three infantry battalions or five cavalry regiments, commanded by a brigadier-general

Caisson: a wheeled, horse-drawn wagon that contained artillery ammunition

Cap pouches: the small, leather pouch in which percussion or detonating caps for a rifle were kept

Canister: bullets contained in a cloth bag that was used by artillery against cavalry or infantry at short range

Carbine: a short musket or rifle carried by cavalry and specialist troops

Chobham: the town in Surrey close to which the first, all-arms' exercises occurred from 1852

Coatee: a waist-length jacket with swallow-tails

Colours: the pair of flags carried by each infantry battalion. They were carried by two ensigns and protected by two colour-sergeants

Commissariat: military logistics train

Company: the basic infantry unit, about seventy men strong, commanded by a captain. Each battalion had ten companies, two of which remained at the home depot for administration. There were two, specially picked companies: the Grenadiers and the Light

Craic: Gaelic for fun or banter

Croppies: Irish rebels of 1798, so named because of their short hair

Division: in the Crimea, six battalions of infantry or ten regiments of cavalry commanded by a major-general

Dress the line: the practise of straightening a line of troops

Dura mater: one of the three coverings of the brain, or meninges, that lie below the skull

Earthwork: fortification made from spoil rather than from masonry

Embrasure: narrow slot cut in the wall of an earth work from which artillery could be fired

Ensign: the most junior, commissioned rank in the infantry, later known as a second-lieutenant

Farrier: specialist cavalrymen who dealt with the horses' shoes and metal-work.

Fermoy: major military depot in County Cork

Field officer: the mounted officers of an infantry battalion, viz the commanding officer, the senior major, the junior major and the adjutant

File firing: the practise of firing by alternate ranks

Firelock: a musket or rifle

Full screw: slang for a corporal

Gabion: large basket that, when filled with spoil, would protect personnel against shot and shell

Gaffs: iron spurs for game-cocks

Gallus: Gaelic for over-confident or showy

Greenjacket: British term for rifle regiments, the slang term being "greenfly"

Haar: Gaelic for mist or fog

Hat: used by grenadiers as a term of contempt for non-grenadiers. It originated when grenadiers were given tall, mitre-like caps to wear which allowed them to hurl a grenade without knocking their headdress off, unlike the tricorne hats of the other companies

Jaunty: small gig or carriage

Limber: the wooden frame used to tow guns and their ammunition into action

Lunette: a crescent-shaped trench or earthwork

Malakoff: the main, Russian earthwork defending Sevastopol

Mamelon: a lesser, Russian earthwork designed to screen the Malakoff from assault

Minié: the principle by which an expanding lead bullet fits into a rifled barrel; named after the French inventor

Musket: smooth-bore firearm

Oltenitsa: battle of 4th November 1853 on the Danube where the Russians were defeated by the Turks

Orlop: deck or decks below the water-line

Overalls: tight fitting trousers worn by all cavalrymen and infantry officers

Parapet: the front lip of a trench as opposed to the parados, the back lip

Parallels: trenches that were used to approach a besieged town

Phoenix Park: Dublin's central park

Picket: a small group of dismounted lookouts or guards

Piece: an artillery gun's barrel

Pipeclay: white dye used to stain leather equipment for parades

Poshteen: Hindi word for sheepskin outer coat

Queen's regiments: units belonging to the Crown rather than the Honourable East India Company

Redan: a technical term for an earthwork of acute, defensive angles, used to name one of the lesser Russian defences outside Sevastopol

Redoubt: an earthwork usually designed to mount artillery pieces

Regiment: a cavalry or artillery unit, but see "battalion"

Sabot: the wooden disc that held a round shot stable in the bore before firing

Scunner: Gaelic for an irritating person. Also used to 'take a scunner' to someone

Sepoys: Indian infantrymen

Sergeant-Major: in the 1850s, the senior, non-commissioned rank in a battalion or regiment

Shamrock: Irish slang for a prod with a bayonet

Sharpshooter: specially trained marksman usually, by the 1850s, armed with a rifle

Shell: explosive ordnance, a "star-shell" being an illuminant

Shell jacket: the waist length, undress jackets worn for informal parades or field work

Sinope: the port on the south coast of the black Sea where the Russian Admiral Nachimov sank a Turkish fleet in November 1853

Sir Harry: Sir Harry Smith, the victor of Aliwal

Subbies: slang for subalterns, the most junior commissioned ranks

Tape: a chevron or badge of rank

Thurible: small container for incense used in religious services

Tranter: a designer of revolving pistols popular with officers in the 1850s

Wing: half a battalion, usually four companies commanded by a major. Also, the heavy, gold bullion shoulder straps worn by officers in the light and grenadier companies

Zouave: French-Algerian troops that saw much service in the Crimea

Historical Note

An infantry battalion on active service tends to exist in a bubble of its own (at least, that was my experience) and all the diaries and contemporary accounts of the Crimea would lead me to believe that things were exactly the same then. Officers and soldiers were consumed with survival and the everyday needs of supplying large numbers of troops in the field whilst keeping the enemy at bay. But, whilst Morgan and McGucken would, doubtless, have told statesmen, politicians and generals to "go hang", readers might like a slightly broader perspective of the war.

First, the term "Crimean War" is a misnomer. Until Kinglake published his eight volume Invasion of the Crimea in 1877, it was more generally known as the "Russian War", and so it should be. Similarly, modern public perception of the war revolves around a single cavalry charge and the doings of a handful of militant nurses, but the reality is rather different.

In fact, the conflict that lasted from 1853–1856, caused more casualties than the American Civil War and ranged over several different fronts from the Baltic to the Atlantic via the Black Sea and the Caucuses, with

Britain playing a mainly maritime part and a less significant role in the ground war than many imagine. It plunged a continent into turmoil, sowed the seeds of revolution in Russia, caused the redefinition of several European countries and their colonial influences, destroyed a government in Britain and, perhaps most significantly, provided the platform for the emergence of a new Germany. Indeed, had the Russian War never occurred or the result had been different, would the events of 1870, 1914 and, arguably, 1939 followed?

There is a strangely contemporary feel to this war, as well. It saw the unravelling of Russia followed by a new regime in that great empire, Germany more powerful, catastrophic friction between Christians and Muslims, Chechens and Russians and the emergence of hotspots like Jerusalem, Istanbul, Sarajevo and Grozny. All of those names continue to make headlines today.

I last served with the descendents of Morgan's Regiment in 1998. Had I said then, with uncharacteristic prescience, that their next, serious, bout of active service would be in Afghanistan not many miles from where their great-grandfathers fought, I would have been laughed to scorn — and quite right too! Today, though, if someone predicted that the same regiment would one day be told to embroider the battle-honour "Sevastopol" on their Colours for the second time in one-hundred and fifty years, how many of them would dismiss the possibility?

Author Note

I have a photograph of Anthony Morgan fifty years after he fought in the Crimea. It shows an old man dressed up in his campaign kit to delight his grandson, a boy of four who's holding his grandfather's hand outside their house in County Cork. Whilst the boy smiles, though, the old soldier lours out at us, his clay pipe firmly clamped between his teeth, his jaw set and determined.

There's another photograph in the Regimental History taken in the same year, 1904, at the Sandbag Battery at Inkermann. A gang of old 95th men, all white whiskers and watch-chains, are visiting the site of one of the greatest feats of arms in British military history.

In 1992 I tried to find this desolate spot outside Sevastopol (I think I was the first Briton to do so since those veterans eighty-eight years before), but after much searching and swearing amongst a tightly-planted fir wood, I still wasn't sure that I had found it. Certainly, there was an eroded bank of the right dimensions facing in the right direction, but it was only when I scuffed my boot through the loose soil and rough grass that I was convinced. Just below the surface were the bones of the men who had perished there. Ribs, femurs, fragments of skull were mixed up with spent bullets, percussion caps, the broken tip of a Russian bayonet and even a British regimental button. The story had to be told.

Tony Morgan was a real man in a real regiment — 95th (The Derbyshire): both were at the heart of some of the most vicious fighting of the Crimean War, but there the similarity ends. I've used the triumphs of the regiment as faithfully as I can as the framework for the fictitious Morgan's story, taking names, personalities and vignettes from the war and bending them around the actual battles and skirmishes.

The characters speak as my soldiers and their women did in the late twentieth century with a veneer of Victorian slang, for I feel sure that whilst weapons and technology have changed, fear, boredom, loyalty and plenty of military mores have not. Where I have used an obscure word, I have tried to make its meaning clear in the context, precise meanings being given in the glossary. Similarly, I hope that the weapons, tactics and formations of the time are explained in enough detail.

Patrick Mercer